RICK COOK

LIMBO SYSTEM

Acknowledgements:

Dr Art Upgrin of the Van Vleck Observatory at Wesleyan University found me my star. What I did with it afterwards was entirely my own fault.

LIMBO SYSTEM

A Baen Books Original

Baen Publishing Enterprises
260 Fifth Avenue
New York, N.Y. 10001

ISBN: 0-671-69835-4

Cover art by David Mattingly

First printing, August 1989

Distributed by
SIMON & SCHUSTER
1230 Avenue of the Americas
New York, N.Y. 10020

Printed in the United States of America

For My Parents

INTO THE FIRE

The pilot hit the main engines. Gradually the *Maxwell*'s mad dash through space slowed as the huge rockets bled off the excess velocity.

"Sir, we have achieved orbit," Iron Alice DeRosa reported formally.

Captain Jenkins nodded. Then the gray haired woman smiled wryly.

"The sixteenth human expedition outside our own solar system. Gets to you, doesn't it?"

Jenkins smiled back at his second-in-command. "Don't let it get to you too much, Al. Just get me the station reports."

And far, far away, millions of miles and hours of light travel, the Maxwell *announced herself to other ears with a burst of radio noise. The others were as quick in reaction as they were tireless in scanning the heavens. Other instruments swiveled onto the radio source. Optical detectors found the brilliant flame of the* Maxwell*'s fusion drive. Infrared arrays followed it too, and as the flame died, they picked up the* Maxwell*'s heat against the background of space.*

From one end of the system to the other the word went out by ways both secret and open. "Others have arrived. Make ready."

Fuseki: The beginning

Joseki: Opening gambits

Chuban: The middle game

Tesuji: Middle-game gambits

Sente: When the player has the initiative

Ko: A move which must be answered, giving the opponent one or more "free" moves

Gote: When the player has the initiative

Semeai: The race to capture

Damezumari: A shortage of liberties

Yose: The end game

Aji: Literally "taste"; the lingering effects of a move

PART I: FUSEKI

The kneeling man settled into himself on the mat, hakima billowing oddly in the low gravity. His palms rested high on his thighs, his elbows were out, and his back straight. He looked down at the mat beneath him and his lips moved as he softly spoke a single phrase.

There was a rustle of motion and suddenly the sword was free of its scabbard, whipping across in front of him as he rose on one knee. Without stopping, the blade came back and overhead, slashing down in a two-handed cut that ended a foot above the mat. Slowly and fluidly the man rose, sword still in front of him. Then the blade swept around the side and over his head, ending with a flicking motion down his front and to the side.

Without looking he flipped the sword up and across his body, catching the back of the blade with the thumb and forefinger of his left hand while the other fingers held the mouth of the scabbard. The blade slid out and the tip clicked into the scabbard. The man dropped slowly to one knee as the sword slid softly home in the sheath. The fingertips of the right hand moved caressingly out to the end of the long handle, partway down the inside of the handle and came to rest on the inner side of the right thigh.

And all was still and calm again.

Around him no one paid attention. The people doing aerobics in the great curved gym gave him wide berth, but the men and women working at the weight machines along the walls well away from him ignored him completely, concentrating on

1

their own internal agonies as weights they could never have handled on Earth rose and fell.

The old man stood, smoothed his hakima and knelt again to repeat the exercise.

Beautiful, thought Sharon Dolan from where she stood watching. *Like a dancer.* Her face was still beaded with sweat from her own workout, but she had stopped on her way to the shower to watch Dr. Sukihara Takiuji in his daily practice. *Beautiful, archaic and deadly all at once.*

That was the impressive thing, she decided. It wasn't the motions themselves. It wasn't the grace with which he handled that sword. It was the utter concentration, as if every cut was directed at the body of a real enemy. Sharon had taken one semester of fencing in college, but that was totally different. None of the fencers she knew gave that sense of actually trying to kill someone.

Dr. Sharon Dolan shivered slightly and it wasn't from the sweat slowly drying on her body.

She turned away from the exercise area and glanced up at the big clock on the wall. Nearly an hour to spin-down. Enough time for a long shower before the ship's living quarters lost gravity. *A good thing, too,* she thought, wrinkling her nose. *I need one and if I don't get a shower now it will be zero-G sponge baths for a day or two.*

"Time to jump two hours, fifty-five minutes."

Captain Peter Jenkins floated in near darkness and watched the stars. He didn't need the pilot's call, but he was glad for it just the same.

In addition to the big three-dimensional screen ahead of him—"above" him when the ship was under acceleration and the term had any real meaning on the bridge—there were actual ports to either side. His own displays showed a multitude of views of essentially the same scene, some with almost photographic realism and others abstracted to a network of colored lines.

Beneath the spangled display of the heavens, the bridge was a blood-red pit lit by the dim glow of screens and the dimmer reddish work lights. It struck groundsiders as eerie, but to Jenkins and the rest of the bridge crew it was just "the office."

As a Space Force officer, Captain Peter Jenkins had spent

most of the last fifteen years working under red lights in an office just like this one.

No, he corrected himself, *not just like this one. Not like this one at all.* He pulled his lank frame down into his command chair and belted himself in extra tight. This one was very, very different.

The annunciator on the edge of his screen lit up. "Doctor Aubrey calling," the synthesized voice announced.

Jenkins shook off the mood. Then he summoned up his patience and punched the "accept" button.

Dr. Andrew Aubrey blossomed into existence in one corner of his screen, the full-color image clashing with the abstract diagrams that filled most of the space.

"Smooth" seemed to have been coined to describe the man. His skin was smooth as if the flesh was packed tightly into it. His brown hair was smoothly cut and laid. His clothes were as neat as if they were still on the rack. But most of all, his manner was smooth. He exuded confidence and an easy grace. It was hard to imagine Andrew Aubrey committing a gaffe of any sort.

"Yes, Dr. Aubrey?"

"Captain, the Ship's Council has asked me to discuss leaving spin on one more time."

"I'm sorry, Doctor, but the decision stands. We will restore spin as quickly as possible after we have jumped and stabilized, but we will jump spun down."

"Captain, may I speak frankly?"

"Of course, Dr. Aubrey."

"There is a sizable faction on the Council who feel that your insistence on removing artificial gravity before we jump is not a matter of safety at all. They see it as a rather crude attempt to assert superiority over the technical staff."

Jenkins kept a tight rein on his temper. "Believe me, Doctor Aubrey, it is and always has been a matter of safety and ship handling. When Spin is spun up it acts as an enormous gyroscope and it makes it that much harder to maneuver the *Maxwell* quickly."

Aubrey nodded sympathetically. "I understand your concern, Captain, and I'm sure it would be ideal to jump spun down. But I ask you to consider the problems and resentment it will cause as well as the human misery involved in leaving us without gravity for two days or more."

3

"I have considered it, Doctor. Believe me, I know how miserable zero G makes most people. But I must have the ship as maneuverable as possible when we jump."

"Surely the matter can't be that clear cut," Aubrey protested. "The *Einstein* jumped spun up on her last two missions."

"With no disrespect to Captain Anguro, I disagree with his decision," Jenkins said, a little more forcefully than he intended.

"Captain, I wish you would be a little more flexible on this."

"Dr. Aubrey, as I have been telling you for the last three months, I must insist on spinning down before we jump. This is a matter of ship safety and handling and no matter how badly the Ship's Council wants it, I cannot compromise."

Aubrey nodded. "Very well, Captain, I won't take up more of your time. Good day."

Aubrey vanished and was instantly replaced by the leathery brown face of Iron Alice DeRosa, Jenkins' pilot and second in command. As number two, DeRosa was automatically cut into conversations on the captain's channel.

"As if we could change now if we wanted to," she rasped. "Christ! Less than three hours to jump and that bozo is still after us."

Jenkins shrugged uncomfortably. "Not him so much as some of the people on the Ship's Council, I think."

She snorted. "The authority of the Ship's Council stops at the edge of Spin. Formally they don't even have that much. There's nothing in the orders for this expedition authorizing a Ship's Council. I still think you're soft in the head for encouraging Aubrey and his pack of trained seals."

No one else in the crew would have dared to speak to the captain like that, but Jenkins and DeRosa had served together for years. Besides, Iron Alice DeRosa was a legend in the Space Force and legend has its privileges.

"I 'encourage' them, as you call it for three reasons." He held up three fingers. "First, we've got almost 600 people, nearly two-thirds of those aboard, who are not Space Force and who are only nominally subject to Space Force discipline. Second, those people arrived at the idea of a Ship's Council consensually and democratically." DeRosa snorted again, but Jenkins ignored her.

"And third," he ticked off the final finger. "The Ship's Council keeps those people out of my hair. Better to deal with Aubrey than listen to the complaints of fifty dropsick passengers."

And fourth, neither of them added aloud, it's the scientists who are running this show and they've got a lot more pull than the ship's captain.

"So now the Ship's Council thinks we can change our plans just like that. What do those yutzes think this is, the Toonerville Trolley?"

"They have a point, Al. Nearly two-thirds of the people aboard are dirtsiders. They're going to be pretty miserable for the next couple of days."

DeRosa looked sharply at her superior. "You going to change plans?"

Jenkins shook his head. "No. But it's important to remember that the Council is expressing a legitimate concern. Now," he said more briskly, "let's get back to business. We've got a long way to go in the next three hours."

DeRosa snorted again and broke the connection.

"Hello, Sharon."

Sharon Dolan turned to the voice behind her and Major Autro DeLorenzo flashed a smile. His tee shirt was dark with sweat and his curly hair damp from whatever exercise he had been pursuing. "Resting?" he asked in his faintly accented English.

"No, I just finished. I'm going to try to get a shower while we still have gravity."

At five-four, Sharon barely came up to DeLorenzo's shoulder. He was broad and heavily muscled. She had the slender build of a dancer. He was darkly handsome, with almost black, curly hair. Sharon had fair skin and a short mop of reddish blonde hair.

DeLorenzo chuckled. "I know what you mean. I tried bathing once in zero G and nearly drowned. Never again."

Sharon found herself warming to him. His charm was infectious in spite of everything and she realized she did enjoy herself in his company.

"How about you? Weights today?"

"Nope, handball." Again the smile. "It never ceases to amaze me what you can do on a handball court in half gravity."

It was Sharon's turn to smile. "You should try it in zero gravity."

DeLorenzo laughed. "I think I'd spend more time bouncing myself off the walls than I would the ball."

"That's part of the fun."

"Well, I'll have to try it sometime, if I can find a partner that is."

"It will have to wait until we get back then," Sharon told him. "The gym isn't open when we're spun down."

"Pity," he said and then his smile froze on his face as he caught sight of something over her shoulder.

Sharon looked around and saw Andrew Aubrey coming their way.

Last night in the Sunset Lounge the pair had another one of their political "discussions" that broke up in a shouting match. She hoped they wouldn't start up again here in the gym.

But DeLorenzo was apparently in no mood to resume the argument.

"I'll see you later, Sharon," he said and walked across the gym floor to ostentatiously strike up a conversation with a man working at one of the weight machines. She turned to greet Dr. Aubrey.

"How are you this morning, Dr. Dolan?"

Sharon smiled at him. "Hello, Dr. Aubrey. Are you down here for the exercise?"

"No, just finishing up a few matters of Council business before we jump." In addition to his regular duties, Aubrey was presiding officer of the Ship's Council.

"Spin down?"

He nodded. "The Council asked me to try one more time. I'm afraid the captain is as adamant as ever, though."

"That's too bad," Sharon said sympathetically.

Aubrey sighed. "I'm sure the captain feels strongly about this, but it is unfortunate he can't see how undesirable it is." He shrugged. "But that's as it is. Where are you off to?"

"I'm going to take a shower. If I don't hurry it will be too late."

"Quite right," Aubrey nodded. "See you at dinner perhaps?"

"If either of us has any appetite," Sharon said.

The director's face clouded. Like most of the non-crew on

6

board he was fundamentally a ground hugger and he didn't enjoy zero G.

"I'm sure it won't affect you at any event."

"Doctor, I'm afraid Spacers get dropsick just as easily as groundlings. We just get more used to it."

Behind him she saw Dr. Takiuji kneeling once again to repeat his sword exercise.

Sharon turned and walked away, vaguely dissatisfied by something about the two men. It wasn't until she had her leotard off and she was standing in the shower stall that she finally pinned it down.

He's a lot nicer than DeLorenzo, she thought as she turned on the water. *Why is it I don't like him as much?*

Aubrey watched the planetologist as she headed back through the gym to the showers. Then he sat down on a bench behind him to see who else came along.

Andrew Aubrey genuinely liked people and the gym was the best place on the ship to meet them. Everyone had to exercise to keep muscle tone and prevent physiological problems in the half-gravity maximum that Spin provided and there was only one gym. By contrast there were four cafeterias and a dozen or more lounges scattered throughout the enormous revolving cylinder that constituted the ship's living quarters.

As president of the Ship's Council, Aubrey conducted a lot of business in the gym. DeLorenzo and his friends might snort and call it "holding court," but a large part of modern management was meeting people on a personal level to understand their concerns. Aubrey was fond of saying that only old-style hierarchical managers tried to run things from behind a desk. A consensual manager should try to meet people in less formal surroundings, he maintained.

He didn't have long to wait. Sharon Dolan was barely out of sight when a dark-clad man in a clerical collar came into the gym and turned toward the locker room.

"Father," Aubrey nodded.

Father Simon looked up, as if he was slightly startled. "Oh, hello, Dr. Aubrey."

Father Michael Simon, SJ, was short, with graying hair and a face that was saved from ugliness only by his air of good humor.

7

Under gravity he was awkward and in zero G he was notoriously clumsy. He was quiet and self-contained in a way that came off as superiority to the less perceptive and as shyness to the keener observers.

"Going to exercise?"

"Oh, no. I've already been today. In fact I left something back in my locker. And you?"

"Just sitting here, enjoying the last of the gravity. I've been talking to the captain about spinning down."

Father Simon nodded. The spin-down controversy had been the main topic of conversation in the sealed little world of the *Maxwell* for the last few weeks. Even someone as resolutely aloof from the ebb and flow of the ship's politics as Father Simon was thoroughly familiar with it.

"Without success, I take it?"

"I'm afraid so. We will spin down on schedule. I'm afraid the captain puts abstract principles of ship handling above the welfare of the people on board. I'm sorry, Father."

"Oh, I expect I'll be all right. I have a fairly strong stomach." The priest smiled shyly. "Mostly I'm just anxious to get to our destination and begin observing." As an astrometrician from the Vatican Observatory, Father Simon was especially interested in the ultra-long baseline observations the *Maxwell* would be making.

Aubrey returned the smile. "I'm excited too, Father. Still, it's a shame that so many people will be made so miserable for such trivial considerations."

"So our safety is unimportant, eh?" Major DeLorenzo said loudly. He had come back when he had heard what Aubrey was saying to Father Simon.

Like a lot of military men, DeLorenzo was slightly deaf from being around explosions. He compensated by talking loudly and even in normal conversation his voice carried. All over the gym people paused and looked. Some of them continued to stare and listen, some of them made a great show of going back to their workouts. Only Dr. Takiuji continued his sword exercises uninterrupted.

"All this fuss over a few upset tummies," DeLorenzo made a throwaway gesture. "The problem with you people is you don't have any willpower. Discipline yourselves and you'd never notice there is no gravity."

"That's hardly fair," Father Simon put in. "You know space

8

sickness is real and extremely debilitating to those who suffer from it, even if you don't." DeLorenzo was one of those lucky people who was naturally immune to space sickness and he delighted in proving it.

"Bull. A couple of days of zero gravity won't hurt anyone."

"But it is unnecessary," Aubrey said. "You know the Ship's Council voted to recommend that we stay spun up."

"And you know I voted against it. If the captain says it's too dangerous, that's good enough for me."

"Of course," Aubrey said deprecatingly. "After all you are steeped in hierarchical thinking. But we need a more consensual approach here."

"Doctor, in this case, your 'consensual approach' is based on the idea that the opinions of a dozen ignoramuses is worth more than the opinion of one expert."

"Those 'dozen ignoramuses' represent a consensus of nearly six hundred people."

"A dozen or six hundred, it doesn't make you any more expert at ship handling."

"It's not really an issue of ship handling. I have no doubt the captain is right in principle," Aubrey said. "But simple calculations show that in practice the added margin is negligible."

"So now you're an expert on ship handling," DeLorenzo retorted. "Look around you. Spin is nearly two hundred and fifty meters across and another two hundred and fifty meters long. Do you have any idea how many hundreds of thousands of tonnes this all masses? What do you think it would be like trying to maneuver this ship with a gyroscope that big?"

"I hardly think it takes an expert to understand the situation," Aubrey said. "The fact is that other captains have made jumps spun up. Captains with more experience commanding starships than Captain Jenkins."

"So now he's incompetent," DeLorenzo flared. "Just because he has the guts to put the safety of the ship ahead of what you and your so-precious Council want, he's not fit to command."

"Oh nonsense!" Aubrey snapped. "I did not at any time question the captain's fitness to command. At most I questioned his judgment on this one issue."

"No, of course not. You'd never do anything as direct as questioning someone's ability outright. They might have a

9

chance to defend themselves. No, you'll just insinuate, you'll just hint. You'll just poison the minds of everyone around that person until everyone looks at him like a monster."

"I think this has gone quite far enough."

"Quite far enough," Father Simon put in tartly. "Especially since you have had this argument a dozen times before and neither of you has budged an angstrom. Unless you propose to resort to something other than argument you will just have to agree to disagree."

DeLorenzo glared at Aubrey. "You're right," he said finally. Then he turned and nodded to the priest. "Father," he said and stalked off to the locker room.

" 'Blessed are the peacemakers,' eh Father?" Aubrey said as they watched him go.

"It didn't seem to be a very productive discussion."

Aubrey sighed. "You're right, of course. I shouldn't let myself be drawn by that man."

"I imagine he feels very much the same way about you."

The administrator smiled. "Father, you have a remarkable ability to see both sides of a discussion. You know, you really should have a seat on the Ship's Council. You have a tremendous amount to contribute."

"Thank you, no," Father Simon said. "I've already told you I have no interest in participating in the ship's government."

"It is onerous, I know, but consensual management works best when widely divergent viewpoints and experience are represented."

"I'm afraid you overestimate my uniqueness," Father Simon said. "I believe there is already at least one astrometrician on the Council."

That wasn't what Aubrey had meant and they both knew it. Catholics were rare in space, so the priest was an object of curiosity and a fair amount of misunderstanding.

"Well, if you should ever change your mind . . ."

DeLorenzo came out of the dressing room wearing the neatly pressed khaki shirt and pants that were his every day wear. Aubrey saw him across the gym and his mouth tightened.

"You're certainly much better qualified than some of our present members." Father Simon followed Aubrey's eyes and saw DeLorenzo. "To have a man like that in close quarters with hundreds of other people for months," Aubrey shook his head. "And then to put him on the Ship's Council."

"Major DeLorenzo is opinionated and rather loud, but his behavior seems civilized," Father Simon said mildly. "As for his Council seat, he was elected, was he not?"

"By the construction workers and technicians primarily," Aubrey said disparagingly. "Oh, I can understand his appeal. He is a forceful speaker and he does have an attraction to people who prefer slogans and simplistic answers to careful consideration of real problems. Very frankly, though, he is a major source of dissension on the Council. A number of our difficulties stem from him and the few he influences."

"I thought you said that consensual management worked best with many different viewpoints represented."

Aubrey raised his eyebrows. "But a man like him? With his background?"

"All I know of his background is rumor and second-hand stories. I am not called on to judge him on that basis, or indeed on any basis."

"You mean you sympathize with him?"

Father Simon sighed. "No, by and large I do not. However, that is not the same thing as judging him."

"Father, I'm not interested in judging him either. But I have to run this ship." Father Simon wondered what the captain would have thought of that claim, but he kept quiet. "He presents an immediate and continuing problem for me. Besides, if even half the stories about him are true, he represents something abhorrent."

"First, we don't know that the stories are true. I think that charity demands we ignore them. Second, even if the outlines of the incident are true, it is not clear he deserves condemnation for his actions."

"But you're a man of peace," Aubrey said, surprised. "Isn't that the essence of the Christian message?"

"I think you misunderstand Christ's position," Father Simon told him, "and the Church's. The Church puts no prohibition on force per se, even on war. Indeed, in some circumstances the use of force is specifically approved."

"The doctrine of the Just War?"

"Properly construed. That and much else."

"I would have thought you would have abandoned that idea by now."

"Self-defense remains as valid a concept today as it ever was."

"Oh, but surely . . ." Aubrey broke off. "Forgive me, Father, I don't mean to argue religion with you."

Father Simon smiled. "Please, no apology necessary. Now if you'll forgive me."

Father Simon was frowning as he left the gym. He shouldn't allow himself to become annoyed with Aubrey and he shouldn't bait the man the way he had. He made a special note to confess that when they returned to Earth and he could go to Confession again.

It was even worse because for all his refined backbiting, Aubrey did have a point, Father Simon admitted to himself. Having someone as notorious as DeLorenzo on board did upset people. Given the lurid incident that had sent the Brazilian-Argentine into exile it could hardly be otherwise.

Ostensibly DeLorenzo was attached to the Construction and Engineering section. He was to help with rigging the giant telescopes which were the reason for the *Maxwell's* mission. In reality, he was in exile, swept under a convenient rug while the Brazilian-Argentine Confederation waited for the storm to die down.

Major Autro DeLorenzo's last job for his government had been roadbuilding, turning a muddy rutted track through the hills along the Bolivian border into an all-weather road.

It was typical of the kind of projects modern armies were used for all over a war-ravaged planet. But this one was more difficult than most. In addition to the usual problems of supply, labor and equipment shortages, a torrential rainy season and atrocious terrain, there were the bandits.

They were called Pacuarequeros, after the fortified hilltop villages where they lived. From time out of mind they had preyed on the people in the valleys below and collected tribute from travelers through the border region.

The hilltop villages were over the border in Bolivia and seemed invulnerable. Neither country had the men or the resources to police the area effectively. Expeditions by either government produced, at most, a temporary end to the raiding and banditry.

At first DeLorenzo tried the traditional solution to dealing with the Pacuarequeros. He paid the bribes they demanded. But that was insufficient. The construction crews were too rich and tempting a target in a poor, backward land. Besides, the Pacuarequeros had an uneasy sense that the road meant change and that the change might destroy them.

DeLorenzo appealed to his government for troops to guard his men, but there were none to be had. The bandits continued their raids on his camps and their ambushes of his construction crews.

Finally, Major Autro DeLorenzo opted for something direct and more permanent. He picked a dozen men, armed them and turned them into a flying squad. Then he commandeered a tiltrotor VTOL aircraft at so close to gunpoint as made no difference.

With a few rifles and a plentiful supply of blasting explosives, he loaded them into the tiltrotor and raided the hilltop villages at night.

While some of DeLorenzo's commandos stayed outside the village and shot anything that moved, the others went from house to house lobbing dynamite grenades into the huts. Surprise was complete. The Pacuarequeros never had a chance. Neither did their wives and children. In less than a month, Autro DeLorenzo effectively ended the Pacuarequero threat that had plagued the high plains for at least a century.

DeLorenzo completed his road and returned home to a hero's welcome. And a simmering pot of political trouble.

His mission had succeeded, but far too many people had died. The confederation government was not unhappy to see the Pacuarequeros destroyed, but it did not want trouble with Bolivia and it didn't want the unfavorable comment the action got from the rest of the world. It seemed prudent to stash DeLorenzo someplace until the heat died down.

What, if anything, the silent brown people of the valleys thought of Major Autro DeLorenzo, no one ever bothered to ask.

From the shuttle bays aft of Frame 23 there is a manually operated scuttle that leads to a trunk paralleling the ventilation risers to . . . no, that's only on Bays 1, 2 and 3. On Bay 4 it's . . .

"Still at it, Mr. Kirchoff?" The voice boomed in his ear. Barry Kirchoff jumped and whirled, lost his purchase on the console and spun helplessly for a second before hooking his foot on the couch to bring himself under control.

Hanging nonchalantly behind him was Karl Ludenemeyer,

the Chief Engineering Officer. His feet brushed the over-head, putting him upside-down in relation to Kirchoff.

"Yessir," Kirchoff said lamely, furious at himself for his own clumsiness.

"You'll never get it all, you know," he said shaking his head. "This ship is nearly four thousand feet long and eight hundred in diameter. There is no way you can memorize the entire layout."

"Perhaps not, sir." *But see if I don't, dammit!*

"Even if you did, what good would it do when you're transferred?" the older man went on, not unkindly. "You'd be better off practicing skills like working in zero G. You should never be so startled you lose your grip. And floating over the couch on your stomach like that isn't smart. One quick burst of acceleration and you'd get the back slammed into your gut."

You're a fine one to talk, hanging upside down. But Kirchoff knew that if he said anything, Ludenemeyer would probably demonstrate some tricky maneuver that would bring him down easily on his feet no matter which way the thrust came from. Once more he felt completely inadequate.

"Spin down's coming up," Ludenemeyer said. "Make sure your station's secured."

"I've already been over it twice, sir."

"Then go over it again, Mr. Kirchoff. Engineering is no place to have something come loose under acceleration." With that he twisted and darted away like a minnow—a bulky minnow in khaki coveralls.

Kirchoff bit his lip. As a product of the new engineering officers' school on Luna he was considerably different from Ludenemeyer and the rest of the engineering crew who had come up through the informal apprenticeship program that served to train most workers in space. That not only made him different, it grated on the other engineering officers.

He knew he had a theoretical grounding that most engineering officers did not. But he was also keenly aware that Ludenemeyer and the other senior officers had years of practical experience that he lacked. That only made him more determined to show the value of the Academy approach. He was also years younger than most engineering officers. It didn't help that he was slender with a shock of dark hair and a fair, almost girlish, complexion that made him look like an adolescent.

With a last look at the diagram, Barry Kirchoff turned away and started to make one more inspection of his area.

All through the ship, the speakers chimed, their voices resonating and beating together like the echoes in some impossibly shaped space.

"Five minutes to spindown. Secure for zero gravity. Five minutes to spindown."

Throughout the living quarters of the ship there was a bustle as fittings were given a last minute check. In the garden spaces near the core the last of the nutrient-rich water drained from the racks of growing plants back into the tanks. The super-humid air around the roots would keep the plants supplied for several days. Further out toward the hull other workers went over their sections looking for anything loose which might float away.

Fore and aft of Spin, the motors spaced around the ship's central core ceased receiving energy from the power system and gradually started sucking energy from the huge turning cylinder within the *Maxwell*'s hull.

It was a slow, tedious process. Spin was almost 250 meters in diameter and nearly 250 meters long. It massed in the hundreds of thousands of tonnes and revolved just under four times a minute. That represented a lot of energy to manage and it was best bled off under careful control. So the computers monitored the motor/generators and humans monitored the computers and everywhere on the ship humans and computers looked for the least sign that something was amiss.

As the rotation drained away, the humans in their bunks around the periphery of Spin felt weight drain away with it. Their bodies became lighter and lighter on the pads. Their blood pulsed in ways unfamiliar to people who had spent their lives in gravity. Inner ears and stomachs also responded to the sensations. Some of the people clenched their eyes tight to try to hold down their stomachs. Some of them forced their eyes wide and stared fixedly at the walls to convince themselves they were not falling, no matter what their bodies told them. Many of them were miserably sick and most of them prayed for it to be over soon.

The speaker chimed again. "Full stop. Spin zero. Full stop. Prepare for jump."

At his station Captain Peter Jenkins rechecked the status display and nodded to the pilot. Grim gray, Iron Alice DeRosa played the sidestick under her right hand gently, delicately giving the final orders to the ship.

At the far rear of the ship Michael Clancy ran his hand through his curly gray hair and checked his instruments one more time. Then he dogged his spacesuit helmet and checked them again. A few feet from him the ship's torch pile stood ready and waiting.

"All stations report ready, sir," Lieutenant Kirchoff told his superior.

The chief of engineering looked coldly at his subordinate. "Don't tell me, Mr. Kirchoff. Tell the captain."

Kirchoff reddened. "Yessir."

Ludenemeyer sighed audibly and turned back to his own display. He hated managing people almost as much as he loved his machinery. If he had his choice would have been back doing Big Mike Clancy's job, but that wasn't possible. The Engineering Officer's place was forward, in front of the ship's main pile and next to the drive room. Although what Ludenemeyer or anyone else on board could do if the star drive malfunctioned, he hadn't the faintest idea.

Just out of curiosity he had asked Dr. Takiuji—or was it Dr. Sukihara?—that question once. The Japanese physicist merely smiled and answered, "perhaps some things." The way he had said it did nothing for Ludenemeyer's confidence.

"Heading on," Iron Alice DeRosa reported. Jenkins looked down at his screens. The captain's console showed him the same information the computers were giving the pilot. DeRosa's announcement was perhaps unnecessary, but it was both correct procedure and comforting.

"All sections report ready," the deck officer called out. Again Jenkins looked at his board to confirm.

"Stand by for drive," Jenkins said. On his touch panel a palm-sized square glowed red, deeper and brighter than the red bridge lights, like a hot coal on the instrument panel.

Jenkins took a deep breath and placed his fingers over the glow, as if to block it out. A timer sprang into existence on his screen, its numbers unreeling frantically as it counted off the hundredths of a second.

Clancy got the signal and increased the speed of the turbo-pumps. The torch was hot and ready, waiting only the fuel.

Once more the signal sounded. Sharon sighed, climbed into her combined bunk and acceleration couch and tightened the safety straps over her shoulders and midriff.

When the clock reached 0 the drive kicked in automatically. There was no lurch, no inside-out feeling, no distortion of the star field in the view ports. One instant they were looking at one set of stars and the next instant the stars had changed as if someone had changed channels. The only sensation was a not-quite feeling of incompleteness, as if they had missed something or blinked at a critical moment.

Instantly Iron Alice DeRosa was very busy.

The most difficult time in using the KOH drive was not travelling between the stars, it was right after you arrived.

A KOH drive provides instantaneous transport, but it does not repeal the laws of physics. You break out with at least the total kinetic energy you went in with, including the energy inherent in your path about a star, and your rotation about the center of the galaxy. It also includes the energy inherent in the galaxy's motion through space, but that can be neglected as long as you stay within the galaxy.

This is both exacerbated and mitigated by two other things. The mitigating factor is that the drive tends to automatically seek points where the ship's energy is most nearly in balance with its surroundings. A KOH starship tends to travel between isogravs.

The exacerbating factor is that there are quantum-like effects at work which add a measure of uncertainty to the ship's position and velocity. A component of the difference in total energy between where you started and where you finish shows up as velocity in a random direction.

You cannot in principle know which way you will be heading when you break out, nor can you predict your exact velocity and position. It is entirely possible to break out with more total energy than you went in with and for various complex and subtle reasons this does not represent a violation of the law of conservation of energy.

Not all this uncertainty shows up in velocity. Some of it is released as heat. A KOH ship that comes out on a really bad vector will cook its crew like microwaving ants in a vacuum bottle.

With careful navigation the mismatch will never get that bad. But preventing a serious mismatch requires detailed knowledge of the target area, especially the gravitational fields. That kind of knowledge is easier to get about the edge of a star system, away from the competing gravitational effects of the planets, so jumps tend to be made to and from the edge of star systems and the ship proceeds in or out on a conventional drive. There is also the fact that coming out of drive in a volume of space containing an appreciable amount of matter will rather nicely reproduce the condition of the universe a few microseconds after the Big Bang on a much smaller scale.

As a practical matter, what happens is that a ship breaking out of drive finds itself in a strange solar system heading in a random direction with an uncertain amount of velocity. The first order of business is to get the velocity under control and that takes very sharp piloting.

The sensors on the ship's hull took a quick and dirty reading on the apparent movement of the star field, the ship's computers translated that into a rough guess as to the ship's direction and velocity, and Iron Alice DeRosa reacted.

Thrusters swung the ship around so the stern was pointed in the direction of travel. Then the pilot hit the main engines.

Far back at the rear of the elongated teardrop that was the *Maxwell*, Clancy's turbopumps poured a river of hydrogen slush enriched with deuterium and tritium into the fusion torch. An appreciable fraction fused to helium, and lambent flame too bright to have a color lanced from the rear of the ship.

Clancy kept his eyes on his displays and his hands on the fusion control panel. In theory there was no need for the torch watch. The computers were capable of overseeing the enormous forces unleashed and channeled by the torch. In practice there wasn't a torch captain alive who trusted the pile that far and the engineers trusted it less than that. Next to the pilot's chair, the torch watch was the most important job on a fusion ship.

Slowly the *Maxwell*'s mad dash through space slowed as the great reaction engines bled off the excess velocity.

"Sir, we have achieved orbit," DeRosa reported formally.

Jenkins nodded. Then the gray haired woman smiled wryly. "The sixteenth human expedition outside our own solar system. Gets to you, doesn't it?"

The captain knew precisely what she meant. The first

interstellar expeditions had belonged to world powers in the southern hemisphere and the vital young states of the Pacific Rim. The old worn-out nations like the United States, Japan and the fragments of Europe had no role. This was a sop, an unimportant voyage meted out as a reward for political favors. *But it's still an interstellar expedition, dammit!*

Jenkins smiled back at his second in command. "Don't let it get to you too much, Al. Just get me the station reports."

And far, far away, millions of miles and hours of light travel, the Maxwell *announced herself to other ears with a burst of radio noise. The others were as quick in reaction as they were tireless in scanning the heavens. Other instruments swiveled onto the radio source. Optical detectors found the brilliant flame of the* Maxwell's *fusion drive. Infrared arrays followed it too and as the flame died they picked up the* Maxwell's *heat against the background of space.*

From one end of the system to the other the word went out by ways both secret and open. "Others have arrived. Make ready."

Again the gongs boomed and echoed through the ship. "Secure from acceleration stations."

Back in the passenger section, Sharon Dolan breathed a sigh and loosened her harness.

The romance of space travel, phooey! she thought, massaging her shoulders. *I bet I'll have black and blue marks for days.* She wondered how long it would take to spin back up and restore gravity. Normally it took at least twenty-four hours. It was a fairly complex process and had to be done carefully.

Then maybe I can stop playing passenger and get down to work.

The *Maxwell's* job was astronomy, part pure science, part practical. The ship had gone deeper into space than any human vessel and the astronomers and astrophysicists who made up the majority of the scientific contingent were hoping to literally see the universe from a new angle.

Sharon was along almost as an afterthought. The main interest was stellar astronomy, not planetology. The system they had entered probably had planets—most single stars do—but there were no plans to come in beyond the fringes of the system.

Like the theoretical part of the mission, the practical part was much more concerned with other stars than this one. Their destination was simply a convenient place to stand while they did their observations.

With the KOH star drive, the limiting factor on how far you could travel was not range, it was location and gravitational energy. Like the Portuguese explorers working their way down the coast of Africa nearly seven hundred years before, the starships needed "landmarks" to work from and information on which harbors might be safe.

The essence of the landmarks were long-baseline observations. That meant an elaborate series of observations taken light years apart and closely tied to an object whose position relative to Earth was well known. A star, in other words.

From this point new observations could be made to precisely locate other stars, and information on the gravitational lay of the land could be inferred from those observations. With that information stars further out could be plotted precisely enough for other expeditions, and crude gravitational maps constructed to help later explorers.

Maxwell's interest was less in this star system per se than in what could be seen from the system. The distance and motion of the star was known and the information gathered here could be tied into observations taken in other star systems to extend the baseline. In turn that longer baseline could be used to send starships even further out to extend the baseline even more.

On the bridge Jenkins scanned the spangled black sky laid out ahead of them.

DeRosa looked over her shoulder. "Try about two o'clock and maybe one thirty down," she told him.

The captain shifted his gaze and picked out "their" star.

Far away the ruddy sun glowed in the depths of space. At this distance it was merely the brightest star in the sky. They were far out from it and suns of its type do not shine brightly in any event.

The star was a perfectly ordinary M2 red dwarf, so ordinary it had no name. Although it lay only seventy light years from

Earth it was invisible to the naked eye and hard to see from an Earth-based telescope.

It had a number, of course. It was AC +37° 30242. There were other designations in other catalogs, but never a name. It was too small and too plain to have ever gotten a name.

It looks so, well, ordinary, Jenkins thought. Intellectually he had known what it would look like, but he still had a feeling that somehow it ought to be special.

Jenkins' contemplation was broken by a chiming on his screen.

"Dr. Aubrey on line two," the synthetic voice reported.

Jenkins touched his panel and Andrew Aubrey's face sprang to life on his screen.

"Captain, do you have any idea how soon we will be able to spin up?"

"Not yet, Dr. Aubrey. We are still checking."

Aubrey nodded. "I'd appreciate if you could let me know as soon as possible. It will make the discomfort easier to bear if people know how long it will last."

Aubrey looked none too good himself. He was pale and his easy air seemed just a trifle forced.

"Of course, Dr. Aubrey," Jenkins said soothingly. "I will let you know as soon as I have the information."

"Thank you, Captain," Aubrey said and cut off.

The cafeteria wasn't crowded, even though it was the only one on the ship fitted out for zero gravity and the only one on the ship serving tonight. Much of the crew was at their maneuvering stations and zero gravity upset too many stomachs.

Still some stomachs are stronger than others and even the weakest stomach has to be fed. There was a slow but steady flow of people through the line and on to the tables beyond.

They wore a variety of costumes. The crew generally wore jumpsuits in the colors that denoted their sections. The civilians dressed in everything from street clothing to jumpsuits of their own.

In all the group Dr. Sukihara Takiuji stood out. Suki was dressed in his normal mode. Which is to say in a manner a pre-Meji Japanese would have regarded as normal and that nearly any twentieth-century Japanese would have considered eccentric for everyday wear.

His hakima, a long divided skirt, floated around his legs.

His tabi, divided socks, were white. His kimono, tucked into the hakima, was brown patterned with white. Suki was completely at ease and after months in space no one else paid any attention.

In modern Japan, Dr. Takiuji's clothing marked him as an adherent of one of the traditionalist parties, trying to revive a country damaged for the second time in as many centuries by atomic fire with the virtues of the past. Sharon knew that the details of his clothing proclaimed more precisely where his loyalties lay to anyone who could read the signs. Possibly his practice of iaido, the art of drawing the samurai sword, and his obsession with the ancient game of go indicated his political beliefs as well.

Sharon noticed that the soles of his tabi had very untraditional dark patches of Grip Sole sewn neatly to them.

Like the decks and bulkheads in the passenger spaces and the corridors everywhere, the cafeteria was carpeted in a short-pile fabric. To the hand it felt slightly stiff. The loops in the pile caught at the special material on the soles of the slippers everyone wore. The result was a slight "tack" that held you to the floor—if you didn't push too hard or try to walk too fast. To Sharon it was like walking on the sticky floor in a busy movie theater, but it was better than floating off the floor every time you took a step.

Tonight the cafeteria's food tended to be sparse and bland. Sharon was thankful there was nothing spicy or pungent or worse yet, greasy, filling the air with an odor that would challenge her stomach.

She selected an insulated bulb of tea from the rack and took two slices of toast, neatly wrapped in plastic.

Ahead of her, one of the crewmen in the tan coveralls of engineering was heaping his tray with wrapped sandwiches. Sharon shuddered.

The watchers did not know yet what to make of their visitors. Typically, they did not announce themselves directly. Perhaps the newcomers were ignorant of their presence or perhaps they believed that the watchers were ignorant of theirs. In either event, best to keep silence and watch.

Suki stopped at the steam table holding sticky oriental rice and a few other equally bland dishes for those who wanted hot food. He heaped rice into a covered bowl as nonchalantly as if they had not come nearly a hundred light years between breakfast and dinner. His appetite was still good, although, Sharon noticed with a slight smile, he eschewed the pungent pickled vegetables that normally accompanied his meals.

The cafeteria was a big room. On special occasions it might feed five or six hundred people. Although there were empty tables everywhere, the diners tended to cluster at the round four- and six-person tables near the serving line. There was something about being sealed in an enormous steel bottle a hundred light years from home that encouraged sociability.

Another mark of how far we've come, Sharon thought, like the murals of Earth scenes on the walls.

The long back wall of the cafeteria was a forest glade. The water in the brook meandering through it and the leaves on the trees moved as if the wall was a picture window. Another wall showed the red rock desert of North America, the fantastically carved spires of pink and buff sandstone soaring out of the reddish soil. An occasional eddy of dust or quiver of the scraggly greasewood bushes in the foreground gave the illusion of wind.

There were no cities on the walls. That might have been too painful.

The catering crew understood the psychology perfectly and had not bothered to activate most of the farther tables. The vacuum intakes in the middle of each functioning table made a slight hissing noise as they sucked crumbs, spills and debris into the cleaning system.

Sharon eased her way in to a vacant seat at the table with the Japanese physicist and several other people.

She watched, fascinated, as Dr. Takiuji produced a pair of chopsticks and began to eat from the bowl, holding it close to his mouth.

A single grain of rice floated free and the Japanese deftly plucked it out of the air with his chopsticks.

"You know that's probably more efficient than a fork in space," she said.

Suki looked up at her and grinned. "Better control," he said in his accentless English.

She sucked tea from a bulb and watched again.

"I wish I had a better understanding of the principles

behind something that's taken us a hundred light years from home," Sharon said.

Dr. Takiuji smiled at her. "So do I."

"But you helped develop the drive," one of the engineering crew put in.

"That does not mean I understand it, I am afraid," Suki said. "It is very difficult."

"What is the maximum speed with the drive anyway?" a stocky man in a vacuum jack's coverall asked.

Suki smiled slightly. "No speed."

"Come again?"

The Japanese physicist gestured. "First we are here. Then we are there. Instantaneous. No speed."

"That's how we avoid the Einsteinian effects," Sharon said. "How does it work?"

Again the slight smile. "Very complicated. It is not easy to describe without mathematics." He turned back to eating.

"But you worked with Kerensky and Omo on the drive?" someone else asked.

Dr. Takiuji picked the last grains of rice out of his bowl. "I worked on it, yes."

"What did you do?"

Suki rested his chopsticks on the edge of his now empty bowl and thought for a moment. "Without mathematics, the best I can think to say is that I helped define the difference between 'nothing' and 'almost nothing.' "

Sharon continued to watch out of the corner of her eye as she sucked on her bulb of tea.

And you, Dr. Takiuji, Sharon thought as she watched him. *What did you do to earn exile?* She knew in a general way. There had been some kind of struggle within the traditionalist parties in Japan and it had been considered politic for Suki to absent himself for a while. In another time he might have shaved his head and become a monk. Now he went out among the stars he had helped open for Man.

But there were no details. Like so much in Japanese society it was closed and opaque, hidden behind a curtain of natural reticence and cloaked in inflections, sub-texts, and things half said.

Captain Peter Jenkins sucked lukewarm food out of a plastic pouch. Then he took the package away from his lips and

24

looked at it disgustedly. The label said it was "turkey dinner with dressing and gravy." The contents were the consistency of thick mush with little bits of stuff in it. Some of the bits were crunchy. That meant they were celery. Some of them were rubbery. That meant they were turkey. Overall it tasted of salt, sage and artificial turkey stock.

Jenkins made a face and put the package down on his console. The opening had sealed itself automatically as soon as he stopped sucking and the pouch stuck lightly to any surface it touched.

It could be worse, he thought, wrinkling his nose. *It could be ham and lima beans.*

One of the privileges of being captain was you got first pick of the food packs in the closet-size duty galley aft of the bridge. Of course, being the captain, you were also usually the last to get off the bridge to choose.

Four thousand feet of starship, a catering staff of nearly fifty and the captain still eats slop.

He knew fatigue was getting to him. He and DeRosa had both been on the bridge for nearly twenty hours. Now their long watch was coming to a close. The ship was in orbit about the star, the systems had been checked and minor damage either repaired or worked around until it could be repaired. There were just a few things left to set in motion before both of them would turn their stations over to other officers. With the next watch the real work of the expedition would begin.

He punched up engineering and Ludenemeyer's face appeared.

"Final status?"

The engineering chief shrugged. "About the same. Pretty good and getting better."

"How soon can we begin deploying the gravitational telescope?" Jenkins asked.

"It's not a telescope," Ludenemeyer said. "According to the astronomers it's an array. A telescope produces images."

"How long, Mr. Ludenemeyer?"

"Probably next wake cycle. There'll be an engineering meeting in a little under an hour and I can tell you more then."

"As soon as you know." He caught himself. "No, make that as soon as I come back on. I don't need to know badly enough to be woken up."

He made to sign off and then he paused. "And what the hell are *you* doing still on duty, Mr. Ludenemeyer? You started before I did."

Ludenemeyer shrugged, a little embarrassed. "You know how it is, Captain. Besides, I sent my seconds to get something to eat in the cafeteria. I'll go off as soon as they get back."

"Lucky stiffs," Jenkins said. "I'm still on zero G rations."

"It could be worse," the engineer told him. "We're on them too. All we've got left down here is ham and lima beans."

Mike Clancy and three others from the engineering section squeezed into an unoccupied table in the cafeteria. Barry Kirchoff followed them through the line and sat down with them. The others made no comment, but they moved over to give him room.

There weren't many people in the cafeteria, Kirchoff saw. A couple of tables away a mixed group of crew, technicians, scientists and vacuum jacks was talking noisily. He noticed it included the Japanese guy who always dressed funny and the foxy little blonde astronomer. They were all eating lightly, he saw.

In contrast, the engineers had loaded their plates and Clancy was holding forth.

"You know what I hate about being spun down on this tub? You can't get anything decent to eat." He gestured at the pile of sandwiches. "Damn galley shuts down." He tore the wrapper off one of the sandwiches and stuffed half of it into his mouth. "Now when we were running from the Moon to L5, last night out we'd always have spaghetti."

"Spaghetti in zero-G?" Kirchoff blurted out.

"Sure," Clancy drawled. " 'Course you've got to learn to suck down an entire strand in one breath. You can't cut it up and eat it with a fork like an officer and a gentleman."

From Clancy's grin and the way the others were smiling, Kirchoff realized he had been caught in another space crew joke. He smiled weakly to show he was a good sport and went back to eating.

Damn, he thought. Space crews were the ultimate insiders. They lived in each other's pockets for months at a time and they had made a whole subculture out of it. He had been

26

catapulted from the Academy directly into the engineering department and he simply didn't have the background.

Clancy had launched into a complicated anecdote involving a catcher ship at L5 and several people whose nicknames apparently meant something to everyone else at the table. Kirchoff kept his head down and tried to concentrate on his food.

Two technicians came in and sat down at the table next to the engineers. They had practically nothing on their trays and they moved slowly and carefully, with the gait of men who expect that their bodies will betray them at any second.

"God, another day to go. I hope that bastard's enjoying this," said one of the technicians loudly enough to be overheard at the next table.

"And which bastard did you have in mind?" Mike Clancy said very quietly.

The technician was too miserable to take the hint. "The captain. I hope he's happy now that half the people on board are puking their guts out."

"Part of the price of space travel," Kirchoff said mildly.

"Bull!" the technician said. "You can jump without spinning down. Other ships do it all the time. But our captain's got to show how important he is. So he makes everyone else miserable."

Clancy shifted in his seat, but Kirchoff leaned over and grabbed his wrist. Their eyes locked and then the older man settled back.

"Have you ever seen a man who's been decompressed?" Clancy asked evenly. "The way his eyes bug out and bleed? The frozen black froth where he's tried to breathe vacuum and his lungs burst? The way the veins ruptured under the skin and his body blows up like a balloon, the way his guts push out his asshole?"

The two technicians shifted uncomfortably and turned even paler.

"And you ever smelled someone like that when you bring 'em back inside and the body warms up? The shit and the blood and all the other juices that get squeezed out of the body in vacuum."

One of the technicians jumped up from the table and made a dash for the door, bouncing along as he barely kept contact with the floor.

"Now you think about that," Clancy went on inexorably, his eyes locked on the complainer. "You think about how it would feel if we hit a piece of ice or rock out here because we couldn't maneuver fast enough and you lost all this nice warm air. You think about it and you tell me if it's worth trying to keep spin on when we jump."

The engineer shrugged. "Now me, I don't care. When we jump I'm back in the ass end of this thing in a pressure suit babysitting the torch. Anything goes wrong, I'm either fine or I'll never know what hit me. You're the one who would be sticking your finger down your throat trying to hold your lungs in place."

The technician muttered something incomprehensible, got up from the table and followed his friend out.

"Assholes," Clancy said conversationally and went back to his anecdote.

Sharon Dolan turned back to her table and started eating again. Nearly everyone in the cafeteria had heard the argument and it had obviously struck a cord.

What had been a casual mix at her own table had suddenly separated as completely as oil and water under gravity. Although everyone was trying to ignore it, a gap had opened between the crew and the scientists and technicians.

The argument, even the whole question of spinning down, were just symptoms, Sharon admitted. The problem was there really *was* a gap between the crew and the passengers and it was getting bigger every day.

Part of it was that very few of the passengers had ever been in space before they shuttled up to join the *Maxwell*. The vacuum jacks who were along to rig and maintain the arrays had, of course, but almost none of the astronomers had. Ironically, only a few astronomers had ever been off Earth. The huge instruments floating in space or anchored to the airless surface of the Moon were mostly run by remote control to meet the needs of scientists at institutes and universities around the globe. Space sickness was something every crewman had learned to handle long ago. To most of the scientists and technicians it was a whole new level of discomfort.

Worse, the scientists and technicians didn't understand the limits and problems of space living that the crew and vacuum jacks took for granted. To them the rules and precautions

28

seemed unreasonable and the crew seemed arrogant bullies. To the crew the passengers seemed like dangerous ignoramuses.

Conversation had picked up again around the table; a strained, artificial chatter as the group tried to recapture the mood of a few minutes ago.

It wasn't just being in space, Sharon thought. The crew and the passengers had totally different styles. The crew was much more hierarchically oriented. They were used to commanding and being commanded, to orders generated at the top and passed down a chain of command. Even the vacuum jacks, that band of happy anarchists, was used to working that way. It was hard for them to understand the more consensual, collegial style of decision making the scientists and technicians were used to.

Over at the other table the crewmen had gathered up their trays and headed for the door. The scientists and technicians at the nearby tables seemed to stiffen and flinch away as they passed with the easy gliding steps of people used to zero gravity.

Put it all together and it spelled friction, Sharon realized. *If someone doesn't do something, we're going to have real trouble before this is over.*

Clancy caught up with Kirchoff in the corridor outside the cafeteria and put his hand on the young man's shoulder.

"Thanks, kid," he said quietly. "Ludenemeyer wouldn't have liked it if I gave that shit what he really deserved."

Kirchoff flushed. "I think what you did was much more effective than hitting him," he said. "Maybe he learned something."

The older engineer looked him up and down. "You know if you weren't such a puke you'd be all right." Then Clancy moved off down the corridor in easy bounds, leaving Kirchoff to wonder if he'd been insulted and complimented.

Iron Alice was already on the bridge when Captain Peter Jenkins came back on watch the next morning.

"What's the word on the gravity array?" he asked as soon as he had formally taken command of the bridge.

"We're about ready," DeRosa told him, still standing next to his console. "Ludenemeyer says we can spin up in another eight hours. Formal report's waiting for you."

29

The captain punched it up on his screen and studied it. "After we deploy the array, then." He had hoped they could spin up first, but the schedule lines on the report chart showed that would mean delaying the deployment.

"Anything else I should know?"

The second in command shrugged. "Not really."

Jenkins looked around to make sure no one else was close. Then he leaned over to her. "I understand Mike Clancy nearly decked someone in the cafeteria last night."

Iron Alice shrugged. "Just a little discussion."

"I'd appreciate it if there weren't any more of those little discussions."

"Ludenemeyer's already talked to him about it." She dropped her voice even more. "But if something doesn't shake some sense into our passengers we're going to have real trouble sometime soon."

"I intend to talk to Aubrey as soon as we're spun up," Jenkins said. "He's the expert on conflict resolution."

"I just hope it does some good. Some of those people need a real attitude adjustment and we're all sealed in here like flies in a bottle for eight more months." She shook her head. "Jesus."

"Just as long as it doesn't turn into scorpions in a bottle," Jenkins told her. "Don't worry. Things will get better when we get down to work." *I hope*, he added to himself.

"Well, the sooner we get these arrays deployed, the sooner we'll know. Any word from Ludenemeyer and the others yet?"

"Any minute, I imagine," the captain told her.

Iron Alice nodded and returned to her pilot's chair. The leathery woman might be pushing sixty, but she was still far and away the best pilot on the ship for anything that didn't take lightning reflexes. A 1,000-meter-long starship doesn't do anything at lightning speed and for this job Jenkins wanted the best he had.

There were only two people in the Telescope Shack. That was one more than necessary, but Dr. Pete Carlotti wanted to be there for the first quick-and-dirty scan.

Not that there would be much to see. The great arrays that made up the *Maxwell*'s real observing power were still stowed in the holds aft of Spin. The only instruments available now were finder scopes, a battery of 24-inch optical instruments and small radio, IR and UV arrays mounted on the ship's hull. Compared to the tools of modern astronomy they were only toys.

The real astronomical work wouldn't start until the riggers and vacuum jacks had deployed the big arrays and the technicians had calibrated them. For now the view wasn't much better than it was from the giant telescopes in the Earth system.

Of course any of the astronomers who wanted to could tap into the data and images flowing back from the instruments on the terminals in their quarters or the public areas of the ship. A few probably had out of curiosity. But no one was going to go to work until the big equipment was broken out. The only astronomer doing anything productive right now was the junior staff member directing the system from the cabin in Spin still called the Telescope Shack.

Carlotti was there because he wanted to be. He felt it was somehow *right* that as the head of the *Maxwell*'s astronomy group he should be where the action was when the ship broke out into the new system. Typically, he was completely oblivious to the effect his presence and nervous energy was having on his subordinate.

Already the subordinate had completed his first quick scan of the neighborhood. Within the limits of their drive, they were where they were supposed to be. Now several of the instruments were trained inward, to check out the sun they were orbiting.

"Doctor Carlotti, what do you make of this?"

Peter Carlotti was small, dark and intense, with a big beak of a nose and a thinning thatch of dark hair. He called up the display on his workstation and scowled at the information coming up on the screen. He was unusual among astronomers in that he had actually spent considerable time in space. That deep space experience was one of the reasons he had been chosen to head up the astronomical team on the *Maxwell*.

"Millimeter wavelength. And strong," he said to his subordinate. "That star is doing some damned odd things." He watched the data a minute more and his scowl deepened.

"I think we'd better let the rest of the team in on this. Call the heads of the astronomy departments and tell them we'll

have an additional agenda item at the First Look meeting."
He glanced at his watch. "When is that meeting, anyhow?"

"A little more than four hours from now." His subordinate
popped up a schedule window. "That will be just after spin's
scheduled to be restored."

"Good. Maybe everyone's stomach will have settled down
by then. Make sure everyone is notified."

The subordinate snorted, but very softly. His job was to
direct the instruments, not to set up a meeting. Carlotti
could do that just as easily from the other console and *he*
wasn't supposed to be on duty.

"Even the deep-sky people and the theoreticians?" his
subordinate asked. The distinction between stellar and deep-
space astronomers and the larger gap between observing
astronomers and theoreticians was centuries old, but it was
still as true as it had been when telescopes were tied to the
Earth.

"Especially the theoreticians," Carlotti grinned. "They're
going to go nuts."

"What about the crew? Should I alert them?"

"No reason. We won't need a maneuver right away and I
imagine they're all busy doing whatever it is they do on this
thing." He paused. "Oh yes, make sure Dr. Dolan's notified.
This could have some very interesting implications for planetary formations and surfaces."

He was almost rubbing his hands with excitement as he
watched the data pour onto his screen.

The gravitational detection array was four cylinders, each
about the size of one of the *Maxwell*'s shuttles. The tanks
were filled with liquid helium and carefully shielded from the
star even at this distance. In each tank were carefully sized
masses of metal with sensors that measured the size of the
masses very, very precisely. Gravity waves moving through
the cylinders changed the size of the masses and the changes
were measured.

In operation, the cylinders were placed at the vertices of a
tetrahedron spaced an exact distance apart and held in position by sensitive maneuvering units. From the six baselines
so constructed—and a mass of highly sophisticated processing
equipment on both the array and the *Maxwell*—the strength
and direction of gravity waves could be determined.

That information would be integrated with the data from the various optical and radio telescopes the ship carried and the data painstakingly reduced both by workers on the ship and later back on Earth.

The array was finicky beyond belief and the gravitational map it produced was coarse and crude, but it was the best humanity had. The map would aid future expeditions as they moved further out in the galaxy.

When the *Maxwell* left the system, the array would be left in place and operating. At intervals, a ship would visit the system to collect the data the array produced.

Jenkins had barely settled into his command couch when Ludenemeyer's face flashed up on his screen.

"We're ready to deploy, sir."

"Then deploy, Mr. Ludenemeyer." He touched another stud. "Pilot, you have the conn."

With that Jenkins became an observer. Ludenemeyer and DeRosa would handle the deployment as they had practiced it so many times on the ship's simulators. He was superfluous unless something went really wrong.

The captain watched on the screen as the enormous doors far back on the *Maxwell*'s hull slowly split open. Except for the spacesuited men hovering gnatlike around the hatch it was impossible to determine the scale.

Slowly, carefully the spacesuited workers brought the first cylinder free of its cradle. They were in no hurry. The cylinder's mass was considerable and the more carefully the cylinders were handled, the sooner the array would stop ringing, settle down and start producing useful data.

Once the cylinder was eased out into space on the shadow side of the ship, the workers erected a sun screen, a shade of thin plastic on thread-like struts. Even this far from the star the differential heating caused by sunlight could affect observations.

On signal, the ship rotated gently to bring the next sensor bay to the shadow side. Again the doors opened and the ballet was repeated.

Gently the scooters drew the four sensors off several kilometers from the *Maxwell*. Two or three spacesuited figures trailed along like pilot fish on a couple of sharks. As soon as they were a safe distance away, Jenkins ordered the ship to slide away on its maneuvering jets.

DeRosa played her sidestick gently and Jenkins heard the low "whoosh" of the bow thrusters and the ship eased away. It was so gentle there was no sensation of motion. Only the tendency of dust motes and other objects to float to the left told him the ship had been briefly under acceleration.

The units still needed to be positioned and aligned, but that was best done without the ship hovering so near. The scooters would ferry the workers back when their shifts were done and in an emergency, their inflatable auxiliary cabins would provide refuge for the crew.

While he watched the work, Jenkins considered the other problems he faced. Like most of the difficulties that have occupied captains from time immemorial, the people problems were a bigger headache than the problems with things.

The worst one, he acknowledged, was to keep the crew and the technicians and scientists from clashing. *Hell,* he thought, *I'm a ship captain, not a social director.* But he was the ship's captain and that made it his problem. For perhaps the hundredth time he wished he had Andrew Aubrey's easy way with people.

Maybe I should try to learn consensual management. The theory and practice of getting groups of people to work together by forging agreement was alien to him. Most of the time in the Space Force you never needed to work at it. Crews were small and most of the time everyone understood their jobs. If there was a problem you tried talking it out and if that didn't work, you gave a direct order.

I feel like a damn dinosaur, Jenkins thought as he watched the intricate zero-G ballet unfold on his screen.

There were nine people in the conference room when Carlotti walked in. Some of them were studying the display on the wall-sized screen at one end of the little room and others were reading off the smaller screens in the wood-grain top of the long table that nearly filled the room. One or two were huddled over a screen speaking in low tones.

"Well," Carlotti said without preamble, "I assume you've all seen what we've got so far. Does anyone have any thoughts on what that star is doing?"

"What is the spectrum on this radiation anyway?" asked

Dr. C.D. MacNamara, a big soft man with a potato face and unruly blond hair.

"Surprisingly narrow," replied elegant little Winston Chang. "Within that spectrum there are three or four strong peaks close together."

Charlie George, the head of the spectroscopy section, ran a liver-spotted hand through his thinning white hair. "That's a damned odd configuration," he said as he scowled at the displays.

"A natural maser!" MacNamara exclaimed. "The star has a thick hydrogen corona and it's masing."

"That's been theorized, of course," Carlotti said.

"And here we have the first true example of it," MacNamara said triumphantly. In astronomical circles he was known for his rather heterodox views on stellar atmospheres.

"I wonder," Chang said. "It doesn't precisely conform to the theoretical predictions for a natural maser. Dr. George?"

Charlie George shrugged. "Hell, I don't know. It's damned odd, but I've seen stranger emission spectra."

MacNamara waved that aside. "Perhaps our initial readings were not completely accurate. Or perhaps the mechanism is more complex than we had imagined. It is certainly coherent or near-coherent radiation."

Sharon Dolan sat at one corner of the table and said nothing. As the only planetologist on board she was the head of her own, one-woman, department. Professional courtesy demanded she be here but no one expected her to say anything.

Carlotti sighed. The eternal problem of astronomy was trying to decide whether anomalies meant something or if they were simply problems with the data. "The data is still coming in. We'll know more as we get it analyzed. If worse comes to worst we can always divert one of the large arrays to study the system more closely." He made a face. Any diversion would upset observation schedules which had been worked out months in advance. Worse, it was bound to produce strains and infighting among astronomers whose observations would have to be delayed.

"I think the appropriate thing to do is to let it ride for now. We can meet again tomorrow afternoon and see if the data makes more sense. Shall we say three P.M.?"

* * *

"I hope you like bread pudding because we're going to have a lot of it. They didn't even eat the toast."

Carmella O'Hara ran a brush through her short dark hair while her friend chattered on.

"It must be rough to cook and then have nobody to eat it," she said to her friend lounging on the bunk in her tiny cabin.

Mary Beth wrinkled her nose. "In catering you don't expect to be *appreciated*. But when you overestimate or underestimate how much food you'll need, you feel like you're a professional failure or something."

Carmella laughed and nodded. That was why she liked Mary Beth, she thought. When she was with the plump little blonde it was easy to relax and laugh. Pilots, vacuum jacks and engineers were so damn serious all the time, and Mary Beth Villa didn't know the meaning of the word.

There was a knock at the door. Hairbrush in hand, Carmella swiveled around to open it.

There was Iron Alice DeRosa.

"Hello Cammy," the older woman said.

Carmella O'Hara's stomach tied itself in the old familiar knot.

"Come in," she said softly.

Iron Alice stepped into the room and at Carmella's gesture settled herself on the bunk next to Mary Beth.

"This is Mary Beth Villa," Carmella said by way of introduction.

Iron Alice nodded and looked at the young woman. "You're not a pilot, are you?" she asked in her gravelly voice.

"No ma'am," Mary Beth used the title automatically. "I'm in the Quartermaster division." She fidgeted and tried not to stare at the legend sitting next to her.

"Well, I won't stay," Iron Alice said. "I just came off shift and I wanted to say hello. How you doing?"

"Just fine," Carmella said.

"Getting your simulator time in?"

"Oh yeah. They keep us pretty busy."

"That's good. Very good." She got up. "I'll talk to you later, then. A pleasure meeting you, Mary Beth." She patted Carmella on the shoulder and was gone.

"Jesus," Mary Beth said, eyes wide. "I didn't know you knew *her*."

"Oh yeah," Carmella said uncomfortably. "Yeah, I know her. She's my aunt."

"Oh. So that's what they meant."

Carmella's antenna quivered. "Who? What did they mean?"

Her friend looked embarrassed. "Well, I heard some people talking once, you know."

"Yeah, I know," Carmella said tiredly. "Look, Mary Beth, I've never asked Aunt Alice for anything. No special favors, nothing."

"Sure. I understand."

Like hell you do, Carmella thought. No one understood what it was like to have a legend for a relative, someone who insisted on doing things for you whether you wanted it or not. Someone you looked up to and were scared to death of at the same time.

When she found out the Americans were going to get an interstellar mission, Carmella had put in for a slot. Naturally. She'd remembered how thrilled she'd been when she had not only been chosen, but had been given the rank of Senior Pilot.

She also remembered how it had all turned to dust when she found out who the Command Pilot for the *Maxwell* was. In addition to acting as pilot for the ship and executive officer, the Command Pilot had a major role in picking the pilots for the ship's tugs and shuttles. Naturally.

The knot in her stomach drew even tighter.

"Carmella," Mary Beth asked at last, "is she always like that?"

"Well, no, I mean she wasn't around home. Look, Mary Beth, let's just drop it, okay? And please don't talk about this. I mean to anyone."

The next "afternoon" a very confused group of astronomers met in the conference rooms in the forward part of Spin. It was a larger room than the one the department heads had used the day before because there were a lot more people at this one. Word of the star's anomalies had spread and as more data had come in more people had gotten interested in this very strange new sun.

In addition to the department heads, a number of other specialists were there. Father Michael Simon had joined the group and even Dr. Takiuji had forgone his usual iaido practice to be in on the meeting.

"This doesn't make any sense," Dr. George said half-disgustedly as he studied the information displayed on the wall-sized screen at the end of the room. "This isn't a picture of a star, it's a portrait of madness."

That wasn't a new observation. For nearly an hour the group had been poring over the data and the results of the analysis programs trying to fit what the instruments were telling them into some coherent picture.

"Are we sure the instruments are functioning correctly?" C.D. MacNamara asked almost petulantly. The new data made it very obvious that if the star was masing nearly everything he believed about stellar atmospheres had to be wrong.

"The instruments, yes," Peter Carlotti told them. "We think the processing and data reduction software is correct as well, but there's always the possibility of an obscure bug of some sort."

He looked like he had just found half a worm in an apple and so did a couple of the others. A major software problem would seriously damage their ability to make meaningful observations.

"A bug like that would hardly be obscure, I think," Father Simon said.

"All right," Carlotti announced, "brainstorming time. Does anyone have a hypothesis, no matter how far-fetched, that might possibly explain all this."

"There is one hypothesis under which it does make sense," Winston Chang said softly.

"Which is?" MacNamara snapped.

"Which is that the system has a high civilization of its own. What we're seeing is produced by intelligence."

For a moment no one said anything.

"Oh my," Dr. George murmured from the end of the table. "Oh my."

"Well, it would explain the readings," Chang said.

"That hypothesis would explain anything," MacNamara said tartly.

"LGM? It has for over a century," Carlotti said. LGM was astronomers' shorthand for "Little Green Men," the explanation that anomalous results are caused by alien civilizations.

In its time it had been suggested to account for phenomena that later proved to be things as diverse as quasars and pulsars. It remained the hypothesis of desperation in astronomy.

"If there was someone out there we would have seen something more concrete by now," someone objected. "Even those small sensors could have picked them up at this distance."

"Not necessarily," Sharon Dolan said. "You have been concentrating on the star and ignored the planets and the space around them."

Carlotti had the grace to look uncomfortable. Sharon had asked for early observing time for the planets on the small scopes and been turned down.

"It's still preposterous," MacNamara said.

"Fortunately it's testable," Carlotti said. "It won't take much to scan those planets and the nearby regions. If there is something there we should find it fast enough." He shifted in his chair, as if to rise. "It will take us several hours to organize a program of observation for these new phenomena anyway. While we are doing that, we might as well check the planets. Shall we meet again in four hours to discuss observing strategy?" There was a chorus of assent and the meeting broke up.

Four hours! Sharon thought as she settled herself down at the workstation in the Telescope Shack. The implication was clear. She'd have the use of the scopes only until the rest of the astronomical team was organized. That was barely enough time to start examining the planets, much less do any serious work. There was no time to implement a systematic observing plan. She'd just have to sweep the inner planets with the instruments and try to analyze the data on the fly. With luck maybe something would turn up that she could use to argue for more instrument time.

Later on she'd be able to use the smaller instruments freely, of course—after the big ones were deployed and the more senior researchers were occupied elsewhere. But that would take weeks and she wanted to know what was going on near that star *now*.

Well, she thought, *maybe I'll get lucky*.

The first information came from the arrays. The images from the telescopes had to be enhanced to be meaningful and even with the *Maxwell's* computers that took time. The array data would benefit from enhancement too, but it could be run through simpler, faster programs to get a first cut.

Sharon called for an overview of the inner system and frowned at the result. The infrared scan was showing point sources everywhere. There was a band of roughly equally active heat sources around the star and many others scattered more-or-less randomly throughout the field of view.

The creases on her forehead got deeper and she punched a few keys. There were objects that produced an effect like that, but the display showed an absurdly large number of them.

Then the second display came up and she caught her breath. Most of the heat sources were at about the same temperature no matter how far they were from the star! That implied that the objects were producing their own heat and that made no sense at all.

Or maybe it does!

"Jaysus," Sharon Dolan breathed. "Oh Jaysus."

Frantically she began punching buttons to train one of the telescopes on the nearest of the heat sources.

Carlotti was on the screen. That in itself was odd, Jenkins thought. The astronomer usually liked to be where the action was and unlike most of the scientific personnel he wasn't afflicted with space sickness.

"Captain, can you turn the ship to a bearing of twenty-seven degrees?" Carlotti was pale and his dark hair was even more unruly than usual.

"Turn the ship?" Jenkins repeated, mystified.

"Slew it, actually. We want to bring all four of the forward telescopes to bear on something."

"Well, we aren't scheduled for maneuvering . . ."

"Captain, please." Carlotti's voice was agonized.

"You in, Al?" Jenkins asked.

"Here." DeRosa's face blossomed in a window at the bottom of Jenkins' screen.

"You heard what he wants? Can we do it?"

"Yeah. Not much of a maneuver. Take us about ten minutes to do it, plus thirty minutes to secure for maneuvering."

"Thirty minutes?" Carlotti sounded like he was in pain.

"This is a big ship, Dr. Carlotti."

"Yes, you're right. Very well, but please as quickly as possible."

40

"Would you mind telling me what this is about?"

Carlotti looked uncomfortable. "We have an anomalous object we wish to observe using all four telescopes as a synthetic aperture optical array. I'd rather not say more until we have more data." With that he blinked off.

Jenkins touched a pad and his pilot's face grew to fill the whole screen.

"What do you suppose that's all about?"

Iron Alice shrugged. "Someone probably spotted a comet or something."

"Think they'll tell us about it when it's all over?"

DeRosa made a face. "For weeks. At every opportunity."

Captain Jenkins and the crew had their own telescopes of course, but they were wide-field instruments trained outward to precisely fix the *Maxwell's* position and relative motion. There were position checks on the star but the navigation software wasn't looking for oddities. It was where it was supposed to be and their relative motion to it was within parameters. That was enough.

Dr. Peter Carlotti was practically beside himself. "Dammit, there can't possibly be life in this system! That's an M2 red dwarf. The life zone's too narrow and none of those planets are the right type."

In spite of efforts to keep the discovery a secret there were nearly thirty people jammed into the conference room and more gathered outside the door. The meeting wasn't supposed to start for another fifteen minutes but already the arguments waxed hot and heavy.

"Not right for our kind of life, but obviously right for someone's," Winston Chang corrected him smoothly.

"Not right for anyone's," Carlotti snapped. "The inner planet is as hot and airless as Mercury and the two others are Mars-types."

"There was a lot of speculation about men from Mars."

Carlotti snorted. "Then where are the signs? Any civilization able to go into space would leave traces all over the surface of its planet and there are none here."

"We would," Chang said. "That doesn't mean everyone would. Besides, what about the Jovians? There seems to be a lot of traffic around them."

41

"If they evolved on a Jovian world then why are the habitats all further in toward the star?" Carlotti shot back.

Chang shrugged. "Insufficient data. All we know is that intelligent life did evolve here."

"Oh, but it didn't," Sharon Dolan put in breathlessly as she elbowed her way into the room. "At least, I doubt seriously it did."

Everyone looked at her and her cheeks grew red.

"I'm sorry I'm late," she said quietly. One of the seated astronomers got up to give her a chair and, flushed with her new importance, Sharon plopped down in it.

"What leads you to that conclusion, Dr. Dolan?" Andrew Aubrey asked from his place at the head of the table. He hadn't been formally invited but no one was really surprised he was attending.

"Well, none of the planets in the system are habitable by our standards. And the placement of the habitats indicates they prefer conditions much like ours."

"Some of those habitats are out to the orbit of the Jovians," Carlotti objected.

"Yes, but those have what appear to be mirrors to concentrate the sunlight. Wherever they live now, they prefer a temperature range much like ours. That argues for a water-based metabolism and probably oxygen/water, although that last is somewhat speculative.

"Besides," she added, "the star's too cool for life to develop here. So they came from somewhere else."

"So not only have we found our first intelligent species, we have also found an intelligent interstellar species."

"But how in the world could something like that remain hidden from us?" MacNamara asked.

"For one thing, we weren't looking," the planetologist told them. "After the shock wore off I went back over our software. It's designed to discard readings that are outside the accepted parameters on the grounds that they are obviously artifacts." She made a face. "Our so-helpful computers were discarding about ninety percent of the readings that indicated intelligent life here."

"Well, why haven't we detected their radio signals?" demanded another person. "We're certainly close enough."

"Two reasons," Dr. George put in. "First, we're still not finding a lot of radio. We suspect they transmit information by laser. At least we've seen some modulated monochromatic light sources at frequencies that would be good for intra-system transmission.

"The other reason is that their signals are digitized and highly complex. At first hearing they sound like noise. If you apply analysis you will find regularities, but it is not something obvious like Morse Code."

"What?" said one of the astronomers and his neighbor, a communications buff, leaned over to whisper an explanation to him while the main discussion went on.

"I wasn't thinking just of this expedition," MacNamara said. "I was thinking of all the time we have spent in the last hundred years looking for intelligent radio signals. Surely they would maintain communication between the star systems even if there wasn't much direct trade."

"Perhaps they don't have a faster than light communicator," Carlotti said. "We don't. Or if all their messages are going by ship we'd never detect them."

"Ridiculous!" someone snapped and that produced another babble.

"Gentlemen," Andrew Aubrey's voice cut through the buzz, "ladies. This clearly needs to be shared with the rest of the people on the ship. I intend to convene a meeting of the Ship's Council in," he looked at his watch, "say, ninety minutes. Dr. Carlotti, do you think you could pull together a presentation by then to brief the rest of the ship on the basics of the situation?"

"Dr. Dolan is really the person to make the presentation," Carlotti said. "It was her discovery, after all."

Aubrey turned to her. "Dr. Dolan."

"Of course I can." Then she paused. "But has anyone told the captain about this?"

Carlotti looked stricken. "Oh dear."

"You mean you have known this system was inhabited for hours and you didn't notify me?" Captain Peter Jenkins demanded.

"We have suspected something for hours," Andrew Aubrey corrected him. "We did not reach a consensus until a few minutes ago."

"Jesus," said Iron Alice DeRosa from the pilot's station. If Aubrey heard he took no notice.

"Did it ever occur to you that this was a circumstance that might affect the safety or functioning of this ship?"

Aubrey nodded. "Yes, Captain, you're quite right. We should have notified you. I am sorry for the oversight, but in the rush of the moment . . ."

"Dr. Aubrey," said Captain Jenkins tightly, "I would appreciate if there were no more oversights."

"Of course, Captain. We will do our best to see that there are not."

The way he said it made Jenkins feel as if he had made an unreasonable request and Aubrey was graciously ignoring his bad manners by granting it.

"I have already convened a meeting of the Ship's Council for an hour from now, if that is convenient?"

An hour! Jenkins thought, but he said, "That will be fine."

As Aubrey twisted and swam clumsily toward the exit and gravity, Jenkins turned away.

"Get me Ludenemeyer," he barked over the intercom. "I want to know how soon we can get out of here."

"I don't suppose there's any chance they don't know we're here?" the navigation officer asked.

"Only if they're deaf," Iron Alice told him. "The blast of radio noise this thing puts out when it breaks in is enough to alert the whole system. By now every one in the system knows something is up. And if they bring their telescopes around they'll have seen our torch flame."

"Damn," said the navigator without heat.

In contrast to the babble and confusion of the astronomers' meeting, the meeting of the Ship's Council was subdued. The twenty members listened intently as Sharon Dolan made her presentation. Occasionally someone's attention would wander to a desk screen as they used hypertext to call up an explanation of a point, but most of them simply sat and listened intently.

Abstractly, Sharon Dolan was glad everyone was so quiet. She had never addressed anything bigger than a poster session at a scientific meeting before and her voice was thin and weak from strain and excitement.

"In conclusion, we know that, first, the system is definitely inhabited. There is absolutely no question of that now.

"Second, the aliens have a high technological civilization.

Since we modified our software, we have found literally hundreds of O'Neill colonies in orbit around this star and we are finding more all the time. There is also a ring of power satellites in closer to the star and there are signs of mining activities in the asteroid belt and in the Jovian systems." She paused to take another drink of water. In less than a half hour she had nearly emptied the pitcher on the table.

"Beyond that we know very little. We can only speculate until we get more data."

"Which planet are they from?" someone broke in.

"We don't know yet," Sharon said. "There are no definite signs of habitation on any of the planets we have examined." By mutual consent she had not mentioned her belief that the aliens came from outside the star system.

"Do we know if they know we're here?" another Council member asked.

"Probably," Sharon said. "They couldn't have missed the burst of noise the drive makes in breaking out and if their instruments are any good they may well have picked up the flame of our torch as we maneuvered."

Autro DeLorenzo slammed his hand down on the table with a noise that rang out like a pistol shot. "That settles it. We leave *now*."

"What?" Sharon said, bewildered by his statement and his vehemence.

"We get the hell out of here," DeLorenzo growled. "We're virtually unarmed and we've blundered into something we can't handle."

"Don't you think you're being a little hasty?" Aubrey said mildly. "There is an enormous amount we can learn here, surely."

"And an enormous amount they can learn from us," the South American shot back. "We're scouts and part of a scout's job is to know when to run for it."

"I don't think our mission was conceived in military terms."

"Well, we'd better start thinking of it in military terms.

"What makes you think they are hostile?"

"What makes you think they aren't?" DeLorenzo countered.

"We've seen no evidence of anything hostile."

DeLorenzo grinned wickedly. "You want to bet your life

45

on that, Aubrey? You want to bet the ship on it? Do you want to bet all of Earth on it? Because those are the stakes. If they are hostile there is enough stuff on this ship to lead them right back to where we come from."

"*Major*," said MacNamara, "I wish you would stop talking like a character in a bad science fiction movie."

"Doctor, I wish you would get your head out of your ass."

MacNamara's head jerked back as if he had been slapped. "I hardly think vulgarity will help us handle the situation, Major." He emphasized DeLorenzo's title with just a hint of a sneer.

"The only thing that will help us, *Doctor*, is to get out of here and I mean right now."

"Gentlemen, please," Aubrey put in. "This is highly premature. Besides, whether we leave or not is really the captain's decision, isn't it? You've always been a strong supporter of the captain's authority, Major, and I'm sure you have no wish for the Council to usurp it now."

"The captain is going to order us out of here real quick," DeLorenzo predicted.

"That is the captain's decision," Aubrey told him.

In the control room Captain Peter Jenkins looked up at the big overhead screen and examined the sight. The scale was compressed and within the orbits of the gas giants the screen appeared spangled with points of silver, each representing a floating habitat. There were already more than five hundred of them and as Jenkins watched another silver pinpoint sprang into existence.

"Fantastic," breathed a voice behind him. "Utterly fantastic."

Jenkins turned and saw Andrew Aubrey on the bridge for the second time today, staring transfixed at the display. He was so engrossed he didn't show his usual discomfort in zero gravity. Then he seemed to shake himself and turned to Jenkins.

"Captain, may I talk to you privately?"

Jenkins nodded. "Of course, Dr. Aubrey, please step into my office."

The office was a cubbyhole off the bridge. There was barely enough room for a desk and the affectation of three chairs—practically useless in a part of the ship that never knew gravity.

"You might be more comfortable if you belted yourself in," Jenkins told his guest, pointing to the restraints attached to the chair arms as he closed the door behind him. Aubrey strapped himself down and Jenkins eased into his seat.

"Now, Doctor, what can I do for you?"

"Captain, the Ship's Council has been meeting to decide what we should do. I wanted to get your thoughts."

"I really haven't had time to think about it, Dr. Aubrey. I do know one thing. If there is any possibility of danger to the ship or the crew, we're leaving immediately."

"I'm sure the Ship's Council would agree with you," Aubrey said. "However, the Council is also concerned that we don't jeopardize this enormous opportunity."

"With all due respect, Doctor, this is a matter of the ship's safety. It is not a matter for the Ship's Council."

"I understand your concern. But surely you would consult before taking any action."

"Not if I believed our safety was involved."

"Captain, may I speak frankly again?"

"You usually do," Jenkins said with a slight smile.

Aubrey returned the smile, charmingly. "I realize this has not been an easy voyage for you because of the, ah, cultural conflicts, and believe me when I say that the Council has done everything in its power to minimize the problems. However I think that on this issue the conflicts come to a head.

"Now obviously we have a common interest here," he went on. "No one wants to see the ship endangered. You do see that, don't you?" Again the smile and Jenkins nodded half-reluctantly.

"Good. Because what we are really dealing with here is a difference in methods, not goals."

Aubrey leaned forward, elbows on knees and hands clasped. "You mentioned your concern for the people on the ship as well as the ship itself. Don't you think that part of that concern should be to involve them in deciding their own fate? What the Council is essentially saying is that it's important for everyone to have some control over what happens to them."

"Of course I agree, to an extent," Jenkins said. "But I'm still the one responsible for the ultimate safety of the *Maxwell*."

"And that's where the clash of cultures enters in. In a

47

hierarchical system, like the Space Force, decision making and power flows from the top down. In a consensual system, decisions are made by those affected. Aside from the military," Aubrey pronounced the word in a way that wasn't quite a sneer, "the Space Force is perhaps the most rigidly hierarchical system left. Scientists, by the nature of their work, are among the most consensual."

He held up a hand to forestall an objection Jenkins had no intention of making. "I'm not trying to be insulting in saying that. Hierarchical organization isn't always a bad thing. I can understand why it has survived so long in the Space Force, for example. But it isn't the way most of the modern world works and it isn't what most people are used to any more. We've learned to do things differently because we had to. And we very nearly didn't learn it in time."

"What's your point?"

"Simply this. No one wants to put the ship in danger. But any danger is not going to be immediate. We're in no danger now and we can see anything coming for millions of kilometers in any direction, correct?"

Jenkins nodded.

"That being the case, there is time for all of us to have a role in making the decision. We would have hours or days to forge a consensus before we act."

"Doctor Aubrey, I cannot abdicate my responsibility for the ship's safety."

"No one is asking you to, Captain. Only that you take us into your confidence before deciding our futures." He paused, studying Jenkins intently. The captain said nothing.

"Captain, will you promise me one thing?" Aubrey said at last. "That when the time comes you will make your decision based on the facts, not fears or speculations."

Jenkins considered, looking for traps. "That seems reasonable enough," he said finally.

Aubrey's smooth face split into a grin. "Fine, Captain. That's all I ask."

"Don't read too much into that," Jenkins said. "If there is any sign . . ." The intercom chimed before he could complete the sentence.

"Captain, you'd better get up here," DeRosa's voice came over the speaker. "There's something I think you should see."

Without another word, Jenkins stood up and catapulted past the startled Aubrey. The scientist hesitated a second and then followed.

One look at the big display told him why DeRosa wanted him back on the bridge. On the screen one of the dots flamed a brilliant green.

"Strong energy emission from that habitat," DeRosa said. "It appears to be monochromatic."

The captain started. "A weapon? An attempt to communicate?"

"Not communication," the pilot reported. "There's no modulation of the beam." A pause. "I don't think it's a weapon either. At least nothing that can reach us this far out." Another pause. "I think it's a launcher. I think they just used a laser to launch something in our general direction."

"A laser launch in space?"

Iron Alice shrugged. "Makes sense of a sort. It's a real efficient way to give something an initial kick. Not the way we'd do it, but . . ." She shrugged again.

"And it would keep the level of pollutants near the habitat," Aubrey said breathlessly as he came swimming through the door. "Beautiful."

The captain crossed to his console and punched into the comm. Carlotti's face bloomed on the screen. "Ah, Captain, I was just going to call you. There's been a change . . ."

"I know Dr. Carlotti, we have it here too. Can your people get us spectroscopic data on that emission?"

The astronomer hesitated. "We can try. I think one of the smaller instruments might be adapted for that sort of work. We'd need a low-power wide-field scan, but yes, I think we have something that will work."

"Fine. And once you get started on that can you come to the bridge? And bring Dr. Dolan with you. And Major DeLorenzo." Out of the corner of his eye Jenkins saw Aubrey wince.

"Doctor, if you're going to stay, please strap yourself into one of the observer's couches," he directed. Aubrey really had nothing to contribute, and Jenkins would have preferred to send him off the bridge, but he knew it would cause more problems than it would solve. He needed Carlotti and Dolan for their technical knowledge and DeLorenzo because of his all-around engineering background, but he doubted that explanation would wash with Aubrey. *Fortunately*, he thought, *we've got the room on this ship.* The control room on the average space force vessel was cramped with just the officers. The *Maxwell's* bridge had been designed to take a lot more visitors.

DeLorenzo came charging onto the bridge in less than five minutes. Carlotti and Dolan arrived a few minutes later. Still the single point flared a brilliant green on their screens. He directed Carlotti to a vacant console and DeLorenzo went to peer over his shoulder.

"Any more information?" he asked as soon as Carlotti was settled in.

"Just that what we're seeing is consistent with a laser launch. And there definitely appears to be something in front of those beams. Possibly a light sail."

The captain punched more buttons and Ludenemeyer blinked up in a corner of his screen. "Mr. Ludenemeyer, is that heading for us?"

The engineer shrugged. "We don't know the mass of the object, but, yes, it is possible that an object launched on that trajectory might intercept us.

"Of course, I really can't tell much with what I've got down here," he added hopefully.

"All right Mr. Ludenemeyer. Come forward to the bridge. You might as well join the party too. But keep the drive hot!" he commanded as the engineering officer grinned and broke contact.

For the next several hours there was nothing for the group to do but watch the unwavering green point of light and do make-work extrapolations as new data arrived. Jenkins moodily sucked coffee bulbs until he knew his stomach was going to pay for it tomorrow and watched as the lines and projections grew on his screen.

Sharon drifted over to look over his shoulder. Normally that would have irritated Jenkins, but he found her presence comforting instead.

"Dr. Dolan," he said as she made a move to drift back to Carlotti's station, "could you explain to me why this system isn't supposed to have life?"

"Because that's an M2 star," Sharon said, surprised.

"Yes, but why does that preclude life?" Jenkins looked apologetic. "Forgive me, but I am not very well versed on planetology."

"Well, there are several things. M2s put out a lot less energy than our sun. Their surface temperature is around half that of the Sun, you know, and that means the life zone—the area where water can exist as a liquid—is considerably closer to the star and much smaller than it is on a G-type like our sun.

"That introduces two problems. First, it's much less likely that a planet's orbit will fall within the life zone and in fact none of the planets in this system do, really.

"The second problem is that the drag from the star's gravity will have slowed the rotations of the inner planets considerably. The outermost Mars-type has a rotation period several times that of Earth and the ones further in probably barely rotate at all. A very slow rotation usually makes conditions on a planet unsuitable for life."

She paused. "At least that's the pattern we've found so far."

"And we've seen a lot of planets," Jenkins added.

Oh yes, thought Sharon, *we've seen lots of planets. But none you'd care to live on. None that could be like Earth again.*

When the star drive had been developed, man had gone looking for real estate. The first expeditions had gone out to the nearest stars that might have Earth-like planets.

The results had been scientifically fascinating and uniformly disappointing. The expeditions had found planets, but none of them Earth-like. Every single star in this neck of the galaxy seemed to have its quota of Jovian gas giants, small desolate Mars-types and a few hot hellish Venerian worlds. But no Earth-like planets at all. No oxygen worlds, no seas of liquid water and no life.

"They've cut off their lasers," DeRosa announced, scanning her console quickly.

"Yes, but there's something else there now," Carlotti said. "There's a rocket exhaust of some kind."

"What kind?" Jenkins demanded.

"Tell you in a minute." He turned back to his instruments.

No one was terribly surprised. Although you could propel a ship all the way to its destination on lasers alone, it made more sense to use them just for the initial launch. Their projections of the object's course had made allowances for a shift to a reaction engine at some point.

"We got a reading on their exhaust, Captain," Carlotti said. "It's hydrox."

"*What?*"

"Hydrox," the astronomer repeated. "You know, hydrogen-oxygen."

Jenkins turned that over in his mind. A H2-02 rocket had considerably less specific impulse than the fusion torch the *Maxwell* used. A culture capable of building advanced laser launchers ought to be able to do better than that.

"If that's the best they can do, then what the hell are they using to power those lasers?" DeLorenzo asked.

"That's another very good question, Major," Jenkins put in. "I hope we can get some answers before we have too many more of them."

The mission had been hasty and ill-prepared. It was driven by a single imperative—reach the strangers quickly! Hence the laser launch.

But even in haste there are rules that must be obeyed and constraints to be considered. As the ship hurtled out, driven first by the bank of lasers and then by the thrust of its rockets, frantic negotiations continued in its wake. Decisions were reached, exceptions made and conventions set aside. At last the permission the ship's captain had awaited since launch came blasting through on a tight beam of laser light.

"Captain, their rockets just went out."

With a flip of his arms and a flick of his leg, Jenkins scooted over to look at the readout. "Where are they headed?"

Iron Alice punched in a few commands and scowled. "It doesn't look like they're headed anywhere," she said. "Maybe it's a rendezvous, but it doesn't make a lot of sense."

"Wait a minute," the astronomer called out. "I think I'm still getting something."

"Cooling engines?" Jenkins suggested.

"I don't know. I don't think . . . hold it." He fiddled frantically with his display and patterns of lines danced across the screen.

"Ion drive," he said, looking up. "They just switched to an ion drive using cesium as the reaction mass."

"Al, what's their acceleration?"

"Take time to be sure. Right now just under one hundredth

of a G. It may go higher." She called up another display on her screen. "Then again it may not. If they hold their acceleration about where they have it now they'll be on an intercept course with us." She scowled at the screen. "It will have to go a little higher since presumably they are going to do a turn-around and start breaking at mid course, but yeah, in about six weeks we're gonna have company."

"Constant acceleration drive," said Jenkins. "Laser launch to give them an initial boost and then drive straight on. They can reach any place in this system in a few weeks."

"So why wait until they were so far out to light up?" the pilot asked. "They could be here a hell of a lot sooner if they had turned on their drive as soon as the lasers shut down instead of using hydrox to start."

"Maybe it takes time to light and they were in a hurry."

The pilot frowned. "Maybe, but they still would have been ahead if they waited until the drive was ready instead of using those boosters."

"I don't think you'd want to turn on that ion drive too close to the habitat," Carlotti said. "Between the electric field and the cesium ions it could interfere with a lot of space-based activities."

"That explains the laser launcher, but not the hydrox rockets," DeRosa said. "Why load yourself down with a lot of tankage and propellant when you've got an ion drive? You just don't gain that much velocity."

Sharon Dolan came up beside Jenkins.

"Captain, can you explain something to me now?"

"If I can."

"If those aliens are as advanced as we think they are, and if they're in such a hurry to meet us, why don't they use a fusion-powered ship?"

"I can think of several possible reasons. For one thing, a fusion torch is big. You need a separate fusion pile to drive the torch, plus whatever power source you use for your ship—in our case a second fusion pile."

Sharon frowned, prettily, Jenkins thought. "But it is still a constant acceleration drive."

"No, it's a high acceleration drive, not a constant acceleration one," Jenkins told her. "It can drive us at a steady acceleration for some weeks if it had to, but that's not what it's designed for.

"Basically a torch is supposed to produce a lot of thrust over a fairly short period of time. It's not nearly as efficient as an ion engine, but it gives a hell of a push when we need it. And we need it. A starship has to be able to shed velocity fast when we break out from KOH drive. That takes very powerful engines.

"Besides that, a fusion torch is hideously expensive to run. It took an appreciable fraction of the deuterium and tritium mined over two years to enrich the hydrogen in the *Maxwell*'s tanks. You couldn't do that for every ship in the system. We can barely afford to do it for the star ships we have operating."

Sharon was silent for a moment watching the displays. Out of the corner of his eye Jenkins watched her.

"Do you think they can build a fusion torch?"

"Probably. A torch is just a modified fusion pile and they must have something like that on the ship to power the ion drive.

"An ion drive is much more efficient. It makes better use of its energy than nearly any other form of propulsion and it is ideally suited to constant acceleration missions."

"Then why don't we have one?"

"Two reasons. First, an ion drive by its nature has a relatively low maximum acceleration. We need a high maximum acceleration because we may not have much room to slow down when we break out. The second reason is we can't build one capable of giving high enough acceleration to a ship to make it worthwhile."

"So they're more advanced," Sharon said slowly, not liking the idea.

"Let's just say they do some things more efficiently than we do."

"If they're so much more efficient why don't they use beamed power to power their ships?" Carlotti put in from where he had been listening. "That would give them efficiency and high-acceleration."

"Maybe they don't know how," Sharon suggested.

"They beam power from those power stations near the star out to the Colonies. For that matter, we use the same technique with our powersats."

"I'll tell you why not," DeLorenzo said, "because our alien friends are not fools. To power a ship you would have to concentrate the beam down to a few square meters. If it jiggles even just a little you have a sword of energy reaching out across your system. Any kind of accident or failure of control and poof!" He made a throw-away motion.

"Makes sense," Ludenemeyer said. "Living in space habitats as they do they would we terribly vulnerable to an accident like that."

Sharon turned back to Jenkins. "What's going to happen when they reach us?" she asked.

"That's a very good question. I wish I knew the answer."

"I wonder what the hell that ship looks like," Ludenemeyer said thoughtfully. "An ion drive needs a long, long accelerator sticking out the back and a laser-launched ship wants some kind of big sail structure to catch the light. It must be an ugly sucker."

"Their standards of beauty may be different from ours," Aubrey said from his couch.

Ludenemeyer shrugged. "Hybrid propulsion systems like that are damned near impossible to make pretty by any standard."

Aubrey smiled tolerantly. "Ethnocentrism?"

"Nope, engineering."

"Can we get a visual image of them?" Jenkins called across the bridge.

Carlotti shook his head. "We don't have anything designed for that kind of work. We could deploy one of the large arrays, I suppose, but that would take several days."

"Damn," Jenkins breathed. "A starship full of astronomical equipment and we don't have anything that will track an object right in the planetary system."

"That was hardly one of the parameters in our planning," Carlotti told him.

Again the Ship's Council met in the large forward conference room; this time Captain Jenkins and Ludenemeyer were present, along with Sharon Dolan and one or two other specialists. Although the meeting had been physically closed to keep down the crowds, screens all over the ship were tuned in. Clearly, this was the most critical meeting the Ship's Council was ever likely to have and no one wanted to miss it.

Aubrey started off by bringing the Council, and through the screens, the rest of the ship's complement, up to date.

"The upshot is," he paused briefly and went on. "The aliens definitely know we are here. They have launched at least one ship out to meet us. We may assume we are under observation by instruments at least as good as our own."

That produced a ripple throughout the room. Almost everyone at the table knew just how good modern astronomical instruments were. Even an object as small as the *Maxwell* could have little to hide at these distances.

"If we stay where we are the aliens will be in physical contact with us in less than six weeks. The question is," he looked up and down the table, "what do we do?"

"Aren't there some kind of rules about alien contact?" one of the Council members asked.

"Very sketchy," Jenkins said. "Anyone who thinks they have seen any sign of intelligent non-humans is supposed to report immediately."

"There was a lot of discussion about fifty or sixty years ago," Sharon Dolan said from down the table. "There were proposals to establish a very elaborate system of rules to govern first contact, but eventually they all fell through. We realized we simply didn't know enough about possible aliens to set firm guidelines." *And besides, we lost faith that there were any aliens*, she thought.

"But the standing orders are to report immediately?" DeLorenzo asked sharply.

"Well, yes," Jenkins said.

"That settles it then," the major said firmly. "We run for Earth. Right now."

"Captain, I believe you have considerable latitude in how you carry out your orders?" Aubrey put in. "Those orders were hardly drawn to cover a starship a hundred light years out. They were drawn up to cover the situation in the solar system and they were not revised when we started sending out starships. Besides, what can we report? We don't know anything."

"We know there's someone else out there," DeLorenzo replied. "That's enough."

"I beg your pardon Major, but I don't think it's nearly enough," Aubrey said. "After all, what can we tell Earth? Only that there are aliens here with a space-faring civilization. We know nothing else about them, not even what they look like. How much good would that information do Earth?"

"That's enough."

"Be reasonable, Major," Aubrey went on. "It will take us months to get home and months to mount another expedition. Two or three years at least before an expedition can reach here again. What harm is there in waiting a while longer until we can report more accurately?"

"Plenty if we never make it home," DeLorenzo told him.

"I see no reason to assume we won't," Aubrey said.

"Captain, what is our armament like?" DeLorenzo asked.

Jenkins blinked. "I beg your pardon?"

"Armament? How are we armed?"

"Well, we aren't. I mean there are the pistols in the provost marshal's locker. Six or eight of them, as I recall, but that's it."

"And Dr. Takiuji's samurai sword," DeLorenzo said with a tight grin. "But we've got nothing bigger. No missile launchers, no fighting lasers. And a ship that's built to commercial standards."

"There is always the fusion torch," Ludenemeyer said. "Makes a pretty good weapon close in."

"With no tracking and the slew rate of an arthritic snail," DeLorenzo said. "No thank you."

"This is a scientific expedition, not an attack," Aubrey said stiffly.

"I'm not concerned about attack, Dr. Aubrey, I'm worried about defense."

"Defense against what?"

"Them," DeLorenzo gestured sunward.

"Major, we have been over this repeatedly. There is not one single shred of evidence they intend to attack us or anyone."

"And there's no evidence they don't," DeLorenzo said. "We need to get out of here now."

"Formally, that is the captain's decision," Aubrey said carefully. "After all, this could be construed as a matter of ship's safety."

Jenkins looked up and down the table. *And there's no doubt which way you want me to decide*, he thought, looking at the expectant faces. He didn't like it, his instincts told him he was wrong. But there was no hard evidence to back him up.

"All right, we make contact," Jenkins said firmly. "But we don't do it here."

"Where then?"

"In the main settlement belt. I want to get close enough to learn something and I want them to know we can come and go instantaneously." He turned to his engineering officer.

"Ludenemeyer, how close to the center of their belt of habitation can you get us?"

"Depends on where we are positioned and what our relative energy profiles are like. I'd say pretty close."

"Fine. We'll jump down into the gravity well and aim for a stable position within the habitation zone. We'll plan to undershoot rather than overshoot and try to close to our desired position on the torch."

"Moving that close to the star will play hell with our observations," Carlotti said gloomily.

"Doctor, I don't think astronomy is our main mission any more," Aubrey said.

"Oh and Ludenemeyer . . ."

"Yessir?"

"Once we jump, the drive stays hot. I want to be able to jump out of there at a moment's notice."

"Yessir, but we can't update our position often enough."

"I'm not concerned about that. I just want to be able to jump instantly. We'll worry about where we are later."

He looked up and down the table.

"If that's all then . . ." Aubrey said, and picked up his computer.

"Not quite all," DeLorenzo said as the others made to rise.

"Major?"

DeLorenzo turned to Jenkins. "Scuttling charges."

"I beg your pardon?"

"I want permission to rig scuttling charges in case we are in danger of capture."

"Absurd!" someone further down the table exploded.

"Captain, your decision carries with it enormous risks for our entire race. We need to be able to destroy the ship, or at least the most important parts of it to prevent their capture."

"I don't see that it's necessary, Major," Jenkins said soothingly. "We can jump out of here as fast as we could blow ourselves up."

"What if something knocks a hole in our hull?"

"That's not very likely."

"But we can't jump unless we can run the drive field over the entire hull, can we? One good hole and we're stuck here."

"Major, long before anything could punch that big a hole in us, we'd be out of here. Meanwhile, a destruct mechanism would be at least as big a threat to us as it would be to our aliens."

Suki sat in one corner of the Maple Lounge intent on the go board in front of him. On every side of him an electronic wind rustled the images of the sun-dappled leaves on the walls. The Japanese ignored them, just as he ignored the two or three other people in the lounge.

He had gotten into the habit of coming here every day at this time to play the ancient Japanese game with anyone who cared to challenge him. Most days that was Father Simon, but today the priest had not come.

"What are you doing?" Carlotti asked as he meandered up to Suki's table.

"Fuseki. Beginnings. Openings, you call them in chess." He pointed out the scattering of black and white stones on the board.

Carlotti stared at the board, divided by dark lines into a nineteen by nineteen grid with a half-dozen stones sitting on intersections near the corners. "You study them like chess openings?"

"Yes. For many hundreds of years. Fuseki are very important in go. They make shape that determines the rest of the game.

"Here," he gestured at two seemingly unconnected stones in the lower left hand corner of the board. "Those two establish that black will be very strong in the corner, but not so strong towards the center. That is an invitation to white to build territory there."

"But those are just two stones. Couldn't white still take that corner?"

"Oh yes. But it would be difficult. Perhaps not too profitable. While white is doing this, black would be gaining advantage elsewhere. Perhaps white would win the corner, perhaps not. But he would lose more than he gains."

The elderly Japanese looked down at the board again.

"In go one must consider the whole board. In fuseki the board is open. There are many opportunities. Each player must decide where his advantage lies."

Carlotti nodded. "What you're saying is that it's more like cooperation than competition. Each player stakes out territory and doesn't try to cut into the other player's territory."

"Each player strives for the greatest advantage. To clash too soon is not advantageous." He paused. "Much like life, you see."

"I see." Carlotti looked again at the board with its few stones. "By the way, we're going to be making another jump shortly. We're staying to study the aliens, but we will jump inward to be closer to their colonies."

The Japanese nodded and continued to place stones on the board in an opening pattern.

Deep in the bowels of the *Maxwell*, Billy Toyoda half sat, half floated and watched the data pouring in. His world was a glowing three-dimensional construct and he was at the very center of it.

The computer room was within Spin, but it was high up toward the central shaft. Gravity was never strong here and it was easy for the Japanese-American computerman to imagine himself floating in a sea of data.

For him cyberspace was a dark vastness shot through with neon-bright lines that wavered and pulsed and broke apart and reformed in ever more elaborate arabesques.

From here he saw the world around him as the ship saw it, in raw inputs or neatly organized ranks of massaged data. He floated and watched as the information poured in, totally immersed in it.

But somewhere a fly was buzzing. Caught in the web of glowing, throbbing sense impressions there was a discordance, something beating futilely against the structures trying to get out—or trying to get in.

What? Oh yeah, the comm circuit. Slowly Billy pulled his way back up to the real world and reached over to answer the call.

Peter Jenkins stared distastefully at the young man with the brush-cut hair who blinked at him out of the screen.

"Yessir?" he slurred. "What can I do for you?"

If Toyoda had been a vacuum jack or even an ordinary crew member, Jenkins would have been all over him for being drunk on the job. But he recognized that the man was coming out of a cybertrance and kept his temper. After all, part of Toyoda's job was to be intimately familiar with the *Maxwell*'s cyberspace.

"Mr. Toyoda," Jenkins snapped, "we're making a major change in the mission. We're not going to deploy the rest of the arrays and I need an inventory of computing resources that frees up and how we can use them to help us contact these aliens."

Billy blinked and smiled slowly. "Oh wow, Telescope's not going to like that."

"Who?"

60

"Telescope. The AI that runs the arrays."

"Right now that's the least of our worries, Mr. Toyoda. How soon can you get me that information?"

"The inventory? Maybe three hours. You want recommendations on what we can use where?" He shrugged. "That'll take a little longer, maybe another five, six hours."

"As quickly as you can, Mr. Toyoda," said the captain and broke contact.

"He's damn good at his job," Iron Alice said neutrally from her little corner of the screen as Jenkins continued to scowl at the place where Toyoda's face had been.

"No argument there."

"So why are you so down on him?"

Jenkins sighed. "I suppose because he represents everything that is wrong with this expedition."

The pilot waited.

"You know why he's aboard?"

She shrugged. "Not my department."

"He's here because his uncle thought it would do him good to get off Earth. And his uncle is a congressman from Middle California. Half the crew is like that and the passengers are worse. Dammit, this crew wasn't selected. It was negotiated!"

"And?"

"And all of a sudden we're in shit up to our necks. It would have been hard enough to run this ship on a simple astronomical mission, but this . . ."

"So why don't we pack up and run?"

"Because the Ship's Council insists we stay."

Iron Alice carefully said nothing.

"Look Al, we're truck drivers on this one. Our job is to take the scientists where they want to go, give them the opportunity to see what they want to see and to 'assist in any way possible' as our orders put it."

"You couldn't convince them?"

Jenkins made a face. "I didn't even try. The consensus was so strongly against me it wasn't even worth opening my mouth."

He paused for a minute before going on. "The Council does have a point. There is no clear threat to the ship or the crew. They want to stay and see what we can learn." He shrugged. "So we stay."

"I wish you'd quit trying to make excuses for them," DeRosa said.

"I'm not making excuses. I'm trying to see their side of it. You know, Aubrey's right in a way. Humans do have to learn how to get along with each other better and that means we need to work by consensus rather than command. We're pretty old fashioned in the Space Force, I guess."

DeRosa made a face. "I'd like to see someone run a ship consensually."

"When it gets as big as this one it just about has to be run that way," Jenkins responded. "At least partially."

"Partially. So we stay. But with the drive hot."

"With the drive hot," Jenkins agreed. "I want to be able to get out of here instantly if we have to."

"Based on the telescope data we have done a reconstruction of those colonies," Carlotti said. Instantly his face was replaced by the diagram. A pointer moved to the center of the picture. "The core is that cluster of rotating cylinders in the center. We think that's where the aliens live. The mirror behind it catches sunlight, reflects it off the smaller forward mirror and that shoots it down the center of the tube cluster."

"Neat," Ludenemeyer said. "I suppose that forward mirror also serves as a radiation shield for direct solar radiation."

"We think so. M-type stars are notoriously variable, sometimes as much as twenty percent. That forward mirror is backed by a thick layer of something that looks pretty dense. There may also be an electromagnetic field around it to help control charged particles. That and the spacing would keep down the secondaries. The outsides of the central cylinders are apparently thick enough to provide adequate shielding from other directions."

Ludenemeyer nodded. "And they control the amount of solar radiation arriving at the colony by changing the size of the mirror. Neat."

"And the mirrors helped to shield the colonies from us," Jenkins said.

"Precisely. The colonies on the other side of the system were hidden by the glare from the sun and the ones on this side were covered by their mirrors. Those mirrors radiate remarkably little infrared from their backs, by the way. The reflecting surfaces must be incredible."

"How big is this thing?" Ludenemeyer asked.

"We're not exactly sure, but we think each of those cylinders is several kilometers long."

Ludenemeyer whistled. "That's a lot of real estate. What do you think the population is, anyway?"

The astronomer shrugged. "Tell me how big the aliens are, how well they stand crowding and how efficient their life support systems are and I might hazard a guess. I'd say it would have to be in the tens of thousands and it might be an order of magnitude above that."

"And how many colonies have you found?" Jenkins asked.

"There are something over a thousand complexes we have identified so far. Most of them have a structure like this in them, but they have other structures as well."

"That makes sense," the engineer said. "With no planet to run to you wouldn't want to put all your eggs in one basket. Besides, there are some jobs that are better done in separate complexes." He grinned. "You don't want to put your petrochemical plant in the same atmosphere as your apartments."

"What about the aliens themselves?" Jenkins asked.

The astronomer pursed his lips. "That is somewhat harder. You understand we are handicapped because we don't have a xenologist on board, or even a linguist. As a planetographer, Dr. Dolan is the closest we have to an expert on alien species since it's a hobby of hers, but we're still severely handicapped. As for the linguists, well, we'll just have to do the best we can." Carlotti sighed. "It's hardly an ideal situation."

"Well, do the best you can," Jenkins told him. "And keep us posted. The more we can learn and the faster we can learn it, the better off we'll be."

The cafeteria was crowded and noisy. Most of the tables were taken by the time Sharon got her tray filled and there was still a long line in by the serving area. In another twelve hours the *Maxwell* would be spinning down again for another jump and this was the last chance many of the ship's complement would have to digest a meal on a calm stomach for several days.

But this time, Sharon noticed, no one was complaining about jumping spun down.

"Sharon! Dr. Dolan. Over here." Major Autro DeLorenzo beckoned to her from a table he shared with several other people.

Sharon wove her way through the room and dropped into the seat next to him.

"Thank you, I was afraid I was going to have to eat standing up." The others at the table, one of the maintenance people and a young Oriental Sharon vaguely associated with computers, ignored her and went on with their own conversation.

DeLorenzo gave another of his infectious smiles. "Eat, drink and be merry. So, what did you think of the Ship's Council meeting?"

Sharon paused, fork halfway to her mouth. "Well, I'm glad we're staying, of course. I suppose of all the people on the ship I have the most to gain from it professionally."

"And we all stand to lose," DeLorenzo said. "I tell you, Sharon, I think this is a dangerous business."

"Why didn't you object when the captain said we'd jump deeper into the system?"

DeLorenzo smiled again, but grimly. "The captain is smarter than that weasel Aubrey gives him credit for. By appearing in the middle of them rather than waiting for them to come to us we gain the initiative. We also make it plain we can flick out of their space in an instant."

"And that keeps us safe?"

"It will help, surely. But the only true safety is in leaving immediately. Unfortunately, the captain will not stand up to the Ship's Council to go that far."

Sharon concentrated on her food and said nothing.

DeLorenzo caught the change in her mood immediately. "Oh, our captain is a good man, Sharon, do not misunderstand me. But at bottom he is weak. He does not have the strength to do what he knows to be right."

"That's the first time I have ever heard running away characterized as courageous," she said tartly.

"Sometimes the most courageous thing you can do is to be a coward." He tapped his chest. "Now me, I am often a great coward. It has kept me alive." He smiled that infectious little-boy smile of his again.

"I think it's blasphemous!" another voice put in. Sharon looked up and saw that a dumpy woman in a technician's smock had put her tray down at the other end of the table. "It's blasphemous to even think about dealing with these things." She sat down heavily, deliberately. "Not that that counts for much on *this* ship."

"Perhaps you are right," DeLorenzo said politely and turned his attention to his food.

"Darned right I'm right," the woman said. "Oh, no good is going to come of this, I can tell you." She sniffed. "Not that this trip deserves any good, the way they treat people."

Sharon kept her eyes on her plate and gradually the woman's litany of complaints dropped to a grumble. Through it all the computer type kept talking to his friend as though there was no one else there.

"Okay look," Billy Toyoda said earnestly. "How do we know what we know? I mean how do you know I'm sitting here talking to you? You don't really. All you know is the input from your senses and what your nervous system tells you after it's processed that shit." He waved a hand airily. "You're constructing your reality, man. You're building it up out of that sense data and you call the result 'reality.' "

His companion frowned, not really liking the course the conversation was taking. "So what's that got to do with you and the computers?"

"It's a different construct is all. Different i/o, different senses. I get a different reality."

"So you're saying there is no real reality?"

Billy grinned and ran his hand through the rough-cut black mop of hair. "Reality? Man, reality is just a bigger simulation. We're all running around inside some computer that's simulating the entire universe. Not even a good one at that."

"Huh?"

"Precision. The thing only goes between plus and minus ten to the thirty-eighth on the constants of the universe."

"How do you figure that?"

Billy waved a hand. "Look at the cosmological constant and some of the other magic numbers. They all fall right around that range."

"Um, interesting. But what do we do about it?"

"Nah, man. We're *inside*, see? We can't do anything about it."

"Well, what happens if the computer gets shut off?"

"We never know. When we're not running, we don't exist. Probably happens all the time."

At the end table Lulu Pine hunched deeper over her meal. *Blasphemy*, she thought. Even for this ungodly place that was a new level of blasphemy.

*   *   *

Sharon Dolan hung in darkness before the port and sang to the stars that bloomed around her.

The song was an ancient Irish lullaby about a woman held prisoner beneath an elf hill. Someone lost and alone and wanting desperately to be back in her home.

The 30-foot bubble about her displayed the stars like a planetarium. But these stars were real, not optical projections. Only the double layer of curved window separated the singer from the depths of space.

Her voice was not strong, but it was sweet and pure as she crooned the words in a language she did not understand. Her mother had sung it to her, long ago in a radiation-scarred land light years away. A neighbor who spoke Irish had told her what it meant once.

On the ship's blueprints the bubbles were called auxiliary observation stations, although what anyone was supposed to observe from them that couldn't be seen by the hull-mounted arrays or the deployed sensors wasn't clear. There were four of them, spaced equidistantly around the blunt nose of the *Maxwell*.

But if you didn't mind zero G you could darken the room and float in the midst of the universe.

For Sharon, the song was comforting and full of yearning at the same time. It held longing for the land half-remembered and the warmer, greener, better land that she knew only through the memory of others.

Sharon was vaguely aware that the door had opened behind her, but she kept her attention on the blazing heavens and continued with her song.

Her voice trailed away and she floated silently in the starry sphere.

"That was beautiful, Miss Dolan," Father Simon said at last.

Sharon flinched at the broken silence and then relaxed. "Thank you, Father," she said without taking her eyes off the panorama.

Father Simon was the only person on the ship who called her "Miss Dolan." Titles for marital status had largely gone out of fashion and everyone either called her Sharon or Dr. Dolan. Somehow the old form of address was comforting in the priest's mouth.

"What does it mean?"

Sharon shrugged, not willing to share the secret of the song with anyone. "It's an old lullaby. In Irish."

He swam forward and for a while they both stared out at the sun before them and the star field all around.

"Limbo," Father Simon murmured at last.

"I beg your pardon?"

"I said Limbo. Souls floating suspended between Heaven and Hell."

"But no Eden," Sharon said.

Father Simon turned to her. "You expected one?"

"No, not really." *But I hoped.* "You know, it's funny. We knew that Earth-type planets would be rare, but we expected intelligence to be rarer yet. And of course we always assumed where we found intelligence we'd find Earth-like planets. But here we've found intelligent beings and we still haven't found our first Earth-like world."

"Still even without the aliens there are planets here for you to study."

"Yes. Mars-type planets." Sharon shrugged. "Oh, the work on the Martiform planets is valuable, but we've seen those before, more than fifty of them in the last eight years. Still, I'm sure there will be things to learn here."

"But you hoped for more."

Sharon sighed. "Yes, Father, I had hoped for more. It would have been tremendously exciting to find an Earth-type planet for a change."

"So far there is only one of those."

"I know," Sharon said quietly.

"You're a Spacer, aren't you?" Father Simon asked.

"I am now. Originally I was Irish."

Father Simon nodded. Ireland had escaped the worst of the War in Europe, but conditions were still brutally hard. The bombs that had brought an end to thousands of years of European culture had not completely spared Europe's westernmost outpost. There were a lot of Irish in space.

"How long has it been since you've been to Confession?" he asked.

"I said I was Irish; I didn't say I was a Catholic. My family was originally from Belfast."

"Oh. Sorry."

Sharon shrugged. "No problem. One of the things the War did was put an end to a lot of the sectarianism."

67

Along with most of the Irish, thought Father Simon.

"Anyway," Sharon went on, "I became a planetographer because I hoped—" she smiled deprecatingly—"I hoped we might find someplace where we could get a second chance."

"A new Eden? That's what drew you to this expedition?"

"Well, in a way." She shrugged. "Oh, I knew by the time I finished my studies how unlikely that was. But I always hoped.

"And besides," she concluded practically, "by that time I was committed to my career. Making an interstellar voyage is a considerable help in my career."

They both fell silent again under the light of alien stars.

"And you?" Sharon asked at last. "Why did you come?"

Father Simon smiled nervously. "Well, astrometry is my field, after all. The chance to get a longer baseline was nearly irresistible. When the opportunity arose I was fortunate enough to be chosen to represent the Vatican Observatory on this expedition. No great story there, I'm afraid. I was available, I was called, and I came."

"You're not an exile, then?"

"Far from it. But are there exiles among us?"

"Lots of them. Major DeLorenzo, Dr. Takiuji. Maybe a third of the ship's complement are exiles in some way or another."

"Even Dr. Aubrey?"

Sharon smiled. "Especially Dr. Aubrey. You know about the disagreement in the Scientists' Union?"

"No," said Father Simon, "I didn't know."

"You are a member, aren't you?"

The priest looked a little embarrassed. "As a matter of fact, no. I'm not much of a joiner, you see."

"Oh," said Sharon, slightly taken aback. "Well, there was a considerable contest for the presidency in the last election and Aubrey lost. So they offered him the leadership of this expedition."

"Exile? That's rather heavy punishment for losing an election, isn't it?"

"Dr. Aubrey called it an 'opportunity,'" Sharon said. "Besides, it wasn't just the election. There were some complaints about tactics, you see."

"My goodness, I wasn't aware that scientific politics got

68

that rough. It sounds like astronomers trying to get telescope time for their projects."

Sharon smiled. "There is a lot of similarity."

"Still, it seems like an odd punishment. To send astronomers out to study the stars."

"Oh, it's not punishment, not exactly. It's just that certain governments or institutions function better when some people aren't around. It's a convenient way to getting them out of circulation until things cool down."

"I see."

"We should be thankful, actually. It had a lot to do with the decision to give this expedition to the Americans, Europeans, Japanese and some of the other lesser powers."

"I thought that was a matter that was worked out nationally."

"It was, but having the leaders of the Scientists Union backing the American proposal on the condition that Aubrey go along didn't hurt."

"You seem very knowledgeable on all this," Father Simon said.

Sharon shrugged. "I'm a people watcher. Or maybe a gossip." She paused. "I guess I'm going to get the chance to watch more than people this time."

"So it would seem."

They stared at the stars for a while. "What do you think they're like?" Sharon asked at last.

"The aliens?" The priest spread his hands. "I really haven't any basis to form an opinion. Besides, you're the planetologist."

Sharon made a face. "That doesn't make me a xenologist. I can probably tell you more about their home world than I can about them."

"Well, we certainly have a mystery," Father Simon said. "I suppose we'll know soon enough."

"Doesn't it scare you?"

The priest considered before answering. "There is a certain unease. But it is confirmation that God's creation is at least as rich and diverse as ever we dreamed."

She turned back to the viewing bubble. "Wonder what they'll make of us?"

"And we of them," Father Simon replied.

PART II: JOSEKI

The conversation sounded like a panic in the zoo, with roars, snarls, shrieks and bugling mixed together. To humans it would have been deafening. To those in the room it was merely normal.

Far, far back on their ancestry had been a thing analogous to a tree-climbing dinosaur. Like the hadosaurs of the Late Cretaceous, these creatures had elaborate hollow crests which could modulate their roars. In their descendants the crest had disappeared and the only resonating chambers were left in the much-reduced snout. Still, their language was as much an outgrowth of the climbing reptiloids bellowing out their territorial challenges from the trees of extinct forests as human languages had grown out of the mating and foraging calls of apes ranging across equally extinct savannas.

"We first detected the object, here," a taloned finger tapped the chart, "when it emitted a strong burst of interference. We examined it and determined it was an orbiting artifact of unknown origin. It was obviously powered, probably crewed and like nothing in our records."

The superior one grunted.

"A ship was launched toward it," the Master of Skies said delicately. "Then permission was granted to use the High Drive to reach it even faster."

The superior's beak twitched open at the reminder, as if to rend someone. The first one hurried on.

"Then, one revolution ago, the thing disappeared."

"You mean you lost it?"

70

The other tossed his head in negation. "I mean it vanished from our instruments."

The other remained impassive. "And then?"

Again the talon tapped on the chart. "Then it reappeared here, within home space."

The superior one froze, neither moving nor blinking. "You are certain you did not lose it? That there are not two of them?"

"It might be possible to lose the thing out here," he gestured to the first position. "But it could not approach *here* without being detected."

"And you conclude?"

The Master of Skies hesitated, hunching slightly in anticipation of what was to come.

"It apparently travelled faster than light."

His superior tossed his head and his beak clacked like a gunshot. The underling flinched away. Then the most powerful being in the system froze in contemplation.

"A complication," the superior said at last.

There were cultures who built faster-than-light ships, but not many of them and usually not for long. FTL ships were wasteful, ruinously expensive and disruptive. It took the resources of an entire system to build one and the craft was as large as a colony.

Still, any culture that travelled by FTL ship was a culture to be treated respectfully. They were obviously young, powerful and suicidal.

"Do we know the lineage?"

The Master of Skies gestured negation. "The design is unfamiliar to us."

His superior indicated assent. That was hardly surprising. Lineages so foolish as to build starships seldom lasted more than a few handfuls of cycles.

"What do they want?"

"They have not communicated with us. They give no sign of wishing us to communicate yet."

"How large is the vessel?"

"We are still trying to find out," the Master of Skies said. Actually he had a figure, but he was not about to trouble his master with it until it had been checked. Very thoroughly checked.

With variations the scene was repeated in more than a dozen floating cities scattered about the solar system.

Captain Peter Jenkins felt rumpled. His stomach was sour from all the coffee he had been drinking. He had been off the bridge for eight hours but the caffeine and his worries had left him with only fitful sleep. Externally he knew he looked as trim as ever, but he *felt* rumpled.

"Are there any signs of anything being launched toward us?" Jenkins asked DeRosa as soon as he reached his station.

Iron Alice shook her head. She looked as neat and calm as always, he noted with just a twinge of jealousy, even though she was coming off watch rather than going on.

"Not that we can tell. Of course the inner system's thick with traffic, but nothing seems to be coming our way."

"Any sign of communication?"

"None of that, either. It looks like our hosts are lying low. Maybe they want to see what our next move will be."

"The next move's up to them, unless the Ship's Council decided otherwise."

His title meant, roughly, "The Leader," or more precisely "The One Who Rules As The Embodied Will Of His People." His name identified an exact place in his lineage, although it no more indicated that he held that place than a human named "Smith" necessarily worked at the shaping of metal. It was irrelevant and simply a tag. Like all of his kind, he preferred to be known by his title.

"It is *how* large?" he demanded.

"No more than one twentieth the size of a small Colony," his Master of Skies said.

The Leader did not clack his beak. Instead he froze and stayed immobile for a space of three breaths.

"Indeed? The others know of it, of course."

That was rhetorical. Space contains few secrets from those with the right instruments.

"We could not estimate accurately at its former position. Now we are certain. It is undeniably a starship and many times smaller than any known starship."

The Leader turned his great yellow eyes on his subordinate, as if measuring him for challenge.

"I thought that was impossible."

The Master of Skies' only reply was the alien equivalent of a shrug.

"Something utterly new then? A new kind of drive."

"It would seem so. Our libraries make no mention of the roar of electromagnetic noise that accompanied its move. Also it seems to reappear with excess velocity which must be bled off to achieve orbit. There is no mention of that either."

Again The Leader froze, for even longer.

"A prize," he said at last. "A very great prize. We must act boldly and decisively now."

"We have already acted boldly in launching a ship without the Council's permission."

The Leader made a dismissing gesture. "We will act more boldly yet, now that we know this thing's worth. Open communication with this ship immediately!"

"There is a difficulty."

"Do not pule to me about difficulties, do it! And do not fear the Council."

"It is not the Council. These creatures do not respond to our invitations." He paused. "They may not be a known species."

Now The Leader did snap his beak.

"It does not matter. Initiate communications."

"Uninvited? But—"

"But do it! You say they may be an unknown species? Then assume they do not follow the conventions. Now leave me."

As the Master of Skies bowed out, The Leader was already beginning to pace the room, his inelegant springy stride carrying him nearly off the floor in the lighter gravity of his headquarters.

The alien turned again to look off the terrace and out over the patchwork under the ruddy sunlight.

The Citadel was a great shining sphere partly buried in the end of the cylinder. From the terrace the surface fell away sharply in a series of steep steps to the floor of the cylinder which stretched away almost as far as the eye could see.

From the floor of the cylinder the Citadel stood out like a sun. It was at the sunward end of the habitat so that every waking when the traditionalists rose to give homage to the sun they also honored the Citadel and the one who inhabited it.

It was not accident that it was so.

Even though The Leader despised the traditionalists and

73

their mire of ancient rituals, he continued to live in the Citadel and did nothing to discourage the waking Rite.

Far, far off, almost lost in the misty distance at the opposite end of this cylinder, he could barely make out the brownish smudge that marked the huddle of workers' quarters where he had been born and grown to adulthood. From there, stretching almost to his feet, was an expanse of carefully landscaped vegetation, an artificial forest hiding the administrative complexes, the home groves of the powerful sublineages and other centers of wealth and power.

The sight soothed him. It always did.

The Council President was not soothed. "So small?" he demanded of his Master of Skies. "This thing is so small and travels between the stars."

"So it would appear."

The Council President's talons twitched, as if to anchor himself more firmly to a tree while a storm blew through the forest.

"There is more," the Master of Skies said deferentially. "We *estimate*," he stressed the word hard, "that these beings' drive must be at least five hands of hands more efficient than the star drive we know." He paused, waiting for a reaction.

"Which means?"

"Which means that—assuming the estimate is correct and the device is not unbelievably difficult to fabricate—faster than light travel to other stars is economically feasible."

The Council President froze, not even breathing, until the Master of Skies almost moved to shock him out of it. Then he inhaled a deep ragged gulp of air and turned back to his subordinate.

"Are you sure?"

The Master of Skies tossed his head. "No, but it seems likely."

"We will have this drive. Open communications with this lineage at once. Do not wait for them to talk to us. Now. Immediately!"

The Master of Skies bobbed low and scurried out the door, leaving his master staring and shaking in his wake.

The Council President lowered himself back into his seating sling. His hands were shaking. What a prize! All-Father what a prize!

74

With a drive like that his lineage could spread throughout half the galaxy in a few generations. And the daughter colonies would be securely tied to the Mother no matter what star they circled. He had to have that drive! Somehow he had to get the secret from these strangers.

There must be a meeting of the Colonial Council, he decided. *We must coordinate, plan together*. And in doing so, he added to himself, he would have to make sure his own Colony came out on top.

To begin, he would act in the Council's name. He would open communications with the aliens without waiting for their invitation. Improper, perhaps, but it was an extraordinary circumstance and demanded extraordinary measures.

"It looks like things are picking up," Pete Carlotti told the group. "In the last twenty-four hours we have gotten modulated laser light from no less than six colonies."

Once again a dozen people were packed into the small forward conference room, halfway up toward the hub at the very forward edge of Spin, including Carlotti, Sharon Dolan, Autro DeLorenzo, Father Simon (for reasons that were obscure even to the priest) and, of course, Andrew Aubrey and C.D. MacNamara in their roles as president and vice president of the Ship's Council—plus Jenkins and Ludenemeyer, at the captain's insistence. They had been constituted a committee by the Ship's Council to oversee contact with the aliens.

For the last three days all they had done was watch and speculate. The huge floating cities throughout the system had remained mute.

"What do you make of it?" Jenkins asked.

"It looks like they are trying to talk to us."

Aubrey nodded. "Can we answer them?"

"Not like that," Carlotti said. "We don't have a laser in that frequency or any of the equipment we'd need to make it work."

"All right then, reply by radio."

"Do you think they will figure it out?"

Jenkins smiled grimly. "One thing I think we can count on, Doctor, is the intelligence of our hosts."

"There's one other problem," Carlotti said. "A linguist.

75

I've checked the files and we don't have anyone on board who is trained in linguistics."

Of course not, Jenkins thought. *Why the hell should we?*

He turned to Sharon. "Dr. Dolan, what about you?"

Sharon shook her head, reddish curls flying. "I barely met the language requirements for my Ph.D."

"Perhaps I could be of assistance," Father Simon put in.

"Do you have a talent for languages, Father?"

"Well, I do know Latin and the discipline that involves is a wonderful basis for learning any language." *Or so we used to tell them at seminary,* the priest thought.

Carlotti considered. "Well, it doesn't look like you're going to be doing much astrometry. If you think you can handle it, do it."

"I'll need help, of course," Father Simon said. "Especially computer time."

"You'll get everything we can give you, Father," Jenkins promised. "Even if we have to strip the programs out of the navigation computers."

To Billy Toyoda it was a sheer waste of time. Why bother reporting to the captain in person when you could call him up on the screen quicker and easier? But the captain wanted to see him in person, so he pulled himself onto the bridge and over to Jenkins' station.

"Toyoda reporting." He even tried to salute like he'd been told to.

Jenkins looked up in distaste. Not only was the computerman's salute ludicrous, the man was nearly fifteen minutes late. But he decided to confine himself to more immediate matters.

"Mr. Toyoda, it is customary when on the bridge to anchor yourself to something," Jenkins said caustically. "This *is* a ship, ships *do* move and it is very distracting for bridge personnel to have to dodge flying bodies when they change acceleration."

"Sorry, Captain," Billy said, unabashed, and did a fairly neat but inexpert maneuver that brought his toes in contact with the deck.

"I would also appreciate it if in the future you would respond on a more timely basis when I send for you."

"Sorry, Captain. I was in the middle of something."

Jenkins decided to leave it at that.

"Mr. Toyoda, we are going to need to use the computers to communicate with the aliens. Your superior tells me you are the best man for this kind of thing, so I'm assigning you to handle it."

"Heavy job," Billy Toyoda told the captain lazily. "We've got MIPS to burn, but this stuff isn't specialized for what you want."

"Specialized or not, it's what we've got. How soon can you get a translation program up and running?"

"Hard to say. I'm gonna have to scrounge around to see what we've got that we can convert." He paused and grinned mischievously. "Probably have to cannibalize stuff from the astronomers' software."

"How long?" Jenkins asked, keeping a tight rein on his temper.

The computerman shrugged. "We can have the basic stuff in a few days. Beyond that, depends on how complex things are and how good their sand is."

"Sand?"

"Yeah. You know, their processors."

Since processors were made of gallium arsenide and other more exotic materials Jenkins was as completely in the dark as he was before he asked the question. But he decided not to pursue it.

"Well, get started Mr. Toyoda, and keep me posted."

Billy grinned and mimed a salute. "Aye aye Captain, sir." He flipped neatly and kicked off a console to dive for the door.

Jenkins watched him go distastefully.

"I just hope that little punk is as good as he thinks he is."

"No one's that good," Iron Alice told him. "But he's very good."

Jenkins just shook his head.

The first part, the easy part, was to translate the signal. The optical channel was pretty well out. The aliens' frequencies were too different from the ones the humans used and there was no easy way to convert the equipment.

That left radio-frequency communications. By responding in the rf band to every laser signal, the humans were able to get the aliens to respond on a mutually satisfactory frequency. The aliens used a very complex, sophisticated encoding scheme to pack the maximum amount of information into their radio beams. But it was still child's play for the *Maxwell*'s computers to determine the scheme and the basic protocol involved. With that information it was the work of only a few hours to translate the signal into audio and video components on the human's equipment.

Jenkins was on the bridge when Billy Toyoda called him.

"Captain, we've got video from the aliens," the computerman said.

"What is it?"

"Dunno. But we've got the signal. You can put it up on your screen if you want. Channel 614."

Jenkins nodded and punched up the image. He expected a diagram or perhaps writing. Instead he found himself staring into a pair of unblinking yellow eyes.

Owls! thought Captain Jenkins when he saw his first alien.

It was illusion, of course. From the front, the great staring yellow eyes and the hooked beak looked owl-like. The downy gray body covering, something between feathers and fur, accentuated the effect. But when the creature moved its head and Jenkins saw it in profile, the illusion was lost. The beak was real enough, but it was the end of a short muzzle.

Jenkins looked down at Billy's image in the corner of his screen. "Is that a live picture?" he asked sharply.

"I think so."

"How fast can you encode a video signal and beam it out?"

"Few minutes."

"Then do it. Apparently they expect to look at the people they talk to."

Once the video channel was established, the real work began. The principle was simple. Take a black box, human or electronic, it doesn't matter. Now give it inputs and compare each output with the desired output for that input. Next introduce a correcting signal proportional to the difference between the desired and actual outputs. Correct the output. Now repeat the process, over and over and over again until the output is sufficiently close to the desired output. Next you move on to a new input/output pattern and repeat the process.

If the black box is a human you call this "teaching," or perhaps "operant conditioning." If the box is a computer it becomes "boltzman programming" or one of a half-dozen or so similar terms. Either way, eventually the system learns to match up inputs and outputs.

The principle may be easy, but the process is not simple. Billy Toyoda became red eyed and haggard overseeing the computers, guiding them and easing them out of local minima and trying to find appropriate strategies for altering the "weights" of the connections to produce the most accurate translations in the least time.

First came the easy things. Numbers, mathematical operations, basic logical operations. The computers handled that part pretty much on their own, although Billy hovered over them in cyberspace like a broody hen.

Then they moved on to the harder parts, the more human parts. First came the concepts of verb tenses. This thing happens now. This thing happened in the past. This thing is a continuing process which stretches from the then to the now and on to the future. This thing was a continuing process which was started and finished in the past. This thing is a continuing process which will start and finish some time in the future.

Even with the computers to help, it was difficult. The verb tenses did not match, but then they seldom do. The aliens' concept of "now" had more in common with the physicist's notion of simultaneity than with the English present tense. Even the distinction between "I" and "those like me" was blurred by human standards.

Father Simon was invaluable for the work. He had no formal linguistic training but he was patient and possessed a keen analytical sense. He was however, only one of a small, constantly shifting group that worked on turning the sounds and images into a comprehensible language. Somehow—part aptitude, part common agreement—the priest was the human who appeared before the cameras.

The aliens took a somewhat different approach. Four or five of the habitats sent signals to the *Maxwell*, with different teams of aliens working at each one. Only one habitat seemed to use the same speaker every time. It was obvious that the aliens were monitoring each other's transmissions and perhaps exchanging information because a word or concept learned by one seemed to be instantly known to all the others.

The diversity had its advantages, but it placed a cruel load on the priest. Father Simon worked at the screen for hours at a time, gesturing, speaking, listening patiently and consulting with Billy Toyoda to improve the translation software.

Beyond the mechanics of translating the words, the software was vital. There was no way humans and aliens would ever speak each others' language unaided. Beaks could not be used like lips to shape sounds, and humans lacked the aliens' resonating chambers in the muzzle. A large part of the alien language was gestural. Posture and movement were critical to interpretation and some "words" would have required a human contortionist.

Sometimes, in spite of computers and beings on both sides working themselves to exhaustion, the results weren't quite what was expected.

Father Simon studied the alien on the screen carefully. This was the one who always appeared for his habitat, he knew, and there was an indefinable something else about him, something that set him apart. Now they were to the point where they could start exchanging referents. Perhaps the source of that difference would emerge there.

The priest pointed at himself. "Simon," he said, pronouncing the word carefully.

The alien tapped himself on the beak and his mouth moved. There was a pause while the computer searched through its data base for the word or phrase that most nearly conveyed the same meaning. Since the word was presumably a name, the program had unusual latitude to seek even non-English words if they matched more precisely.

"Der Fuhrer," the computer announced.

Father Simon started. *Well, if that's the translation of the being's name . . .*

"Der Fuhrer," he repeated, pointing at the screen.

Gradually both sides built up their store of concepts until they could begin to discuss substantive issues, even fairly abstract ones.

"What do you call yourselves?" Father Simon asked the alien on the screen.

The literal answer was something like "the descendants of

80

those who chose to live in space." The computer boiled it down to one word.

"Colonists," the image on the screen said.

"Where are you from?"

The great yellow eyes regarded him without blinking. "Another star. Thousands of cycles ago our great Branch arrived here."

"In a ship like ours?"

Again the unblinking stare. "Not like yours. Bigger. Much bigger."

"Ah, yes," Father Simon said. The alien's stare was making him nervous. "Do you have ships like ours?"

"Yes."

"Forgive me, it was just that since we came we have not detected any faster-than-light ships in the system." The alien showed signs of agitation. "I do not mean to pry," the priest added hastily.

"Why have you come here?" the alien asked.

"We came looking for knowledge," Father Simon told him. "At first astronomy—star knowledge—then when we found out the system was inhabited, we wished to learn about you."

There was a pause while the computers at both ends of the link translated what the priest had said. Then the alien's mouth moved.

"Knowledge is good," the alien said. "Do you offer knowledge in return?"

"Yes, we would offer knowledge in return."

"Knowledge of your . . ." the words stopped and there was a long pause while the computers went looking for the correct meaning ". . . thing that moves between stars?"

"Our star drive?" Another long pause while the computers conferred.

"Yes, the star drive."

Father Simon frowned. "I thought you had faster-than-light travel."

"Yes."

"Then why do you want to trade for that?"

The alien froze and suddenly the screen went blank.

"What in the world . . ." Father Simon checked the link. It was intact, meaning the alien had deliberately shut off transmission.

Then just as suddenly the screen cleared and there was the

alien again. Or rather, Father Simon corrected himself, *an* alien. Looking closely, he didn't think it was the same one.

"A problem," the alien said. "Sorry."

"Quite all right," the priest said, nonplused by the jack-in-the-box routine. "Ah, I had asked about the star drive."

"We have a star drive."

"Then why do you want to trade for ours?"

The alien's mouth moved for a long time before the computer spoke.

"Knowledge is good. Knowledge is always good."

Father Simon frowned. Obviously he wasn't getting the full meaning of what the alien had just said. That was one of the problems with the programs at this early stage. He didn't suspect that he had just missed an elaborate equivocation because of the imperfect translating software.

"Knowledge is good," Father Simon agreed. "But you do not keep starships in this system?"

Again a long answer and a long pause for translation.

"We know of starships."

"Yet there aren't any coming and going here?"

"Sometimes."

"But not while we have been here. We would have detected them."

"You cannot detect a starship until it makes its presence known."

"That's not . . ." Father Simon stopped, his mouth hanging open. "It isn't the same kind of drive, is it?"

"It is faster-than-light travel."

"But not our kind. That burst of RFI is characteristic and inherent in the drive. If you knew about our drive, you would have known about that."

"We have faster-than-light drive," the Colonist repeated, obviously agitated.

"But not like ours?" Father Simon pressed.

The alien hesitated. "No," he said finally. "Not like yours."

"How is it different?"

"Many ways."

"It's not as good, is it?" Father Simon asked shrewdly. "It doesn't work as well. Otherwise you wouldn't try to hide it."

The screen went blank.

"Well, that's a confirmation of a sort," the priest said to the blank screen. Then he punched up a second frequency.

*   *   *

The Ship's Council met in one of the large conference rooms down on the A deck—the part of Spin furthest out from the core with the highest gravity and hence the most desirable part of the ship.

Affectation, Peter Carlotti thought, looking out over the empty seats. The room was big enough to hold nearly a hundred people, but aside from the members of the Council only Sharon Dolan and Father Simon were present. Anyone else who was interested was tuned in on a screen. He sighed inwardly, turned his attention back to the Council meeting and waited for the others to pounce.

The meeting had droned through twenty minutes or so of routine business and Carlotti's report was the next item on the agenda. He didn't expect it to be routine at all.

"And the next item is the report from the contact committee," Aubrey said. "Dr. Carlotti?"

"There's not a lot to report," Carlotti told his fellow Council members. "We're making significant progress, but it's slow work."

"Excuse me, Dr. Carlotti," MacNamara interrupted, "but I'd like to know when we will be able to talk to the aliens."

There was a murmur of assent from the rest of the Council.

"I wish I could give you a definite time frame, Doctor, but it's not easy. There is still a great deal we do not understand about the aliens' language, and communication is painful and full of difficulties."

"But we can communicate?" MacNamara asked. "We can start actually talking to them?"

"We communicate, but only on a very elementary level. That's one problem." He took a breath. *Here it comes.* "The other problem is that so far the software is only trained on Father Simon."

"You mean Father Simon is the only one who can talk to the aliens?"

"Right now, yes. To speed things up we didn't attempt to train the computer on other human voices."

"Doctor Carlotti, we have been in communication with the aliens for nearly four weeks," MacNamara said. "There are nearly two hundred scientists on this ship who are eager to start learning from them. But so far Father Simon is the only one who has spoken to them and except for their language we have learned nothing from them."

Carlotti hesitated. "We have found out one other thing. They don't have our star drive."

"What?" Aubrey interrupted. "They haven't told us that."

The astronomer shrugged. "I don't think they intended to. It slipped out when they were talking to Father Simon. Or he deduced it rather, and forced it out of them. He is amazing." Father Simon looked uncomfortable.

"But no star drive . . ."

"Oh, they know of a star drive, but it isn't ours. It is a lot clumsier, apparently, and a lot more expensive to use. Also their ships have to be huge. The one called Derfuhrer says their starships are nearly as big as one of their colonies."

"Well, if you have to move a lot of people to start a colony . . ."

"I said they know of a star drive, I didn't say they use it."

"How do they move?"

"Generation ships."

"You mean they take hundreds of years to travel from system to system?"

Carlotti shrugged. "It apparently suits them. They live their entire lives in artificial structures, so it doesn't matter much whether the structure is in orbit or moving through interstellar space."

"They're cut off then. One star system from another."

"Physically, yes. But they seem to maintain communications with other solar systems by laser. I gather that travel doesn't count for much with them. Even within this system most of their contact is electronic. Not many of them have seen more than one colony."

"Makes sense of a sort," DeLorenzo said. "The energy cost of moving from one colony to another isn't negligible. They aren't in orbits around planets, most of them, so they can't do the kind of gravity well maneuvers we use so much." He smiled. "Planets are handy things to have around, even if you don't live on them."

"But they did originate on a planet somewhere?"

"Oh, yes," Carlotti said.

"From what I've seen, I'd deduce the Colonists' home system was a dwarf, possibly a high M," Sharon put in.

"Their planet was probably close to it and it was almost certainly smaller than Earth."

"How do you know that?"

"I don't know it, but it's a good guess. The kind of light they prefer tells us something about the sun they evolved under. They keep their habitats at about one-third earth normal, although I suspect that may be less than the gravity on their home planet. Their air is thinner and colder than ours. There are a number of other things too." She sighed. "It must have been a very atypical system to allow life to evolve."

"Where is their home planet?" someone else asked.

"They're unclear on that," Father Simon said. "I suspect they simply don't know."

"Or they won't tell us for security reasons," DeLorenzo put in.

"No, I honestly don't think they know. They settled this system from another where they lived in orbiting habitats and they settled that one from another where they did the same. They have been doing this for a long, long time."

"How long?" someone asked uneasily.

Father Simon shrugged. "Again, that is unclear. Certainly for thousands of years and perhaps for hundreds of thousands of years."

There was dead silence all down the table.

"They are a very old civilization," Father Simon added half-apologetically.

Sharon Dolan caught up with the priest after the meeting broke up.

"I still can't believe it," she said by way of starting a conversation. "Even now, I just can't believe it."

"It is remarkable," Father Simon agreed.

"It's so mind boggling and it goes off in so many ways. Do you realize we've also found the answer to the Fermi Paradox?"

"You mean 'Where are the intelligent aliens'?" Father Simon asked. "Why here, of course."

"No, no I mean why we never found them before, or why they never found us."

"That is a question," the priest said. "Especially considering how widespread their civilization must be."

"Yes, but we were looking at it from the wrong perspective, a planetbound perspective. These aliens don't need planets. Do you know that except for some mining outposts on the surfaces of the larger moons of the gas giants there isn't a single settlement anywhere on a planet in this system? It's all space habitats."

"And that has kept us from finding them?"

"Or them from finding us. Part of the Fermi Paradox was that we had calculated that even a slow rate of expansion at sub light speeds would send a culture to all the habitable planets in the galaxy in a galactic eyeblink. But because we were thinking in terms of planets, our 'slow' expansion was much too fast. These aliens almost never have to go further than the next star to find suitable habitation. They don't bother looking for Earthlike planets—or whatever their equivalent might be. They just colonize in orbit.

"More than that, because they exploit the entire resources of a solar system, not just the planets, a single system can support many more of them without crowding than it could if they were planetbound."

"So they spread slower and they have less incentive to colonize," Father Simon said. "I see. And since we're the farthest out any human expedition has ever gone, we have finally run into them."

"Farthest out and in the right direction." Sharon agreed. "Precisely. And when you realize that they communicate within the system by lasers and over interstellar distances by very tight beam you can see why we never found radio emissions."

"So we may have been neighbors for centuries and never known it. Remarkable."

"It is remarkable," Sharon agreed. Then her face clouded. "The question now is what do we do with our new neighbors?"

The steps stretched up before him, growing steeper as he climbed the end wall of the great cylinder. There were no transport lines reaching up to the Citadel. It had to be approached on foot, like a supplicant coming within the sacred precincts of a temple.

In some of the less advanced colonies, the Citadel was a temple. Their rulers claimed divine rights by virtue of their exalted position under Heaven. In 246 The Leader merely claimed to rule as the living embodiment of the will of the entire lineage. There was no longer a religious aspect to the Citadel. But neither was there a transit line.

Gravity lessened as he climbed, but it did not go to zero. The entire group of cylinders spun around a common central axis. This meant that not all the surface area inside each cylinder was habitable, but there were compensating advantages.

He looked up. Between the great windows running the length of the cylinder that admitted light from the central shaft, were dense mats of green. This close the Master of Forests could see workers suspended in harnesses moving among the hanging gardens, harvesting the vine crops and tending the plants. Production was up again, he thought approvingly. That will be something to tell The Leader if he asks.

He ascended to the terrace that ringed the Citadel and swept across it, past the guards and through the great open doors of the airlock. One of the functions of the Citadel was to protect its inhabitants even if the cylinder lost atmosphere in some barely imaginable catastrophe.

There were others there, the Master of Forests saw. The Masters who counted for most in the colony. The Master of Bounds, who dealt with relations with other colonies; the Master of Skies, who handled space transportation and engineering; the Master of Seas, who regulated the colony's water and climate; the Master of Makers, who handled manufacturing and some parts of trade. As Master of Forests his concern was food and agricultural production.

The summons had said nothing about any others, but then The Leader's summonses never did.

So it was to be one of *those* sessions, he thought. The Leader never gathered them to ask advice and seldom to issue orders. For those he saw them separately, often dealing by screen. The only time he talked to his subordinates in a group was to set out some new policy.

The Master of Forests felt a tingle of apprehension. What new plan did their leader have to announce to them now. He could see the others felt it too. The Master of Cities and the Master of Bounds seemed the most nervous. Were they privy to The Leader's new policy? Or were they its victims?

An inner door opened and the Master of Masters, the head of his lineage, swept in. He moved with the too-springy stride of someone who had spent his formative years under the colony's maximum gravity rather than the easy glide of one who was born to the Citadel. But there was power in his walk. He seemed to radiate an elemental force, unstoppable and unquenchable.

"We have come a great distance," The Leader began. "When we started we were weak, disorganized and no one would have given us a chance to ascend to the Inner Grove.

"And yet, my brothers, here we are today." He gestured expansively.

The Leader's voice was not clear and pure as a herdmaster's was supposed to be. Nor did it have the strength to carry great distances. A human listening through alien ears might have described it as "hoarse" or "reedy." That did not matter. In a manner unmatched by any other elder in any colony, The Leader could catch and hold his listeners.

As we are all fliers fluttering in his net, the Master of Forests thought.

"Now Heaven offers us a new opportunity.

"A new species has entered our system in a faster-than-light ship of unknown and vastly superior design. It is less than one twentieth the size of the faster-than-light ships we know.

"That ship is the key to 246 reclaiming her rightful place under heaven. I mean to seize it for our lineage."

The Master of Forests went cold. Here was audacity indeed! This meant a direct confrontation with the Colonial Council and every other colony in the system. But The Leader kept speaking, as if what he had just proposed was a routine bit of business.

"With it we shall be great as no lineage has been before us. It is my unshakable desire that we shall learn the principles of this new alien drive before any other colony."

"Perhaps easier said than done," demurred the Master of Bounds, the lone member of the group who had not risen to position with The Leader.

"But it will be done! We will do it because it is my will that we do it. And our will is greater than that of any other lineage."

He stopped and looked over the group.

"I do not claim this as special virtue for myself," he said more softly. "I am the representative of the collective will of our lineage; a pawn, a puppet to be moved hither and yon as Heaven commands.

"And it is the Right Order of Heaven that our lineage be returned to its proper place. That the bonds placed upon us by our oppressors be loosened. To this end I have unshakably dedicated my life."

He stopped his pacing and struck a heroic pose, a herd guardian looking out over the forest for signs of danger.

Not for the first time the Master of Forests wondered how much of this his leader actually believed.

"We know what the policy of the so-called Colonial Council will be. They will attempt to monopolize this thing as another prop to their illegitimate grip on the system. They will strive mightily to deny us the fruits of our rightful place in hierarchy of lineages.

The Leader relaxed and swept his gaze over the assembled group. Then his beak clacked like a gunshot and all his subordinates flinched away.

"*No*," he bellowed. "It shall not be. They may plot and they may scheme. But we shall *act*. We shall smash their plots. We shall seize what is rightfully ours. We shall not be denied!"

He turned to the Master of Bounds. "Open negotiations for the star drive at once with the visitors."

"The Council will forbid it."

"The Council cannot forbid what they do not know. I said begin negotiations, not ask the Council's permission. The Council has not yet decided upon a policy so we are not in violation. That makes it easier. Now at once!" The minister craned his neck submissively and bounded from the room.

"We stand on the threshold of a great new era, my friends. All that we need is the will to seize it."

Father Simon and Sukihara Takiuji were playing go in the Cypress Lounge. Or more correctly, Suki was demonstrating a point.

"From here, this is joseki," the Japanese said, laying down black and white stones in alternate order. "It builds strength to the outside." He scooped up most of the stones and laid them down in another pattern. "This is also joseki, but it emphasizes the side of the board."

Father Simon nodded and looked up from the board. Three of the walls showed a misty swamp with trees hung with moss looming out of the oily black water. A heron preened itself in a "nearby" tree, startlingly white against the gray mist. There was no sound, but then the picture didn't call for any.

"A joseki is a gambit, correct?" Father Simon asked.

"Much like a chess gambit, yes. But there are many, many more of them. More possible combinations than chess, you see?"

Father Simon shook his head. "I don't see how you remember them all."

Suki considered. Behind the Japanese, the image of the heron took flight. "You remember them when the time comes," he said at last. "The context of the game reminds you."

"Gentlemen," said a familiar voice behind them, "may I join you?" They looked up to see Andrew Aubrey.

"Please, sit down," Father Simon said and Suki nodded amiably.

"I'm glad I found you both together," Aubrey said briskly. "I need your help."

"What's the problem?"

"More an opportunity than a problem." He turned to the priest. "Father, the Ship's Council needs to work out details for trading the KOH drive to the aliens in return for their knowledge—assuming of course that they really don't have it. Since you're the only one who can speak to them yet and since Dr. Takiuji knows more about the drive than anyone on board, naturally we will need your assistance."

"Are you sure that's wise?" Father Simon asked.

"Wise?" Aubrey sounded surprised by the question. "We can learn an enormous amount from the aliens and I gather they want knowledge of our drive very badly."

"Yes, but are we authorized to do anything of the sort? And is it in our best interests to do it?"

"As to authorization, naturally it would be better to consult with Earth. But Earth is months away. Sometimes the people on the spot have to make the decision.

"And as to our best interests, isn't it in our best interest to establish friendly relations with these people?"

"What does the captain think of this?"

"This really isn't the captain's decision. It is a decision to be made by all of us, acting consensually."

The heron was back, Father Simon noticed, sitting motionless on a moss-draped snag barely out of the water with its head cocked to one side.

"I don't think we can form an intelligent opinion at this time," Father Simon told him. "I think we at least need to know more before we start thinking about making a trade."

"You say they want to trade," Suki said diffidently. "How do we know what they will offer us?"

"A great deal," Aubrey said. "I gather they want the drive badly."

"But one person's 'great deal' is sometimes very little to another person."

"You sound as if you doubt their sincerity," Aubrey said.

The Japanese looked down at the loose formation of stones on the go board. "I believe they are very sincere. But perhaps it is better to go slowly and avoid any possible misunderstanding."

"Delay or outright refusal could also provoke misunderstanding," Aubrey pointed out. "They might even think we mistrust them."

The heron's yellow beak flashed down, striking the water with a soundless splash. The bird jerked its head back with a fish flapping in its beak. With a practiced toss of its head, the heron started the still-wiggling fish down its gullet.

"It is a very difficult question," Suki agreed. "But since we can barely understand each other, misunderstandings now are very possible, eh? Maybe in a little bit we can make sure of understanding." He began picking up the stones and putting them back in their bowls. "Besides, it would be difficult to make such a trade with just the information we have here. It is incomplete. Completing it would be very time-consuming."

Aubrey knew when to beat a tactical retreat. "You are the expert on that, of course, Dr. Takiuji," he said. "I suppose we will have the opportunity to learn more about the aliens before we make a decision." He smiled winningly. "I would appreciate if you gentlemen would think about this over the next few days. Now if you'll excuse me. . . ." He got up and left the table.

"It is something to think about," Father Simon said after Aubrey had left the lounge.

"Perhaps it is also something to tell the captain about," Sukihara Takiuji said, replacing the last of the stones in the bowls. "It may be that he does not know what Dr. Aubrey is thinking."

Behind him the heron flapped off into the mist.

The Pine Lounge was busy that night. The whole ship was buzzing like a hive of disturbed bees with the latest discoveries, so naturally the lounge was packed.

At the large center table Father Simon was hemmed in by nearly two dozen people who wanted to hear the latest report straight from him.

"Father, do you mean that we have discovered something that these aliens, whose civilization is ten times as old as ours have not?"

Father Simon shrugged apologetically. "It appears so."

"But how can that be?" the questioner persisted.

"Easy," Ludenemeyer spoke up from further down the table. "Our drive is not intuitive."

"Well, not to humans, perhaps . . ." the other began.

"Not to anybody," Ludenemeyer cut in. "At least not to anyone sane."

"But there are many different ways of describing the universe; surely in some of them it is obvious."

"Not if they're sane. Look, Dr. Takiuji could probably explain all this better, but let me take a stab at it.

"The KOH drive only makes sense if you look at the universe in a pretty damn peculiar way. And if you look at the universe that way, almost nothing else makes sense, if you follow me. In the math that best describes the drive, a simple vector is damn near indescribable and indeterminate when you do describe it. You can construct a mathematical system like that, but unless you know about the drive it is useless."

"Oh come now," MacNamara protested from the edge of the group. "Hawking suggested the foundation for the KOH drive nearly a century ago."

"That's the myth created by popularizers," Ludenemeyer retorted. "There is some stuff in Hawking's later work that sort of touches on the drive, but Hawking was as wrong as Einstein about it. Hawking was such a romantic figure—the Crippled Giant and all that—that those hints got picked up and turned into the precursor of Kerensky's and Omo's work.

92

That's why we call it the Kerensky-Omo-Hawking drive. But Hawking didn't invent it.

"And the problem's worse than that," he went on. "Even if you think in Kerensky Spaces and Hawking Attractors, the drive is still hard to pin down. You have to make just the right choices and you need the right technologies to prove it out. Do it wrong and you don't even get an interesting explosion. The drive just sits there and puts out a lot of heat."

He grinned. "And once you figure out the drive, you need to take it pretty far out from your sun. Someplace where the geodesics are—ah—nice and 'flat' to run your first tests."

He took a pull on his stein of beer. "Besides," he added, "I don't think they had our incentives to find an efficient star drive. That's Dr. Dolan's theory anyway."

"That's an odd thing to say about a star-faring culture," Carlotti put in.

"Not as odd as it sounds," Ludenemeyer said. "I gather they spread from star to the next nearest star and they don't much care about spectral type.

"With their culture they don't need habitable planets and within broad limits one solar system's pretty much as good as another to them. I doubt they go as much as ten lightyears in a hop and in this part of the galaxy, stars are only an average of three lightyears or so apart.

"We never thought of that. We went into space looking for habitable planets—new Earths. We had to have something that would let us travel fast between stars, so we looked and looked until we found it. They simply went from star to star, so they could settle for something less.

"It's more than that. The physics underlying the KOH drive are extremely subtle, indeed counterintuitive. The formalism that expresses the possibility is damn clumsy for expressing the normal range of physical phenomena."

One of the other scientists grinned. "What he's saying is it's not the sort of thing you stumble across by accident. You got to go looking for it and then there's a lot of luck in finding it."

"And they don't have a KOH drive?"

"Not at all."

"It is a remarkable situation," Father Simon said.

"I imagine we will find many more remarkable things as we

learn more about them," MacNamara said. "Or whenever the rest of us can talk to them."

"That's being worked on right now," Father Simon assured him. "The computer crew is retraining the translation programs now."

At the same time, Aubrey was having a very uncomfortable interview with the captain.

"Dr. Aubrey," Jenkins said for the third time. "I don't want anything more said about the drive, at least until we know where we stand."

"Captain, it is not really your decision."

"Doctor, everything that bears on the safety and welfare of this ship is my decision and in my opinion the details of the drive definitely do."

"You're arrogating a great deal to yourself, Captain."

"I'm trying to protect my ship in a difficult and possibly dangerous situation."

"So the stranger is the enemy," Aubrey said bitterly. "Haven't we had enough of that attitude? Hasn't it cost us enough?"

"Dr. Aubrey, I am not assuming anything of the sort," Jenkins said, stung. "It seems to me you are the one who is taking a great deal on yourself."

"The Ship's Council is the focus of decision making for everyone on this ship."

"The Ship's Council has not discussed this matter," Jenkins retorted. "Until it agrees on a course of action you are acting unilaterally. And if it agrees, I still must decide to go along."

Aubrey smiled. "What do you propose to do, Captain? Censor every man and woman on this ship?"

"I propose to exercise my prerogative and take the ship out of here immediately if I do not like the trend of events," Jenkins snapped back. "We can argue about it later and you can present information at my court martial if you like. But until that time, neither you nor anyone else will discuss details of the drive with the aliens."

A throwback! Andrew Aubrey fumed. *A 20th-century throwback in command of this of all expeditions*. He stalked the corridor alone, trying to work off some of the blind rage. He had known the captain was difficult, and wedded to the archaic methods of the Space Force, but *this* . . .

He was so angry and so wrapped in his own thoughts he nearly knocked Sharon Dolan down when she came around a corner.

"Oh, I'm sorry, Dr. Dolan," he said, recovering. "I didn't see you."

"Are you all right, Dr. Aubrey?"

He let his breath out in a long sigh. "Yes, I'm all right. I just had a rather—unsatisfactory—interview with the captain."

"About the aliens and the drive?"

Aubrey chuckled brittlely. "News does travel, doesn't it?"

"Well, no. Just that everyone knows you want to give the principles of the drive to the aliens. What else could you be talking to the captain about?" She paused. "I take it he didn't agree?"

"No. He actually threatened to jump us out of the system if we tried to reveal the drive. Subconsciously Captain Jenkins still confuses the stranger with the enemy."

"I don't believe that!" Sharon said, more sharply than she meant to.

"I think it's true nonetheless. Oh, I can understand it to an extent. They are frightful looking enough. But Dr. Dolan, we can't afford that kind of thinking! Fear of the alien almost destroyed us when the alien was nothing more than a human who didn't think exactly as we did. We can't afford another war, ever."

"I know," Sharon told him. "My family is Irish."

No one knew who started it and there were almost as many reasons why as there were scholars studying it. The important thing was that as the 21st century dawned, the United States and the Soviet Union fought a brief, futile and suicidal nuclear war.

Compared to what could have been, it wasn't much of a war. Both sides had spent nearly two decades building defenses against nuclear-armed missiles. Neither nation's missile defense system was perfect, but they both worked. The Americans stopped nearly ninety-nine percent of the warheads aimed at their territory and the Soviets somewhat less, perhaps ninety-five percent.

As a result only about 400 million people died worldwide.

Most of Europe and vast tracts of North America and Eurasia were turned into blasted ruins and the economic and political face of the planet was turned upside down. But by the skin of its teeth humanity survived.

Technically, you could say that the United States won. After all, the United States of America still existed—or rather a country bearing that name and with more-or-less the same territory still existed. The Soviet Union had dissolved into a welter of competing republics. The European Community existed only as a pale shadow. But a twentieth-century American would have had a hard time seeing his country in what now called itself the "USA."

Aubrey grinned without humor. "Do you know how I spent my weekends in high school? I was a ghoul."

"A ghoul?"

"I grew up in upstate New York, in one of the safe zones. Right after the war there was a refugee camp there. Tens of thousands of people packed in from New York City, Rochester, Buffalo, all over."

He licked his lips. "Well, nearly all of them died, of course. You know how it was, no food, no medicine, radiation poisoning, disease—plus the winters. They have terrible winters there." He sighed and hurried on. "Anyway, they died and were buried in mass graves. Row after row of trenches, hacked out by hand because they couldn't afford to use a bulldozer and the bodies dumped in without coffins or shrouds and then they'd mound the earth over them. Forty years later and those mounds were still two or three feet high."

"I know," Sharon whispered. "I've seen the like."

Aubrey took another deep breath. "Well, that was fine at the time, but the land where the camp stood was good farmland. As the population built back up they saw they couldn't let it lie fallow. Besides, they thought that even after all that time the bodies were contaminating the water. We had a lot of sickness in the summertime. So the remains of the camp, including the graves, had to go."

"And you . . ."

Again the drawn, deathshead grin. "I got the job. I was away at school during the winter so I didn't have regular employment. So I was thrown into the labor pool with all the drunks and bums they could corral and that was our job for two summers.

"We went out there with shovels and picks and opened the mounds and turned the soil, sifting out every bone we could find, ignoring the stench as best we could, and piling all of them up for hauling and disposal."

He paused. "I was luckier than some. I never got sick. But I would get back to camp and I would wash and wash and wash until my skin was raw and I could still smell the death on me."

Aubrey looked as if he would throw up. Then he took another deep, shuddering breath and turned back to Sharon, apparently the old Andrew Aubrey again.

"Anyway, that's when I decided that we had to change or it would be all humanity in those pits the next time. I think we are changing, too. But now we're at a critical point and we have to deal with someone who is still infected with the old ways of doing things."

"Captain Jenkins is a reasonable man," Sharon told him. "I'm sure you can reason with him."

Aubrey relaxed. "Perhaps you're right, Dr. Dolan." Then he smiled. "Yes, I'm sure the captain will be reasonable when we have more evidence to convince him."

One by one the screens lit up, showing the faces of the leaders of the most powerful colonies in the system. The meeting was not to exchange information, it was to decide what to do. They had all been monitoring negotiations with the aliens.

"We meet to seek common direction," the Council President said after finishing the opening ritual. "There are strangers among us and we must decide how to deal with them.

"They are not of any known lineage," he continued, knowing full well this was news to no one. "They are a new and undiscovered kind of being.

"Their ship is vastly smaller than any known faster-than-light craft. The aliens admit they have a drive which works on new principles, but they refuse to share it with us."

"Then let us take it!" one of the smaller colonies trumpeted. "They are deep within our system."

"They can also vanish in an instant," the Council President retorted. "Since they discovered we do not have the drive, their ship is held constantly ready to leave. At the first suspicion of trouble they will disappear."

"What is it they want?" asked the leader of the conservatives, the oldest member on the Council.

"That is unclear. They seem eager to trade knowledge with us, but they insist that they must refer matters back to the elders of their lineage. They will offer nothing of value."

"Then why don't they leave?" the elder snapped. "Why do they remain and cause dissension?"

The Council President made the equivalent of a shrug.

"Apparently they hope to gain from us without giving us anything substantial in return."

"Do they think us such weaklings?"

Again the shrug. "That, too, is unclear. Seemingly there is some uncertainty among their elders as to the proper course to pursue. They say that others will come after them who will be more willing to discuss their drive." He made a dismissing motion, as if to brush off an insect. Long experience had taught the colonists that cultures which built starships seldom visited a system more than once. They collapsed too quickly.

"As long as they stay there is hope," one of the other councilors observed. "Let us wait and watch."

"There is one other cause for hope. They desire to communicate with us. If we talk to them perhaps we can resolve the uncertainty and gain what we want."

Not altogether unsatisfactory, the Council President mused. The meeting had not gone badly at all. There had been the usual interminable wangling as the leaders of the factions squabbled and jockeyed for advantage. There had been the heightened tension of having a great prize dangled before them. But in the end the Colonial Council had agreed on a general course of action. The conservatives had stayed pretty much in line and even 246 had been less obstreperous than usual. All things considered, the Council President decided, it was more than he had hoped for.

The Council President's screen lit up. There stood the leader of the conservative faction.

"A proposal," the old one said without preamble.

"I will entertain it," the Council President replied. *By the All-Father, what now?*

"We have taken counsel among ourselves. We desire to destroy the newcomer."

The Council President's beak snapped in response. "Unacceptable!"

"Hear what we offer," the old one said.

"It is insufficient," the Council President trumpeted. "No matter what it might be it is insufficient."

"These—things—are dangerous," the old one said. "They threaten the stability of the entire system."

"These 'things' are very powerful," the Council President countered. "Can you be so sure we can destroy them?"

"They are merely young and crude." The old one made a dismissive gesture. "There is only one small ship of them. An easy mark for a combined attack."

"We know little about them."

"We know enough. They can be destroyed and destroyed they must be."

"Are you so certain we can learn their drive from the wreckage?"

Again the dismissive gesture. "Their drive is unimportant."

The Council President blinked. "No one else thinks so."

"Then they are blinded fools! The Order of Heaven is important and that must be preserved."

"The consensus is that we can do both."

"No!" The old one's beak snapped. "We exist in a very tight orbit within many competing fields. Already we are threatened to be pulled from our course. We do not need another potential to further complicate our calculations."

"New opportunities open up new orbits," the Council President responded. "With the drive we could spread our lineages through the galaxy in our lifetimes. We would become the greatest Founders of all."

"When blinded by the sun be very careful how you reach for the next branch," the old one warned. "Already they produce dangerous strains. Consider 246's action."

The Council President repeated the old one's dismissal. "246 is acting as always."

"He broke the Covenants. He broke the Covenants and got away unpunished."

"We should add new conflicts merely to punish an upstart for a technical violation?"

"His violations will not always be technical," the old one warned. "And since you are so infatuated with these creatures' star drive, consider what would happen if 246 were to obtain it."

"246 will not obtain it. They are a weak lineage with deep obligations yet to be discharged."

"Are they so weak as they were two hands of cycles ago?" the old one asked sharply. "With each cycle beneath the yoke of that madman they grow stronger. They build, they ignore their obligations and they grow."

The Council President snorted. This was an old, tired argument. "246's obligations are so heavy there is no hope of meeting them in the approved fashion."

"Then let them suffer for their foolishness," the old one retorted. "They attempted to upset the Order of Heaven and now they collect the consequences. Let them serve as an object lesson to all would-be rebels against Heaven."

"You would drive them to desperation and to the unthinkable. It is our policy to defer their obligations and that is a settled matter."

"It is your policy to let them grow so strong they can threaten us all."

"It is my policy to maintain the Will of Heaven so long as the Mandate rests with me."

"Or," he asked shrewdly, "would you rather that all Colonies acted together to give 246 a generation ship and send its present leaders out to start a new founding?"

The oldster tossed his head in negation, the folds of flesh shaking from the violence of the gesture. "Why should we deprive our own lineages of the opportunity of our own Foundings merely to be rid of this upstart and outlaw?"

It was a rhetorical question, just as the Council President's had been. Launching a generation ship to another star to Found a new system was enormously expensive even for the Colonial civilization. There was enormous prestige in being part of a Founding Branch, but also great risk and hardship and huge expense for the sponsoring Colony. True, launching a Founding was one of the civilization's standard ways of averting open conflict between irredeemaby opposed groups, but the primary expense was always borne by the sponsoring Colony.

"Very well, then," the Council President said. "It is my policy—and the will of the Council—to gratefully accept the gifts that Heaven puts within our reach."

100

"This is not a gift of Heaven. It is a snare that will set us one against the other and ultimately destroy us all."

"So you wish to throw it away?"

The old one shrugged. "We have lived long and well without it. Why should we nurture a thing that threatens us?"

"This thing does not threaten us," the Council President repeated. "It promises to enrich us. Your request is rejected."

The other stared at him in challenge. "We will speak of this again in Council."

"So we shall," the Council President agreed.

Old fool! the Council President thought as the image disappeared from the screen. *So mired in the past that he cannot see the future.* He froze, considering the other's possible moves and his counter-moves.

The conservatives could not win on the issue of destroying the strangers. Even most of the conservative faction saw the value of this new drive. The threat was that the conservative faction would align against him on other issues, hoping to build a challenge that would topple him.

The Council President made a gesture like brushing off an annoying insect. Let them! The conservatives had never been among the core of his support. So long as he remained strong and the orbits of the Council did not perturb too greatly there was nothing to fear from them.

Still, the Council President thought, there was one truth in all that muck. When it fell, the aliens' drive had to fall into the right hands. It could not be allowed in the hands of 246.

246 was a perpetual thorn in his side. An outlaw colony ruled by a madman. Who was outrageous and grew bolder with each passing cycle. An upstart. A rebel with only the most tenuous claim on his own lineage. Well, one day he would go too far and lose the Mandate of Heaven. His own people would deal with him then.

In the meantime, however, he had to be reckoned with.

The root of the trouble was that nearly a hundred cycles ago 246 had been led by a genuine lunatic.

246 had been one of the powers of the system, a first founding, a Great Branch of the One Tree of the parent lineage. It had dependencies and a web of mutual obligations

101

that spread across the entire system and its voice echoed in the Council.

That a colony should fall from such an exalted state was part of the Natural Order of Heaven. But the way 246 had fallen was strange and inglorious in the extreme.

The leadership of the 246 lineage had fallen to one of great personal force and pronounced cultish leanings. For sake of a quasi-religious ideal he had attempted to turn an entire planet into a colony.

That such a thing was unheard of and clearly against the Order of Heaven mattered not at all to him and very little to his people. He determined that to honor his mad gods a planet should be made over into a place where people could live unaided. Even more incredibly, his people, rather than withdrawing his Mandate, went along with him.

For two lifetimes the people of 246 labored at their great work. Resources enough to build twenty colonies or to launch expeditions to two other stars were poured into 246's dream.

Enormous mass drivers were built in the Jovian systems and huge chunks of water ice were hurled onto the surface of the planet. Settlements were established at the bottom of the planet's gravity well, under pressure structures more massive than those surrounding a colony. Construction started on a vast system of mirrors to focus additional sunlight on the planet. Cultures were bred to transform and stabilize the planet's atmosphere when it was finally generated.

And always the leader drove his people on with the vision of the paradise they would have on the surface of the planet. A place to stand and defy Heaven itself.

It was madness, of course. It was contrary to the collected wisdom of tens of thousands of cycles and thousands of Foundings. But the leader was mad and he infected his people with his madness. Under the incredulous eyes of the other colonies, 246 pushed ahead with its project. In the process it beggared itself and its future.

First 246 spent its available capital. Then it called in its accumulated rights and obligations with other colonies. Then, as the huge unproductive works dragged on for cycle after cycle, it mortgaged its future and placed itself under heavy obligations to other colonies to get the resources to feed its leader's obsession.

Finally, inevitably, it all collapsed. The project was too

great and the available resources were not enough. The old leader had spiraled slowly down into madness and senility. For a while his successor had attempted to carry on the project until he too was overwhelmed. In the end he lost the Mandate of Heaven and 246 emerged embittered and impoverished.

For perhaps another lifetime 246 alternated between periods of weak leadership and direct control of the Council as one or another of its obligations became overdue.

During these recurrent periods of chaos and foreign rule, the present leader had risen out of obscurity to take control of the Inner Grove. In the process he had swept away the old lineage leaders and changed the social structure of 246 forever.

There was a shred of legality for the leader's position, the Council President admitted. Leadership of a lineage was a matter of limited election. Although the choice was normally made by the Elders of the Inner Grove, their authority rested on their claim to represent the entire lineage. It was theoretically possible for the lineage as a whole to instruct the elders as to who was an acceptable candidate. But in all the long recorded history of the race there were only a few times when that had been done and never before in this system.

But for the Council President, whose lineage was a Great Branch stretching back through Elders of the Inner Grove for three Foundings, Derfuhrer was an insolent upstart.

As a politician, Derfuhrer's constant stream of complaints about how 246 had been stripped of its rightful position and his constant demands were more than annoying, they were dangerous.

Dangerous, but manageable. The Council President had even briefly allied with 246 to help tame the conservatives. Now he must be checked before he could expand his insolence even further.

Meanwhile, there were other alliances to consider and other demands to balance as each colony attempted to use its resources and obligations to take advantage of this new situation.

There are too many resonances, the Council President thought. *Too many competing influences. The orbit is perturbed and its future path is beyond prediction.*

And now this new thing, this shipload of strange creatures with their fantastic drive. What new perturbation would they bring with them, the Council President wondered. What price would they extract for their secret?

Andrew Aubrey stared into the Colonist's eyes and tried to avoid looking at the great beak in front of them. *This being is just as civilized as you are,* he told himself sternly.

"Uh, you are one of the leaders of a colony?"

"I am," Derfuhrer told him. Aubrey had asked to talk to one of the leaders and since Derfuhrer and the Council President were the only ones willing to spend time personally on screen with the humans, he ended up with Derfuhrer.

"I am interested in the way your society works."

"It works very well," Derfuhrer told him. "All join together harmoniously for the greater good." He saw no point in mentioning the machinations of the illegitimate usurpers who made up the Colonial Council.

"How long has it been like this?"

"Thousands of cycles."

"And you have been at peace all this time?" Aubrey asked, his excitement growing.

"We have always lived in harmony. It is the Way of Heaven."

"But no war?"

Derfuhrer hesitated. What was this strange being asking him now?

"Explain please."

It took a long time for the translation to come back.

"War. Open hostility between lineages. Killing and destruction of colonies."

Instinctively, Derfuhrer flinched. *Open hostilities! Were these creatures truly mad?*

"We do not do that," he said at last.

"How . . . how long?"

Again the alien shrug gesture. "I do not know. Never in this system."

"But when you have disputes, how do you settle them?"

"We talk. We trade. We strike balances. There are many ways."

"Fantastic," Dr. Andrew Aubrey breathed. *No war! These people had no war.* This was a race at peace for thousands of years.

There was an undercurrent of excitement running through

104

the entire ship when the Ship's Council met again. In the packed auditorium where the Council met, the air was almost electric.

All the seats had been taken long before the meeting was scheduled to begin and from engineering to the bridge nearly every screen on the *Maxwell* was tuned in on it. Most of the Council members were early as well. They whispered back and forth as they waited, sometimes gathering in huddles of two and three. At either end of the table sat the invited guests, Captain Jenkins, Ludenemeyer, Sharon Dolan, Father Simon and the others who had technical knowledge to offer.

At precisely the appointed hour Andrew Aubrey strode onto the stage, polished, trim and smooth as always, to rap the meeting to order.

"Since this is a special meeting of the Ship's Council, we will dispense with the regular business and go straight to the heart of the matter. As you all know, we have to discuss trading information with the Colonists. Before we try to make policy, however, I think we need to understand what the advanced civilization of the Colonists has to offer." He turned to Pete Carlotti. "Dr. Carlotti, I believe you have been talking to them about astronomical data."

"Well, under the circumstances the aliens are unwilling to discuss theories," Carlotti said. "But they have given us some notion of the scope of their observational astronomy. Gentlemen, ladies, the only word I can find for it is 'breathtaking.'

"These people have astronomical records going back literally thousands of years. They include observations made from an area which must be hundreds of light years across. It is an unbelievable treasure trove in both scientific and practical terms.

"I'm sure the scientific benefits are obvious to all of you. I will simply add to that with the aliens' knowledge we could extend the range of our starships manyfold. I was shown samples of the data and from those samples I would estimate we would be able to navigate safely out to nearly a thousand light years in at least some directions. The implications are stunning."

"And what do they want in return?" DeLorenzo asked.

"Our own astronomical data, of course. And the details of our star drive."

105

DeLorenzo muttered something in Spanish.

"I think we had best leave that until we have heard all the reports," Aubrey said. "Dr. Dolan, I believe you had something?"

"There is even more than astronomical knowledge here," Sharon said, almost breathless with excitement.

"Dr. Aubrey mentioned how far ahead the Colonists are," Dolan said. "There is another area where they are ahead of us. Space engineering. We don't know how to build anything like those colonies."

"They are enormous," Carlotti agreed.

Sharon shook her head. "Size is the least of it. The impressive thing is that they are completely self-supporting and have been for thousands of years." She looked up and down the table excitedly and her face fell at the lack of reaction.

"Let me summarize," she said more dryly. "We supply about ninety-five percent of the needs of our space colonies from space resources. The rest represents material that has to be transported from Earth at enormous cost.

"This isn't just a matter of making some things on Earth and not in space. There are a number of things that *have* to come from Earth because we cannot produce them in space. The classic example is that every so often we have to replace the seed stocks and cultures for our farms.

"These people don't. They supply *all* their needs from space and they have been doing it effectively forever.

"Not only that, but they are much more efficient at managing their life support systems. The implications of that alone are huge. Our colonies are limited because we have to have a fairly large amount of room for each colonist, far more than we really need to support him or her. All that extra air, space and biomass make an environmental flywheel effect. That makes it easier to manage the environment on the colonies, but it also makes our colonies very inefficient. These people have much finer control over their ecologies so they don't need that flywheel. That fact alone makes their colonies much more productive than ours.

"The signs are everywhere. Their ships, their propulsion systems, the construction of their colonies. All of them far, far ahead of us and all perfectly adapted by thousands of years of life in space.

"If we can learn their technology we have the chance to

leap millennia in just a few years. Our space populations can explode. We can even start exporting food from space back to Earth!"

That caused a stir, Sharon noted with satisfaction as she sat back down.

"I have a report I'd like to add," Aubrey said, standing up. "We have heard about the Colonists' scientific knowledge," he nodded to Carlotti, "and about the practical skills they could teach us," a nod to Sharon Dolan. "But there is something even more significant here."

He paused dramatically.

"The Colonists do not have war."

"Huh? Are you sure?"

"I said war is totally unknown in their culture. They were horrified at the thought of violent conflict."

"But surely they must have some disagreements," Carlotti said.

"Of course, but they have perfected a system of handling them without resorting to violence." He looked down the table.

"Over thousands of years the Colonists have evolved a nearly perfect Sixth Wave society. They have moved beyond the age of Industrial Scarcity and Information-Age conflict into a post-Information-Age culture built on conflict resolution.

"Think about it," Aubrey went on. "In the first place what do they have to fight over? The natural resources of the system are plentifully distributed and free for the taking. The Colonists haven't begun to bump against their resource limits and since they control their populations carefully, it is doubtful they ever will."

Jenkins thought about resource distribution and the energy cost of reaching them from various points in the habitable belt, but he kept silent.

"Beyond that, they have had to learn to live together. Those habitats are fragile. In the event of open hostilities it is all too probable that both parties would be destroyed. They have lived with that for thousands of years and they have learned to adapt to it."

"Humans have had millions of years and we still haven't learned how," DeLorenzo put in skeptically.

Aubrey looked annoyed. "We have not lived in structures in space which could be easily damaged by missiles or even rocks. No, they are far, far ahead of us in the techniques of conflict resolution.

"If we can apply their lessons to our own society we can advance centuries in a single generation.

"Earlier someone said the potential here is enormous. It is more than that, it is nearly inconceivable in human terms. There has never been an event anywhere in human history fraught with such great potential for constructive human change!"

"Human change into what?" DeLorenzo snapped.

"I beg your pardon?"

"Since you're harping on the Colonists' long history, let me give you a quote from our own history: 'beware of Greeks bearing gifts.' We are sitting ducks for these people."

"Just because we were fortunate enough to come across something they did not . . ." Aubrey began.

"Exactly. We're damn lucky we've got one bargaining chip."

DeLorenzo let out his breath in a gust of exasperation and ran his hand through his hair.

"Look, I said this in the beginning. The thing to do is to cut and run. Earth wants to negotiate with these people? Fine, let Earth send out a team of negotiators—and the armed force necessary to back them up."

He looked up and down the group.

"We aren't authorized to conduct negotiations. We aren't equipped to conduct negotiations. And we sure as hell are in no condition to defend ourselves if the negotiations go sour."

"We are not conducting negotiations," Aubrey said.

"No? What do you call it then? Earth has exactly one advantage in dealing with these aliens and that is the FTL drive. The only thing we can do here is blow that advantage by giving it away to them. It's too damn dangerous for us to stick around."

There was a muttering from the crowd.

"Captain," Aubrey asked. "Do you think it is too dangerous to stay?"

"Not if we keep the drive hot," Jenkins said. DeLorenzo scowled at him. "But that's not the same as saying we're going to tell them how the drive works."

"I beg your pardon?"

"I said we are not going to discuss the drive with them, Doctor. We do not have the authority."

"You're agreeing with Major DeLorenzo?" Aubrey said incredulously.

"Only to the extent that we are not empowered to give the Colonists the principles of the drive." Again the audience muttered and Jenkins realized he had driven a wedge between himself and most of the people on the ship.

"Very well, Captain," Aubrey said at last. "We all know you have the power to enforce that decision—at least while we are here."

"Doctor," Captain Jenkins replied, "my only concern is while we are here."

The ship was still buzzing at dinner that evening. Characteristically, Billy Toyoda didn't even notice. He barely noticed what was on his tray as he talked shop with one of the other computer crew.

"That's heavy sand the Owlies have got," Toyoda said for perhaps the sixth time since they had sat down. "There are some smart Owlie computer architects out there."

Neither of them saw Andrew Aubrey come up behind them and stop short when he heard what Toyoda was saying.

"I really don't think it is appropriate to call them 'Owlies'," Aubrey admonished. "It sounds derogatory."

Billy turned to look up at the scientist. "So who cares? They never hear what we call them anymore than we hear what they call us. They probably call us something worse."

"Calling them names promotes prejudice," Aubrey said.

"That's what everyone calls them."

"The proper term is 'Colonists.' I'd appreciate it if you'd use it in the future." He walked away from the table.

"You know that guy crottles my greeps," Billy said as Aubrey moved out of earshot.

"Why?"

"He's a control freak. He wants to run every one and every thing he comes in contact with."

"That's a funny thing to say about Mr. Consensual Management himself."

Toyoda nodded. "That's the other thing. That he's not even honest about it."

To the great relief of nearly everyone on the ship, including Jenkins, the Colonists were willing to continue talking even once they understood the secret of the drive was not up for trade. However, they had their own conditions.

"It would be best if we avoided contamination," the Council President explained. "So we wish to limit physical contact between us."

"Disease?" Aubrey said. "The possibility hadn't occurred to me, but yes, I can understand your concern."

The Council President froze. *Physical illness between species? Are these things even more fragile than they appear? Or is the translator malfunctioning?* Never mind. The creatures had agreed and that was the central point.

"With your permission we will establish a station near your ship where we may meet in safety and mutual comfort to discuss and to trade physical objects. Naturally we will keep you fully informed of all movements of ships and materials near your vessel."

"Naturally," Aubrey agreed.

"Now," the Council President said, "I have another proposal for communication . . ."

"The Colonists have suggested that we limit our physical contacts to the greatest extent possible," Aubrey told the next meeting of the Ship's Council. "They are concerned about the possibility of disease."

"Between species?" C.D. MacNamara asked. "But surely that is exaggerated."

Captain Peter Jenkins considered it more than exaggerated, he thought it was insane. But he wasn't in this "working session" of the Council, sitting at the foot of the table, to voice an opinion. He was here as a half-welcome guest because Aubrey had finally realized that the Captain held effective veto power over dealing with the aliens. Like it or not, he needed to know what the Captain thought before the Council established a policy.

"Perhaps," Aubrey replied to MacNamara. "Perhaps not. They have much greater experience with these things than we do, after all. However in view of certain other concerns," Aubrey glanced significantly at DeLorenzo, "it appears a reasonable suggestion."

"How can we learn anything if they limit contact?" someone asked.

"The Colonists have also proposed free and open communication with us."

"Just what does that mean?" DeLorenzo growled.

"It means, Major, that any of us can talk freely to them. They will open as many channels as we desire and make available as many of their people as we wish to speak to."

"While they pump us dry?"

"Certain subjects will not be discussed, of course," MacNamara said. "We have already agreed upon that."

"And did any of the people doing the agreeing stop to consider the security risks?"

"We have already agreed not to discuss the drive or anything relating to it with them," Aubrey said firmly.

"And what about the rest of it? What about the location of Earth?"

"That too, is not a subject for discussion."

"Aubrey, do you know what the first principle of interrogation is? Get the subject talking. Talk about anything. The weather, soccer, anything, but get him talking. You do that and you're halfway to finding out anything you want to know."

"I very much doubt the aliens will be subjecting any of us to the third degree," Aubrey said stiffly.

"Third degree, third degree," DeLorenzo mimicked nasally. "Jesus Christ man, you don't have the faintest damn idea of how an interrogation is conducted! Let me tell you something. I've done plenty of interrogations, and I *never* resorted to force." *Well, almost never*, DeLorenzo admitted to himself. "I found out what I wanted to know, too. If you follow this idiotic policy, the aliens will have the secret of the drive and the location of Earth in six weeks."

"Absurd," MacNamara snapped.

"Is it, Doctor?" DeLorenzo's smile was more like a snarl. "Do you know how pitifully easy it is to trick someone into saying more than they should?"

"Major, we are talking about scientific discussions here."

"Remember how much the Soviets got from the West by 'scientific discussions'?"

"Now really . . ."

"You know, you're awfully damn eager to end up as some-

111

one else's slaves," DeLorenzo's voice cut through Aubrey's smoothly modulated tones.

"I beg your pardon!"

"Slaves," DeLorenzo repeated firmly, looking up and down the table. "The whole human race. You've already heard that they're centuries ahead of us. If they show up at Earth how do we stop them?"

"Slaves went out with the industrial revolution," Carlotti said.

"Call them 'colonies,' or 'protectorates' then." DeLorenzo's smile was ugly. "It puts a better face on it. But the result's the same. Economic and cultural domination of Earth by these aliens."

"Oh come now, Major," Aubrey said patiently. "We have been all through this before. What conceivable reason could an advanced culture have for trying to dominate another culture?"

"I bet the Indians couldn't figure out what Cortez hoped to get out of them either. The only thing that stands between us and slavery is the star drive. And now you want to put yourselves in a position where the aliens are sure to get it." He shook his head. "Talk about selling someone the rope to hang you. You people want to *give* them the shackles to enslave you."

"It never ceases to amaze me," Aubrey said coldly, "how we read our own basest motives into those we mistrust."

"And it never ceases to amaze *me* how some people confuse their rosy fantasies with reality. Man, these are *aliens*. We know nothing about them!"

"We know the Colonists are not guilty of genocide," Aubrey shot back.

DeLorenzo went white. A single vein in his forehead throbbed. Without speaking he pushed back his chair, rose from the table and stalked from the room.

No one said anything until the door had closed behind him.

"Now," Aubrey murmured, "if there are no *logical* objections . . ."

No one said anything.

"Of course," Aubrey went on, "since this is a matter affecting the safety of the ship, the Captain has the final say in the matter." He turned toward Jenkins.

112

Jenkins cleared his throat. "If we are going to learn anything from these aliens we are going to have to talk to them. The more of us there are talking to them, the faster we can learn it." *And the sooner we can get out of here.*

"Subject to the provision that nothing bearing on the drive, the location of Earth or certain other sensitive matters is discussed, I'll support open communication with the aliens."

Aubrey paused. Obviously he hadn't expected the captain to do more than rubber stamp the Council's decision. "I suppose we all agree to that," he said smoothly.

MacNamara and the other Council members nodded.

"All right then. It's settled," Aubrey said briskly. "How quickly can we have the channels open?"

"That depends on how fast we can get them set up and how long it takes to draw up a list of prohibited topics. I'll want Dr. Takiuji's advice on that."

"I think a committee would be more appropriate," Dr. Aubrey said.

"If Dr. Takiuji wants help I'm sure he will ask for it," Jenkins said. "But he knows much more about the drive and what is likely to be sensitive than any of the rest of us."

Aubrey turned that over for a minute.

"All right. But we need to do this as quickly as possible."

After the meeting broke up, Jenkins did not return to the bridge immediately. Instead he went to the North Bubble and swam over next to the port to float alone in an ocean of stars.

The star field was familiar but not identical. At 100 light years there are differences. Shift a few light years and you lose most of the G and K suns and all the M type dwarfs. But the big bright stars, the O, A and B suns, still shine brightly in the sky. Their positions change, sometimes radically, but by concentrating on the brightest stars you can pick out the general outlines of the sky from the Solar System. That m. the effect even stranger than if all the stars were new.

"It is different," a voice said in the darkness behind him. He turned and there was Father Simon.

"I'm sorry, you startled me."

"I seem to be making a habit of that," Father Simon said ruefully. He caught Jenkins' puzzled look.

"Never mind," he said. "I'm sorry to have disturbed you."

"That's all right. Please, stay if you want to."

For a while both men looked at the stars without saying anything.

"You know, Father," Jenkins said at last, "this is a damned unusual situation."

"I rather imagine so," said the priest with feeling.

"No, I don't mean the aliens, although God knows that's earthshaking enough. I mean the situation I'm in."

"How is that?"

"Normally a ship captain has superiors no more than a few hours away—by radio, I mean. A captain can consult with his or her superiors on any major decision." He sighed. "That's a good feeling. I never realized how much I relied on that chain of command until now."

"But surely you didn't ask for instructions on every little problem?"

"No, of course not. Captains have a lot of freedom of action and especially in an emergency you act first and then ask permission. Still, it's a tremendous comfort to know there's someone out there you can call on when you're not sure what to do."

"I am familiar with the feeling," Father Simon said, fingering his clerical collar.

Jenkins was staring out into space and didn't notice. "Here we're alone. I'm not used to it. Not with something like this."

"But it isn't unknown for a captain to be in this situation," Father Simon said quietly. "Historically ship captains have usually had to make decisions without direct reference to higher authority."

"Historically? Oh, you mean naval captains, on Earth's seas. I suppose so, but commanding a clipper ship doesn't have much to do with commanding the *Maxwell*."

"True," the priest agreed. "But the traditions, and I believe much of the law, relating to captains and their ships comes from that time."

"I suppose so," Jenkins repeated. "But I don't see the connection."

"Forgive me, but it occurs to me that perhaps there are lessons to be gleaned from those traditions for our present situation."

"No one's ever been in *this* situation," Jenkins said wryly.

"Perhaps, but I venture to say that people have often been in similar situations." He paused and Jenkins turned toward him. The ruddy light of the alien sun caught the priest's face from below, etching the cheekbones and accentuating the hook of his nose.

"I think the reason humans value tradition is that there is so little we meet that is truly new. Oh, new facts, certainly, and new combinations of circumstances. But so much of what we must deal with is merely old wine poured into new bottles. Traditions tell us how others have coped with similar circumstances, for better or worse."

"So you think I should do what an old-time sea captain would do?"

"No, I think you should do what *you* would do. But in deciding that, perhaps you should also consider the lessons embodied in the traditions that grew up when captains were truly 'masters under God.' "

"There may be something to that," Jenkins said noncommittally. "I wonder what an old-time sea captain would have done in a situation like this."

"You could always look in the library," Father Simon suggested.

Logically there was no need for a ship's library. Screens in offices, cabins or anywhere else in the ship could call up data just as easily as ones in study carrels.

But humans are not entirely creatures of logic. They need to break their routine, to see different people and places. Hence the library. A place of quiet and rest where anyone could go to browse through the available knowledge carried on the *Maxwell*.

But it was not restful to everyone there.

The damn fools, Major Autro DeLorenzo fumed, *the damn blind stupid fools*. All they could see was the bait being dangled in front of them. And that wimp captain! *Madre de Dios* how did a cretin like that ever achieve command?

115

So they would not protect themselves, eh? Very well, it was up to him to protect all humanity from them.

The library had the complete plans of the ship and all its systems. He had the training to put it to use.

Carefully and methodically, Major Autro DeLorenzo began planning his sabotage.

In the observation bubble Captain Peter Jenkins floated in space and watched the stars. *Have I really done the right thing?* he wondered. *Can we trust beings we have so little in common with? DeLorenzo's right. The risks are enormous. But so is the reward.* He had taken action only after consultation and, indeed, at the urging of the Ship's Council. However this turned out, he was sure there was no board of inquiry in the Solar System that would find fault with his actions.

But somehow the thought didn't reassure him.

How to reach them, the Council President wondered. *How to reach these peculiar creatures and wrest from them the secret of their drive.*

Already the ship was under intense scrutiny. Alien instruments studied it from every colony that could bring them to bear and from many other places in space as well. Every emission from the ship was sampled and exhaustively analyzed by the Colonists' computers. Scientists scrambled through the accumulated knowledge of millennia seeking correlations between the ship's shape and performance and anything that might possibly offer a clue to the drive's function. Hypotheses were formulated, argued violently, modified, discarded and formulated anew.

So far, nothing. The scientists and savants talked at great length of what they learned, but none of them could offer the slightest clue as to how the drive might work. There seemed to be nothing in any library anywhere which could shed the slightest clue as to how the drive worked.

For now their best hope, their *only* hope was to induce them to part with it.

"I'm sorry," Aubrey told the alien, "but our Council has decided to leave discussion of our star drive until a later expedition. Personally it was not my choice, but . . ."

116

There was a pause while the computer translated the statement and a longer pause while the alien considered it. Aubrey did not realize that the word the humans translated as "council" referred to a governing and arbitrating body between different, independent groups.

"You represent different lineages, then?" the Colonist asked.

"No, we aren't related, if that's what you mean. We are many different races and several nationalities."

The Colonist stood with his head cocked to one side for a long time, apparently listening to a complex translation. When he spoke, he spoke at length and the translation was slow in coming.

"How do you resolve conflicts, then?"

Aubrey looked embarrassed. "We try not to let such notions interfere with us. We strive to work together in peace and harmony."

Aubrey didn't realize that the sentence translated into: "We must work constantly and strenuously to achieve an absence of open conflict within our primary group and to find a stable orbit." Even if he had, he probably would not have seen the difference in the sentence.

The alien froze. He stayed motionless so long Aubrey wondered if something had gone wrong with the video. Then the Colonist flicked his nictating membranes over his eyes and his mouth moved.

"You strive for this?"

"We try to achieve it, yes." Aubrey sighed. "It is not easy for us. We are a young species and we tend to be combative."

"It is not good to be too combative," the alien said without special emphasis.

Yes! The Council President replayed the transmission for the fourth time and tried to stifle the excitement welling up in him.

He had it, he realized. The answer was unbelievably simple and now he had it!

The aliens did not represent a single lineage. There were many lineages and they were bound together by only the most rudimentary agreements. They seemed to have no Covenant at all. Not even for their species as a whole!

117

As a result they were in constant conflict with one another. Their lineages were weak and seemed unable to enforce more than the most rudimentary discipline.

It was not necessary to deal with these creatures' entire lineage. They could be dealt with individually. One by one they could be bribed, suborned, coerced and threatened into giving up their most precious secret.

And, most incredibly of all, from the sound of it, it could be done with ease. These aliens had no real concept of security. Their channels of communication were almost completely unguarded and their computers were poorly protected.

The Council President spared a thought for the society that lay behind this starship. How had the leaders of their lineages survived so long? It was insanity to send out a ship with so little protection and a crew so hopelessly disunited. Did the Elders of the Inner Grove simply not care what happened to these ships?

Incredible. But then the entire situation was incredible.

It really did not matter. They were here, they were as they were and they carried with them a thing of great value. It would be a simple matter to get that information from them now that he had the key.

Turning individuals against their lineages was a technique which had been old among them long before this system was founded. Yes, the Council President thought, the weapons were well in hand to take what was wanted from these strange beings.

He turned from the recorder to the map inlaid on the wall behind him and thrilled again at the vision of power it spread out before him.

There were complications, he admitted to himself. He was sure this same recording was being played and replayed in every Colony in the system. The others were undoubtedly aware of the same weakness and they would move to exploit it.

That would not be easy to control. Concessions would have to be made, of course, and the full Council authority doubtless invoked to keep the colonies from trampling each other in their haste to take advantage of this. But ultimately the Council President had no doubt in his ability to perturb the orbits to his benefit. As always in the scramble of bargaining, coercion, cajoling and arguing, he would emerge on the upper branch. And his lineage would benefit accordingly.

So, the Council President thought. *The pieces are all in place. Now let the game begin. The great game for the greatest stake of all.*

PART III: CHUBAN

Heavy sand, Billy Toyoda thought approvingly. *Really heavy sand.*

He was floating disembodied in cyberspace admiring the structure spread out before him.

The aliens' computer net was as complex as a Mandelbrot Set, with the same kinds of intricacies and unexpected excursions into near chaos. Overall there was a plan to it. It was elaborate and subtle but Billy could definitely sense an ordered structure to it all.

Much of it Billy couldn't interpret yet. But he could understand enough to know that this net tied together all the colonies in the system. Stretching off from the main structure were tenuous gray extensions, links that reached across interstellar space to tie into other Colonial civilizations through laser links. The signals were slow but the bandwidths were huge.

Probing gently, Billy Toyoda delicately tried to grasp the Tao of this alien cyberspace.

"Excuse me."

Billy opened his eyes and the vision of the alien net faded away. In its place was the image of Dr. Sukihara Takiuji standing in the door of the computer room.

The computerman shook himself mentally and regarded the Japanese physicist.

"Please excuse the interruption, but you are in charge of the translation programs, I believe?"

"Sure. What do you want?"

"Can it be arranged so certain words are not translated correctly?"

Billy frowned. His interest in the doings on the ship outside of his computers was limited, but he did know that Dr. Takiuji was drawing up a list of forbidden topics for conversation with the aliens.

"You mean take them out of the tables so they won't come across? Yeah, I guess so."

"Not so they do not come across. So they are not translated meaningfully. I do not know, perhaps the word is translated differently each time." He smiled. "It would be best if it were done so the speakers did not know what was happening."

"That'll screw up communication."

"That is precisely the point."

"Oh! You mean stuff about the drive? Yeah. Is that what the captain wants?"

"I am sure that it is," Dr. Takiuji said.

"I am sorry," Suki told the alien. "We are not allowed to discuss anything which might bear on the drive."

The owl-like face remained impassive. "Of course not. However, there are other areas in which it would be mutually profitable to exchange information."

"It is not an easy decision," Suki said. "I must think on it."

Derfuhrer was content with that. The creature had not refused outright and as long as communication remained open there was the possibility of learning what he wished to know. Besides, there was the other one, this 'Aubrey.' He was coming along nicely.

Most of the Colonial leaders assigned the job of contacting the humans to their intelligence specialists and each of those specialists dealt with only one human on a regular basis.

Derfuhrer spent hours cultivating two humans personally.

In part that was a measure of the importance he attached to learning the secret of the drive and in part it was a mark of his confidence in his own abilities. Derfuhrer was a very convincing speaker and he knew it.

"Did you hear what Dr. Takiuji did with the computers?" Jenkins asked DeRosa. "He had Toyoda gimmick them so they wouldn't give a straight translation of anything dealing with the drive."

"Cute," Iron Alice said. "But you don't look so happy about it."

"I'm not sure if I am or not. It's useful security, but the Ship's Council wasn't consulted. I don't think they'd like it at all."

"You could take the matter up with them."

Jenkins shook his head. "If I did that they would probably disapprove on general principles. I think I'll let it ride."

"What is this you do?" Derfuhrer asked Sukihara Takiuji.

"I play a game. Do you have games?"

There was a hesitation while the computers dealt with the concept.

"We have games. What is the purpose of this one?"

Suki made a deprecating gesture. "To pass time pleasantly. Perhaps to learn. It is called 'go.' It is very old."

Derfuhrer had no time for games, but he had identified this human as one of the critical ones.

"Would it violate convention for you to teach me this game?"

"Not at all. Let me call up a board from the ship's computer." He made the adjustment and the nineteen by nineteen grid appeared on the screen.

"The game is played by the players alternately placing black and white stones on the intersections. Beyond that there are only four rules."

"It seems simple," Derfuhrer said dubiously.

"Perhaps not so simple," Suki replied politely.

For the first game Suki spotted Derfuhrer fifteen stones, far in excess of the traditional nine. As the lines of stones grew, the alien quickly recognized that this was not a mere pastime. This was a battle game designed to develop and hone skills for conflict. He became absorbed in the flow of the play, dimly sensing the subtle logic that underlay the moves.

Even with a fifteen-stone handicap, Suki beat Derfuhrer easily.

"That was most interesting," the alien said as the stones were counted and territories tallied. "Thank you."

"It was an honor," Suki replied.

"I wish to learn more of this game," Derfuhrer said.

"I am sorry we do not have time for another game right

now. But another time. Meanwhile there is some information in the ship's library," Suki said. "I could supply it to you."

"I would be honored," Derfuhrer said.

What is this creature offering me now? Derfuhrer thought after the screen went dark. *Why is it giving me insights into its strategic thinking?* An alliance? Possibly, but to what purpose? And against whom? *It is imprudent to share matters of such import until the agreement is sealed and we have not yet agreed on terms.*

Or are these beings just stupid? He nipped that thought off quickly. Beings who travel faster than light are not unintelligent. There had to be some deeper meaning here.

Derfuhrer was willing to wait to discover what it might be.

Steven Bustamonte held the capsule under his nose, exhaled and crushed it between his fingers. He inhaled sharply, filling his lungs to the very bottom with the sharp, sweet chemical reek. Then he collapsed backwards on his bunk and let the drug take him.

Goddamn those Owlies are good, Bustamonte thought as the waves of warmth spread through his veins and radiated out from the very center of his being, beating time with his own pulse. *Goddamn good.*

"You know," Iron Alice said, "we've got another problem here."

"What?" Jenkins asked, running his eyes down the oxygen/food production figures from hydroponics in another window on his screen.

"The crew. They were supposed to be kept busy rigging those scopes and running experiments. Now they're just sitting on their asses. It's not healthy."

Jenkins turned his full attention to her. "Spacers are used to waiting."

"I'm not so worried about the spacers," DeRosa said. "But most of these people are scientists, technicians and construction workers. They're not used to doing nothing and most of those scientists and techs haven't been off Earth before."

"There's no point in rigging those arrays, not this close to a sun."

"Maybe not, but it would be a good idea if they had something else to do to keep them occupied."

"I'll take it up with the Ship's Council. It'll give them something constructive to do."

"Speaking of which, how is the Ship's Council?"

Jenkins shrugged. "Not doing much of anything. Most of the members are too busy talking to the Owlies and the rest of them are debating nitpicking procedural details."

"Ain't consensual management wonderful?" Iron Alice said cynically.

"Let's just say dealing with them isn't the best part of the job."

The dice bounced high under half gravity and settled slowly to the groans of the losers and the applause of the winners. William Jewett turned over in his bunk and tried to concentrate on the book he was reading.

Not too long ago he would have been down there on the blanket yelling his lungs out with the rest of them. But he was married now and he needed all his pay.

The noise and the excitement was too much. Finally he set the book down and rolled out of his bunk.

"Hey, here comes fresh blood," said one of the shooters, a burly crewman named Bustamonte.

"Not tonight," Jewett said and made his way out the door to a chorus of good-natured catcalls.

Now what? he wondered as he made his way up the corridor. There just wasn't a lot to do in the section of Spin that the vacuum jacks had claimed for their living quarters and from long tradition named the Construction Shack. There was some sappy historical drama on the tridee in the lounge— which was why his roommate had moved the crap game into their compartment. He wasn't much of a reader under the best of circumstances and he'd already worked out in the gym twice today. In the old days he would have hit the bar and tried to find some female companionship, but that was out too.

God I miss you, Cherry!

There wasn't even any point in writing her. He'd get back almost as fast as the letters would and besides, there wasn't anything to tell her. The big instruments he and his fellows were supposed to rig and maintain were still stowed and the crews were down to half days of make work every other day. The pay was the same, but even so . . .

Well, what about doing something that would be worth talking about? How about trying to talk to the Owlies?

The procedure had been explained to every one on the ship. All you had to do was punch 663 from any comm screen and you'd have a private line to the aliens.

Well, there was a comm screen in a corner of the lounge.

He skirted the dozen or so people clustered around the tridee and pulled down the screen's hush hood before he punched the number.

The screen dissolved into a kaleidoscope of colored sparks and then Jewett was looking at his first Owlie.

As usual, the view was face on. The fierce yellow eyes and hooked beak dominated the face from this view. The eyes fixed on him without blinking or wavering.

"Yes?" the computer synthesized voice sounded surprisingly human. Jewett almost lost his nerve and broke contact right there.

"Hi," Jewett said lamely. "I'd like to talk to someone."

Still the unblinking stare. "Have you spoken with us before?"

"No."

"What is your special interest?"

"No special interest. I, uh, just wanted to talk to you guys. So I'd have something to tell my wife, you know."

"What is your function?"

"My job? I'm a vacuum jack. Hey look, if this is any trouble . . ." But the alien was gone, replaced by a panoramic view of the inside of one of the colonies. To Jewett it looked like a jungle in a greenhouse.

"Hello." The alien was back. Or rather an alien was back. Jewett wasn't sure, but this one looked different.

"Hi," Jewett responded. There was a long pause. "Uh, my name's Bill Jewett. I just wanted to talk to an Owlie. I mean an alien."

The unblinking eyes never left Jewett. "I am called Splicer. I work on an outside maintenance and repair crew," the Owlie replied.

In point of fact he did no such thing. But Splicer was a quick study and a very convincing liar.

Sukihara Takiuji and Derfuhrer studied the go board on the screen as they went over the results of their last game.

"Here you see," the Japanese physicist said as he flicked

the cursor to a group of stones, "your play is very strong, but perhaps a little heavy. You enclose my stones firmly, but your shape is not good. Too compact."

The cursor moved over the board, rearranging the stones. "Now if you had extended here instead of drawing back you would have made better shape."

"I see," Derfuhrer said. "Thank you." He studied the configuration again.

"You were correct. This is not a simple game. But very interesting."

"I am honored you find it so," Suki told the alien. "You learn very quickly." He didn't tell Derfuhrer that he was already better than anyone on the *Maxwell* aside from himself. He only had to spot the Colonist five stones and Father Simon, the strongest human player, required a six stone handicap to play evenly against him.

"Have we time to play again?" Derfuhrer asked.

"If you wish," Dr. Takiuji told him.

William Jewett made his way across the metal plain with all the skill of an experienced vacuum jack. From where he stood with a toe hooked through a safety line, the *Maxwell*'s hull curved away from him before and behind and ran off straight to either side. Momentarily he felt like an ant on a stainless steel sewer pipe.

Goddamn, this thing's big, he thought for the hundredth time.

As a vacuum jack Jewett had worked on some of the biggest manmade structures in the solar system, but the *Maxwell* and her sister starships were among the largest constructs in space. Only the L-5 colonies were larger, but they weren't designed to go anywhere. The *Maxwell* was and that added to the air of unreality.

And so far from home, Jewett thought. *So damn far. God, I miss you, Cherry.* He tried to pick out the Sun from the star fields around him. He knew he was looking in the right direction, but he was a construction worker, not an astronomer and he could not make sense out of the myriad of lights before him.

Oh well, this would be his last one. With the money he'd make on this trip and his skills he'd be able to buy on to one of the colonies. Then he'd spend his days doing outside maintenance or something and come home to Cherry every night.

Not much help right now, though, he thought.

Automatically Jewett checked his safety line before starting out again. With an expert twitch, he shook out the line and then used his toes to propel himself forward toward the curve of the hull.

Splicer's instructions had been specific, but he had been mysterious about their goal. *Go to this place on the hull and turn on your short-range communicator to this frequency*, the alien had told him in their last conversation. *I think you will find something of interest.* Jewett was bored enough to try it. Splicer was an odd sort, but he was a space worker and that gave him and Jewett a bond.

Normally the search would have been a lot more difficult. Jewett could only have gone out on his shift with his work party and would have been restricted to the area where he was working. But with no real work to be done, discipline and security were both lax. He had bluffed his way out the active lock with a lame story about taking a needed tool to a work group. He suspected the lock watch didn't really believe him, but they were vacuum jacks too and sympathized with a jack's need to get outside.

Jewett switched on his personal communicator, although there was no one else in sight on the vast pocked metal plain of the ship's hull. He tuned his receiver as he had been instructed. Cautiously he swiveled his head, listening for a tone.

The personal communicator was a line-of-sight device using infrared radiation. The unit was designed to work with digitally encoded transmissions, eliminating the background noise produced by simple heat sources. However, it was possible to cut the encoder/decode circuits out of the loop and that was what Jewett had been told to do.

He had turned halfway around before he heard a low hum in his earphones, as if someone was sending a single tone on the communications channel. He picked his way carefully toward the sound, stopping every few feet to listen.

It took him a few minutes to find the source of the sound. The package was white, whiter than the *Maxwell*'s skin and about the size of Jewett's clenched fist, but otherwise unremarkable. Without the infrared beacon, Jewett would never have been able to find it.

As he picked it up, the vacuum jack saw there was no sign of a power source or an emitting element anywhere on the package. The wrappings themselves must emit, Jewett realized. They could soak up IR when the package was in sunlight and retransmit the energy on a single narrow frequency.

Jewett wasn't enough of a technician to know how sophisticated that cloth was, but he had a practical spaceman's appreciation of a clever engineering hack. He tucked the package into a leg pocket and turned to make his way back inside the *Maxwell*.

Back in his compartment, William Jewett hefted his present from the aliens. The package was heavy and it felt like there were several hard objects inside. The wrappings weren't immediately obvious and he fumbled with them for a minute before they fell off and the contents went bouncing and clattering to the floor.

Jewett goggled and then dove for the floor, grabbing at the items with both hands. There were six of them, each a multi-sided prism about the length and diameter of the first joint of his thumb. One of them had a mashed corner where it had hit the floor, all of them were metallic and very heavy and there was no mistaking their color.

With shaking hands William Jewett shoved the prisms down into the bottom of his laundry bag. Then he tore out of the room, heading for the lounge and the hush-hooded communicators.

Harry Waddell was no more ambitious than any up-and-coming astrophysicist who had spent the last eight years knocking about between universities and observatories without a permanent appointment. Which is to say he would have cheerfully killed for tenure at a second-rate cow college.

"You mean you have a complete theory of stellar evolution?" he said incredulously. "No anolomies?"

"We have found none in thousands of cycles," the Colonist on the screen informed him.

"That's incredible! . . . I mean, how does it work?"

"It is somewhat complex. But we can provide you with the information—privately."

"What do you mean—privately?"

The alien made an odd gesture that Waddell had been told was the equivalent of a shrug. "It is not necessary that we even be mentioned. If you were the human discoverer of this thing it would help you, would it not?"

"Well, sure, but . . ."

"That can be arranged," the Colonist told him. "I can see to it that none of my colleagues convey the complete information to other humans. You would seem to have taken what you learned from us and developed it further. And if later it were discovered that some of us had evolved a similar theory— well, your culture recognizes priority of independent discovery, does it not?"

A complete theory, Waddell thought frantically. *My God, that's a Nobel for sure!* Visions of a chair at a major university in Niarobi or even Djarkata danced before his eyes.

"It would not necessarily be an untruth," the alien went on. "We could supply the basis and you could work out the details yourself. In that it would be no different than building on the work of others."

"Yes," Waddell said at last. "It's irregular of course, but, yes, I'll do it."

"We would require some assistance on other matters, of course," the Colonist said.

"Like what?"

"As you know, we are interested in the details of your star drive. Unfortunately, your captain refuses to share the information with us."

"I don't know a lot about the drive. It's not my field."

"But as an astrophysicist you have an understanding of the basic phenomena. That is all we would require."

Harry Waddell thought very hard for maybe ten seconds. "Nuts," he said. "It's a stupid rule anyway. Okay, I'll tell you what I can about the drive."

The alien quivered.

"The basic principle is that you go with the flow," Harry began. "For any appropriate set of coordinates the X flow is connected to the Y flow, the Z flow is connected to the X flow and them bones naturally gonna rise again."

"I do not understand," said the alien. "Is this flow gentle?"

"Gentle, hard, it doesn't matter. The important thing is that round and round and round it flows and where it stops is Heisenberg-indeterminate."

"Let us go back to the beginning," the alien said. "The flow runs from high potential to low potential, correct?"

"No, you see the harbustrang murfitzes the weebitz and then a thousand flowers bloom."

The alien said nothing for a long time.

"You mean that the sternchaser outpumps the impalement gryonny?"

Man and alien stared at each other incredulously.

"No, that's not what I mean at all. There's this flange, see? And on the flange there is a spacetime node . . ."

Eventually they gave up by mutual agreement.

"That was gold!" Jewett exclaimed as soon as his alien friend appeared on the screen.

"It has value for you?" Splicer seemed only mildly interested.

"Hell yes it's valuable! Where did you get it?"

The Owlie made the equivalent of a shrug. "We have a sufficiency of it. Would it please you to have some?"

"Well, yeah, but we're not supposed to have physical contact with you."

"We did not have physical contact when I gave you this. Why should that change?"

Jewett thought hard. "What do you want in return?"

The Owlie started. "Want? Why should I want anything? We have much of this and we obtain more every time we smelt an asteroid. I can easily acquire some and it pleases you. It is a simple enough thing to arrange."

"Well . . ."

"Consider," the Owlie went on. "You have but a single thing we do not and that is your star drive. My bosses want that, but what has that to do with you or me? You do not know the secret and it would profit me nothing to have it."

"Yeah, but, I mean gold," Jewett protested.

"If it causes you anguish, forget that I said anything," the Owlie urged. "I will not mention it again. It is just that among my people such—unofficial? yes, unofficial—arrangements are common among workers in spite of what the bosses say. I did not realize it was so different for you."

"Now wait a minute!" Jewett's mind was working furiously. "We do the same sort of thing. It's just that this is a special deal, see, and . . ." he sighed. "Oh hell, what can it hurt? Yeah, sure I'd like some more of that gold. How can we do it?"

The Owlie opened his beak in the equivalent of a smile.

"Let me know when you will be out on the hull next. Give me four or five hours notice and the package will be waiting for you."

Not all of the trade with the aliens was illicit. In a matter of weeks a softly glowing construct had blossomed not far from the *Maxwell* for exactly that purpose.

Meetpoint's proportions were wrong for human eyes and it stuck out in unusual places, as if someone had draped gold foil around a milkweed seed, but to Andrew Aubrey it was the most beautiful thing he had ever seen.

"Wonderful!" he breathed as he floated into a golden chamber near the center of the station. "This is wonderful!"

The light was reddish and dim by human standards. In another context it might have been called gloomy. But to Aubrey the room seemed like part of a fairy castle.

"We are glad you like it," said the Colonist.

He turned to the alien floating easily in the room. "It is a pleasure to meet you in person at last."

The Colonist nodded acknowledgement in a very human fashion.

"It is quite remarkable. You have taught us so much already."

The Colonist was prepared for this. He had studied tapes of Aubrey's conversations carefully, as well as the reports of the psychologists assigned to study the humans and he had his responses thoroughly worked out.

"You have been most apt pupils. We have been very pleased with your progress."

Aubrey almost dimpled. "Thank you. I hope we can continue to learn from you. And I hope we have the opportunity for further discussions as well as the exchange of artifacts."

"Yes," said the alien. "We have many more things to discuss."

"Lulu, have you got those results yet?"

"I'm working on them," Lulu Pine said sullenly, not looking up from the bench. She was a doughy, lumpy woman with a potato face, coarse complexion and wiry black hair pulled back in a bun. Even in low gravity, she moved with a heavy, flatfooted gait that made it seem her body weighed too much for her to bear.

"I need them now, Lulu," Albers said with a hint of exasperation.

"I can only work so fast," Lulu snapped.

Albers hesitated and then recognized it for a losing game. "Well, as fast as you can, please." He turned on his heel and tried to stalk out of the lab—but the low gravity betrayed him and he bounced jerkily each time his foot hit the floor.

Lulu never looked up so she missed it. *Assholes. Goddamn assholes giving orders all the time. And all of them acting like their little project was the most important Goddamn thing in the world. Well Mr. High-And-Mighty Albers, your images just got shoved to the bottom of the pile. I'll tell Dr. Wadsworth they came in late and I couldn't get the time on the computers.* She snorted. *Talk to me like that, will you? Asshole!*

Albers was still muttering when he ran into Wadsworth in the corridor.

"What's wrong, Luke?" his superior asked when he saw the look on his face.

"Oh, that Pine woman."

Wadsworth nodded sympathetically and fell in beside Albers.

"How in the world did we ever get saddled with her?" Albers asked his boss.

"Sanchez recommended her very highly. I'm afraid I didn't figure out why until it was too late."

Albers grunted. "Meaning dumping her on us was the simplest way to get her out of his lab. We'll have to think of a way to return the favor when we get back to Earth."

"Meanwhile I'm afraid we're stuck with her. The best we can do is keep her on jobs where she'll do the least damage."

"It's ironic. I was talking to DeLorenzo yesterday and he says his biggest problem is to find something for his construction crews to do. Yet we are so understaffed our work is suffering."

"Are you proposing we re-train a couple of vacuum jacks to work in the lab?" he said jokingly.

Wadsworth flinched at the thought of the stereotypical vacuum jack, huge, clumsy and hairy-eared, turned loose in his lab.

"A couple more run-ins with that woman and even a vacuum jack would look good," Albers told him.

Dressed in an engineering blue coverall, DeLorenzo half bounced and half swam down the corridor. This close to the ship's central axis there was almost no gravity.

And almost no people. The walls and floor were light blue above, brown below without any of the murals or decorations that marked the ways further out to the hub. This was an engineering corridor and a place of refuge in time of solar storm. In any event, not a main passage. DeLorenzo didn't expect to meet anyone here and he was not disappointed.

A quick turn brought him into a shallow alcove with three blank walls and a closet without a door. He reached up and with an expert twist of a screwdriver-like tool he released the fasteners holding the panel. Setting the panel to one side he stepped through into a cramped little room lined with cables.

Consulting his compad, he found a gray metal box with ranks of cables leading in and out of it and counted over until he found what he was searching for.

The gray box was called a punchblock, DeLorenzo knew, just as this space was called a wiring cabinet. Both names were misnomers now. There were no wires running through this area, only hair-fine filaments of glass that carried optical signals. And they were connected through optical switching ICs in the box, not by being punched down into connector strips.

The names had nothing to do with the reality, he thought, but they had survived, just as what he was doing now had nothing to do with the wooden shoes disgruntled workers used to throw into machinery. But they still called it sabotage.

From his tool belt he drew out a black plastic box just too large to fit comfortably in his hand. There were leads dangling from each end of the box, in colors matching the cables.

DeLorenzo hefted his version of a wooden shoe and smiled slightly. The box was a standard components container from the *Maxwell's* stores. The leads were the appropriate colors and the code stenciled white on the top was appropriate for a part in this punchblock. The smart tag embedded in the box would read out a reasonable but quite confusing description of the box's contents, complete with references to a logical set of change orders that somehow never quite described what this box was actually supposed to do.

He set the box aside and plugged a hand-held programming unit into the punchblock. A few quick strokes and one of the switches was programmed to tie two additional connections in parallel with one of the cables. Then he carefully connected the leads from his box to the connection points and carefully stuck the box to the side of the punchblock case with the approved nine dabs of the approved adhesive. Another command to his programmer and the cable's original path through the block was deactivated. Now all the signals on that line had to flow through his black box.

And that line was a key link in the ship's command system. DeLorenzo closed the punchblock cabinet and wiped his hands on his coveralls. For now the box would do nothing. As long as he gave a certain command to the ship's computer every twenty-four hours, the box would do nothing. But if he failed to give that command, or if he gave a different command, the *Maxwell*'s nervous system would be cut into pieces.

Among other things. There were similar boxes on other punchblocks around the ship. There were other devices elsewhere attached to pipes, gas lines, electronic circuits and equipment all over the *Maxwell*. At his command he could cripple and ultimately destroy the *Maxwell*.

Whistling, Major DeLorenzo replaced the panel over the wiring closet and headed down the corridor to place his next box.

Lulu Pine shifted and snuffled in front of the screen. The yellow-eyed, beaked face in front of her repelled her, but she wasn't going to have anyone say she was afraid of these unholy creatures. Besides, this one seemed almost sympathetic—although what she had to put up with would make a stone weep.

"Your bosses oppress you, then?" the Owlie asked gently.

"They're always after me. Just yesterday I was up to my elbows in plates and Dr. Albers comes in and starts harassing me. For no reason at all! I told him I'd get to his stuff as soon as I could, but he was on me for just no reason at all!" She snuffled.

"They use you harshly."

"Well, I'm a Christian and I try to keep a Christian attitude," Lulu responded. "But it's hard. When those high hats start ordering me around it's hard to keep my principles."

"I wonder that you can stand it."

"Oh, it's a trial, I can tell you. And you know what the worst of it is? All the time they look down on you. Who gets them their plates, huh? But they're always riding me. All the time getting on my case."

134

"Perhaps things could be different," the alien told her.

"Yeah," Lulu said suspiciously, "how?"

The image of the heron perching on the sun-dappled limb in the wall of the Cypress Lounge seemed to eye Andrew Aubrey and his little knot of admirers.

"They are fantastic," Aubrey was saying. "They truly are an elder race. Their history goes back hundreds of thousands of years, their civilization spans light years. They have so much they can teach us."

From where she was sitting, a little apart, Sharon noticed the heron, but Aubrey was oblivious to everything but his audience and the others around the table listened raptly. He was back from three days at Meetpoint and that made him one of the few humans to have direct physical contact with the aliens.

"It's not just the material things. Those are the least of it. They have no war. Just think of it! No war for thousands and thousands of years."

The talk made Sharon uncomfortable. She understood better than Aubrey what the aliens could offer humanity in technology and she knew well enough what war had cost Earth, but there was something in his manner of speaking that bothered her. It was as if he were a worshiper reciting a creed.

She knew he had been spending more and more of his time talking to the aliens and leaving the business of the Ship's Council to C.D. MacNamara and the others. That bothered her too.

Deep down, Dr. Sharon Dolan felt that things were not at all right on the *Maxwell*. She prayed they would get out, back to Earth, before something went really wrong.

PART IV: TESUJI

"Captain, may I speak to you?" Father Simon asked from the door of Jenkins' office.

"Sure. Sit down."

The priest pulled himself in clumsily and settled into the chair. "I would have called you, but I wanted to be sure our conversation was absolutely private," he said half-apologetically.

"What's the problem, Father?"

"Temptation."

Jenkins frowned. "That's more your business than mine, I'd think."

Father Simon shook his head. "I'm afraid this kind of temptation is your concern." He hesitated and took a deep breath.

"As you know I have spent a good deal of time talking to the Colonists. Very frankly I am quite disturbed by some of the things I have seen and heard."

"Like what?"

"I think they are deliberately trying to manipulate us. I think to obtain the secret of our drive, and possibly for other things as well."

"Dr. Aubrey sees them differently," Jenkins said noncommittally.

"I suspect Dr. Aubrey is not completely unbiased on this point," the priest said. "He has, shall we say, an unusually high regard for the Colonists."

"What makes you think they are tempting us?"

"It's a combination of a number of things. First, this policy of open communication. Anyone on the ship who wants to talk to an alien can always find someone to talk to. Someone who is interested, a good listener and as sympathetic as you can expect an alien to be."

"So?"

"Captain, how much information have we gotten out of this 'treasure trove'? The Colonists will talk to us, and talk and talk. But they don't *tell* us anything. As far as I can tell we have learned very little about their culture or their society and practically nothing about their science." The priest rubbed his graying temple.

"What we *do* get is a constant, subtle probing under the guise of friendly curiosity. They are interested in everything about us. Including especially our gossip and most especially anything about our individual foibles and weaknesses."

"I certainly haven't seen that."

Father Simon smiled. "Captain, with all due respect, I doubt very much that you would. You're not attuned to it and I suspect they have written you off as hopeless."

"Have you been offered anything directly?"

"You mean as a bribe? No. But there have been very delicate hints. If I express interest in anything there is an intimation that it could be available. Once or twice I have been asked to do things—very small things—that would violate the ground rules. As soon as I made objection the suggestion was immediately withdrawn with apologies, or passed off as a bad translation."

"I don't know," Jenkins said. "Besides their knowledge, what could an alien culture possibly have to tempt humans with?"

"Captain, these people have the resources of an ancient culture and the wealth of an entire solar system behind them. If I am right they are very skilled at this sort of thing."

The priest gnawed the back of his thumb and looked off past the captain, as if deciding whether to say more. Jenkins waited.

"There is something else," he said at last. "I believe I have gotten some insight into their philosophy and that is the most troubling thing of all."

"I beg your pardon?"

"Don't make the mistake of assuming that philosophy is an

excrescence, Captain. It is not. A person's philosophy goes directly to the heart of his or her beliefs."

The priest leaned forward in his chair and the straps creaked slightly against his middle.

"Philosophy is always an expression of the fundamental ways we see the world. A society that produces Scholastics is not going to produce Political Economists or Logical Positivists. Those schools not only have different views of the world, they arrived at those views by asking very different questions and by making totally different assumptions about what is important."

"You're assuming the same would be true for aliens," Jenkins said skeptically.

"I think it would be true for any thinking being. Philosophy is the organization of thought about the broadest possible questions. Next to Theology it is the Queen of the Sciences."

"Very well. What do the Colonists' philosophies tell you?"

"It's what they don't tell me. They have an elaborate and vigorous philosophical tradition, richer than Earth's in some respects. But their political philosophy is very rudimentary. As nearly as I can tell they have no activist political philosophers. No Mill, no Locke, not even a Marx. For them philosophy seems to be entirely concerned only with individual morals and personal ethics in a world which is at best neutral and often hostile, uncaring and unjust."

"You're assuming you've seen all their schools of thought."

"No Captain, I almost certainly have not. But the troublesome thing is that what I see as gaps they don't see at all."

"Very well, what do you want me to do?"

Father Simon looked down at his hands. "I'm not really sure. I thought you should be aware of what is happening."

"Very well," Jenkins said, "I'm aware. Thank you."

"I'm sorry to have disturbed you, Captain."

Jenkins sighed. "You've disturbed me more than you know, Father. I've been thinking along these lines already—about the temptation, I mean."

The priest rose, but Jenkins held up a hand.

"One other thing. Why did you come all the way up here to tell me this? Why not call me?"

Father Simon looked self-conscious. "Perhaps it was melodramatic of me, but it occurred to me that if the aliens were tempting us, they might already have found a way to tap into our communications system."

After Father Simon left, Jenkins sat scowling down at his desk for several minutes. Then he left his office and made his way down and deeper into the ship. Like the priest, he did not want to use the screen for this.

The computer room was several decks "down" from the bridge complex. The door was open and inside Billy Toyoda was sitting crosslegged with his eyes closed and the headset on, swaying gently in time to some imperceptible rhythm. His eyes opened and then focused when the captain rapped on the door.

"Hey man, what's up?"

"I need some information," Jenkins said.

Toyoda gestured around the cubicle grandly. "That's what we deal in. Welcome to cyberspace."

Jenkins pulled himself in and closed the door after him. "Two things. First, is there any way to know if the ship's communication system has been tapped?"

"You mean like eavesdropping? Sure. Happens all the time." He grinned. "People like to gossip, you know."

Great! Jenkins thought. "Okay, can you tell if information is being transmitted off this ship?"

Billy shrugged. "I haven't been looking for anything like that, but if whoever it was didn't get too fancy, yeah, I could probably find it if I was looking."

"Then start looking, Mr. Toyoda. Also, is there some way to make communications circuits secure?"

"No such thing as absolute security, man. But I could make some circuits more secure—at least stop the casual listeners."

"Then do that too. I especially want secure circuits to the bridge, back to engineering and on the other ship maintenance circuits."

"You got it. Anything else?"

"Yes," Jenkins said. "I need to know who is talking to the Colonists and what they're talking about."

Toyoda shook his head. "Hey man, you know that shit's private. Ship's Council says."

Jenkins' first reflex was to chew the computerman out for refusing an order. He swallowed that and looked knowingly at Toyoda.

"I also know you. And unofficially, *very* unofficially, I'm asking you what you've picked up."

Billy hesitated a second and then grinned. "Okay. Very

unofficially nearly everybody on the damn ship's talking to the Owlies."

"What are they talking about?"

"Hey man, I don't know. I don't listen to everything and I don't waste the space storing it, all right?"

"Very well then, do you have any feel for who's doing how much talking?"

The computerman shrugged. "Like I say, everyone's talking. The scientists are probably doing most of it, but some of the crew are pretty heavy too. Hell, I'm spending a lot of time tied into their net."

"Learned anything interesting?"

"Only that their security's damn good."

Jenkins flicked a smile. "Okay. Who are our big users?"

"Dr. Takiuji's probably the biggest one. I think he spends three or four hours a day tied in."

The captain went cold. "What is he talking about?"

"He's not exactly talking. He spends most of his time playing go, him and the one they call Hitler."

"Derfuhrer," the captain corrected absently. "Well, that seems harmless enough."

Billy shrugged. "The Owlie's getting pretty good. Nearly had Dr. Takiuji on the ropes with a four-stone handicap last time."

"I thought you said you didn't listen in."

"I don't mostly. But I'm recording the moves to add to the database for my go program."

"All right," the captain said. "I'd appreciate it if you'd keep me posted and let me know if there's any change. Unofficially, of course."

"No problem," Billy said, and closed his eyes again.

Wonder if I should have told him about DeLorenzo? Billy Toyoda thought after the captain left. *Nah, that's got nothing to do with the aliens and it's probably authorized somehow anyway.*

Playing go, eh? Jenkins thought as he made his way back up the corridor. *Well, that seems harmless enough. The aliens aren't going to learn much from that.*

Fascinating, Derfuhrer thought as he placed the black and white stones on the board. *Utterly fascinating.* The game itself was intriguing, but the insights it gave into human psychology and strategy were even more so.

A subtle and complex lineage, he decided. Bold to the point of rashness, but with a well-developed sense of strategy to support them.

And yet so completely alien. This fixation on territory, for example. The entire game was based on gaining and holding territory by *surrounding* it. How archaic! How two-dimensional!

Clearly the lineage had territoriality impressed into its very genes. As if space were something to be controlled by occupying it. There was no hint in the game of resources and how they might be employed, nothing to represent the dynamics or energy profiles of movement. You placed your stones and that was that.

And yet there was something atavistically satisfying about the game. You only had one enemy and the outcome was always determinate. You either crushed him or you were crushed. There were no ambiguities, no carryovers to a future game. You crushed your opponent and he was wiped from the board, vanished. The conflict was open and direct.

This must be what open war was like, Derfuhrer thought with a thrill as he watched the walls of stones develop and grow.

"Bustamonte! Watch out, Goddammit!"

Stephen Bustamonte checked himself by grabbing the safety line and hauling himself back down onto the hull.

"You fucking idiot!" the foreman yelled. "Don't you know any better than to let yourself float like that? Now Goddammit, keep your fucking feet on the fucking hull where they fucking belong."

With that the foreman turned away and went back to directing another part of the crew. Since he had been using the infrared direct link only Bustamonte and the people around him had heard.

As soon as the foreman's back was turned, Bustamonte's buddy, Walt Jabobs, came over and touched helmets for a private talk.

"Man, Steve, you got Padilla some pissed," he said. "What'd you do a dumb stunt like that for anyway?"

"Fast way to get over there," Steve's voice was slurred and hoarse in Jacobs' helmet.

"Are you okay? Man, you sound awful."

"I'll be fine," Bustamonte assured him and waved him away.

Yeah, baby, I'll be fine as soon as we get inside and I can get another hit of that stuff the Owlies turn out! His breath sounded harsh and labored in his earphones, but he ignored it. He grabbed for his safety line, missed, grabbed for it again and caught it, but the muscles in his hand wouldn't quite close. The third time he got it firmly and followed it back to where he was supposed to be. *Just two more hours and I can toke up again.*

Bill Jewett knew something was wrong as soon as he called his Owlie buddy. Splicer was slow coming to the screen and he had his feathers puffed out like a sick bird.

"There is a problem," the Colonist said without preamble.

A tiny quiver of fear stirred in William Jewett. "What's wrong?"

"My bosses found the gold missing and they are some pissed. They want someone's ass."

"Oh shit. Well look, I can give it back to you."

"It is not that simple. They already know it is missing and soon they will know I took it."

"What's going to happen?"

"I am in the shit up to my neck. When they find I was the one who took it, they will make me tell where it went. Then they will go to your bosses and demand the gold back."

Oh shit. There goes my bonus. Without the bonus it was goodbye habitat. *Damn!* Jewett went cold and still as his dreams came crashing around him.

"How the hell did this happen? I thought you told me gold was worthless to you people."

"It is not worth much to us, but we use it for some things," Splicer told him. "It happened that the gold I gave you was to be used in an important repair. I did not know and now more must be brought from somewhere else. That will require a special trip there. That is expensive and it will take time. That puts us behind schedule. Worse, the project is the pet of the boss who found the gold missing. He looks bad and that makes him even madder."

The alien paused; a genuine pause, not a halt for computer

translation. "I am truly sorry. I meant my action as a gift of friendship and now it has turned back on both of us."

"Well, why can't I just give it back?"

"First, because my bosses already know it is missing and I am sure they suspect me of taking it. Second, how could you get it back to me? Can you place a package in the precise trajectory from the hull of your ship?"

He couldn't, Jewett realized. He didn't have the equipment or skill to fling a tiny package into space so exactly that his friend could pluck it out. The method used to get him the gold was a one-way trip.

"This tears it, you know that?" Jewett said bitterly. "This fucking tears it. I'm ruined, totally ruined."

"I know," Splicer said sadly. "I feel like shit about this." The Colonist froze for a second, which Jewett recognized as meaning he was thinking hard.

"There may be a way out of this," Splicer said at last. "I must talk carefully to someone else. If you are willing to help there might be a way to keep us both out of the shit." He paused. "I will try to call you on my next shift," and then he broke the connection before Jewett could say anything.

The next days were an agony for William Jewett. Twice he almost went to the captain and confessed. But that meant ruin. He had gone against strict explicit orders and there was no way the captain was going to overlook that. He'd lose his bonus for sure, probably be fined and maybe lose his rating. Even if he didn't no one would hire him when he got back to the system. He'd end up cocooning asteroids out in the Belt. A two-year trip each way and a five-year hitch. Cherry couldn't come and there was no way the marriage could survive that.

It was two days before Splicer called back.

"Well?" Jewett demanded.

"I have found a way to keep us out of the shit. If it works no one would ever know where the gold went. You could keep it."

"I don't want the damn gold," Jewett growled. "I just want out of this mess."

"Very well," the Colonist said. "First I must tell you some things we have been keeping from you. You must promise me you will not repeat them to any other human."

As if I wanted anyone else to find out about this, Jewett thought, and nodded agreement.

143

"Very well," Splicer gave a human-like nod. "You must understand that the bosses are not nearly as united as they have led you to believe. There are many differences among them and not all the bosses favor keeping you so completely isolated.

"One of the bosses here belongs to the faction that wants to know more about you. They want to see more so they can learn more. This boss also has a supply of gold intended for another project.

"I talked to this boss, very quietly, and he has agreed to help us out of the shit. He can take some of his gold and give it to the boss whose gold is missing. He will claim the gold was mixed in with his by mistake. No one will be able to prove otherwise and as long as the boss stirring up the shit gets his gold, he will not care."

"Where do I come in?" Jewett asked suspiciously.

"I told you. This boss wants to know more about humans. If we help him he will do this for us."

"I'll be glad to talk to this guy."

The alien made a gesture of negation. "That is not what he wants. Instead he has prepared monitoring devices and he wants you to place them around the ship. They are harmless. They only record what goes on around them. In this way he and his friends will be able to learn more about humans without arousing either his bosses or yours."

"I don't know," Jewett told him. "This could be worse than the gold."

"It is our only hope for staying out of the shit," Splicer told him. "The devices are small and they emit no detectable radiation."

"This could get me in more trouble than the gold."

"No one has to know. This boss will not tell anyone. He is breaking the rules. Once the devices are in place you never have to go near them again. Even if one of them is discovered, no one will ever know who put it there. It will be easier than the gold was."

"How big are these things?"

The alien held up a plain black object the size and shape of a brick.

"Like this," Splicer said.

* * *

"Bad shift, Lulu?" asked the alien as soon as Lulu Pine made contact.

"Just like always. They're on me all the time. You know that jerk Albers? He accused me of messing up his reports! I told him that if he'd label the images right in the first place this wouldn't happen. But no, he's not going to take the blame if he can put it on me."

"Shocking, shameful," the Owlie said. "I wonder how you can stand it." Then he changed the subject. "Did you put out those packages as we asked?"

"Of course I did," Lulu said defensively. "Right where you told me to."

"Very good. Excellent. You do very well. Soon you will no longer have to bear their insults and slights."

"We'll fix them," Lulu said, falling into the well-worn conversation. "We'll fix them good. I'll get what's rightfully mine." She licked her lips in anticipation. "Tell me again how it's going to be."

Shuttle Bay 4 was sealed and under pressure when Jewett entered. It was also unoccupied.

Jewett was floating almost under the blunt rear end of the craft where it rested in its cradles.

The gold-and-black bulk of the shuttle filled the entire bay. The plug nozzle and reentry shield above him came to within a few feet of the rear bulkhead. Overhead, the great egg-shaped body of the vehicle stretched almost to the huge doors that formed the roof of the bay. Forward, the equally blunt nose nearly touched the spinward bulkhead. The landing jacks were flexed to draw the landing pads up close to the sides of the vessel and the cradles supported and held the shuttle within the bay.

He scanned the open space cautiously before stepping out. Vacuum jacks had no real business in the shuttle bays. Jewett had a carefully prepared excuse for his presence, but the black box under his jacket was burning a hole.

He was so nervous he briefly considered simply lunging upward to the plug nozzle thirty feet above his head. But only very briefly. A space worker learns early to keep one hand or foot attached to something solid at all times.

Quickly he swam to the access ladder that led up the cradle to the nozzle and its twenty-two surrounding burners. He moved off onto the inspection catwalk that led around the rear of the nozzle and pulled himself around.

In flight the blunt cone of the nozzle formed the inner bell of what were, in effect, twenty-two separate rocket engines arranged in a ring around it. In reentry the plug was cooled by liquid hydrogen and protected from the worst effects of thermal heating by the plume of gases from the engines.

For right now, it was simply the place where the alien boss wanted one of his damned boxes put.

What the hell that bastard expects to see from here I don't know, Jewett thought as he placed the box against one of the burners.

Still, this was the place where the boss wanted a box, one in the same place in each of the four shuttle bays. According to Jewett's alien friend, the boss still hadn't come across with the gold, so Jewett didn't have a lot of choice.

The tacky surface of the box adhered instantly when Jewett snugged it against the burner. Relieved, the rock jack turned and pulled himself back to the access ladder.

I wish to God I'd never seen that damn gold, he thought.

"Hey Steve, time to get moving," Walt Jacobs yelled as he pounded on his friend's door. He looked at his watch again. Today was duty day for both of them and most of their gang of vacuum jacks was already suited up and headed for the airlock.

"Hey Steve, time to get a move on," Walt Jacobs called from the door. Bustamonte didn't move.

"Come on, you lazy fucker. Get your ass in gear before Padilla comes down here and kicks it between your shoulder-blades."

Still no sound from the huddled mass on the bed.

"Steve?" Jacobs called again. "Steve?" He stepped across the room and reached out to touch his bunkmate's shoulder.

There was a low animal moan from beneath the blanket and the mass jerked and moved spastically. The blanket fell away and Bustamonte's head thrashed against the pillow. Blood ran from his mouth where he had bitten his tongue and his eyes rolled back in his head so nothing but white showed. Again he moaned.

Jacobs slammed the communicator button next to the wall

screen. "C-23 medical emergency," he yelled. "Medical emergency C-23."

"Do we have any idea what happened to him?" Jenkins asked the doctor.

"Not really. Obviously he suffered a seizure of some kind. There is evidence of severe neural deterioration and his cognitive processes as well as his motor function appear to be affected. We'll know more in a couple of days, of course . . ."

"Of course. Meanwhile, what's your best guess?"

The doctor pursed his lips. "If I had to guess now, I'd say it's a toxic reaction of some sort. Probably a drug."

"Do we have anything on this ship that would produce that kind of reaction?"

"Oh yes, but how he could have come in contact with it, I cannot imagine. His bunkmate appears to be completely unaffected, you know, and there are no other symptoms anywhere else in the crew."

Jenkins turned to DeRosa who had been standing silently by. "You're the ship's Provost Marshal. I want you to deputize as many reliable people as you need and search this man's cabin and locker."

Jenkins was still at his station on the bridge when DeRosa swam through the door. Her lips were pressed into a tight, white line.

"Did you find anything in Bustamonte's locker?"

"These," she said, holding out her hand. Cupped in the palm were five shiny capsules filled with what appeared to be golden oil.

"Are those standard?"

DeRosa shook her head. "Medical's got one for analysis, but they don't match anything on any of the manifests. I'll tell you something else. I don't think they came from anywhere on this ship."

"I'm afraid you're right," Jenkins agreed. "Okay, that's it. I want you to deputize enough people to search this ship from one end to the other. Parties to work at least in pairs with pairings chosen at random. Each searcher is to watch the others and each part of the ship is to be searched at least twice. I want to know what the hell *else* is on this ship."

"Right," said DeRosa and turned away.

"Oh yes. Break out those pistols in the PM's locker and issue them to crewmen you can trust. Two to guard the bridge, two to guard the drive and two for life-support control. And put those guards in spacesuits." He shook his head. "Al, I've got a very bad feeling about this."

It didn't take long for Jenkins' premonition to start coming true. Within forty-five minutes there was a call from C.D. MacNamara acting as vice-president of the Ship's Council.

"I understand you have ordered a search of the ship," MacNamara said without preamble.

"That is correct."

"By whose authority?"

"By my authority as captain."

"Your authority as captain does not cover the non-military people on this ship," MacNamara said tightly, "and it most assuredly does not run to searching their personal belongings."

"Doctor, my authority runs to anything that affects the safety and proper functioning of this vessel. Would you care to see the relevant regulation?"

"Why was not the Ship's Council consulted about this?"

"Because there wasn't time."

"Surely, a matter of an hour or two . . ."

Jenkins cut him off. "Dr. MacNamara, I already have one man in sick bay apparently suffering from God knows what kind of drug reaction. I have reason to believe there is other contraband on this ship. I did not have an hour or two to convene the Council."

"So you intend to violate the civil rights of every person aboard without so much as consulting their representatives? No consultation, no attempt to win their cooperation, just, *boom*, pry into everything."

"I intend to protect my ship."

"Captain, the Ship's Council will take a most serious view of this matter."

"I certainly hope so, Doctor, because believe me, I am very serious about this."

He broke the connection and DeRosa's face replaced MacNamara's.

"Well, I was expecting that," Jenkins said.

"Yeah," Iron Alice agreed. "But I expected Aubrey to deliver the message. Wonder where he is?"

"Probably lining up Council votes to have my head on a platter."

"That going to stop you?"

Jenkins grinned. "Hell no. They can't do that until we get back to Earth. Meanwhile this ship is my responsibility."

MacNamara sat in front of the blank screen, drumming his fingers on the console. Dr. Aubrey was off somewhere and unavailable and this would require an emergency meeting of the Ship's Council. That meant he would have to be the one to call it.

But first he made another a quick call over a private channel.

What in the hell? Fawn Wilson went over the wiring in the riser again and checked it against the image on her hand terminal for the third time.

With an effort she wiggled backwards out of the access hatch. At 157 centimeters and 84 kilos, Fawn was spectacularly misnamed. No one with her build had any business trying to fit into the riser access spaces. But she was also a very good internal maintenance tech and there weren't enough of them to be choosy about who went where.

"Hey Henry, take a look at this."

Her partner, a slender blond man with a beak of a nose pulled his head out of the panel he had been checking and came to peer over her shoulder.

"Looks normal to me," he said, playing his light up and down the riser.

"What about that?" Fawn put her own light on a black metal box fixed to the wall of the riser.

"Standard mod box." He punched it up on his own terminal. "It's on the schematic."

"Yeah, but what the hell's it doing there? There's no reason to cut anything into the circuits here. If you want to make a mod, the place to do it is in the wiring cabinet up on the next level."

Henry just shrugged. "It's listed, isn't it? That's good enough."

"Bullshit," Fawn Wilson said, punching up a number on her terminal.

* * *

"Well, it's listed here as an authorized modification," Clancy told the chunky woman on the screen, "but I don't remember it." He called up another document in a window and scowled. "This doesn't look right to me. Stay where you are and I'll be right up."

He spun away from the screen and made for the door. "Maintenance found something funny in a riser up on Spin-3," he called over to his boss. "I think someone's been tampering with the ship's drawings."

"Shit," Ludenemeyer said without any particular heat. "The way this day's going that wouldn't surprise me. But get the hell back as fast as you can, will you? We've got people all over the damn ship and just about no one left in engineering."

Clancy waved and kicked off down the corridor.

"Well," DeRosa said, "so far we've turned up two caches of drugs—Earth type, a vacuum still, several gallons of moonshine and a submachine gun."

"A submachine gun?"

Iron Alice smiled. "DeLorenzo brought it aboard in his luggage. Maybe he sleeps with the damn thing instead of a teddy bear."

"Anything else?"

DeRosa turned grim again. "Yeah. Eight items of indeterminate function but probably alien origin and about a kilo of gold that isn't on the manifest. We're questioning a couple of the technicians, a lab worker and one of the scientists now."

"One of the scientists? That's going to rile the Council even more."

She shrugged.

"Hell, ask me if I care," Jenkins told her. "Anyway, where are you finding these things?"

"Most of it wasn't in living spaces. In the last few hours all that we found has been stashed outside quarters, some obviously hastily."

"Making them nervous." Jenkins nodded. "Good. Now what have you done with the contraband?"

"The alien stuff's in the labs being examined—being very cautiously examined. The rest of it we gave back to the owners or left where it was."

"Even DeLorenzo's submachine gun?"

"I figure we've got bigger fish to fry. We can worry about DeLorenzo and his toy later."

The search of the *Maxwell* did not go unnoticed elsewhere.
"Something has gone wrong."
"I don't know, but they are searching the ship."
"That topples the tree. Tell our agents among the humans to act immediately."

"What happened to stir them so?"
"Apparently 312 was giving drugs to some of the humans and one of them became ill."
"Maladroit idiots! We must move now."

"Quickly! The others are moving. Strike before it is too late."

"Strike now!"

"Now!"

"Now!"

Nearly twenty humans get messages over the communications channels. *"Now! You must act now."*

PART V: SENTE

Once again Billy Toyoda floated in cyberspace and watched the patterns of information converge, melt and flow away in neon swirls against the blackness. *Heavy action today,* the computerman thought as he watched the rise and ebb of shapes.

It was all information, he knew. Each of those shapes and lines indicated a different kind of information flowing into or out of the ship's computers, or control signals rippling out over the ship's nervous system. He could put names to nearly all of them, but he preferred not to. To Billy, the patterns themselves were reason enough.

He shifted, relaxed—and then tensed again as a flash of movement caught his eye. Off in a neon cage skyscraper at the far reach of his vision something had flickered where there should be no flicker at all.

There! There was another one out in another direction, an instantaneous bit of wrongness disturbing the pattern he knew intimately.

And there! And there! Bright bits of information glimmered and flashed in ways that were totally, dangerously wrong. The whole structure of the ship's cyberspace was being subtly distorted.

Billy Toyoda had never seen anything like it before, but he knew what they were. "Security breach! We have a breach of the computer systems!"

All through cyberspace the dark forms were multiplying.

* * *

Lulu Pine was grumbling over a series of images when her terminal chimed. With a muttered curse, she flicked the incoming call onto the screen. There was her Owlie.

"Now Lulu. The time has come. The Judgment is at hand."

Lulu dropped the papers in her hand and her face lit up with a pure, clear joy that the alien had never seen before. As the papers fluttered to the floor unheeded, the Colonist realized they might have trouble with this one.

Further aft, the shuttle bays were racked by a violent explosion as William Jewett's "observation devices" blew up with enormous force.

The charges were directional and the explosions sliced through the shuttles' plug nozzles like so many knives. Composites shattered, metal warped and tore and control electronics were reduced to dust. In milliseconds, all four of the *Maxwell*'s shuttles were put out of action.

But that was only the beginning in Bay One. Unlike the others, Shuttle One was kept fueled for trips to Meetpoint.

The blast slashed through the ablative coating of the plug nozzle and ruptured the hydrogen and oxygen lines beneath. A gout of colorless flame erupted as the hydrox ignited.

Normally the fuel in the cooling lines running through the nozzle would have been only enough to scorch the paint and warp the bulkheads in the shuttle bay. However, the blast had ruptured the main valves and hydrogen and oxygen from the main tanks fed unobstructed into the fire.

Alarms screamed in the bay and trouble lights blossomed red on the panels in engineering and the bridge.

"*What the hell?*" Ludenemeyer yelled as his board lit up.

It took him only a few seconds to decipher the warnings and only seconds longer to grasp the import of a fire in Bay One. He blanched and hit the general alarm.

Like some comic book avenger flying through a city of neon skeleton skyscrapers, Billy Toyoda zoomed in on the dark skittering things that threatened his realm.

He reached into a crevice between two glowing constructs and yanked out one of the invaders. Heedless of its struggles, he opened it up and turned it inside out, exposing its full workings. He paid special attention to the shape of its "mouth" parts, designed to suck information and to the "egg sacs" beneath which would encapsulate the stolen data and send it back along the glowing paths to where the thing's masters waited.

The design was alien and very clever, but Billy started weaving a defense almost instantly. First a gesture and dark portals dropped across the furthest extensions of the neon rivers, isolating the *Maxwell*'s cyberspace from the outside world. Next he raised a series of internal barriers like walls of smoke to separate the cyberspace into parts.

In the back of his mind Billy was aware that he was sitting at a terminal pounding keys and manipulating other input devices, but he ignored that as much as he possibly could. The secret to working in cyberspace was to keep your visualization of the whole intact and not get distracted by the physical forms of input and output.

Ruthlessly he forced his attention even more completely into his glowing neon city under siege.

Major Autro DeLorenzo was asleep in his room when Toyoda sounded his alarm. Normally he wouldn't have gotten it, but one of his "modifications" had taken care of that.

DeLorenzo was awake and out of his bunk like a cat. He grabbed his compad to check as the fire alarm from the shuttle bays came through. That was enough. DeLorenzo hit the button that activated his sabotage devices.

Then he got dressed and started loading magazines for his submachine gun.

Thousands of kilometers away, an alien snapped his beak in frustration. The Master of the strangers' computers was fighting back with unusual effectiveness. The thing shouldn't even have detected the invasion yet and already half the Colonist's approaches had been shut off.

And he was not alone. There were at least two other sets of worms loose in the ship's computers, interfering with his own and making it harder to locate the data he needed.

Worse, his worms had not yet located the critical data. Even though the enemy's entire cyberspace seemed to be open to his probes, he could not find what he sought. Somehow, primitive as they were, the visitors had come up with a way to seal off part of their cyberspace. Well, he would find that hidden information space nonetheless. He had his own skill and thousands of cycles of his culture's experience behind him.

Grimly the Colonist set his worms to coursing back along the information paths, seeking the one that led to the treasure he sought. It never occurred to him that a culture that had used computers for less than two centuries might not keep everything online at the same time.

"Engineering, what's going on back there?" Jenkins yelled into his screen. But the screen stayed blank.

"What the hell?" He punched an alternate circuit. Still nothing.

"Communications, what's wrong?"

The communications officer came on the screen. "I don't know, sir. The circuits have been interrupted all over the ship."

A window opened in the corner and Iron Alice DeRosa broke in. "That's not all that's been interrupted. We've lost control to engineering, life support and just about every place else."

"General quarters," Jenkins snapped. "Pass the word any way you can—relay through suit radios if you have to. Or use runners." He turned back to the communications officer. "And get me some circuits!"

He looked up at his second-in-command. "Al, I want you to go back to the secondary bridge in engineering. As soon as you're established there you have command. Get us out of this system and do it fast!"

DeRosa nodded and the screen blanked. She got up from the pilot's station and passed Jenkins wordlessly as she headed aft. The two guards at the door moved aside to let her pass.

One of the ships hovering off Meetpoint suddenly fired its engines and swooped toward the *Maxwell*. In the confusion, no one on the starship noticed. The ship scooted in close to the hull of the starship and stopped over the lock with a quick burst of braking rockets. Two dozen figures in shiny suits tumbled from the hatch and dove for a lock in the hull.

The lock was one of the engineering locks designed for use in transferring medium-sized loads. It lay aft of Spin in an area of cargo holds. It was not designed to be opened from the outside, but that didn't matter. It opened before they reached it and a single spacesuited figure beckoned them in.

"Quickly," Andrew Aubrey urged. "You must move quickly."

Nearly twenty-five spacesuited raiders moved past him and set off in a springy, alien stride.

Unerringly the aliens moved down the corridor to the lift shaft and in threes and twos launched themselves up the shaft toward the ship's core. The raiders had excellent maps and they had gone over their mission again and again on their journey out to Meetpoint.

Albers was in Wadsworth's office when the lights flickered, dimmed and went over to emergency lighting. "What in the hell?" he exclaimed. Both men rushed into the main lab just in time to see Lulu Pine dog the door.

"Lulu, what's wrong?" Wadsworth demanded.

The technician turned toward them, her pasty face lit by an unholy glee. "It's the day of divine retribution," she chortled. "Hallelujah, it's the time of judgment. When the elect are saved and the rest condemned to the eternal fires of hell!"

She fumbled in her dress and pulled out a knife, the kind they used in the kitchen to carve meat. "Vengeance is mine!"

Albers tried to shove past her to the door, but he massed barely half what she did and for all her dumpiness she was very strong. Wadsworth shrank back against the wall and whimpered.

Communications had been cut to the bridge, but some of the auxiliary engineering circuits were still working—to an extent.

"Mr. Clancy."

"Here, sir."

"Where the hell are you?"

"Forward in Spin, sir."

Ludenemeyer swore under his breath. "Get the hell back here. We've got a fire in Shuttle Bay One."

The chief engineer cut the connection and did a quick calculation. The order to search the ship had completely disrupted Engineering. Instead of a full watch, the spaces were manned by himself and the two guards the captain had posted. Almost all his people were well away from their assigned damage control stations. He knew the crew would be in the same fix. That left the passengers, and Ludenemeyer had no confidence at all in their ability to handle an emergency without skilled assistance.

He swore again, out loud this time.

At best it would take Clancy time to get back and get things organized and that fire needed fighting *now*.

He suppressed the urge to head for the shuttle bay himself. If that shuttle blew he was going to be needed here in a big way. Instead he gritted his teeth and hit the communicator again.

"Lieutenant Kirchoff, report immediately." He waited a moment, fuming. "Kirchoff, dammit report!"

"Here sir." There was no visual.

"Where the hell is here?"

"660-18—ah . . ."

"Never mind that. We've got a major fire in Shuttle Bay One and Clancy's unavailable. Get up there on the double and take charge of firefighting and damage control."

Lulu Pine's "packages" had been smaller than Jewett's and were less destructive. They were intended to disable the nexuses of communication in Spin. The aliens had given her very specific instructions on precisely where to plant them, but Lulu was as unreliable an agent for them as she was an employee for the imaging section. She had "planted" most of the charges in storage lockers along the Central Corridor through Spin, meters from where they were supposed to be.

Nevertheless they were destructive enough. They blew the lockers apart, destroying power, communication and control lines that ran through the trunks that paralleled the central shaft. One of them cut an oxygen line that ran through its own trunk and oxygen hissed out onto hot metal and organics.

In theory, almost nothing in Spin would burn, especially not in critical areas like the Central Corridor. In practice, there is very little that will not burn when pure oxygen is played on it. The aluminum-magnesium supports went off like Fourth of July sparklers. The composite panels of the corridor warped, melted and began to burn, filling the air with choking black smoke.

Once more alarms shrilled, indicating a mortal danger to the *Maxwell*. Automatically emergency doors slid into place throughout Spin, cutting the entire rotating section of the ship into hundreds of smaller compartments.

By Earth standards it didn't make much sense to compartment off all of Spin because of a fire in just one region. But the men and women who designed the *Maxwell* didn't think in Earth terms. They thought like Spacers, and Spacers have a pathological and very well-founded fear of fire in space.

The emergency systems in the *Maxwell*'s shuttle bays were both autonomous and automatic. Sensors reported the hot spots and told the computers that hydrogen and oxygen were burning in Bay One. The computers sized up the fires, realized they were beyond the ability of the firefighting systems to control, and opened the shuttle bay doors, venting the atmosphere in the bays.

That would have stopped a normal fire, but the shuttle carried its own source of oxygen as well as fuel. The fire raged on unabated.

The concussion slapped Mike Clancy in the back as he pulled his way down the central corridor. The force of the blast knocked him off balance and for a moment he twisted in mid-air, trying to get purchase. *What the hell. . . ?*

His hand brushed a wall and he quickly planted himself, clinging to the wall on all fours like a spider. Then he looked forward along the corridor just in time to see yellow flames and dense smoke pouring out of a section of the corridor wall before the automatic doors slid into place, cutting the corridor into segments.

Clancy looked back toward the aft section. His emergency station was in the engineering spaces. Abstractedly he realized there wasn't much chance he was going to make it. Acrid smoke curled forward and reached his nostrils. The engineer coughed and realized there was at least a fair chance he wouldn't make it out of here alive.

"What happened?" someone yelled further down the corridor. Still clinging to the wall, Clancy swiveled around and saw he wasn't alone. There were a man and a woman in the same section of corridor. The woman was wearing a dark blue crew coverall with the patches of a pilot and pulling herself along like someone who had experience in zero G. The man was wearing street clothes and standing shakily, obviously unused to the environment.

"We've got a fire in the next section forward," Clancy said as he scuttled along the wall to meet them.

"But fire won't burn in zero G," the man protested. "There's no convection so the flame smothers in its own waste gases."

Clancy grinned mirthlessly. "In practice that's a damn nice theory. It only works if the air's still and it's never still on a ship."

"What do we do?"

"We get the hell out of here. Come on. Let's try an alternate passage."

"I think I remember seeing an emergency hatch a little further down the corridor," the young woman said.

Clancy looked at her for the first time. He'd seen her around. One of the shuttle pilots, what was her name? Carol? Carmen? He'd thought she was cute and a little standoffish. Now she looked young and very scared.

"Sounds good. By the way, I'm Mike Clancy from engineering."

The pilot looked a little relieved. "Carmella O'Hara, shuttle pilot."

"I'm John Martin," the man said. "I'm a spectroscopist."

The lights in the corridor went out, replaced by the glow of the emergency lights.

"Glad to know you," Clancy said as if nothing had happened. "Now let's get the hell out of here before something else blows up."

They moved out with Clancy in the lead and Carmella helping Martin along.

"Just a minute, ma'am."

Iron Alice DeRosa had almost reached the Central Corridor that ran down the center of Spin when the four men stopped her. Two were obviously vacuum jacks and the other two looked like technicians. She didn't recognize any of them. All of them were wearing white armbands, torn from sheets, with "PSC" crudely lettered on them.

Iron Alice looked at the men.

"Just what the hell do you think you're doing?"

"Ma'am, we're placing you under arrest by order of the

Provisional Ship's Council," the big one in front said, almost politely. "You'll have to come with us."

DeRosa shook her head. "I didn't think Aubrey had the balls for this."

"Dr. Aubrey's got nothing to do with it," another smaller man said. "We take our orders from the *provisional* council. Dr. Aubrey and the other members of the old council are already under arrest."

"Come along, ma'am," the big one said and eased closer.

Iron Alice DeRosa let him get almost close enough to put his hand on her arm before she kicked him in the groin and used the momentum to carry her back into the wall near the ceiling of the corridor.

A fight in zero G is very different from a fight in a place where "up" and "down" mean something. As soon as the trouble started the two technicians were worse than useless. One of them instinctively lunged forward, lost contact with the floor and flailed helplessly in midair. The other stood rooted, his club floating lazily out of his slack hand.

The vacuum jacks knew about rough-and-tumble in zero G, but they didn't know anything about Iron Alice DeRosa.

While the second vacuum jack was coiling to spring, DeRosa flipped over, planted her feet on the ceiling, lunged off and flipped again so she descended on the men feet first. The vacuum jack launched himself just in time to put his head in direct line with Iron Alice's booted feet. His head snapped to the side under the impact and he went drifting away head over heels as DeRosa landed, sprang and rammed the heel of her hand into the man's nose. He yelled as bones crunched, but DeRosa was already spinning away again, using the push to change her direction and miss a clumsily swung club in the hands of the other technician. She twisted her body and lashed out with her foot to strike the man in the solar plexus before he could recover from his swing. He whuffed and went slack. One more twist and a push with her toe on the wall and Iron Alice went flying past the first vacuum jack. A well-aimed kick to the side added to his agony.

A final push and somersault and Iron Alice DeRosa was standing on the floor again, almost where she had been when the fight started. One of the vacuum jacks was doubled over clutching his ribs and retching feebly. The second vacuum jack and one of the technicians were out cold. The other technician floated back against the wall, moaning and holding his broken nose with both hands.

"Breathe through your mouth or you'll suffocate," Iron Alice told him coldly. "Take your friends here down to sick bay. Then put yourselves all on report."

With that she turned and kicked off down the corridor.

About halfway between the fire doors there was a small oval door with a light over it. It was perhaps one and a half meters high and maybe a meter wide.

"Emergency scuttle," Clancy said as they came up on it. "Leads to the service corridor that parallels the central corridor."

Martin pushed forward to open the scuttle.

"Wait a minute!" Clancy commanded. He pulled himself up and put his palm flat on the door. It was so hot he yanked it off almost immediately.

"We're not going that way," he told the group. "Now, what's the best alternate?"

"Is there a service corridor on the other side?" Carmella asked. Most of the *Maxwell* was ruthlessly radially symmetrical, especially in Spin.

Clancy thought hard. He carried a map of the engineering spaces in his head but no one could possibly remember the complete configuration of a 4,000-foot-long spaceship. Spin was alien territory to him and he had only a vague notion of this area.

"No," he said finally. "There's too much stuff that has to run along the central axis so there was only room for the one service run." He rubbed his chin. "I think the best bet is to open the door at the other end of the corridor and go out that way."

"I thought they couldn't be opened," Martin said.

"How the hell do you think emergency crews can get around?" Clancy said. "If there's air and no fire on the other side, I can open the door."

The smoke was getting thicker in the corridor and they were all coughing by the time they reached the aft door. Clancy popped up an unobtrusive panel set in the wall and punched a number into a keypad. Then he frowned and punched in another number. The door stayed closed.

"Damn!" Clancy pounded his fist on the bulkhead.

The override was supposed to let the door open unless the conditions on the other side were unlivable. There was even an override on the override so that spacesuited emergency workers could get through when things on the other side were unlivable. However all those overrides depended on a measure of central intelligence and thanks to DeLorenzo's sabotage that was not available. The door stayed closed.

The other two looked at him as if they were afraid to ask what happened next. He scowled and tried to dredge every fact he could about the Central Corridor out of his memory.

Maybe the little puke had the right idea after all, Clancy thought, *memorizing the whole fucking ship.* Well, the little puke wasn't here and he'd have to make do with what he knew.

Think of a wheel, or a tin can rotating around its axis. The axle of the wheel, or the center line of the tin can, was the Central Corridor. It ran straight through Spin at the center of rotation.

Now imagine a straw thrust down the center of the axle. That straw would be the corridor that Clancy and the others were in. The Central Corridor was more than just the corridor. It was a whole complex of cable runs, piping, conduits and shafts enclosed in a larger axle that carried the enormous load of the rotating Spin section. It was one of the most complex parts of the ship.

"Where are the emergency crews anyway?" the pilot asked.

"Probably spread all over the fucking ship," Clancy told her. "Everyone was out searching and then we got hit with a whole series of emergencies. This is the second fire we've got on board."

And that puke Kirchoff is back there leading the crew fighting the one in the shuttle bay. Ludenemeyer must be shitting bricks. Well, I hope he's doing better than I am.

Kirchoff struggled into his emergency gear. Twice he made a mistake in the attachments and cursed to himself as he undid them.

The most important thing is to keep command, he reminded himself. *A leader's job is to lead, firmly and decisively. He must know what to do and see that it is done.* That had sounded wonderful when he was memorizing it in a classroom on Luna. Making his way down a darkened corridor in a badly fitting spacesuit he suddenly wasn't so sure.

Kirchoff reviewed his map of the ship. Aft of Spin, most of the ship was taken up by six enormous pressure cylinders, each more than seventy-five meters in diameter and hundreds of meters long and each holding either enriched hydrogen or oxygen. The shuttle bays sat inside the main hull nestled between the curves of those cylinders. If that shuttle blew . . .

He shook off the thought and concentrated on getting to his destination.

"What the hell are you doing back here?" Jenkins demanded when Iron Alice DeRosa kicked her way onto the bridge.

"Couldn't get through. The emergency doors in Spin closed before I had a chance. I'll have to go through the spaces between Spin and the hull or out over the hull. Oh yeah, I met four bozos back in the corridor claiming to represent the Provisional Ship's Council or whatever." She smiled wolfishly. "They tried to arrest me."

Jenkins didn't bother to ask what had happened to the bozos. "Mutiny too?"

"Looks like."

Jenkins swore savagely and then sobered. "Well, we can worry about them later. I'm glad you didn't get through. The doors on the shuttle bays are all open and there's a hell of a fire in Bay One. We can't button up until they get that beat."

DeRosa nodded. Any hole or discontinuity in the hull would keep the drive from working. "You got communications back?"

"We've got a relay of space suit radios, but all the regular channels are out. That looks like sabotage too."

It was DeRosa's turn to swear. "What about the Central Corridor?"

"Explosions and fire. We've got a scratch team trying to fight their way through from this end and we're trying to get one organized to hit it from the other side. We think we got most of the people out of the corridor."

"God help anyone left in there," DeRosa said fervently.

*　　*　　*

Mike Clancy took a deep breath. "Okay, people, there's something else we can try."

"Another scuttle?" Carmella O'Hara asked.

"Not that official. There's a water main that parallels this corridor and there's a crawl way that runs along it. It's tight but we can get through."

"How do we get to it?"

Clancy fished in the pocket of his coveralls and held up a thing that looked like a screwdriver with a funny tip. "With this," he said.

The trio worked their way back up the corridor with Clancy leading the way and counting panels on the walls. The smoke stirred sluggishly as they pulled themselves along, but it didn't seem to be getting any thicker. The corridor grew noticeably warm as they moved in the direction of the fire, but it wasn't uncomfortable.

At last Clancy stopped in front of a section of wall seemingly indistinguishable from the rest and applied the tool to it.

"These walls are full of stuff," he explained to no one in particular as he released the fasteners. He grunted as a particularly stiff one refused to loosen. "The panels aren't really part of the structure. They just cover things." Another grunt and the last fastener came loose. Clancy lifted the panel out of the way and peered into the narrow space behind. Several pipes ran through the center of the closet, but nothing else showed.

As Carmella and Martin watched, he crawled in, eeled his way around the pipes and attacked the fasteners at the bottom of the closet. "There," he sighed as he backed out and wiggled the panel free.

The opening was perhaps two feet square and pitch dark. "It's a tight squeeze, but I think we can all make it," the engineer told the other two. He reached into a breast pocket and handed a penlight flashlight to Carmella. "You're the smallest so you go first."

Hesitantly, Carmella took the flashlight and wiggled through the opening.

There were a dozen men waiting for Kirchoff in the corridor just beneath Shuttle Bay One. Quickly they filled the engineering officer in on the situation.

The obvious thing to do was to get the shuttle out of the hangar. But the mechanisms in the bay were not responding. The bay itself was a raging inferno and open to vacuum besides.

Worse, Kirchoff knew they didn't have a lot of time. So far the fuel feeding the fire was only coming out of the ruptured line. But if the tanks themselves leaked, the shuttle would turn into a bomb that could set off the *Maxwell's* adjacent tanks and destroy the ship.

Meanwhile the fire from the shuttle's stern was licking against the rear bulkhead of the shuttle bay, heating it and threatening to warp and broach the bulkhead.

"What's in the storeroom behind the shuttle?" Kirchoff demanded.

"That's Hold 48. General cargo, sir."

"What *kind* of general cargo, dammit? Is it going to blow or just burn?" The man turned back to the screen.

"Listed as dry stores, sir. Nothing hazardous or flammable."

"All right," he ordered, "open that hold to vacuum." One of the men moved off down the corridor to the nearest set of manual controls.

Kirchoff looked at the other men. "Okay," he told them, "the doors are already open. We have to free the shuttle and get it out of the bay."

He turned to an engineering crewman who had a compad plugged into an access panel. "What's the status of the release mechanism?" Kirchoff asked.

The crewman consulted his compad. "I'm not getting any readings," he said. "At the very least the controls and sensors are out and the shackles are probably damaged as well."

The engineering officer nodded. "Someone's going to have to go in there to assess the damage to the shackles." *And we all know who that someone is going to be*, Barry Kirchoff thought bleakly.

"Hell, we *know* the damn shackles are munged," one of the vacuum jacks said.

"Perhaps and perhaps not. The first thing to do is check them to make sure they can't be released manually."

"That's going to take time, sir," one of the engineering crew pointed out in a neutral voice. "Do we really have the time?"

"The first thing to do in a situation like this is get a precise assessment of the damage. Once we have that we can formulate an action plan."

Someone snorted. Kirchoff decided to ignore it.

"All right, I'm going outside to find out what's happening in the bay," he said, hoping his nervousness didn't show. "You men move down the corridor and wait for me around the corner. You'll be less exposed there."

As if that's going to help if the damn shuttle blows.

"How are we coming on clearing the Central Corridor?" Jenkins asked the soot-streaked runner who had just reached the bridge.

"Making progress," the man gasped. He had come forward at top speed and even in zero G moving fast takes energy. "We're having to force the doors as we move through, but we're about a third of the way back. Fire's confined to a wedge about 250 to 270 degrees from the corridor proper to about halfway out." The man coughed and shook his head. "If we had communications and control to the systems in there we would have had it out a long time ago."

"But now?"

The man grinned and even under the red gloom of the bridge lights his teeth gleamed in contrast to his smoke-stained face. "We're getting it, sir. It's just taking a little longer."

As he made his way along the hull to the shuttle bay, Kirchoff looked up. There, laying a few hundred meters off the *Maxwell*, was a Colonial ship.

What the hell? Kirchoff thought. But he had his own troubles.

With the penlight clenched in her teeth, Carmella O'Hara led the small party down the crawl space. It was dank, musty and every motion stirred so much dust Carmella was afraid she would sneeze and lose the light. Her nose tickled unbearably, but she restrained herself and every so often pressed her nose into her shoulder.

Suddenly Carmella stopped so suddenly that Clancy nearly ran his head into her butt.

"What is it?" he demanded.

Carmella took the flashlight out of her mouth. "There's a

wall here." She groped ahead. "It fits right down on the pipe and it fills the whole tunnel."

"Shit! It's a Goddamn firebreak." Clancy realized his imperfect knowledge of this part of the ship had betrayed him. *Of course they'd have firebreaks across spaces like this, you shithead! And naturally they match up with the fire doors.* This crawlway was only intended to give repair crews access to patch leaks in the water pipe. There was no need to go all the way along the Central Corridor in it.

"What do we do now?" Carmella couldn't keep a quiver out of her voice.

"We back up and we look for an access panel on the other side of the crawlway," Clancy said with a lot more confidence than he felt.

"We can't turn around in here," Martin protested.

"That's why we back up," Clancy told him. "And we don't bother about turning around when we get to the place we came in. Give me the flashlight." Wordlessly, Carmella handed it to him.

"All right, ass-end first. Let's go."

And the three crawled back down the tunnel.

Shuttle Bay One was, to put it mildly, a mess. Part of the cradle was provided by the bay doors themselves. Opening them had half-freed the shuttle, but the rest of the mechanism was on the other side, toward the center of the ship. That part was hung up.

The rear end of the bay was glowing dull red from the hydrox fire spewing out of the damaged rear of the shuttle. The hydrogen-oxygen flame itself was colorless, but flakes of paint and other debris caught in the torch flared, sparked and smoked. Even from where he stood, Kirchoff could feel the heat radiating off the hot metal.

Dear Lord! the young engineer thought, staring down into the pit. Then he began to work his way down the handholds on the front wall of the bay, headed for the deck and the shackles that were clasping a bomb to the *Maxwell's* breast.

Ludenemeyer flitted back and forth among several stations nervously.

He wanted all his top people on duty, but everything seemed to have gone wrong. Clancy was somewhere forward and Kirchoff was fighting the fire in Bay One. That left him and one engineering technician, young Carson, plus the man the captain had sent down to help guard the engine room.

A cook! The captain had sent a Goddamn cook to engineering!

And now communication with the bridge had gone completely out. It was too much.

"This is ridiculous," Ludenemeyer said at last. "I'm going forward to try to establish communication."

"Orders were to wait here, sir," the cook said neutrally.

"My orders are to run this department as efficiently as I can and I can't do anything until I know what's happening elsewhere."

The man only looked at him.

"Look Mr.—what did you say your name was?"

"Francis, sir. Joe Francis."

"Very well, Mr. Francis," Ludenemeyer said patiently, "there is an emergency comm on a different circuit a hundred meters down this corridor. It will take me less than five minutes to reach it."

He turned to the younger man. "Carson, you're in charge." With that he twisted and flicked off through the door.

The engineer eyed the older man suspiciously. Not only wasn't he an engineer, he wasn't a technician of any kind and to Carson's way of thinking he had no business at all in the engineering spaces.

When he had been dishing up food on the serving line he had been completely unremarkable. Now he had an air of easy superiority that the young engineer found both irritating and a little unsettling.

Besides, he wore the pistol on his hip with suspicious ease. The younger man was acutely conscious of the pistol flapping at his own side, not to mention how completely ludicrous he looked with a gunbelt strapped over his spacesuit.

The other man ignored Carson and made himself comfortable for the wait.

It seemed as if they had been crawling forever. Carmella's knees were raw and sore and several times already she had planted a booted foot on one of Mike Clancy's hands as they crawled backwards down the tiny access space. Unlike Martin, Clancy didn't complain when a foot landed on his fingers.

The tunnel seemed to squeeze in around Carmella and the

dank, musty air was becoming harder and harder to breathe. Her breathing was becoming ragged and she was hoarse from coughing due to the dust everyone was kicking up. *Are we going to die like this?* she wondered. *On our hands and knees crawling backwards into a fire?* There was a part of her that wanted to scream and flail against the tunnel walls and that part was getting bigger and bigger the further they crawled in the darkness.

Suddenly Clancy stopped and Carmella nearly rammed her butt into his nose.

"Access panel," the engineer said. Carmella twisted her head around and in the flash of the pen light she saw him running his hands around the edges. "This one wasn't designed to be opened from this side," he said conversationally, "but . . . give me some room will you?"

Carmella crawled forward and Martin crawled back. Then Clancy writhed around in the narrow tunnel until his back and shoulders were against one wall. Then he lashed out with both feet.

On the second kick the panel began to tear loose. On the fourth it floated free and all three of them tumbled out into a small compartment lit only by a single emergency lamp. While Carmella rubbed her knees and sucked in great lungfuls of the dry dust-free air, Clancy opened the door and played his light on the numbers stenciled on it.

"Not bad. We can't get out of this section unless we can get one of the fire doors open, but we should be safe here."

"Thank God," Carmella said.

"There's another scuttle down that corridor, but it leads up to the service corridor forward—the part that's on fire."

Clancy came back into the room. "Wait a minute," he said as his light played on the wall behind the other two. "That's firefighting equipment!"

Carmella turned and saw the familiar red symbol and the word "fire" stenciled on the door.

"I'll bet there's a fire riser coming off that main above us and down through that closet," the engineer said. He paused, thinking.

"Wait here just a second," he said and dashed out into the corridor.

* * *

The inside of the bay was even worse. By the time he reached the deck, Kirchoff could hear the fire. The sound was conducted by the deck and came up through his boots, a low rumbling roar that rattled his teeth.

Doing his best to ignore the inferno raging at his back, Kirchoff took the tester from his belt and clipped it to the test point on the shackle. The controls were stone dead.

He looked at the clamps skeptically. They were basically hydraulic and without power they couldn't be moved. They would have to be cut, but that was going to be a major job, especially so close to a loaded shuttle.

Although tiny compared to the *Maxwell*, the shuttle was massive. It would take a lot of energy carefully applied to get her moving out of the bay. It couldn't be just any push, either, Kirchoff realized bleakly. The shuttle was essentially a light shell. It was fairly strong along the line of thrust, but it was much less strong laterally. Too much pressure against the already weakened shell and it would rupture, guaranteeing an explosion.

Whatever they did they were going to have to do fast. By rights the shuttle should have exploded long ago and Kirchoff doubted their luck would hold much longer.

Ludenemeyer pulled himself down the corridor keeping close to the righthand wall. Ahead was a cross corridor leading to one of the stores sections that lay along the central tube beneath the enormous fuel tanks that made up most of the rear two-thirds of the *Maxwell*. It was on the logistics circuit, not engineering, so there was a chance it would still be working.

Not much of a chance, Ludenemeyer admitted to himself. The engineering comm circuits had more redundancy than the logistics circuits, but it was an excuse to move around, to do something. He would probably end up having to pass the word forward using spacesuits' radio sets, but he didn't like that at all. Too insecure.

He reached the cross corridor and turned the corner with a quick kick. He only vaguely saw the mass of grayish shapes before a dozen clawed hands grasped him.

"It's like I thought," Clancy said as he came back. "The doors are sealed at each end of the corridor and the scuttle leads back up into the next section of the service corridor."

"So we stay here until someone comes to get us," Martin said.

"Wrong! The first thing we gotta do is get that fucking fire under control."

Carmella bit her lips and nodded. Like Clancy, she had a Spacer's fear of fire in space.

Martin was a groundsider and he didn't. "Fighting that thing's a job for the fire crews," he protested.

"See any fire crews around?" Clancy said with a nasty grin. "Between the damned search the captain ordered and whatever the hell has happened, it's gonna take a long, long time to get those crews up here. Meanwhile we're here and if we don't get that thing knocked down in a hurry the whole ship's gonna be in trouble."

He rummaged through the locker. There were hoses, extinguishers, and some hand tools. But there were no suits or breathing masks. *Of course,* Clancy thought savagely, *no one but a fucking idiot tries to fight a fire on a spaceship without at least an ordinary spacesuit and more likely a full engineering suit.* Normally he'd be fighting a fire with a trained crew in engineering suits. But his suit was aft with his crew. He'd have to make the best he could of what he had here.

He began dragging out the fire hose and the fog nozzle.

"He's right," the young woman said. "It's not standard procedure but he's right." The thought of trying to fight a major fire with three people and no suits terrified her, but she knew Clancy was correct.

This sure as hell ain't a standard situation, the engineer thought as he broke out the hose and set the nozzle for fog. He reached into the closet and turned on the valve, the hose bucked and fought as it plumped up with water. He flipped the lever on the nozzle and a clammy burst of tiny water droplets blossomed out.

"Okay," he told them, "I'll go up through the scuttle first. You," he nodded to the astronomer, "come up after me to help me hold the hose." He looked at Carmella appraisingly. *He knows I'm scared,* she thought. *I can see he knows.*

"You stay here and watch the water flow. If that gauge starts to drop, come up after us and let us know immediately. I think there's a broken oxygen line in there someplace. We'll try to work back to the manual cutoff for that, shut it off and then damp everything down good."

171

Carmella nodded, glad she was being left behind and ashamed at the same time.

As Barry Kirchoff made his way forward along the hull he realized he didn't have the faintest idea what he was going to do. None of the procedures they had taught him on Luna would work on this one. He had gone through his check list, run off the end and gone through it again and he still didn't have the faintest idea what to do next.

The men were waiting for him in a little knot as he came up the corridor.

Command, he told himself. *You're in command. Whatever you do you can't let them know how scared you are or that you don't have any idea what to do.*

The men gathered in front of him, instinctively arranging themselves so they would all be able to pick up the emissions of his short-range infrared communicator.

Command. Act decisively. A leader always knows what to do. The lessons from the Academy kept running through his head. But he didn't know what to do, none of what he had learned covered this and there was no higher authority to refer to. As the men looked at him expectantly Kirchoff felt terribly alone and completely naked.

Finally he nudged the communicator switch with his chin. "All right, gentlemen," Lieutenant Barry Kirchoff said. "If anyone has any suggestions, let's hear them."

"Well," said one of the vacuum jacks, "we could always knock a hole in the tank."

Ridiculous! But for perhaps the first time in his life Kirchoff bit back his own response. "How would that work?" he asked carefully.

The raid commander couldn't believe his luck. Here was one of the three critical ones he had been sent to seize, blundering into his grasp like a light-mazed night flyer. He checked the moments into the raid and already his mission was one-third accomplished. Now, if only the others were so lucky!

He watched as the enemy's Master of Engines was trussed and hustled to the rear. A secondary mission was to examine the engine room of the alien ship and if possible sabotage enough equipment so that the vessel could not flee faster than light.

Peremptorily, he signaled his fighters to attack and two scouts darted around the corner and charged down the corridor.

Clancy put his hand on the scuttle. The door was only slightly warm. "Okay, here we go," Clancy said. Martin nodded and the engineer undogged the scuttle and turned on the fog.

The high-pressure mist billowed out of the hose and the recoil nearly knocked them off the ladder. Clancy locked an ankle through the rungs and thrust the nozzle through the opening.

The heat was like a blow to the face. The corridor was so full of choking black smoke it was hard to get a breath. Bracing himself against the hot wall of the service corridor, the engineer opened the nozzle all the way.

The air in the compartment turned jungle-like as the fires flashed the water droplets to steam. Clancy flinched and gasped as the heat and live steam struck his face. But he shifted his stance and took a firmer grip on the hose. Behind him Martin scrambled through the hatch and grabbed the hose behind him.

Step by step they fought their way down the corridor, fogging everything as they went. The atmosphere got closer and more stifling as they put more water vapor into it.

Mercifully there was no problem with electrical lines. Almost all communications and control signals were carried by fiber optic cable. There were some electrical cables in this section, but all shipboard equipment was fitted with automatic interrupters which cut off power at the first sign of a short. *Thank heaven for small favors*, the engineer thought as he shoved the nozzle ahead of him. *Now let's just hope the water pressure holds.*

Behind him Martin gasped and loosened his grip on the hose.

"Hold the line, Goddammit!" Clancy yelled over his shoulder.

"I'm trying," the astronomer called back. But he took one stumbling, weaving step forward and collapsed.

"O'Hara, get up here!" Clancy bellowed.

Carmella's head poked through the scuttle. "Get him out of here," he yelled.

Carmella was white and shaking.

"Goddamn it! Move your ass!" Still she couldn't respond. It looked like the fires of Hell in the corridor and it was all she could do to cling to the ladder.

"Goddammit, you silly bitch! Get him!" Clancy got a lungful of smoke and collapsed back against the wall in a fit of coughing. "Get him!"

The young woman roused, seemed to shake herself and scampered through the hatch. She grasped the fallen man by the shoulders and pulled him back to the hatch. The astronomer floated behind her like a swimmer being rescued by a lifeguard.

She'll know! Carmella thought miserably as she maneuvered the unconscious man down the hatch. *He'll tell Aunt Alice and she'll know.* The knot in her stomach wrenched even tighter. She looked back up the open scuttle and with an effort of sheer will began to climb.

Carson was poring over the displays when a movement in the corridor caught his eye. Someone dressed in gray was coming toward the control room. He looked up and frowned at what he saw.

The muffled gray figure was *wrong*. The proportions were wrong, it moved wrong and the thing in its hand was hideously wrong.

While Carson gaped, another one came caroming off the corner and arrowing down the corridor at them.

Three loud explosions rang in his ear. The lead figure seemed to pause in its headlong flight and a cloud of pink bloomed around it. Then the second one crashed into the first and they tumbled bonelessly together into one of the corridor walls.

Carson gaped and then hit the emergency transmission switch on his suit. "Aliens! We've got aliens on the ship."

"'Get down, you fucking idiot!" his companion yelled. Carson dragged himself behind a pump as a beam of blinding light flashed down the corridor. In the afterimage Carson could see part of a figure sticking around the corner.

"What the hell was that?" the young engineer yelled.

"I don't know, but it sure as hell ain't supposed to be here."

Another laser beam lanced down the corridor, leaving a stinking scorchmark on the wall.

"Can they come around us?" Francis yelled over his shoulder.

"Doors are sealed," Carson yelled back. "We'd better get this one closed."

"So they can sneak right up on us? No way."

Voices were chattering at him on the emergency circuits, confused reports of fires and aliens on the ship, people rioting, equipment out and other unspecified kinds of trouble. Without taking his eyes off the corridor, Carson repeated his warning of aliens in the engineering spaces and requested that the word be passed forward to the bridge. Somehow he didn't think it would help.

Carmella came up behind Clancy and took Martin's place. With the extra support and friction from another body to counterbalance the recoil of the hose they started forward again, one painful step at a time.

"Are you all right?" Carmella yelled to be heard over the nozzle and the fire. Clancy nodded and they pushed ahead.

They could see the flames now, licking feebly or burning with eye-searing brightness depending on what they were consuming. Clancy turned the hose on them with a fierce joy. The bright spots burned on undiminished but the fire flickered and died under the fog.

For the first time they could also see the effect of the explosions, panels blown off the walls of the ceiling, twisted and crumpled by the force of the blast. The heat and the steam were nearly unbearable and Carmella was already shaky when they heard a new sound.

At first Carmella thought it was an echo of the "whoosh" of their own nozzle. Then as it got louder she realized it was another fog nozzle in action. Someone else was fighting the fire as well.

Suddenly a scuttle clanged open a few feet behind them and a spacesuited head thrust through. The man saw them and reached up and opened his visor. Carmella saw he was grinning broadly.

"Hell Clancy, I might have known it was you."

Mike Clancy grinned back and they took several steps away from the fire to bring them even with the man as he came completely out of the hatch.

175

Clancy coughed again. "What the fuck took you so long?"

"We've been working our way back," the other one told him. "Are you coming forward from engineering?"

Clancy shook his head. "Scratch party. We got cut off in the Central Corridor."

"Yeah," he said, looking Clancy and Carmella over. "Well, I think we'd better take it from here." Behind him other figures in spacesuits came through the hatch and two of them moved to take the hose.

"We got one down on the next level. Smoke got to him."

"I'll send someone to have a look."

"How we doing?"

The man in the spacesuit nodded. "We got this one whipped, I think. Anything burning behind you?"

"Not that we know of."

Slowly they made their way back down the corridor they had fought to save. Clancy was smudged, scorched and hacking up mucus black with soot. The girl wasn't much better. Back in the lower corridor, the astronomer was moaning weakly and trying to rise.

"I'm sorry I let you down," Carmella said.

Mike Clancy grabbed her and hugged her to him with one arm. "Hell lady, you didn't let me down. If you ever want to shift to engineering, I'll take you on any day." He coughed up more mucus. "Now let's get our friend and get out of here."

Again Barry Kirchoff made his way across the hull. But this time he had company.

When they reached the rim of the bay, Kirchoff stood aside and watched as the vacuum jack got ready. Kirchoff's training implied that he should lead the way into a dangerous situation instead of standing aside and watching. *Don't be a bigger ass than you already are,* he told himself. *This man knows what he's doing and you don't.*

The vacuum jack posed on the edge of the bay, tucked in and pushed off gently. He floated down into the hole with his safety line snaking behind. He landed on the surface of the shuttle on all fours, turned and waved with one hand to show he was all right. Then, slowly, carefully, he inched his way along the shuttle's side, moving only one arm or leg at a time. The shuttle vibrated and bucked under him from the effects of the fire. Even from the edge of the bay, Kirchoff could hear it as a dull rumble, transmitted through the structure of the ship and up through the soles of his boots.

At last the vacuum jack arrived at a point slightly ahead of the shuttle's greatest width. He paused for a minute and then reached behind him for a small package attached to his belt. Carefully he placed the bundle against the shuttle's hull. Then he turned and scuttled back to the bay's forward bulkhead. He swarmed up the bulkhead and joined Kirchoff on the hull.

"We better lay down for this next part," he told him.

Behind a blinding burst of laser fire, four aliens came flying down the corridor. Unlike the first two they weren't easy targets. They bounced crazily off the walls and ceiling, using reaction jets on their suits to vary their speed and direction. They came on firing their laser rifles, roaring and shrieking.

Again Francis got off the first shots. The lead alien spun out of control almost as soon as he turned the corner. The second one slammed into the floor like a sack of sand and barely rebounded. Carson fired again and again and the third one was tumbling end over end. The fourth one didn't make it as far as the third one had.

The entire end of the corridor was hidden in a ghastly cloud of pink and carmine. The positive pressure ventilation in the engine room gently pushed the bobbing, drifting bodies back down the corridor the way they had come.

Carson smelled the acrid reek of gunpowder, almost like burning insulation, he thought. A shell casing went floating lazily by and instinctively he reached out and grabbed it. A part of his mind kept telling him he should be sick at the sight of the floating abatoir in the corridor, but he was too excited to care. His mouth tasted like metal and his breath came hard and rough.

He looked over at the man crouched across from him. Francis' eyes never left the door but he was as calm as if he were dishing out mashed potatoes on the serving line.

"Where'd you learn to shoot like that?" Carson asked.

"Chicago."

"New Chicago? On the Moon?"

The older man grinned mirthlessly. "Old Chicago. On the Cicero Crater."

177

"Fire in the hole," the jack called over the comm channel and hit the button.

The effect was totally unremarkable. A small hole, perhaps the size of a dinner plate, appeared in the shuttle's hull where the package had been. The shuttle jerked slightly in its cradle and that was all.

There was no roar, no cloud, not even a slackening of the flame from the other end of the shuttle. But the jerk told Kirchoff all he needed to know. Hydrogen gas was pouring out the hole, venting the tank and eventually depriving the fire of needed fuel.

It would have been impossible in an atmosphere. But in the vacuum there was nothing but the shuttle structure to conduct heat back to the new hole and nothing to oxidize even if there was heat to ignite the hydrogen. The curve of the hull meant the jet was angled away from the fire so there wasn't even the chance that the two would come in contact.

Kirchoff continued to watch from the lip of the bay. The fire was weakening, he saw, the flame gaining color as it got an excess of oxygen. It was a long ways from being out and there would still be a first-class mess to clean up, but the *Maxwell* wasn't going to blow up in the next few minutes.

"That was damned fine work," Lieutenant Kirchoff told the man on the radio. "What did you say your name was?"

"Jewett, sir. William Jewett."

It was sheer bad luck that brought Sharon Dolan into the path of the Colonial raiding party.

When the alarm sounded and the emergency doors slid closed she was coming back to her cabin from a visit to the ship's library. The doors trapped her in the section of the ship next to the one where her cabin was. A quick check of a wall screen showed her communications were out, she had no assigned emergency station and she didn't know anyone in this section except Dr. Takiuji and dropping in uninvited on him didn't seem right.

So Sharon decided to violate the standing rule on travel between sections when the emergency doors were closed and headed for the section's main shaft. Although unauthorized personnel couldn't open the emergency doors, the lower levels of Spin were organized somewhat differently from the higher ones. The compartments on different levels overlapped like bricks in a wall and the elevators in each section's main shaft continued to function. By going up one level Sharon could cross to her section's main shaft and take the elevator back down.

She met no one coming through the corridors, of course. The people with emergency stations had reported to them and everyone else was in their cabins, awaiting orders.

She was almost to the elevator when she turned the corner and ran smack into three aliens in spacesuits.

The voices were calling to her again. High and faint, talking too fast to understand. But that didn't matter. Lulu Pine knew what they wanted and she ignored them. This was the day and time. To hell with the Owlies. She was going to do this her own way.

She was smiling when she turned to face her captives.

Major Autro DeLorenzo fitted the last cartridge into the last magazine and put it into the web pouch. *Four clips. One in the gun and three extras.* A full combat load. Not enough to hold off an invasion singlehanded, but enough for what he had to do. He tapped the bottom of the magazine in the gun, then pointed the weapon at the ceiling and pulled the bolt back. He released the handle and the bolt ran forward with a satisfying clatter. DeLorenzo didn't bother with the safety.

But the submachine gun wasn't his real weapon. The controller was in a pocket of his battle jacket and with that controller he could bring the *Maxwell* to a complete standstill. Now he was the real master of the ship, although the people on the bridge didn't know it yet. He could do what he had to do from here, but he could do it more thoroughly from engineering.

Cautiously, Major DeLorenzo eased the door to his cabin open with the barrel of the gun and scanned the corridor. Nothing moved. He slipped out the door and started for the drive room.

Karl Ludenemeyer had never thought of himself as a brave man, in fact he was terrified. But as alien hands hustled him out onto the hull of the *Maxwell*, he knew that his capture represented more than a personal disaster. With the possible exception of Sukihara Takiuji he knew more about the drive than any other person on the ship. He had never had much feeling one way or the other about the aliens, but he remembered DeLorenzo's warnings.

If they'll do this, they'll do anything, he thought as three Colonists jetted him across the gap between the ships with their maneuvering packs. And that told Karl Ludenemeyer what he had to do.

If he wasn't brave, Ludenemeyer had a simple, direct, uncomplicated approach to problems that grew out of years of dealing with space ship engines. It wasn't a question of courage, it was that there was only one logical solution. So Ludenemeyer took it.

A spacesuit is designed to be as idiot-proof as possible, but men must still work in them. Ludenemeyer had deliberately chosen a model that sacrificed safety for flexibility. The hose to his air pack, for instance, was not completely within the pack shroud. A section of it stuck out at the back of his neck and could be pulled further free if needed. And in the middle of that section was a coupling so that a knowledgeable wearer could change airpacks in vacuum.

Of course, if the wearer forgot to shut off the air valve on his helmet before he changed air packs . . .

Suddenly Ludenemeyer tucked into a ball. The maneuver, precisely performed, threw him into a cartwheeling spin. His guards grasped for him and they were spinning too, all of them a confused tangle.

Ludenemeyer reached behind him and manipulated the fitting automatically. The hose whipped loose, spraying fog and ice crystals around him and his captors.

The Owlies gestured frantically and twisted about him, trying to get the hose back into its unfamiliar fitting to save their prisoner. But the hose fitting was designed to be hard for untrained hands to remove and that made it equally hard for untrained hands to replace.

Ludenemeyer kept twisting his body to make his captors' job as hard as possible. He felt his ears pop and then there was a trickle down his upper lip. His vision reddened and his chest felt as if a giant were sitting on it.

Damn, thought Karl Ludenemeyer abstractedly as the stars whirled about him and consciousness drained away. *What a silly, silly way to die.*

The door thrust open and the three aliens with Sharon Dolan in tow burst into Sukihara Takiuji's room.

The Japanese was kneeling on the mat-covered floor, his go board in front of him and his scabbarded sword on the mat at his side.

"Come," the Colonist commanded, gesturing with his weapon.

Suki said nothing, but his breathing slowed. In and out. In and out.

"Come!" the Colonist barked and gestured to the two behind him. The one holding Sharon shoved her roughly to one side and both moved to pass their leader and grab the kneeling man. Suki breathed in again and rocked back on the balls of his feet as if to rise, his left hand resting on the mat next to the sword.

Then suddenly he launched himself across the room, his sword a glittering arc in front of him.

The aliens' suits were designed to resist accidental tears and provide some protection against laser beams, but Suki's katana sliced through the fabric effortlessly and bit deep into the flesh underneath. The leading alien was down before his companions could do so much as start, the blood floating in the cabin brighter than a human's.

The other two Colonists started to raise their weapons, but Suki slashed left and right in a continuous motion and they too were falling slowly away, blood flowing through great rents in their suits.

The only sound was Sharon's ragged breathing. As if she was not there, Sukihara Takiuji brought the sword over his head and then flicked it down and to one side, just exactly as she had seen him do hundreds of times in the gym. Too-bright blood sprayed off the blade and splattered onto the wall.

"Called 'gama,' " Suki said to Sharon casually. "Means 'bullfrog.' " He brought the blade up and sheathed it with the same unhurried fluid motion he always used in practice.

Just like in the gym, Sharon thought dazedly. *Like he's explaining something in the bloody gym!*

The Japanese picked up his wakazashi, the short that was the mate to the long sword already in his belt. Sharon thought briefly of grabbing one of the dead aliens' lasers but the thought of touching one of them revolted her and she realized she had not the least idea how to use the weapon.

"Now come quickly," Suki said, drawing the long sword again. "We must be away."

There was no one in the corridor outside. Suki gripped his unsheathed sword and looked carefully both ways before letting Sharon follow him out.

"You must go forward, quickly, to the bridge," Suki told her.

"I'll not run from a fight," Sharon said indignantly.

"Not to run. To warn. The captain must be told. Now go quickly."

"What will you do?"

"I must destroy books and paper. Then I follow you."

Sharon looked dubious. "Go. The captain must know. And be careful!"

She nodded and set off down the corridor at a near-run. Suki stepped over the bodies and crossed to the bookshelf next to his bed. His professional library contained a great deal of information about the KOH drive which was not in the ship's computers and his notebooks had even more. It could not be allowed to fall into the Colonists' hands.

Quickly he pulled several electronic books onto the floor and ground them under his feet. The plastic cases cracked and the delicate crystal membranes inside ruptured, rendering them effectively unreadable.

The paper books and his notebooks made another pile in the center of the room. He started to pile them on the hot plate he used to brew tea and then stopped. The room's sprinkler system would automatically douse any fire. Instead he carted the load into the bathroom and used his short sword to cut everything to pieces in a few flashing strokes. Then he flushed the shreds and the pieces of the electronic books down the toilet.

Satisfied, he stepped out over the dead aliens again and padded off down the corridor.

At every corner Suki stopped and listened. He was almost at the main shaft when he flattened himself against the wall and whipped out both his swords. There were voices coming up the corridor. Human voices.

Suki waited until the men were almost on top of him

before he stepped out in front of them, swords lowered to either side.

Both men jumped back and one of them raised a pistol halfway before he realized who it was.

"Jesus buddy, don't do that!" the man with the gun said.

The pair were wearing the green coveralls of the life-support section. The one with the pistol was short and dark with a sheen of sweat beading on his face. His companion was larger, fairer and equally nervous. He was carrying a half-meter metal bar like a club.

"I am very sorry," Suki told them. "But what are you doing here?"

"We're from Life Support. When everything went to hell they sent us to find out what was going on. Then Spin compartmented and the regular codes wouldn't open the emergency doors," the man said with a trace of panic in his voice. "There's a fire in the Central Corridor and we think there are Owlies on the ship!"

"There are."

"Oh God!"

"How long since you came down the shaft?"

"I dunno, half hour maybe."

Suki nodded. "Then come with me." Re-sheathing his swords he started down the corridor.

"Come," Suki ordered. "Quickly."

With the ship compartmented off the aliens had to have come down the shaft and it was obviously the way the raiders intended to go out.

Like all the main shafts, the door of this one was round, man-high and thick as a bank vault's. It wasn't nearly that heavy, Suki knew. Most of the thickness was insulating foam with between layers of metal and sealing compound. But it was thick enough that no one was likely to shoot through it successfully with any kind of hand weapon.

Suki flexed his thighs experimentally. The gravity here was ship-normal. Weight enough so that conventional tactics would work.

There was no sign of life at the lock.

Suki turned to the two men behind him.

"We must secure the lock," he whispered. "Else the enemy escape."

"I got a better idea. Why don't we just let them go?"

Suki looked at the man.

"Well, it was just a thought," the crewman muttered.

"I will go first into the lock and you follow. Be ready to shoot as soon as they show themselves."

"The lock's empty," the crewman whispered.

"It is not," Suki told him.

Without another word he loosened his sword in its scabbard and padded forward. The two men looked at each other and then set out after him.

Suki hugged the wall of the corridor until he was a few feet from the door. Suddenly he whipped out his blade and charged through.

Without apparently looking, the Japanese thrust to his right and cut to his left in a sweeping arc. There was a cacophony of shrieks and roars from the lock and two brilliant flashes of laser light.

The crewman took a tighter grip on his pistol and ran forward, toes barely touching the matting. The other man followed him.

As they came through the lock, Sukihara Takiuji was just wiping the blood off his long sword. There were three more alien bodies on the floor.

"Oh my God," the man with the pistol moaned.

"The door," Suki commanded. "Quickly, close it halfway."

The other crewman, still shaking, pulled the heavy circular barrier partly shut.

"Excellent. Now they are trapped." Suki slid down the wall and squatted back on his heels. "Now we wait."

"Hey," Francis said, "we got company."

Carson shook himself out of his daze to see DeLorenzo striding down the gore-smeared corridor carrying a submachine gun.

"You're needed on the bridge," he snapped as soon as he crossed the threshold. "I'm to guard the engine room."

"We haven't been properly relieved," the engineer protested.

"Dammit man! The ship's under attack and communication's out. Now go!"

The engineer looked doubtful, but DeLorenzo shifted the submachine gun significantly. "I relieve you," he said.

Carson looked over at Francis and the cook shrugged.

For the first time in years Carson saluted. "Sir, I am relieved."

"Good. Now get up to the bridge. And be careful. We may not have all the Owlies off this ship."

For Sharon Dolan, speed was more important than stealth. So when she came around the corner she literally ran head-on into the main Colonist raiding party.

The alien in the lead was as surprised as Sharon but he recovered quicker. Before she could back away, the Colonist grabbed her and thrust her back to the aliens behind him.

Damn! thought Sharon Dolan as she was hustled back to the rear of the group. *Damn, damn damn!* By the time she reached the knot of human prisoners huddled under guard she was crying from anger and frustration.

Once the crewmen were gone, DeLorenzo shut and dogged the main access hatch. A check of the boards showed all the other entrances to the engineering space were sealed and a quick search showed he was alone.

That done, DeLorenzo slung his submachine gun and got down to the second and final phase of his plan.

It isn't difficult to unbalance a fusion reactor. The astonishing thing is that it stays in balance as well as it does. There were interlocks and safety features, of course, but DeLorenzo had spent weeks working around them. Now he needed only a few minutes to activate his program and to keep anyone from reversing his handiwork for the hour or two it would take for the reaction to destroy the *Maxwell*.

DeLorenzo had an alternate plan, one that didn't require his presence in the control room. But that would have only blown the ship to pieces. DeLorenzo wanted to make sure there were no pieces left for the Owlies to analyze.

The only drawback was time. It took a while for the unbalanced forces within the reactors to override the system's natural homeostasis. How much time was unpredictable. But unless someone could get to the controls in the next couple of hours the *Maxwell* was doomed.

What Major Autro DeLorenzo intended to do next had nothing to do with the destruction of the ship, but it was important to him personally. With a couple of quick modifications through his compad, he reactivated one of the circuits

185

to the bridge. Very quickly someone would be trying to reach him, and DeLorenzo had every intention of telling him what was in store and why.

There were about a dozen human captives with the aliens, all of them in spacesuits. As soon as Sharon was handed back among the other prisoners one of her captors thrust a spacesuit at her and motioned her to put it on.

Sharon looked at the garment dubiously. It was a man's suit and much too big for her to wear comfortably.

She started to say something to the Colonist but he silenced her with a ferocious gesture and raised his weapon threateningly. The protest died in Sharon's throat and she tried to fit into the suit.

By pulling the adjustments as tight as she could she more-or-less got the suit to fit. Her hands didn't reach down into the gloves, the legs bunched and bagged at the ankles and the air pack hung down over her buttocks in back, but at least the suit would stay vacuum tight.

Once Sharon had the suit on, the guard gestured her back to join the other prisoners, most of them in equally ill-fitting suits. Obviously the Colonists had grabbed the suits from a lock area without worrying about getting the right ones.

One of the other prisoners in an ill-fitting spacesuit shambled up to her.

"Hello Miss Dolan," Father Simon said. "They got you too?"

With the prisoners in the rear, the raiders made their way toward the section's main shaft. As the first of them rounded the last corner, a shot rang out.

The bullet went high, zinging evilly over everyone's heads as it ricocheted down the corridor. The Colonists in front scuttled back around the corner just ahead of a second, lower, shot.

Using a fiber optic periscope, the raid commander peered around the corner. The door to the central shaft was partly open and he could see shapes inside. Switching to infrared, he saw that there were at least two humans in there and at least one other cooling mass which was obviously one of the guards he had left at the lock. A human force strong enough to eliminate his blocking party must have retaken the lock and they obviously intended to make a fight of it there.

The alien leader considered his options. The lock was clearly strongly held and he couldn't afford the men and the time to take it. With the ship compartmentalized, reaching another lock would mean blasting through a series of pressure bulkheads and doors. Again that would take time. A more direct approach was in order.

Beckoning his group, he led them back down the corridor away from the lock. Several twists and turns later they came to a larger room used as an informal lounge. The human prisoners were herded into one corner and the Colonial commander pointed to a spot in the center of the floor. Two troopers moved forward and placed several packages around the area. Then everyone moved out of the room and several yards down the corridor.

The commander waited, obviously counting off time. Meanwhile two of his men moved among the humans, checking their spacesuits and making sure their visors were down.

The commander signaled and the entire ship rocked and bucked as the explosive charges ripped a hole through the bottom of Spin, the outer hull and into space.

The charges slashed through the Spin floor, ripping huge metallic petals outward to stab into the hull beneath. The jagged edges tore into the outer hull and with a lurch that shook the entire ship, Spin stopped spinning. At the core, the motors heated and smoked at the sudden overload. Everywhere in Spin, people and things lurched, slammed against the spinward wall and began to float away from the floor.

The shock of stopping Spin knocked Sharon and several of the other humans off their feet. The air whistled and screamed around the aliens and their prisoners as it rushed out the hole. Sharon felt her ears pop and her suit inflate as the pressure dropped. Around them she could hear the banging as the secondary emergency doors throughout the section had automatically sealed, locking their inhabitants inside.

The alien commander gestured and the Colonial soldiers hustled their prisoners forward, toward the hole and deep space beyond.

*　　*　　*

Stopping Spin threw the two crewmen to the floor of the lock. Suki, who was already sitting on the floor, had to put out both hands to brace himself.

"What was that?" one of the crewmen demanded, picking himself up. Under the impulse of his push he floated clear of the floor.

"It was Spin!" the other crewman said wide-eyed. "Spin's stopped!"

The first man did an expert flip and planted his feet on the floor again as the alarms howled and the secondary doors started to bang closed. "We've lost pressure in this section!"

The other man clutched his pistol more tightly. "The aliens must have blown their way into the ship."

"More likely they blew their way out," Suki told the men. "Is this shaft airtight?"

"Yes," one of the crewmen told him, looking at the indicators above the elevator door. "There's no power to run the elevator, but it looks like the shaft is clear and under pressure all the way up."

"Good," Suki rose and grasped his long sword. "I do not think the Colonists will come this way again. If they do, it will be in numbers too strong for us to stop. The captain needs to be told what has happened. Can we climb up this shaft?"

"Captain, we are here as representatives of the Ship's Council," C.D. MacNamara said rather sententiously.

Jenkins eyed MacNamara and his companions coldly. "If you want to complain about the search, do it later, please. I'm very busy now."

"That's not why we're here," Winston Chang said.

"The Colonists know that we have problems and they have offered to help."

"I'll bet they do know," Jenkins said. "Since they caused them."

"That's hardly proven, Captain," MacNamara said. "But in any event the ship and everyone on her are in danger. The Colonists want to help. They can have ships here very quickly from Meetpoint and they are offering us assistance."

"Surrender, you mean," DeRosa bit out.

"Assistance," MacNamara repeated firmly. "Captain, there is simply no rational reason to refuse their offer."

None except you've been bribed to turn over the ship,
Jenkins thought angrily. *You and half your Goddamn council.*
But it would be worse than useless to say that. They'd simply
deny it and who would care?

"Dr. MacNamara, that is simply out of the question. We
cannot allow Colonists—more Colonists—aboard the ship."

"Captain, we have been willing to acquiesce on this point
in the past, but I am afraid the time of pandering to your
phobias is gone. Need I point out that we can open the locks
ourselves? We are prepared to do so."

DeRosa ran her hand slowly along her waist to the holster
on her hip. "First you've got to get off this bridge alive," she
said quietly.

"Commander DeRosa, please!" Jenkins cut in.

But MacNamara was right and they both knew it. The crew,
disorganized and immobilized by the fighting, was outnumbered
by the Council and the people who supported them.

Before he could say anything he was interrupted by two
new arrivals on the bridge, both in spacesuits and both
wearing pistols.

Carson saluted and Francis mimicked him. "Reporting as
ordered sir," Carson said.

"As ordered?" Jenkins asked, ignoring MacNamara and the
others.

"You're supposed to be in the engine room," DeRosa cut
in. "Who the hell is standing watch?"

The engineer looked confused. "Major DeLorenzo, ma'am.
He relieved me when he told me I was wanted on the
bridge."

"DeLorenzo ordered you forward?"

"Yessir," said the engineer, relaxing slightly. "Well, he
relayed the order. He came to the engine room with a
submachine gun and told me I was to report to the captain up
in control."

"Shit!" Iron Alice muttered and spun for the comm system.

"I don't see . . ." MacNamara began.

"You couldn't see to pour piss out of a pressurized boot,"
Iron Alice snapped, punching the button savagely.

"Hello, Captain," Major Autro DeLorenzo said. He looked
as calm and unruffled as if they had met by chance in the
cafeteria.

"Just what do you think you're doing?"

"Saving humanity from slavery." He smiled and the tension showed through the surface calm. "You wouldn't take precautions against these creatures? I did. The ship's mine, Captain." He held up his control box. "I've got cutouts on all the communications and control circuits. I've also seen to it that the *Maxwell* will never fall to the aliens, no matter what Aubrey and the rest of the whores on the Ship's Council want."

"What have you done?" Jenkins asked hoarsely.

"Don't worry, Captain, no one will feel a thing. Pretty soon we will all disappear in a blaze of light." He stopped, as if for a new thought. "Oh, and don't bother trying to get me out of here. I'm armed and I'm not at all afraid to die a little sooner than the rest." He reached out and the screen went blank.

"Oh my God," said MacNamara finally.

"Can he be gotten out of there?" one of the other delegation members asked.

DeRosa grinned nastily. "Sure. In two or three days. That whole damn area is the heaviest shielded part of the ship."

"We'll have to go in and get him," Jenkins said.

He and DeRosa exchanged looks. DeLorenzo was heavily armed and the only professional soldier on the ship. Getting to him would be a suicide mission.

"It might be possible," a soft voice said from one corner of the bridge.

They all swiveled and looked at Sukihara Takiuji standing off to the side. "I would be willing to try if you will allow me."

Everyone looked back at Jenkins. "If you think you can do it, then do it," the captain said.

The Japanese smiled and bowed. Then he took his long sword from his sash and held it out horizontally resting on the palms of both hands. "Captain, if you would do me the honor of keeping this until I return?"

"Suki, what are you going to do?" Jenkins asked as he took the sword by the scabbard.

The old man smiled. "Captain, you have never heard the story of Kamiizumi Hidetsuna and the two rice balls?"

"No."

"Then you must check the ship's library when there is time." He paused. "Oh, and Captain . . ." he added in a

190

lower voice. "While you are at it, you might read the story of Alexander Kerensky and the Russian Revolution. Now please excuse me, there is not much time and I must visit my cabin." He turned and padded out the door.

Jenkins watched him go, thinking furiously.

"Captain?" MacNamara called behind him. "Captain, there is still the matter of the Colonists' offer of aid."

"Yes. Very well then, since we have no alternative, we will surrender." Alice DeRosa started, then looked narrowly at her captain and settled back waiting.

MacNamara smiled broadly. "Excellent. Perhaps they can help us get that madman out of the engine room."

"I think it would be inadvisable for them to approach the ship until we have that settled."

"Stalling, Captain?"

"Not at all," Jenkins said blandly. "But there is no reason for Colonists to die if the ship goes up. Besides, there is an excellent chance Major DeLorenzo has tied into the ship's sensors and will blow us up at the first sign of boarding."

"But if the Colonists help us . . ."

"I'm sorry, we must wait. With DeLorenzo's overrides in place I'm not sure I *can* hand over the ship. There's no way of knowing what he has rigged up."

"I see. Very well, we will wait and hope Dr. Takiuji can reason with him."

I don't think that's what Suki has in mind, Jenkins thought. "We all must hope so," he said piously. "Now, about the surrender, ah, excuse me, 'turnover.' It will have to be done properly."

"What do you mean, 'properly,' " MacNamara said, frowning slightly.

"That is for the Ship's Council to decide. As I'm sure you're aware there are a number of details which will have to be worked out."

"Details?"

"Oh, everything from exactly who we turn the ship over to, who will man the engineering and life-support stations, inventories, all those things."

"I'm not sure . . ."

"I want the Ship's Council to make the arrangements. The Council will negotiate with the Colonists and give me a precise procedure, in detail, which I will follow in turning over the ship."

"Captain, the Colonists are ready now. Why not do it immediately? Or as soon as Major DeLorenzo is out of the drive space?"

"Dr. MacNamara, this is too important for our future and Earth's for any detail to be left to chance. As soon as you have told me exactly what you want me to do, I will initiate the procedures."

"But . . ."

"Come, Dr. MacNamara. I need the Ship's Council's help in this. Is that too much to ask?"

"Well . . ."

"It sounds reasonable to me," Chang interjected. The other man nodded.

MacNamara sighed. "Very well, then. I will convene the Council immediately." He turned to go and the others followed.

"Remember, Dr. MacNamara," Jenkins said, "I must know *exactly* what to do."

"Cute," Iron Alice DeRosa said as soon as the trio was safely down the corridor. "You think that will hold them?"

"It will buy us some time anyway. Now, let's get back to the bridge and see what we can do about getting this ship under control again."

Major Autro DeLorenzo cradled the submachine gun and kept his eyes on the door.

What the hell was that story? Old, old one about the officer who seized the nuclear weapons stockpile on the Moon to keep his superior from setting off a war. Written back before space travel even. Anyway he died in the end for his duty. They honored him for it. Shit, if I succeed no one will ever know. No human anyway. He sighed and shifted the submachine gun. *Well, no one ever said life was fair.*

Behind him on the wall the gauges crept ever closer to critical. DeLorenzo didn't bother to look. As the pressure built up the containment fields became ever weaker. Soon they would be weak enough and, for a few seconds, this solar system would have two suns.

This wasn't like combat. He wasn't afraid of dying. This was something that had to be done and he was the only one

192

to do it. There was a kind of sadness to it and a genuine tranquility.

Something moved in the shadows. Reflexively DeLorenzo swung the muzzle toward it.

"Come out with your hands up," he called.

Sukihara Takiuji stepped out, palms out in front to show he was unarmed.

"Please do not shoot."

"How the *hell* did you get in here?" DeLorenzo demanded.

"The aft engineering hatch," Dr. Takiuji said, smiling nervously.

"That's disabled and locked."

"Very true, but there is a way to open it when there is no power. An instrument access port left over from the test program. Not widely known."

Hell! thought DeLorenzo. *That wasn't in the plans. Well, he helped design this thing.*

"What the hell are you doing here?" DeLorenzo growled. He kept the submachine gun pointed unwaveringly at Suki's belly.

"Waiting to die."

"Wait somewhere else."

"I prefer here," Suki said imperturbably. "Close to those." He nodded at the KOH drive generators.

He sat down crosslegged on the drive room floor as if oblivious to the gun trained on him.

"I'm warning you," DeLorenzo said tightly. "If you don't get the hell out of here . . ."

Suki looked up at him. "You will what, Major? Kill me? A rather empty threat under the circumstances, don't you think?"

"You're crazy, do you know that?"

Suki just shrugged. Slowly and carefully he reached into the sleeve of his kimono and brought out a white plastic flask and a tiny handleless china cup.

"What the hell is that?"

"Saki. Twenty years old. It should be served at body temperature." Suki set the plastic flask down in front of him. "It was given to me by a student. 'For a special occasion,' he said. I think one's death is special enough."

"You're Goddamn coldblooded about this."

"Would it do any good to become excited, Major DeLorenzo? It is truly said that the way of the samurai is to keep death always before one." He squeezed the sides of the container and caught the bubble of yellowish liquid in a tiny porcelain cup, moving so slowly and carefully that it did not splash. DeLorenzo watched, fascinated.

"In this gravity the tea ceremony could take on new elegance, do you not think?" Slowly and fluidly he raised the cup to his lips and drained it. Then he looked at the major.

"Would you care for some?"

DeLorenzo nodded and Suki recapped the flask and stood up.

"No closer!" the major barked and gestured with the submachine gun.

"Ah, of course," Suki smiled apologetically and tossed the flask to him underhand.

The flask sailed lazily across the room, turning and wobbling. Suki put his arms in the sleeves of his kimono and waited.

It was not a good toss. The flask passed to DeLorenzo's right about three feet from his body. Instinctively he twisted toward it and stretched out his arm.

Suki was halfway across the distance when the major realized his mistake and turned. Too late. As he closed, Suki batted the submachine gun aside and pulled a wakazashi from his kimono sleeve.

The gun fired three shots into the ceiling and the short sword flashed. DeLorenzo gasped, his eyes widened and then he collapsed bonelessly. Bright crimson droplets floated in the air as Sukihara Takiuji pulled the sword from DeLorenzo's chest.

"I'm sorry," the Japanese murmured and wiped the blade on the sleeve of the dead man's jump suit. Then he turned to the communications console.

"Captain, I have the control room," Suki said. "Send a crew down immediately."

"That was a hell of a job you did," Jenkins told Sukihara Takiuji when the Japanese returned to the bridge a few minutes later.

"I am sorry Major DeLorenzo had to die," Suki said. "I was not proficient enough to be certain of disarming him and I thought the stakes too great to risk failure."

"I don't think anyone will blame you for that," Jenkins told him. He reached down beside his console. "Here is your sword."

The physicist accepted the weapon with a slight bow and slid it back into his sash.

"How is the fusion pile?"

"Getting stable again. The engineers had to cut the output down to practically nothing, but they've got it under control and they're starting to bring the power back up. We're running on accumulators right now, but we've got plenty of power." *Especially since we're not going anywhere,* he thought.

"Excellent. You must be very busy so I will leave you now." He turned to go.

"Oh, Dr. Takiuji."

Suki turned back. "Yes, Captain?"

"I never did find the story of the two rice balls."

Suki smiled. "I fear the incident may be too obscure for our library. It concerns Kamiizumi Hidetsuna, one of the great masters of the Shinkage ryu—school, you would say —of swordsmanship.

"Hidetsuna was travelling the country, seeking to perfect his art when he and his disciples came to a village which was in an uproar. A notorious brigand had been cornered in the village, but he had seized a child and fled into a barn. Now he was holding a sword on the boy and threatening to kill anyone who came close.

"Naturally everyone was very excited, but no one knew what to do. At the least move the thief would kill the child.

"Hidetsuna saw a priest in the crowd and asked to borrow his robe. Then he sent the villagers to get him two riceballs and had his son and disciple, Toyogoro, shave his head like a monk's. When the riceballs were brought, Hidetsuna put on the monk's robe and, unarmed, took the riceballs into the barn.

"When the thief saw him he became agitated and threatened again to kill the child. But Hidetsuna allayed his fears and told him he had brought them food out of compassion since neither the thief nor the boy had eaten for a day and a night. He would not approach, he told the thief, but rather would throw him the riceballs.

"Hidetsuna threw the first riceball and the thief let go of the child to catch it with his left hand. Then he threw the second riceball and the thief dropped the sword from his right hand.

As soon as he released the sword, Hidetsuna sprang at him and wrestled him to the ground.

"I am no Kamiizumi Hidetsuna," Suki concluded sadly. "Not only did I take a sword with me, I was unable to capture my opponent alive."

"You saved a lot more than one child, though," Jenkins said. "So that really happened? I saw it in a movie once."

"It is a very famous story in Japan. May I go now, Captain?"

"One other question. What did you mean by suggesting I study Kerensky?"

The Japanese physicist smiled. "I think you have already worked that one out, Captain." He nodded and swam out of the door.

It took four men and a cutting torch to get the lab door open. The portal was still smoking when the first man played his flashlight around the darkened interior.

The first thing he saw was the blood splattered and smeared everywhere.

The second thing he saw was what was left of Dr. Albers—part of what was left.

He gasped and jerked his head and arm out of the door. "My God!" he yelled into his microphone. "Get a medical team down here immediately."

Off in the corner Lulu Pine heard but she paid no attention. She was of the Elect and the Judgment had come and gone.

"Captain, we've got a ship closing on us," the communications officer told him. "I think it's one of the ones from Meetpoint."

Another raid? And they were effectively helpless!

"See if he'll answer us."

"Yessir."

The communications officer's face vanished to be replaced by a gray, beaked head with unblinking yellow eyes.

"Who are you and what do you want?"

"We offer aid from the Colonial Council," the alien said.

"Go away. We do not require your help."

"But we carry aid."

"Your aid is not needed," Jenkins snapped. "You cannot dock."

"Your Council has approved."

"The Ship's Council has not agreed to anything," Jenkins grated. "I am in command of this ship and I will not allow you to approach." He glared murderously at the Colonist. "If any Colonist approaches this ship, we will leave this system under our drive and never return."

The Colonist froze. "I understood this was impossible."

Jenkins grinned, not at all nicely. "Want to try it? I've got the control under my hand right now."

"I must consult," the Colonist said and hastily broke the connection.

"Can we use the drive?" DeRosa asked in an undervoice.

The reddish ready light of the bridge etched the captain's face in harsh planes. "I doubt it. But they don't know that and they're obviously too scared to test it."

"I wonder how long that will last."

"They're firing their bow thrusters," the navigator called. "They're breaking off and moving away."

"Every day is a victory." He turned away from the screen to face his second in command. "Now, get Ludenemeyer or whoever's in charge up here in person. I want to know how long it will take to be sure we can get out of here on the drive. And see what you can do about rigging a secure command circuit, one that the Colonists or our own people can't listen in on." He paused and frowned. "Has our external comm system been restored?"

"You mean aside from the auxiliary bridge circuits? No."

"Then maybe it would be best if it wasn't restored. Not yet, at least."

C.D. MacNamara pulled himself back onto the bridge a few minutes later.

"Captain, you turned away a Colonist ship," he said accusingly.

"Yes."

"But you agreed . . ."

"Dr. MacNamara," Jenkins broke in, "I agreed to turn over the ship once I had specific instructions from the Ship's Council on how to do so. So far I have not received those instructions and until I do, no Colonist will set foot on this vessel."

"But surely one ship . . ."

"I thought we were quite clear when you and the others were here. As soon as I have a detailed, specific plan from the Ship's Council I will turn over the *Maxwell*. Not before. If you want to expedite matters then get the Council to prepare that plan."

MacNamara started to say something more, but Jenkins cut him off.

"If you want to protest formally, it should come as a Council resolution."

MacNamara clenched his jaw, turned and stalked off.

MacNamara had no sooner vanished than the screen chimed. It was Kirchoff, and the young engineering officer looked as if he was going to cry.

"We found Ludenemeyer," he said tightly. "He was outside the ship. I think they had captured him when his air hose came undone and they left him there." The man's eyes filled with tears and his teeth clenched tight.

"Captain, they just threw him away. He wasn't any good to them dead, so they threw him away!"

"Very well, Mr. Kirchoff," Jenkins said numbly. "Have the body brought back inside. There's a morgue down on S7." He stopped. *Ludenemeyer, My God!* "That makes you senior engineering officer, I believe?"

"Yes sir," Kirchoff said miserably.

"Then you are in charge of engineering. I want a report on damage as soon as possible. Oh, and Kirchoff . . ."

"Yessir?"

"Clancy is a good man. I'd suggest you make as much use of his experience as you can."

"Don't worry sir, I will." Kirchoff sketched a salute and blinked off.

"Jesus Christ!" Mike Clancy exclaimed as he made his way down the main corridor to the engineering spaces. The passage was a charnel house. The walls were streaked and smeared with alien blood where the air currents had pushed the invaders' bodies against them. At the far end of the corridor the corpses hung in a little knot whose position was determined by the air currents.

Blood was everywhere. Globules of blood wafted lazily about like soap bubbles on a breeze, drops of blackening blood floated and shimmered through the air and the air was pink with a fine mist of alien blood that coated everything and made contact with the corridor slippery and uncertain. In spite of his urge to vomit for the first time in nearly twenty years in space, Clancy kept the visor down on his suit.

"Well," he said after a minute. "At least the biology section will have something to dissect."

The Council President tried to shut out the uproar. They had crawled this tree from roots to topmost branches two hands of times already and still the argument continued.

". . . violation of Council agreement."

". . . if you had not . . ."

". . . but you insisted . . ."

"Who was the fool who . . ."

Squabbling and snarling like cubs! he thought disgustedly. But he did not interfere. Let them vent their rage and argue themselves out. They would be more amenable to reason once they were exhausted.

He maintained his outward calm and dignity as befitted his station, like the parent of a brood at unruly play. But inside he too was seething.

Fools! he raged. *Greedy, stupid fools. All you had to do was act in concert and the greatest prize in the history of our race would have been ours. But you could not manage even that. You all had to go off on your own and you got in the way of each other's schemes like an untrained hunting pack.*

The miracle was that not everything had been lost. The aliens' ship was still here, although the ship's elders were in disarray and the captain was threatening to leave the system at the least sign of further trouble.

"You want the bad news in ascending or descending order?" Iron Alice DeRosa asked the captain.

Jenkins looked at the dozen or so faces mosaicked on his screen, the officers and department heads who had spent the last fourteen hours assessing and surveying the results of the alien attack. None of them looked like they had anything good to say.

"Let's start with the worst and work down," he told her.

"Okay," DeRosa said. "The worst of it is that the Colonists managed to grab about twelve of our people and get away clean."

"Not so clean," Clancy said grimly. "They left a hell of a mess in the corridor leading to engineering."

"Aubrey was apparently one of those kidnapped," Carlotti said.

DeRosa got even grimmer. "I'm not so sure he was kidnapped. According to a couple of the survivors, he was helping direct the raiders."

"Oh my God," someone said softly.

"Father Simon was one of the ones taken," DeRosa went on, "and they got Sharon Dolan too."

"That was an accident, I think," Suki said. "They were after me and she was in the way."

"Well, thank God they didn't get you, Dr. Takiuji," Jenkins said. "That would have been the ballgame."

Although I don't know how much of a game we've got left.

"Did they get any more key personnel?"

"Apparently not." DeRosa scanned the list of the missing. "When they realized the raid had failed, I think they just started grabbing people at random."

"What about computer data?"

Billy Toyoda shrugged. "Hard to say. Those damn worms raised so much hell in the cyberspace you can't say for sure what they were able to swipe. But if you mean information about the drive, I doubt it. That isn't kept online and I don't think they were expecting that."

"What about navigation data?" asked DeRosa. "Like the location of Earth?"

"Oh yeah. They could have gone in and cleaned that area out if they wanted to."

"Then we have to assume they did," Jenkins said heavily. "They know where we're from. Okay, what about overall losses in personnel? Not the ones we think were taken, but everyone we lost."

"It's pretty bad," Iron Alice said. "All told we lost nearly fifty people."

Jenkins closed his eyes in pain. No one said anything for a moment. "What about functionally?" the captain asked at last. "Did we lose any critical people?"

DeRosa considered. "Engineering is hit the worst. Ludenemeyer and DeLorenzo are both dead and that takes out the whole top echelon. Clancy and Kirchoff are good, but with Ludenemeyer gone we don't have anyone left who has hands-on experience with the drive." Neither Clancy or Kirchoff said anything. "There's Dr. Takiuji, of course, but he's a theorist."

"And our systems status?"

"Still checking. We do know we have a hole in our side. There were explosions in the shuttle bays and they are vented. Bay One's a real mess. The spin mechanism is damaged, a lot of corridors burned. As far as we know, though, there is no damage to life-support or critical systems—except for DeLorenzo's damn disconnects."

"Thank God for that," Jenkins said.

"That Brazilian son of a bitch saved our bacon," Clancy said. "If it wasn't for those disconnects they probably could have taken control of the entire ship."

"The Lord do move in mysterious ways," DeRosa put in. "Okay, there's a lot more, but those are the high points. We can't run, we can't fight, we've barely got our own people under control and the Colonists are knocking at the doors wanting in." She sighed and looked up. "The question is, what do we do now?"

On the screen a dozen faces swiveled to look at Jenkins.

Derfuhrer looked down over the sweep of the colony and felt the warm glow of satisfaction. Of all the leaders in this misbegotten business, he had been the most successful. He had fully understood the humans and anticipated what they would do and now the largest prize was his.

He had known it was hopeless to try to seize the ship. One or more of the humans were sure to destroy it or, in the end, the lineage loyalty would tell. Foolish also to raid their computers. The humans were innocents, but did the other Colonies really believe they were so utterly trusting as to leave such information accessible? 348 and 579 had been badly burned on that one, he thought with a smile.

No, he and he alone had seen that the important thing was the knowledge of the individual humans. Only he had made adequate use of his agents within the human colony and only he had conceived the daring plan of physically raiding the ship itself.

Derfuhrer settled back and watched the forest spread out under his feet. Then he swiveled to look at the wall-sized screen displaying a view of space spangled with stars. His stars.

PART VI: KO

"I'm sorry gentlemen," Captain Peter Jenkins said, flipping through the surrender document and looking up at the three men, "but this simply isn't sufficient."

C.D. MacNamara, acting president of the Ship's Council, shifted uncomfortably. He didn't like zero gravity and neither did Winston Chang or Henry Parker, the other two Council members who had come with him to present the document to the captain. Worse, the trio was crowded cheek by jowl into the captain's small office. There was no room for them to sit so they were standing, trying hard to maintain their positions in zero G.

MacNamara would have much preferred to meet the captain alone, but with things the way they were on the Council just now, that wasn't possible.

"What do you mean it's not sufficient?" MacNamara demanded.

"Why, it isn't nearly specific enough," Jenkins told him. "It doesn't even say to whom we are handing over the ship."

"To a group of Colonists mutually agreed upon," MacNamara pointed to the document. "Can't you read?"

"Yes, but which Colonists? I can't very well turn my command over to the first Colonist who comes through the air lock. Are we to hand over to representatives of the Colonial Council, one of the colonies, or who?"

"That will be settled later," MacNamara snapped.

"I'm sorry gentlemen, but that simply is not acceptable. You must specify to whom the surrender is to be made."

MacNamara looked at his companions. The Council was

split into no less than four factions on the question of who to turn it over to and in three days of arguing, the best they had been able to do was to postpone the question by making vague reference to it. Now the captain was demanding specifics on issues on which the Council could not agree.

"In the opinion of the Ship's Council this is more than sufficient," MacNamara said testily. "We formally call on you to implement it immediately."

Jenkins shook his head. "Gentlemen, I cannot implement what isn't there. I'm sorry the Council feels so strongly on this issue; they will have to do a better job than this."

"You agreed to hand over the ship," Chang protested.

"I agreed to hand over the ship when the Council spelled out the *precise* terms for that action. This," he tapped the papers, "doesn't."

MacNamara realized he didn't have a lot of options. United, the Ship's Council could easily control the ship. But he knew that at least one and possibly two of the factions would not support any direct action at this time. Besides, the document wasn't really satisfactory to the Colonists he was dealing with. The Captain was holding the Council's feet to the fire and that might give him the leverage he needed to get something his Colonists would like better.

"Very well, Captain. We will further refine the document." MacNamara turned and maneuvered out of the room, Chang and Parker trailing him like discouraged pilot fish.

"You know," said Jenkins into thin air after they were gone. "I'm beginning to like this consensual decision-making."

The ship holding the captured humans flew true, but it flew anything but straight. The hydrox engines fired at precise but carefully irregular intervals, slewing the ship and moving it off course. Sometimes when the engines were shut down, mass drivers mounted on the hull would throw out chunks of nonmetallic mass, changing their course even further with no rocket signature to make the ship easier to track.

The prisoners were never warned about maneuvers, so they were knocked about every time the engines cut in. They became exquisitely sensitive to the sounds that might precede a firing.

Sharon Dolan awoke sick and weak, as she always did from the effect of the aliens' drugs. She had no real memory of the time under the drugs, just a vague feeling of having floated in a gray place for some indeterminate amount of time. Like a dream, but she was not rested.

She felt dirty and *used* by what had been done to her. Unclean.

She swallowed and tasted the bitter drug residue on her tongue as saliva trickled down her aching throat. They must have kept her talking for hours, she realized.

At least there was no physical torture. No beatings, no electric shocks. Not even questioning under bright lights. Instead at intervals their captors would remove one of the prisoners to be interrogated under the influence of drugs.

"Are you all right, Miss Dolan?"

Sharon turned her head and saw Father Simon sitting on the floor beside her bunk.

"I'm sorry," he said. "I must have dozed."

"How . . . how long?" Sharon croaked.

"Quite a long time I'm afraid. They had you nearly two days."

"No, how long have you . . . been here?"

"Oh, since they brought you back. I really don't know how long."

Sharon reached out and the priest took her hand. "Thanks," she forced out.

Father Simon looked embarrassed. "Quite all right, Miss Dolan. Would you like some water?"

"Captain, I must speak to the Colonists."

Jenkins looked up. "Why, of course Dr. MacNamara. Surely you don't feel you need my permission to do that?"

"I am told there is only one channel available. An *open* channel."

"That's true," Jenkins said. "Because of the damage our facilities are stretched extremely thin. We only have one channel available."

"But an *open* channel . . ." MacNamara shifted from foot to foot unhappily.

"We have very little computing power left, Doctor, and almost all that is needed to help us run the ship. I'm sorry, but we don't have the capacity to provide scrambled communication with the Colonists."

"But Captain, our negotiations are in a very delicate state.

The Ship's Council must communicate privately with the Colonists!"

Jenkins spread his hands helplessly. "I'm sorry, Doctor, but we simply do not have that capacity. Perhaps in a few weeks when we have been able to repair more of the systems."

"*Weeks?* Captain, I must speak with the Colonists now!"

"I'm sorry, Doctor, but that is simply impossible. Surely Doctors Chang and Parker told you."

"Told me?"

"Why yes, they have both spoken to me about opening a secure line of communication to the Colonists. Didn't they tell you?"

The Council president's face had taken on a glazed expression, as if he was thinking hard. "Ah, why yes, they did tell me. But I was hoping . . . well, I see how it is. Please let me know when a secure link is available." He turned to go. "Oh, and there is no reason to mention this to Dr. Chang and Dr. Parker is there? I wouldn't want them thinking I was going behind their backs."

With that he beat at hasty retreat.

Terrible when thieves fall out, Jenkins thought to himself as he turned back to the screen.

The Owlie guard watched the priest approach with unblinking yellow eyes. He stood at the door leading out of the captives' quarters with no weapon except his formidable talons and a flexible truncheon.

"I want to talk to Dr. Aubrey," the priest said firmly. The guard cocked his head to one side, listening to the translation coming in through his helmet. He spoke into his microphone, a collection of hoots and roars that made the priest flinch back.

"Wait," the speaker on his harness said. Then the guard settled back into his attention posture and ignored the priest again.

At last there was a rattling noise on the other side of the door. It slid back into the wall and Andrew Aubrey stepped through. Originally the aliens had kept Aubrey with the rest of the humans. After he was repeatedly beaten by the other prisoners, he had been taken out and kept separately. The other prisoners only saw him in glimpses and none of them before had tried to talk to him.

"You wanted to see me, Father?"

There was still that old geniality and air of easy superiority, but it was more strained now, almost forced. Father Simon saw that he had lost weight and appeared drawn.

"Doctor Aubrey, I have come to ask you to use your influence with the Colonists to stop the interrogations. They are damaging and they are producing nothing of value."

"I'm sorry it upsets you, Father, but it is necessary."

"Dr. Aubrey, you must put a stop to this."

"You're being unreasonable."

"This is torture."

Aubrey made a dismissing gesture. "Oh come now. You exaggerate."

"I have just come from Dr. Dolan. If you saw her you would not say I was exaggerating."

"Father, I have been examined several times by exactly the same techniques. I tell you you are exaggerating. The Colonists are far too superior to resort to something as crude as torture."

"So superior they raid our ship, kill people and kidnap us? That adds up to superior force, perhaps, but hardly superiority in any other area."

"Father," Aubrey said testily, "by blind luck we have stumbled across one thing the Colonists do not have. We insisted on withholding it from them like petulant children. In spite of all they offered us, all they can do for us, we refused them this one thing. So finally they took it from us, just as a father would take something from a child. Do you blame them in that?"

"Yes, I blame them," the priest said angrily. The guard shifted threateningly, as if to interpose between the arguing humans. Aubrey seemed to gather strength from it.

Aubrey shook his head. "I thought that as a priest you would see more clearly the essential brotherhood of all intelligent beings."

"Doctor, there are a great many things brothers should not do to one another. What Joseph's brothers did to him comes to mind."

"Yes, but Joseph became one of the mightiest men in Egypt because of it," Aubrey said triumphantly.

"Joseph was also a slave," Father Simon bit out. "And his people became slaves as well."

"Father, I am afraid you are blinded by your prejudices."

"There is certainly blindness here. Now, once and for all, will you tell the Colonists to stop torturing us? None of us have the secret of the drive and we cannot help them."

"I hardly see how putting someone to sleep for a few hours can be considered torture," Aubrey said stiffly.

"Then I have nothing further to say to you," Father Simon turned and stalked off.

"Even if I did believe it, there is nothing I can do," Aubrey whispered to his back.

"The prisoners have told us little," the Master of Bounds told Derfuhrer. "We know most or all of what they know about the drive. However, none of them were directly concerned with it and they are able to describe it in only the most general functions. Further, there are some inconsistencies in their stories apparently arising from different understandings of the drive."

"What have you learned then?" Derfuhrer said impatiently.

"Enough to offer a solid basis for beginning our own research. We know the manifestations of the drive, much of its limits and how it is used. The Master of Skies has already started our scholars to work."

Derfuhrer said nothing. In fact, the Master of Skies had been given pathetically little to work with and both of them knew it. Just as both of them knew that the raid had been botched and the one key prisoner captured had managed to commit suicide with disgraceful ease. But the Master of Bounds hoped that the Master of Masters would forget and it did not suit Derfuhrer's purposes to bring the matter up yet.

The leader looked out past his Master of Bounds, out across the terrace at the green vista beyond.

"And the other colonies?" he said at last.

"They find our possession of the humans most convincing. Already they are ready to listen to our words with new ears. A few of the weaker ones already heed our call. Many of the others listen carefully and begin to waver in our direction."

The question was more for the Master of Cities and the Master of Forests than Derfuhrer. He himself had spent long hours at the screen negotiating, cajoling and threatening, using the force of his remarkable personality to help forge a coalition that was nearly strong enough to overturn the Colonial Council itself.

"Shall we call for a higher seat on the Council?" asked the Master of Cities.

"No!" Derfuhrer snapped. "The Council is a powerless farce and illegitimate besides. We shall not beg for a higher seat. We shall not whimper and pule to be raised in their sight.

"Instead we shall pursue the true path. Let the Council do as it will. Soon it will do little enough."

"What about the other humans?"

"They mend their ship and heal their internal hurts," the Master of Skies said. "What their plans are we do not know."

"Will they give over to the Colonial Council?"

The Master of Bounds gave a fizz of laughter. "Some on the Council still think so. But no, their stroke there has failed. Their agents are divided as the Council is divided and the Leader of the humans seems to use that skillfully."

"We could always put an end to the others," the Master of Cities suggested.

"No," Derfuhrer said. "I know it would increase the value of the ones we hold, but there is still the possibility we can win the secret of the drive from the ones on the ship. As long as the surrender of the ship is not imminent it is not a wise move. Besides, it would not help our political position to move openly against the humans. We have made a spectacular leap from branch tip to branch tip. Now it is time to hug the trunk and wait."

Once again the conference room was packed. Jenkins deliberately had taken a seat halfway down the table. Aubrey used to insist on sitting at the head when he presided over a meeting. Unlike most of Aubrey's meetings, this one was not being shown all over the ship. This group of a dozen or so people comprised the reconstituted alien study team.

Carlotti was still the leader, but many of the old faces were missing, either through capture or because they were tainted by their dealings with the Colonists.

Damn, I sure wish Sharon Dolan was here, the captain thought, *and Father Simon, too*. He shook the thought off and got down to business.

"Okay," Jenkins said, not really calling the meeting to order. "What do we know so far?"

"Well," Carlotti said carefully. "Since the attack we have obviously had to seriously rethink our view of the Colonists and Colonial civilization."

Someone down the table snorted.

"It turns out that some things make much more sense in light of recent developments."

"Meaning we've been conned," Lewis put in.

"Meaning we were shown only part of a culture," Carlotti said. "It's not an unknown phenomenon when studying another culture. Anthropologists run into it all the time."

"Save the theory for later," Jenkins said. "Just give us the highlights."

"Well, most of what we were told about the Colonists' overall culture still appears to be true—or at least remains self-consistent. However it is obvious that they are nowhere near as peaceful as we had been led to believe."

"We know they are warlike."

"No," Carlotti shook his head. "I don't think warlike is precisely the right term."

"Well, you can't exactly call them peaceful!" Lewis said.

"No, but the reasons they gave us for avoiding open war are just as valid. Those habitats are too fragile and their economy is too finely balanced. If I may resurrect a term from the last century, I would say the Colonists exist in a state of perpetual cold war.

"One of the reasons the attack failed is that we weren't subjected to just one attack, we were hit by five or six simultaneously. Most of them were launched prematurely and they got in each other's way."

Jenkins made a note on his comm pad. "There ought to be a way to use all that factionalism. Think about it and see what you can come up with." He looked up.

"Now, how much danger are we in right now?"

"I'll make a guess," Barry Kirchoff said. "I'd say if they wanted to they could wipe us out in minutes. The only thing that would save us would be to jump instantly."

"Probably correct," Carlotti said. "But they won't make the attempt for a variety of reasons. The main one is they want the secret of the star drive."

"How close are they to getting that?" the captain asked.

"I'd say not very close at all," Carlotti replied.

"I disagree," Kirchoff put in. "Granted the mathematics and physics behind the drive are as screwy as everyone says they are, once you know it's possible and you've seen it in operation, you can work out the basic principles in a matter of months."

Carlotti shook his head. "*We* would have the basic secret in a few months. I am not convinced the Colonists can."

"You're saying their science isn't as good as ours?" someone said skeptically.

He hesitated. "Properly speaking, I'm not sure they have science."

Kirchoff gestured toward the star. "What do you call all that then, magic?"

"No, scholarship."

"Eh?"

"I exaggerate, of course, but only slightly. The Colonists are heirs to an old, old culture. Our best estimates vary from 50,000 to 250,000 years. In any event, very ancient. They have enormous libraries, but they do little or no original research. Judging by our contacts, they conceive of 'science' as a matter of going through their libraries and finding the appropriate information. Their store of information is huge, but their rate of addition is minuscule. Even their engineering seems to be mostly of the cookbook variety. Sophisticated, but not at all original."

"Still, if they want something badly enough . . ."

He shrugged. "Oh, undoubtedly. But it will take them much longer than it would take us. They aren't flexible, you see. Remember also that the basic principles underlying the Karpov Omo Hawking Effect are extremely subtle. Finally, the directions their mathematics and physics have taken do not lend themselves to an easy formulation of the underlying phenomena.

"I would say that even if they had, ah, obtained the services of Dr. Takiuji, it would take them several years to unravel the drive. As it is, even with the willing cooperation of their captives, it will take them much longer. A decade, perhaps two."

"Are you suggesting we abandon the prisoners here?"

"That wouldn't work, I'm afraid. I said their progress would be slow, but not nonexistent. Eventually they will solve the problem."

"So we're damned if we stay and damned a little slower if we run?" Jenkins asked.

"That is essentially my assessment, yes."

"And if we get the prisoners back?"

A pause. "I think it would materially decrease their chances," Carlotti said. "In fact, without the prisoners there is a fair chance they would never get the drive. Well, perhaps not never, but it would take them much longer."

The captain turned the situation over and decided he didn't like it no matter what angle he viewed it from. Up and down the table the people were looking at him expectantly.

"All right," he said at last. "We stay for the time being."

As Jenkins glided back up the corridor toward the bridge, Billy Toyoda fell in with him.

"You know, Captain, I've been thinking about Aubrey."

"Oh?" said Jenkins in a tone that didn't encourage further comment. Typically the computerman ignored it.

"I don't see how the Owlies suckered him like that."

"I don't either, Mr. Toyoda."

"I mean all that shit about them being peaceloving. Hell, it was obvious that was a crock."

"How obvious?"

"*Real* obvious. First off, peaceloving people don't build Goddamn fortresses around their systems. Hey, I mean security's one thing, but those fuckers are Goddamn paranoid and paranoids usually have real enemies somewhere."

Jenkins kept moving and didn't look at his unwanted companion. "Dr. Aubrey didn't know about that."

Billy sniffed, indicating his opinion of someone who took so little interest in computers. "Yeah, but he was talking with them. The words should have clued him in."

"What words?"

"Well, for example, did you notice that the main word for 'stranger' is the same as the word for 'enemy' or 'spy'? And that they don't have a simple word for 'neutral'? They've got to use some big long phrase."

Jenkins stopped and looked at Billy. "No, Mr. Toyoda, I had *not* noticed that. How did you come to see it?"

"By looking at the translation tables. Hey, someone must have studied them when you were optimizing them, right?"

"Mr. Toyoda," Jenkins said slowly, "just what is a translation table?"

"That's the list of our words cross-referenced against their words—or really the map of our meaning clusters onto their meaning clusters. You mean you never looked at it?"

"As far as I know, no one ever looked at it directly."

"Oh shit man," Billy cried, "you didn't!"

"Why should we? I thought the computers took care of that part."

"Because the damn things aren't that good, not as they come out of the computer. Translation tables always got to be hand optimized or you lose all kinds of meaning."

"Why the hell didn't you tell me this before?"

"Oh man, I thought you knew."

"Mr. Toyoda, I would appreciate it in the future if you would assume that we know a little less and tell us a little more. Now what else can you tell me about the Colonists' language?"

"Not a lot," said Billy, looking considerably chastened. "I didn't study it systematic-like. I just spotted some things hanging out in cyberspace."

"Well, study it 'systematic-like,'" Jenkins snapped. "I want to know anything you can tell me about their language and what it indicates about their culture. If you need help I'll see that you get it."

"Yes, uh, sir. You think it will help?"

"Mr. Toyoda, at this point *everything* helps." *Even grasping at straws*, he did not add.

Sharon Dolan was dreaming of Earth when the pounding on the bulkhead jarred her awake.

"Get up!" The guards roared down the corridor, slamming the walls with their truncheons as they went. "Everyone out-out-out."

Groggily Sharon pulled herself up and stumbled out into the corridor with the rest of the captives. The guards paced back and forth, brushing by the humans in the narrow space and counting as they went.

"This way, hurry," the commander's translator roared out. His own voice was so loud it hurt the humans' eardrums in the confined space. With the guards pushing from behind, the prisoners were herded down a cramped, narrow corridor to an open air lock.

The guards gestured with their weapons. "Inside."

One by one the humans filed through into what was obviously a second, smaller ship. They were forced back into a compartment barely big enough to contain a dozen or so acceleration couches.

"Strap in," the guard commanded and then the door was shut and locked behind them.

Jenkins was on the bridge, staring at the stars and sucking on a bulb of coffee when his screen chimed.

He touched the stud and his communication officer's face appeared, looking excited. "Sir, I've got the Council President. He wants to speak to you."

"What in the . . ." The captain automatically checked the status display. The drive was hot, manned and ready to jump. Slightly mollified, Jenkins reached over and touched the stud. The screen lit with the familiar image and great staring yellow eyes. Jenkins, who still couldn't tell one alien from another, nodded to the image. "Mr. President."

"I have a proposition," the alien said without preamble.

"Speak on."

"I propose an agreement-of-convenience-between-lineages-with-only-slight-mutual-debt."

It took Jenkins a second to decipher the phrase. He frowned and touched a screen button before he spoke.

"You want an alliance?" he asked. Then he looked down at the English retranslation that flashed on the bottom of the screen. "Alliance" had become "mutual-benefit-agreement-nature-unspecified." He used the pointer to change the translation to the form the Council President had used and touched another screen button to send the sentence.

"I so propose."

"Why?"

"The resultant of forces changes. The social orbits shift inauspiciously."

Jenkins scowled at the screen. Billy Toyoda's optimized translation tables might be more precise, but sometimes they got in the way of clear meaning.

"You mean the balance of power is shifting? In what way?"

"That is what I said. Derfuhrer's vector lengthens. He perturbs other colonies into 246's orbit. We wish to restore equilibrium."

"How?"

"He uses his possession of humans to increase his virtual mass. This is inauspicious."

As soon as I get the chance I'm going to have Toyoda work on this damn thing again. Then he brushed the distraction away and thought hard.

"Such an agreement might prove beneficial," he told the Council President. "I will consider it and then decide."

"How long will it take you to consult your Council?" the Council President asked.

Jenkins punched up the retranslation of his sentence and saw "decide" had been translated as "consult with the elders of the inner grove." *Damn!*

"Pardon. My translator erred. I alone will decide and I will inform you of my decision."

The Council President's nictating membranes flicked in surprise.

"I await your decision," he said, making a gesture Jenkins had never seen before.

As soon as the screen blanked, Jenkins replayed the sequence and queried the translator on the gesture's meaning.

EXACT MEANING UNKNOWN/ the message came back. /PROBABLY ACKNOWLEDGEMENT OF STATUS BETWEEN HIGH-STATUS EQUALS/

Well, well, well Jenkins thought. Then he punched up his second in command.

"Al, get the alien team together right now. We need a meeting."

"Screen's faster."

"Screen may also be less secure."

"Well, what do you think?" the captain asked his hurriedly assembled team after playing them the recording of the Council President's message.

"I think you'd better get that translator fixed," Lewis said. There was a quick ripple of laughter.

"Right, but what about the offer?"

"I'd say he's probably sincere," Carlotti said. "If Derfuhrer was the one who pulled the actual raid on the ship, he's probably upset this system's applecart in high style. As the

214

guy on top, the Council President has the most to lose so he's the most eager to put Derfuhrer down."

"We may assume it was Derfuhrer who ordered the attack," Sukihara Takiuji said. "It is very much in his style and not, I think, the style of the others."

Jenkins looked up and down the table. "Any contrary opinions?"

There were none.

"So you all think the Council President's sincere in his offer?"

"Sincere is perhaps too strong a word," Carlotti said. "I think the alien phrase expresses it nicely—the Council President wants," he touched a stud on his electronic note pad, "an 'agreement of convenience between lineages with only slight mutual debt.' "

"That's not a phrase," Billy Toyoda said. "That's one word in their language."

"Which is significant in itself," Carlotti said. "The main thing is that we can trust the Council President to turn on us as soon as it's to his advantage."

"I rather expect that," Jenkins said. "But in the meantime, I think we might be able to gain something from this."

The Limbo System was covered by a net of sensors, but every net has holes. For the next few hours this particular area of space would not be under hostile observation.

At precisely the right moment, the ship ejected the smaller ship and did a spectacular burn to make a major course correction. Hidden in the flare of the larger ship's rockets the smaller ship fired its own rockets and dropped swiftly away on a very different course.

Again Jenkins faced the broad gray face and unblinking yellow eyes on the screen.

"I have decided to agree on an alliance," he told the Council President—checking the screen to make sure the correct translation was rendered.

"I so agree," the Council President replied.

"I further propose that it is to our mutual advantage to locate our missing people," he told the alien.

"That is unnecessary."

"You know where they are?" Jenkins demanded.

215

The Council President gestured in a way the humans interpreted as a shrug. "Not now. I know where they will be."

"Where? And when will they be there?"

"On Hasta." The computer scrambled for a minute and then identified "Hasta" as the outermost of the Mars-type planets. "Colony 246 has an old base there from when they tried to turn the whole planet into a Colony. It is Derfuhrer's most secure dungeon. They will arrive in a few more days."

"I found out something else interesting, too," Jenkins told Carlotti later as he recounted the conversation. "The Council President says his people can mount a rescue in a few weeks."

Instinctively Carlotti looked out the great bridge windows toward the star. "A few weeks?"

Jenkins shrugged. "They have to modify ships to land on the planet. Most of theirs aren't made for it."

"So we let them make the rescue?" Iron Alice asked.

Jenkins scowled. "No good for two reasons. First, I don't think we have that much time."

"Second?"

"Would you trust the Council President with hostages?"

The pilot snorted.

"Precisely. We need to be in on the rescue."

Iron Alice did a quick mental calculation. "They're damn near on the other side of the sun. We could get there in four or five months if we don't worry about fuel reserve."

"No good. What we need is some way to get there fast."

Iron Alice pressed her lips together even more tightly. "Wishing doesn't make the impossible happen."

"No, but thinking about it may. Let's see what we can come up with."

PART VII: GOTE

Lulu Pine stood before the table. Her dark hair was stringy and her potato face was sullen. Her mouth clamped shut tight.

Captain Peter Jenkins, sitting in front of her, pressed his mouth into a grim line.

"You have heard the evidence. Do you have anything to say for yourself?"

Lulu said nothing. Her eyes were fixed off in the far distance, as if staring at a goal she could never reach.

"Very well then." He shifted slightly and began to read. "Whereas the defendant, Lulu Pine, did, on or about the twenty-third day of August, 2092, willfully commit murder, to wit, the murder of Dr. Luke Albers and Dr. James Wadsworth."

He licked his lips and went on. "And whereas, the defendant having been tried by a duly constituted captain's court has been found guilty of the said murders, she is hereby sentenced to death."

There was a ripple in the conference room being used as a courtroom, but Lulu Pine gave no sign of noticing. "Execution to be by lethal injection no later than seventy-two hours from now."

Lulu said nothing. She glared at Jenkins.

"Remove the prisoner," Captain Jenkins said firmly. DeRosa took Lulu by the elbow and steered her out the door.

As Jenkins gathered up the papers on the table, the spectators drifted out after the prisoner until only Jenkins and C.D. MacNamara were left.

"This is quite improper you know," MacNamara said to Jenkins.

Jenkins looked at him coldly. "The captain is responsible for administering justice on board a ship under way."

"Yes, but she is a civilian."

"Doctor, the law makes no distinction between civilian or Space Force."

"But at least a panel of co-judges . . ."

"Doctor, justice is my responsibility just as the safety of the ship is my responsibility. I cannot pass either off to anyone else."

When Jenkins got back to the bridge there was a vacuum jack waiting to see him.

"Captain, my name is William Jewett and I have to talk to you. Privately."

"Jewett? Oh, you're the man who controlled the fire in Shuttle Bay One. Come into my office." The vacuum jack followed as he led him to the cubicle.

"That was good work, Jewett," Jenkins said as he sat behind his desk.

"Thank you, sir." Jewett didn't look pleased. "That's what I wanted to talk to you about." The man licked his lips. "Sir, I know who planted those bombs in the shuttle bays."

Jenkins looked hard at him. "Well, who?"

"I did, sir," Jewett said miserably.

Jenkins touched his screen. "Commander DeRosa, come to my office immediately. I need a witness."

". . . and that's the story. Sir, I swear to you I didn't know what those things were. Splicer told me they were communication devices."

"And it never occurred to you that planting communication devices might help the Colonists learn more than we wanted them to know?" the captain rapped out.

"Well, I . . . no sir, it didn't. I was in trouble already and the way Splicer explained it to me it wouldn't hurt anything."

"This Splicer sounds like quite a smooth talker."

"Yessir. Later, I mean after the attack, I got to thinking about it. I think he was a spy of some sort."

"Mr. Jewett, you have a genius for the obvious—when it's too late."

Jewett wilted. "Yessir."

"Since the gold has already been confiscated you haven't gained anything from your actions."

"I wish I had never seen that gold, sir," Jewett said miserably.

"So do I, Mr. Jewett. But that's past. The question now is what to do with you."

"Yessir."

"You realize you very nearly destroyed the ship."

"Yessir," Jewett said, bracing himself.

"As captain, I have the authority to impose very severe penalties in a case like this."

"Yessir," Jewett said, thinking of Lulu Pine. Behind him, Iron Alice DeRosa rested her hand lightly on the butt of her pistol.

"But I can also be lenient if I choose and right now I'm inclined to so choose. Mr. Jewett, none of this will ever go beyond this cabin, if, *if*," he waggled a finger for emphasis, "you have nothing more to do with the Colonists."

"Yes sir!" Jewett said fervently.

"One other thing. I want you to keep your eyes open. If you suspect anyone is still talking to the Colonists, you are to tell me. Is that clear?"

The vacuum jack shifted apprehensively. "Yes, sir."

"Just contact with the Colonists. I don't care about vacuum stills and crap games. But if you think anyone is still dealing with the Colonists in any way, I want to know about it.

"Very well," Jenkins said, leaning back, "as far as the record is concerned, none of this happened. Don't give me cause to change that, Mr. Jewett. Now get out of here."

"Yessir!" The man rose and swam out the door.

"Lenient, aren't we?" Iron Alice said after Jewett had left.

Jenkins sighed. "Al, half the crew and two-thirds of the passengers are guilty of dealing with the Colonists."

"Most of them didn't come close to wrecking the ship."

"Most of them didn't have the opportunity. And if he nearly wrecked us, he also saved us. Besides, I keep thinking about what Father Simon said about temptation. The Colonists are experts at it. It's a wonder they didn't get us all.

"I don't need convictions," he made a face, "and I sure as hell don't need more executions. What I need now is loyalty. I think that man is going to be loyal come hell or high water."

"If he isn't you've got him by the short and curlies," DeRosa said.

"That too, but I don't think that's what's going to motivate him." He made another face. "There's one thing about guilt. It's a great driving force."

And when was the last time you heard a vacuum jack call anyone in the Space Force "sir"? DeRosa thought as she left the Captain's office.

The small ship bucked and roared as it entered the atmosphere. Even strapped in as they were, the prisoners were bounced about as the vessel shuddered and pitched.

Considering the shape of the ship there was no way the ride could have been completely smooth. Considering how little practice Colonial pilots got in atmospheric reentry, it was remarkably smooth. But the prisoners didn't know any of that. To them it was one more indignity to be borne as best they could.

Then the rockets kicked in again, slamming them back into their couches, bruising them cruelly against shapes never designed to support a human being.

And then with a thump and a final roar, it was quiet again. Sharon moved her arm to the extent the restraints allowed and realized they were under gravity, perhaps one third of a G.

"Well, we're here," Father Simon said.

Wherever here is, Sharon Dolan thought.

"It's as good as it's going to get," Clancy said irritably. He had managed perhaps four hours of sleep in the last forty-eight and he was in no mood for perfectionism.

Kirchoff continued tracing over the diagram on the screen, punching up the status of each part of the system in turn.

"This still isn't right."

"You want right, you get us back to Luna Yards," the older man replied. "It's the best we can do. It will hold." *I hope.*

Kirchoff ran his finger over the diagram once more. "Okay," he said. "Let's do it then." He reached for the comm unit.

"Stand by for spin up. Spin up in five minutes. Stand by for spin up."

The *Maxwell* had been ready for hours. All over the ship last-minute checks were run, but gear was long since stowed and everything had been checked and rechecked. Everyone on board had been anticipating the word.

Slowly and carefully, Kirchoff fed power to the spin motors.

As energy flowed into the motors, electromagnetic currents grabbed at the central shaft. There were three motors less than there should have been and the remaining ones heated rapidly. Clancy kept his eye on the temperature gauges, watching them climb to normal temperature and above. In the motor rooms improvised fans blasted off air onto the motors, cooling them somewhat. Clancy watched the temperature readings climb and kept his hand over the cutoff switch.

Ponderously, imperceptibly, the Spin section began to move.

With his attention fixed on the readouts, Kirchoff kept inching up the power. In response, Spin picked up speed gradually.

It took twice as long as normal, but all over the spun section, people and things began to float gently toward the decks.

It wasn't the smooth, easy spinup of normal conditions, but Spin was moving again. With the load in motion, the motor temperatures leveled off, then began to drop.

Kirchoff brought the speed up to a little more than two RPM and held it there. The process took nearly four hours with both Kirchoff and Clancy babying the system all the way.

Two RPM gave slightly more than one-quarter G at the rim. Not ideal, but it would be enough. Between the patch in the rim and the missing motors, neither engineer wanted to try to restore a full half-G.

Finally Kirchoff took one last look at the board. The forces on the bearings were within acceptable levels, the motor temperatures had dropped back into the normal range and everything else seemed to be working as well as expected.

"See, I told you it would hold," Clancy said tiredly.

"We'll need to patch the control system to keep a special eye on the temperature of those motors," Kirchoff said.

"Toyoda's already working on that," the older man told him. "Me, I'm going to work on getting some sleep."

"Sounds good to me. You got time for a drink?"

"Nah, I'll take a raincheck."

Side by side, the two engineers glided off down the corridor.

*　　*　　*

The humans were hustled down the corridor, stumbling on the slightly rough floor in the dim reddish light. Where the corridor joined another at right angles they were herded off to the left and up an incline.

For the most part the corridors were deserted. There were no windows and very few doors or cross corridors. Only occasionally would they glimpse a space higher or wider than the corridor.

Here and there were small groups of other Colonists dressed in shapeless ragged smocks. Mixed with them in ones and twos were Colonists in pressure suits with the terrible flexible truncheons the humans had come to know so well dangling from their belts or carried loosely in their hands.

A prison! Sharon Dolan realized. *This place is a prison.*

The others would be pressed back against the wall by their guards as the humans were rushed by. They regarded the strange prisoners with unblinking yellow eyes, showing neither interest nor surprise.

Bleak. Bleak and blasted as no place on Earth ever was. A gray-blue landscape set against gray-blue hills rolling off into the gray-blue distance with a blue-black sky pressing down upon them like a lid.

And deadly. Sharon did not have to be told that beyond the clear viewport lay death. The surface was so cold that carbon dioxide was a fine powdering of frost in the shady side of the rocks. The frail wind which stirred the finer particles was a toxic mixture of nitrogen and noble gases. The atmospheric pressure was less than one percent of Earth's.

They were in a partially buried complex on the surface of a planet. Sharon didn't know for sure, but she thought it was the furthest out of the Martiform worlds. There seemed to be miles of corridors, some tunnels burrowed into the rock and some corridors covered with a thick layer of soil.

The humans were confined to a small section of a tunnel complex. They had two large central rooms like the one Sharon was in and a number of smaller rooms off them for sleeping. Crude human-type sanitary facilities had been installed in one of the smaller rooms and the light in here was brighter and yellower than elsewhere in the complex, but that didn't make Sharon feel any more at home.

She looked out the port again and shivered. "It looks like Hell with the fires out."

"Not Hell," Father Simon corrected. "Purgatory."

They had been there only a few hours and they had already explored their new home. Now the humans were settling in as best they could. Most of them had gone to sleep, or at least retired to their own rooms. Only she and Father Simon were left in the large room.

"So," she turned away from the window and sighed. "What do we do now?"

"What all souls do in Purgatory. We wait. We endure."

On the third day in their prison they were issued portable translators, boxes about the size of a shoebox with a strap to go over the shoulder. They were heavy, bulky and not as efficient as the ones used on the ship, but they sufficed.

"I wonder why they gave them to us at all," Sharon said.

"Probably to keep track of what we say," Father Simon replied, turning the alien device over in his hands. "Presumably the actual translating is done in a central computer and undoubtedly records are kept." He smiled ruefully. "Prisoners deprived of normal means of communication are highly ingenious at inventing new ones. Presumably it is easier just to let us communicate and listen in on what we say."

"You seem to know a lot about prisoners."

The priest shrugged. "An aberration of my youth. In the meantime, we would be well advised to keep in mind that everything we say can probably be overheard."

Within a few days life had settled into a routine as dreary and gray as the landscape outside. In spite of the two guards posted constantly at the entrance to the humans' section, they were not confined to their own area.

However there was no incentive to wander. The other parts of the complex were colder and the light redder and gloomier. There was nothing to see except more tunnels and occasional knots of prisoners. Leaving the human section of the warren meant seeing aliens. The prisoners preferred to stay with their own kind and try to shut the Colonists out of their minds.

One of the worst things was there was nothing to do. Except for occasional drug interrogation sessions, the guards ignored the humans. The other prisoners were either kept away from them or kept away of their own accord.

Mostly the prisoners just slept. Sixteen hours a day was the norm and those who could manage spent twenty hours a day asleep.

Their food was mostly a porridge with no discernible texture and a sharp chemical aftertaste. The prisoners ate and ate, but still they were unsatisfied. The aliens seemed to be doing their best, but it was obvious that nutrients were missing from their diets. All the humans lost weight. Their hair grew thin and coarse and their skin became rough and scaly. Their energy level dropped even further until sometimes just staying alive was almost too much effort.

Father Simon took to walking through the tunnels for hours at a time. He didn't go far because he didn't want to get lost, but he would go for miles through the same circuit of the nearly empty corridors.

"Would any of the rest of you like to come with me?" he asked one day before he set out.

"I don't want to see another Owlie," Sharon said.

"The corridors are deserted," Father Simon told them. "Aside from the two at the door we probably won't see any Colonists at all."

Sharon thought about it. "Well," she said finally. "It sounds better than sitting around here." She stood up. "Anyone else want to come along?"

"Sure," said a little vacuum jack named Diaz. A technician named Shaw stood up and moved to join them.

At first they saw no one. Just dim corridors that echoed to the pad and scuff of their feet. No one said anything and there really wasn't much to see. There were almost no visible doors and the only breaks to the monotony came with the occasional branching of a corridor. Some of the corridors were faced with the native grayish rock and some were lined with a gray-blue paneling. There wasn't quite enough light for humans and the red tinge made colors dark and dull. The air was chill and dry and soon the others were shivering in spite of the exercise.

The route Father Simon had chosen led to a larger, wider corridor that angled back toward their quarters. But this corridor wasn't deserted. A few hundred meters along they met a small group of prisoners and four or five guards under an officer coming toward them.

The humans shrank to the side to let the Colonists pass. As the aliens drew alongside, one of the prisoners was falling behind. The guard at the rear roared at him and brandished his truncheon, but the prisoner replied weakly and continued to lag.

The guard came up to the prisoner and waved his club again. The corridor rang with the shrieks and roars of alien speech, too fast for the humans' translators to decipher.

Then the guard whipped his truncheon sideways across the muzzle of the prisoner and the prisoner's head snapped to the side as if his neck was broken. He dropped limply to the stone floor. The guard stood over him and kept bellowing at the fallen Colonist.

The prisoner shook his head and tried to rise on all fours but the guard hit him again and again across the back with his club.

Sharon turned her face to the wall and bit her lip to keep from screaming. The men stood wide-eyed and shocked, too horrified to turn away.

The prisoner made one more effort to rise and then crumpled and lay still. The guard stood over him, breathing heavily through his slightly open beak. Then he grunted explosively and turned away.

As if he was sleepwalking, Father Simon moved away from the other humans and walked to the fallen alien. Two guards moved to block him, their truncheons raised. The priest looked levelly into their huge yellow eyes and kept coming. When he was almost close enough to touch them the guards fell back.

Father Simon knelt over the alien. The Colonist shivered and his breath came in great racking sobs. Then he convulsed and lay still. The priest bowed his head and his lips moved as he recited a prayer. Then he crossed himself and rose to face the guards.

"What did you do?" the guard commander demanded through the translator.

"I offered a prayer for his soul."

It took a long time for that to translate, but apparently the explanation was satisfactory. The alien backed away and motioned the other prisoners to drag off the corpse.

Father Simon and the others watched until the procession was out of sight.

Sharon was white and shaking. "Does this happen all the time?" she asked.

"I have never seen anything like it before," replied the priest, equally white and just as shaky.

"All the same, I think I'm going to stay in our rooms. This place is horrible!" She raised her face to glare at the priest. "And what in the *world* possessed you to do a thing like that?"

Father Simon frowned. "I really don't know," he said slowly. "Reflex, I suppose."

"Not smart, man," Diaz said. "They could have killed you."

"No, it wasn't very smart," Father Simon agreed. Then he sighed. "Come on. Let's go back."

There were no repercussions, no reprisals. The aliens ignored the incident as if it had never happened and the humans didn't talk about it. But after the scene in the tunnel no one wanted to accompany Father Simon on his walks.

The priest wasn't eager to go out again either. For two days he stayed in the human quarters. But finally the need for movement drove him out.

He didn't go far. He stayed on a circuit close by that brought him past the entrance to the human area and its two guards every few hundred yards. The guards ignored him as they always did and the priest tried to ignore them and the flexible bludgeons hanging from their harness.

He was making his fourth or fifth circuit when a Colonist stepped out of a side tunnel and blocked his way.

"I would speak with you."

The alien was tall and lean, even by the standards of this race. To Father Simon's eye he looked old, although the priest wasn't sure how to tell the age of Colonists. But the most remarkable thing about him was that he was missing an eye. A ragged scar ran from his muzzle back over the socket and almost to the top of his head leaving bare dark skin showing. The scar and the missing eye made him look piratical and sinister.

"You are the truth-seeker among the humans." The voice came out of the translator as a statement, not a question.

226

"I am a scientist, yes," Father Simon said uneasily. It was almost unprecedented for any alien prisoner to talk to the humans and there was nothing in the appearance of this one to inspire confidence.

"Not science, *truth*."

"I beg your pardon?"

"Truth," the alien repeated, so loudly Father Simon's ears rang. "The thing-ness of all things. The nature of the first and the last. That which separates that which *is* from that which is *not*. The forces which regulate beings in their orbits."

The Colonist stopped and looked expectantly at the priest, head cocked to one side like a bird's.

"Ah, you mean philosophy?" Father Simon asked.

"Truth," the Colonist bellowed firmly.

He laid a hand on Father Simon's arm. It was the first time the priest had ever felt an alien's naked skin. It was soft and warm.

"I too am a truth seeker. I wish to speak of truth with you."

The priest looked at the alien. *It would be a diversion*, he thought. "Very well," he said. "Where shall we go?"

A few yards down the tunnel from the humans' quarters there was an alcove cut into the rock with a rock shelf or ledge running around it waist-high. From the holes drilled into stone and the oil stains on the floor, Father Simon assumed it had housed machinery of some sort. Now it was empty and it made a convenient place to sit and talk.

"Here I am called One-Eye," the alien said, squatting down on the stone floor.

"I am called Father Simon."

"Fathersimon," the Colonist repeated, although what came out of his mouth bore little resemblance to the translation. "Are you named or titled?"

"I beg your pardon?"

"Are you called by a rank-name within your lineage or the name of the function you perform?"

"Both. My name is Simon, which corresponds to what you call a rank-name. I am a priest, so I am given the title 'Father.' "

"Priest?"

"A member of a religious order."

The Colonist tossed his head in assent. "A cult leader as well as a philosopher, then."

"And you?" the priest asked. "Are you named or titled?"

"For us there are no titles here," the Colonist told him. "Nor rank-names either. We are named or pick names that suit us. But, come, tell me of your kind's truth."

Where to begin? "We call it 'philosophy,' which means 'love of wisdom' in one of our ancient languages."

"It is good to love wisdom," One-Eye declared. "From Wisdom flows true happiness."

"What does this wisdom consist of?"

"To know the truth. To separate the true pleasures from the false."

"This is important for us as well," Father Simon told him.

The man and the alien talked for nearly three hours in the chilly alcove cut into the gray rock. Most of the time was spent trying to define terms. Finally, when Father Simon had talked himself hoarse and One-Eye seemed to have taken on as many foreign philosophical terms as he could absorb, they parted.

"This is most excellent, Fathersimon," One-Eye said. "Perhaps we can continue again tomorrow."

"I would be honored," the priest told the alien.

"You were gone a long time today," Sharon said to him when he got back. "What happened?"

"I'm not sure," Father Simon said. "I think I made a friend."

As the days dragged on, Father Simon spent more and more time with One-Eye. The alien would squat in the alcove while Father Simon perched on the ledge and they would talk for hours.

"Won't you get in trouble for talking to us?" Father Simon asked One-Eye one day.

The alien made a hissing sound Father Simon knew for a kind of laughter. "What would they do?" he asked. "Separate me from my lineage? Deprive me of my title and honors? Imprison me?" He gestured about him.

"The truly wise man cannot be imprisoned. His body, of course,"—One-Eye made an overall twitch that was the Colonists' equivalent of a shrug—"but his essence, his is-ness, cannot be confined, save by his own action or by wrong thinking."

"They could kill you if they thought the offense serious enough," the priest pointed out.

"Killing me would take me out of this place," One-Eye said. "It would free my essence from this world and its evils and that does not seem to me to be a punishment. Besides," he went on more practically, "as long as we stay in our places they do not care what we do here."

"I do not mean to pry, but why were you sent here? What crime did you commit?"

One-Eye drew himself up. "Crime? I committed no wrong action. I was simply inconvenient to the Elders of the Inner Grove and Derfuhrer." He twitched a shrug again. "It is true of almost everyone here."

"That's terrible," Father Simon said.

"It is so in all Colonies. There are always inconvenient ones and they are always sent to a place of detention. The difference is that in this planet Derfuhrer has a bigger, better place than most." He looked around and hissed. "It is most excellent, do you not agree?"

"You said that if you died your soul would go someplace else. Where do you believe your soul will go?"

One-Eye considered. "That is a matter of debate. Some, such as the followers of the True Form, think that essences are forever reborn according to merit. Others say that at death our essences will reunite with the Essence of the Universe. For myself, I think that when we die our essence is extinguished with our bodies. How say your philosophers?"

"We have schools that believe all of those things," Father Simon told the Colonist. "My own—ah—school's teacher told us that our souls live after us and that after death they will be judged. If we have lived rightly and in wisdom, our souls will live with our God, who is much like the essence of the universe. If we have not lived rightly or refused wisdom, then we will be punished."

One-Eye froze. "Your school has a god? Like a cult?"

"I am not sure this is translating correctly, but, yes, what you call our school is a direct outgrowth of our religion."

"Strange, Fathersimon. Strange indeed. Perhaps we had best leave this until your translator becomes more fluent."

"Very well," the priest said. "But what about your gods?"

One-Eye made a dismissing gesture. "There are no gods. Or if there are, they pay no attention to our affairs."

"Some of us believe that there is a single God and that He is constantly active in human affairs," the priest told the alien.

"Outworn doctrine," One-Eye snorted and changed the subject.

The next time Father Simon came to the alcove, there were two other Colonists with One-Eye. One of them was about One-Eye's height and the other was smaller and more slender. Both of them wore the dark tan smocks of prisoners.

"Jawbone and Fruitpicker," One-Eye introduced his companions. "They are also seekers after truth."

"I am of the students of the True Forms," said the one called Jawbone proudly. "Before, I was a teacher among them."

Fruitpicker said nothing.

"Tell me of the differences between your truth and ours," Jawbone demanded, settling himself on the floor next to One-Eye.

Father Simon leaned back against the rock wall.

"There are many differences and many things the same," he said. "Our seekers after truth have had many of the same thoughts, followed many of the same lines of speculation. But there are also differences.

"Now you center your philosophies on ethics, the search for right action. Some of our philosophy is concerned with that, but more of it deals with other issues."

"What else should philosophy deal with than truth and the search for right action?" Fruitpicker asked.

"Some of us believe that the fundamental questions of ethics have been answered, so many of our philosophers have moved on to other matters."

All three aliens leaned forward. "How did you answer them?"

"Our religion provides the answers to those questions."

"Your cults deal in such matters?" Jawbone asked.

"Our religions—great cults—do," Father Simon said. "They are the legacy of great teachers and their followers strive to live according to their precepts."

"Strange, to mix cult and wisdom so," said Jawbone.

"Don't your cults command you to right action?"

Jawbone and One-Eye looked at each other.

230

"That is a matter on which we differ," One-Eye said. "As I told you, I do not believe there are gods. Cults have no place in the search for wisdom."

"I too do not believe there are gods as the cults teach of them," Jawbone said. "But there is a Universal Essence and the essence in each of us is a clouded mirror of that great essence.

"When one dies, one's essence returns according to his merits," Jawbone went on. "Those who have lived a virtuous life are reborn to a higher station closer to the trunk of the Great Lineage. Those who have done evil are reborn further out on the branches or even as animals. Thus are we rewarded and punished according to our desserts."

"But tell me," said Father Simon, "does an essence remember its previous life?"

"Of course not," said Fruitpicker.

"Then the essence does not know that it is being punished when it is reborn as an animal or rewarded when it returns as a higher person?"

"That is so," the Colonist admitted.

"Then tell me, how can this be effective reward or punishment when the essence is unconscious of it?"

Jawbone snorted explosively.

One-Eye hissed with laughter. "Most excellent, Fathersimon. Most excellent indeed."

"I did not originate the argument," Father Simon said. "A man we call Justin Martyr stated it two thousand years ago."

"Was he named or titled?" One-Eye asked.

"Both," Father Simon told him. "Justin was his name and he was a martyr."

There was a long pause for the translation.

"Explain martyr," One-Eye commanded at last.

"A martyr is one who died voluntarily for our faith or for the preservation of some Christian virtue."

"Voluntarily? You mean such a one deliberately chose death?"

"Yes."

"And this was in accordance with the will of your Teacher?"

"We believe so."

The alien snorted explosively. "Foolish to order one's followers to commit suicide in such a way."

"We believe there are some things worse than death here

231

and now," the priest told him. "What would you do if you were commanded to deny your beliefs on pain of death?"

"Deny them of course. Saying a thing is not so does not make it not so."

"We are commanded always to speak the truth about what we believe."

One-Eye snorted again.

"If what I say bothers you so much, why do you keep talking to me?"

"Because it passes the time," One-Eye told him. "Because I find your cult's school of truth-seeking strange and perhaps in some ways superior to others I have known. It is always wisdom to seek to learn new truths, even when they cannot profit you directly, is it not?"

"And besides," the Colonist added practically, "perhaps some day I shall walk among the living again. Then I could open a school and grow rich teaching this new wisdom." All three aliens hissed with laughter.

One day Father Simon came out to find that Fruitpicker was not there. One-Eye and Jawbone carried on as if nothing unusual had happened, so Father Simon said nothing. But the next day Fruitpicker was still missing, and the day after that as well.

"Where is Fruitpicker?" Father Simon asked after several days.

"He has turned his face to the wall," Jawbone said. "He will be with us no more."

Father Simon crossed himself. "You mean he died?"

"His essence is still in his body, but not for long," One-Eye told the priest.

"What's wrong with him?"

"He has turned his face to the wall," repeated Jawbone.

"But why?" demanded Father Simon.

One-Eye twitched a shrug. "Why does anyone do this? There are many things. Some die in their proper time. There is much sickness here. The food is sparse and poor. Some decide to die or simply give up. Of course the weight of this place presses cruelly."

Father Simon realized that although the gravity here was little more than a third of Earth-normal, it must be terrible to creatures who had never known anything more than one-quarter G.

"Life is hard," Jawbone said simply.

"But what's wrong with Fruitpicker?"

"I do not know," One-Eye said.

"Have you seen him?"

"We do not share a roost."

"I mean have you been to visit him?"

One-Eye looked surprised. "No. Why should I?"

"He is your friend."

"Friendship like all things of the here-and-now is fleeting," One-Eye said. "We meet, we part. To fasten onto such happenstance is to trouble oneself unnecessarily."

"It doesn't trouble you that your friend is dying?"

One-Eye gave another of the alien shrugs. "It is not a cause for regret. Each of us dies soon or late and we can do nothing to stop it. Soon Fruitpicker's soul will be freed. Then he will be happier than those who are left behind. There is no need to visit him."

"Well, he is *my* friend," Father Simon said firmly. "Will you take me to him?"

"This shows lack of wisdom," One-Eye grumbled.

"There are many different kinds of wisdom," Father Simon told the alien tartly.

"My wisdom commands me to stay here," One-Eye said.

"My wisdom and my Teacher tell me to go to a person who might need me. Will you show me the way?"

Jawbone rose. "I will take you."

The room was as large as the common room of the humans, but there were perhaps fifty Colonists packed into it. They squatted or lay along the walls or shuffled listlessly about. The cold dry air was thick with the smell of them.

Off in the distance he could hear a Colonist bellowing. The voice lacked the modulation and differentiation he had come to associate with the aliens' speech. It was merely the sound of pain, or perhaps madness.

"He is there," Jawbone said, pointing. Heedless of the alien stares, Father Simon picked his way over to him.

Fruitpicker lay on a pallet against the far wall. His feathers were fluffed out and his great yellow eyes were glazed. His beak was slightly open and his breath seemed to come irregularly.

233

"Hello, Fruitpicker," Father Simon said.

The alien started and his eyes seemed to focus.

His taloned fingers clutched Father Simon's arm until the points pricked the skin and drew blood.

"How are you?" the priest asked.

"I progress, Fathersimon. I move in my ordained path."

"Are you in pain?"

Fruitpicker hissed weakly. "What is pain to a philosopher, eh?"

"Is there anything I can get you?"

"Water."

Father Simon turned back to Jawbone who was standing by the door. "He wants water. Is there any here?"

The Colonist motioned to one side of the room and the priest saw a metal fitting on the wall with a large flat bowl under it. One or two of the other Colonists snorted and grumbled at him as he picked up the bowl and filled it with water, but none of them tried to stop him. He brought the bowl back to where Fruitpicker lay and the Colonist lapped greedily with his thick black tongue.

At last he raised his head from the bowl. "Thank you, Fathersimon," he said. His voice dropped to a mutter and his breathing became more regular and less labored. The priest whispered a prayer and blessed him.

"I will come again tomorrow if I can," Father Simon told him and left the room.

"The others in the room didn't seem to care what happened to him either," Father Simon said to Jawbone as they made their way back through the corridors. "Are they philosophers too?"

Jawbone hissed. "Not them. But they have seen it many times before."

"Why didn't they try to help him?"

Jawbone twitched a shrug. "We are many different lineages, sub-lineages and clans all mixed together here. Fortunate is the one who has lineage-mates to aid him. But most of us owe little or nothing to those around us and we can expect little or nothing from them."

They walked along in silence. "Does this happen often?" Father Simon asked.

"All the time."

The priest stopped and faced his companion. "Can you find out for me when others have turned their faces to the wall?"

"Why would you want to know a thing like that?"

"So that I can go to them and give them what help I can."

"But they are not of your school," Jawbone said. "You do not know them."

"We are taught that whether of our school or not, all men are bound together. That what we do to the least of them is as if we did it to our Teacher himself."

"But we are not men," Jawbone objected.

"Our Teacher defined 'man' very broadly," Father Simon replied.

So Father Simon added visiting sick and dying aliens to his daily routine. There was nothing he could do for any of them. He had no food to give them, no medicine. He could not even minister to their hurts. All he could do was sit and talk to the Colonists, bless them and pray for them. But something compelled him to go on.

In Fruitpicker's case it didn't matter. When Father Simon returned the next day, the Colonist was gone. He didn't have to be told what had happened to him.

One-Eye disapproved of the priest's new habits and he wasn't shy about saying so. Jawbone was more tolerant, if no more understanding. The school of the True Forms believed that acts of merit could affect a soul's rebirth, but the alien didn't understand how what Father Simon was doing could be considered meritorious.

"You blur the boundaries ordained by the Universal Essence," Jawbone complained one day as they sat talking philosophy. "You treat strangers as kin. Next you will be treating enemies as friends."

"Our Teacher told us we must love our enemies as we love ourselves."

Jawbone hissed with laughter. "Even those who imprison you here?"

"Especially those," Father Simon told him. "Especially those are we commanded to love."

"Yes," said One-Eye with growing excitement. "Yes. By loving those who wrong you, you free yourself from bondage to them. You gain closure on the past and your essence is free to move onward."

"Uh, that's certainly part of it," the priest said.

"Oh excellent," One-Eye said, rocking back and forth and holding onto himself. "Oh, most excellent wisdom. Thank you Fathersimon. Thank you."

One-Eye and Jawbone weren't the only ones who had opinions about Father Simon's actions. The humans thought he had cracked up, and the priest was developing a reputation among the other prisoners as well.

"They call you a sorcerer," One-Eye told him one day, hissing with amusement. "They think you visit those who have turned their faces to the wall to steal their essences."

"I am sorry to hear that," Father Simon said.

"There are others who deny that you steal essences. Some who had turned their faces to the wall turned them again after you visited them. They proclaim you a great healer who comes among us to do good." He hissed more loudly. "Of course that makes you an even bigger sorcerer to them."

"How can I show them that I am not a sorcerer?"

"You cannot," One-Eye snapped. "You cannot because they are credulous fools. Although they are less to blame than you. They have no notion of what constitutes wisdom. You know wisdom and you twist it by mixing it with cult-stuff."

"For me, wisdom grows directly from my religion. It is not alien to religion, it is an integral part of it."

"It leads to dangerous confusions," One-Eye said.

"You have not yet found a logical flaw," Father Simon said mildly.

The old philosopher snorted explosively.

Father Simon had noticed that One-Eye had been growing more intense in his arguments for some time. Ever since the incident with Fruitpicker, the Colonist had been questioning him more sharply, probing harder for weaknesses or holes in his arguments. The easy, scholarly air that had pervaded their earlier discussions was gone and in its place was almost a hostility. Occasionally One-Eye would find something in what Father Simon said that would make him rock back and forth with excitement, but mostly he was an inquisitor determined to find flaws.

The final break came in a discussion of the nature of God. Specifically while he and Jawbone were talking about the differences between the True Forms' Universal Essence and the Christian God.

". . . So you believe this force being directly influences other beings?" Jawbone asked the priest while One-Eye sat by and fidgeted.

"Yes."

"He influences your life?"

"Yes. I have felt Him. Just as I have felt gravity."

"But gravity *is*," Jawbone protested.

"Show me gravity," Father Simon challenged. "Measure me off a meter of gravity, weigh me out a kilogram, or just draw me a picture."

"Absurd," said One-Eye. "One does not see gravity. One knows it by its effects."

"So it is with God's love," said Father Simon.

"Preposterous!" said One-Eye. "Your god is filled with love for all beings, is he not?"

"Yes."

"And your god is all-seeing and all-powerful."

"So we believe."

"Then why is there pain and misery in the world? Eh?" He cocked his head. "Why do we suffer so?"

"Because one of God's gifts is free will. God leaves each being free to choose his or her own orbit. We may act rightly or wrongly and although it pains God greatly when we act wrongly, He will not interfere. He leaves us free to work out our own destinies."

"A difficulty," Jawbone put in. "How can beings' orbits be unconstrained if this all-powerful, all-knowing force exists?"

"The force itself is a being with its own will. It wills that we should be free to choose our own orbits. God knows the outcome because God's knowledge is infinite. He comprehends all space and time because He stands outside space and time. Thus He knows what the outcome will be, but He chooses to allow us to exercise our free will."

Jawbone grunted, a harsh, coughing bark. "Plausible."

"But let us return to the main point," said One-Eye. "You say that your god knows the outcome?"

"He does."

"And he knows that many beings will choose wrongly?"

"He knows that."

"And further, that because of those wrong choices these beings will be punished?"

"Yes."

"Then why does this god who loves all things allow them free will when it means eternal misery for many of them?"

"We do not know the complete answer to that," the priest said. "God is beyond complete human understanding. We do know that God can draw good out of physical evil and that pain and trial can draw us closer to God."

"So your perfectly good being, for reasons you cannot know, sanctions wrong actions and then punishes those who make it? He stands idly by and watches as the innocent are murdered? He countenances condemning the blameless to a living death? This is absurd!"

"It is a difficulty, certainly," Father Simon replied. "But as you recognize, a difficulty does not necessarily make a doubt. Further, I can demonstrate to you that the problem cannot be so stated as to show any absolute contradiction."

The philosopher froze. "This is not wisdom, this is madness!" One-Eye roared at last. "You confuse and corrupt us with your unnatural ways. I will have no more of it." With that the Colonist rose and stalked out into the corridor.

Jawbone hesitated and then got up and followed.

". . . And he just walked off," Father Simon said when he told Sharon Dolan about the incident that evening.

"It sounds like you offended him," Sharon said.

"I know, but I can't for the life of me understand how."

"Some people don't like to lose arguments. I guess Owlies are the same way."

Father Simon frowned. "One-Eye didn't seem like the kind of man who'd get mad just because he was bested in a philosophical discussion."

"He's not a man," Sharon said sharply. "He's an Owlie."

"Right now he's a mystery," the priest said. "I still wish I knew what I did."

It was several days before Father Simon saw either One-Eye or Jawbone again. By this time he was familiar enough with the warrens that he was able to continue his rounds without a guide. He missed the aliens and their talks, but he didn't understand what had happened. And even if he knew what to apologize for, he didn't know where to find either of the Colonists.

Then one morning, Father Simon found One-Eye waiting for him outside the door.

"I came to admit to you that you are right," One-Eye said. "For many cycles I have sought the tranquility that wisdom and right action could bring me." His beak was slightly open and he was panting as if in pain. "I thought that I had found it, but I see now that I was in error. You have shown me a better way and I wish to understand it fully."

One-Eye crouched before the priest.

"Fathersimon, I beg you to initiate me into the mysteries of your cult."

"What?" Father Simon gasped.

"Please Fathersimon. I wish to be of the body and blood of the Christ."

"That . . . that's not a simple matter, One-Eye," Father Simon licked his lips.

"I will do whatever is necessary."

"I will have to think on this," the priest muttered. "Excuse me." He turned and hurried back through the guarded portal into the human quarters.

Next to Father Simon, Sharon Dolan left the human quarters the most of all the humans. She didn't go far, but sometimes the boredom and the cabin fever drove her past the guards at the door and out into the nearby corridors.

She was very careful where she went and at the least sign of a Colonist she would backtrack or hide. Thus she was all the more surprised when an alien voice boomed out behind her as she was coming down the corridor. Sharon screamed and jumped.

There was One-Eye. "I would speak with you," the translation came.

Sharon recognized him, of course. "If—if I can," she said, placing her hand on her chest.

"I did not mean to perturb your harmony," the alien said, making a conscious effort to lower his voice.

"That's all right," Sharon told him. "You just startled me."

"You are the one called Sharon who is the friend of Fathersimon?"

"I am one of his friends," Sharon told him. "All humans are friends here." *Except for Aubrey!*

"Yes, Fathersimon has told me." The alien hissed. "Most excellent wisdom. You have influence with him, is this not so?"

"Well, some I suppose," Sharon said hesitantly. "What is it you want?"

"Truth!" exclaimed One-Eye, forgetting to modulate his voice. "I wish to learn the cult wisdom of Fathersimon. Please Sharon, I beg you to use your influence that he will resume teaching us."

Sharon found the priest alone in the common room, sitting slumped over with his hands clasped between his knees.

"Father, I just met One-Eye in the corridor. He had an odd request."

Father Simon looked up. "What was that?"

"He wanted me to use my influence with you so you would teach him." She paused, unsure. "I think he wants to learn about Christianity."

Father Simon closed his eyes and sighed.

"I know," he said softly. "I know."

"Father, excuse me, but what the hell is going on?"

The priest smiled a strained smile.

"I seem to have started something quite by accident. One-Eye and I got to talking because I wanted to learn more about the Colonists' philosophies. He was apparently a philosopher of some note before he was imprisoned, you know.

"Of course I talked to him about human philosophies and one thing led to another and I told him about Christianity."

"Catholic Christianity, naturally."

"It *is* the kind I am most familiar with," Father Simon said dryly. "In any event, the next thing I knew he wanted to convert."

Sharon goggled. "An *alien* wanted to become a Catholic? Forgive me Father, but you must be one hell of a preacher!"

Father Simon grimaced. "You find that odd?"

"Well, Christianity is a human religion."

"Strictly speaking, it is not. Our Lord commanded that the Gospel be spread to all men and unless you want to limit the term 'men' to male humans only . . ." he trailed off and sat wrapped in thought.

"Yes, but don't the Colonists have their own religions?"

"Well, yes and no apparently. They have a huge number of cults, including a major cult of ancestor worship, and they have a kind of state ritual centered around the sun and civic virtue. They also have a strong belief in what we'd call astrology. But those aren't complete religions."

"And Catholicism is."

"Christianity is. Catholicism is the most fully developed version of Christianity in this regard. But for that matter most of the major religions are complete religions."

He sighed and shifted position again.

"Miss Dolan, religion meets some of the most fundamental needs of a thinking being. It answers questions like 'who am I' and 'why am I here.' All the major human religions—Christianity, Judaism, Islam, Buddhism, even Hinduism—share certain characteristics. They provide an ethical system, a basis for philosophy and a source of spiritual comfort. They appeal to the whole being.

"Cults generally don't. They may provide part of that, especially spiritual comfort, but most are deficient as a source of ethics and their philosophical underpinnings are anything but consistent—or even coherent in most cases."

"And that's important?"

"For some people that's vital. If you move beyond the simple act of belief it becomes increasingly important. First ethics—what is right action?—and then the larger, philosophical questions."

"You're saying that the Colonists don't have that?"

"Not in one piece. These people supplement their cults with philosophies. Their philosophy is quite sophisticated, but like human schools of philosophy they are not very comforting. And the ethics commanded by their philosophers are an uneasy mix with their cults."

He sighed again. "It's an old, old story. It happened a lot on Earth and that had a great deal to do with the spread of Christianity. Christianity has something that these people seem never to have encountered before. Apparently some of them find it very attractive."

"Why won't you teach them then?" Sharon asked.

The priest looked pained. "Miss Dolan, it's not that simple, believe me."

241

"Is it that you're afraid they might not have souls?"

"No, no. It has been generally accepted for years that aliens that have sufficient intelligence are presumed to have souls." He flicked a nervous smile at her. "Subject to contrary proof, of course, but I see none of that here."

"Then why won't you convert them? Isn't that what a priest is supposed to do?"

"It is what *some* priests are supposed to do. Miss Dolan, I am not a missionary. I do not have permission from my superiors to act as one."

"Is *that* all?"

"Believe me, that is quite a sufficient impediment. There are strict canons about who may act as a missionary, a legacy of some of the excesses of the twentieth century. Without the proper license I cannot work as a missionary."

"But you're here and they are not."

"That does not change things. I do not have the authority for missionary work." He shook his head.

"The Church foresaw some situations when we went into space. We are no longer bound to use only olive oil, wine and wheaten bread in the sacraments, for instance, not in an emergency. We saw the need for so many things. But this . . . this goes beyond anything anyone imagined."

"What are you going to do?" Sharon asked, resting a hand on his shoulder.

He reached up and patted it. "I don't know, Miss Dolan. I honestly don't know."

When he came out the next day, One-Eye and Jawbone were waiting for him.

"Did Sharon tell you my request?" One-Eye asked the priest.

"She did." He sighed. "I am very sorry, but I cannot do as you ask. Under the rules of my kind I am not allowed to make converts. I was not given that authority before we left because we did not know we would meet other reasoning beings."

One-Eye stood motionless for a long time. "Then I will live as you have taught us that I may share in this wisdom as far as you will allow and that I may be a constant reproach to you."

"And I also," said Jawbone.

"I am sorry," Father Simon said again.

Whenever Father Simon left the human quarters, One-Eye would be waiting for him. He accompanied him on his visits to the other prisoners and he and Jawbone took to visiting the sick prisoners as well. They still talked philosophy, but Father Simon tried to steer the discussion away from theology as much as he could.

One-Eye wasn't always in attendance on Father Simon. He would go off on his own visits to the sick or on other alien business. But the priest never knew when he would look up and find the one-eyed philosopher standing quietly behind him, watching him with his single good eye.

Father Simon had a general idea what One-Eye was doing but he didn't find out the details until some time later, and quite by accident.

The priest was out on one of his solitary walks, increasingly rare now because of the press of other business. He had reached the furthest point on his circuit and he was getting ready to turn back when he saw someone in the distance coming down the corridor.

Father Simon wasn't afraid of the aliens like Sharon Dolan, but he tried to avoid them in deserted areas. So he slipped back into an alcove off a side tunnel. It wasn't until the Colonist was almost on top of him that he recognized One-Eye.

The alien was moving down the corridor with a sack over his shoulder. At every intersection he stopped and looked in all directions, swivelling his head nearly all the way around to look over his shoulders with his single good eye. Then he padded stealthily on.

Father Simon waited until the Colonist was well out of sight. Then he walked back in the other direction and sought out Jawbone.

The Colonist was squatting in a corridor talking to two other aliens. When the priest approached, Jawbone's companions withdrew respectfully.

"They still fear you a little, Fathersimon," Jawbone explained with a hiss of laughter. Then he looked at the priest with his huge yellow eyes and became more serious. "Since it is not time for our talks, you must want to see me about something else. What?"

"What is One-Eye up to?"

Jawbone twitched a shrug. "Inspired by your cult he seeks wisdom. What else?"

"What does seeking wisdom have to do with sneaking around carrying a sack?"

The Colonist looked at him intently. "Who told you this thing?"

"I saw it. Just now. He was carrying something in a bag and he was trying very hard not to be seen."

Jawbone looked up and down the corridor to make sure they were alone. Then he leaned close to the priest.

"One-Eye has been collecting food from the other prisoners to take to the ones in the outer tunnels."

"Outer tunnels?" Father Simon asked blankly.

"This was once a much larger place," Jawbone explained. "There are many tunnels which are unmaintained and uninhabited. Some of them still have pressure."

"What is out there?"

Jawbone stared at him. "You do not know? No, for your kind are valuable and kept safe and cosseted. Well, we are not. Not all of us have the breeding or wisdom to turn our faces to the wall when this place becomes unendurable. Others become lost within themselves, sometimes quietly, sometimes dangerously. When one becomes so lost as to be uncontrollable, the guards drive that one into the outer tunnels. There they wander to live or die as Heaven wills."

Father Simon stared at him. "And One-Eye has been going there alone?"

Jawbone tossed his head in agreement. "The ways in to the Outer Tunnels are sealed and guarded. But One-Eye is very old. He has been here longer than any other one, I think. Certainly he knows things about this place that not even the guards know. Including how to get in and out of those places."

"That is dangerous, isn't it?"

"More than you know, perhaps. We are not allowed to go outside our tunnels and the guards would kill him if they caught him. But worse, he gets other prisoners to cooperate with him. The one thing the guards fear above all else is that we will make alliance against them. They do not know about his trips to the outer tunnels, but they do know that he causes prisoners to cooperate. It is all very dangerous."

"If he is not careful something terrible will happen to him," Father Simon said.

"He tests them and through them himself," Jawbone told him. "This will end badly, I think."

The next day, Father Simon sought out One-Eye in one of the tunnels near the sleeping quarters.

"I understand you have been going into the outer tunnels to help the people there," the priest said as they walked along.

"I have," One-Eye said serenely.

"I appreciate your efforts and I honor you for them, but I urge you to be careful."

One-Eye hissed. "I am always careful, Fathersimon."

"I would also urge that you do not throw your life away."

The alien stopped and faced the priest. "Fathersimon, you are not my priest so you are not responsible for my conscience. I must do as my conscience commands me."

"I think what you do, you do for pride," the priest told him. "That is a sin."

One-Eye fixed him with his yellow unblinking eye. "Perhaps I err, for I have no teacher. But I try to help those who need help that I may grow in wisdom."

The guards came early in the morning.

Roaring and screaming, they rousted the sleeping humans from their beds and hustled them out into the corridor in a confused, shivering knot.

There were more guards waiting there, with an officer to direct them. Two of the guards held a Colonist in a prisoner's smock slumped over between them. It took Father Simon a second look to realize that the prisoner was One-Eye.

He was shrunken and quivering, with dark patches of blood on his fur/feathers. The talons of one hand were twisted and crushed and the forearm hung at an odd angle. But when he saw the humans with Father Simon in the front he straightened up and stood as proudly as the guards holding him would allow.

The officer gave One-Eye a contemptuous look and then stalked over to the priest.

"This one has acted wrongly," the alien roared, sticking his beak in Father Simon's face and speaking so loudly that the priest's ears rang. "You are commanded to command him to stop."

"If he has acted to harm you then of course he should

245

stop," Father Simon replied. "But he is not under my orders and he will not obey me." He breathed deeply. "Even if he were I cannot order him to go against his own beliefs."

"I obey only my own conscience," One-Eye said from where the guards held him. One of the guards smashed him across the back with a truncheon and he lurched forward in the grasp of his captors.

The officer snapped his beak in Father Simon's face and in spite of himself the priest flinched back. Then he stalked away from him to where the guards held One-Eye. He thrust his muzzle into One-Eye's face and yelled at him.

The words came too fast for the humans' translators, but the din was terrible. Several humans clasped their hands over their ears to try to shut out the noise.

One-Eye waited without moving until the officer finished with a beak snap like an explosion.

"No," One-Eye told him.

The officer bristled. His fur/feathers puffed out away from his body and his beak clacked like a gunshot ringing through the tunnel. The guards let go of the Colonist and stepped away from him. Sharon paled and clutched Father Simon's arm. The priest bit his lip.

One-Eye stood unmoved and apparently unaffected by the display, calmly waiting what might come next.

The officer gestured and the guards with him raised their lasers. Even as the beams lanced out One-Eye raised his arm as if to bless them.

Three streaks of searing brightness crossed and struck the Colonist in the chest. Father Simon gasped and Sharon screamed, but One-Eye crumpled without a sound.

"You must be proud of him," Sharon Dolan murmured as the guards dragged the body of One-Eye off down the tunnel.

"I did not come here to make martyrs," Father Simon replied stiffly and turned away.

The other humans filed wordlessly back into their quarters. Father Simon remained outside, looking at the stained spot on the rough rock floor where it had happened and praying for the soul of One-Eye.

He was still there several hours later when Jawbone motioned him further down the tunnel, out of earshot of the door guards.

"I am sorry, Fathersimon. They would not let any of us near this place."

"I am sorry too, Jawbone," the priest said sadly.

The alien twitched a shrug. "One-Eye was not sorry, I think. He had found what he sought." He hissed. "A strange place to find ultimate wisdom, no? In death?"

Father Simon didn't say anything for a long time. "I hope he found what he sought afterwards as well."

"Is such a reward possible for one who is not a member of your cult?"

"Well, there are exceptions of course . . ." he started. "Oh, I don't know!" he burst out. "I'm sick of theology, I'm sick of philosophy. And I'm sick of this place." For the first time since seminary, Father Michael Simon began to cry. "God help me, I just don't know any more!"

Jawbone reached out a taloned hand and patted the priest's shoulder gently.

"Forgive me, Jawbone," Father Simon said finally. "I'm . . . well, please forgive me."

"I understand, Fathersimon. It comes to all of us here." He paused, his great yellow eyes fixed on the human.

"There is one other thing. One-Eye knew this would come soon. So he showed me the secret ways to the outer tunnels." He shuddered slightly. "Truly it is terrible there. But his work will go on. I will do it and now there are others besides."

"Please be careful," the priest urged. Then he paled.

"Oh my God! The translator! They've heared every word we've said." He looked down in horror at the box slung off his shoulder.

Jawbone hissed. "The recording? No one ever listens to them. Do you think I would talk to you like this otherwise?" Then he made the alien gesture of negation. "No, never fear, Fathersimon, I will be very careful. I am not so willing as One-Eye to learn ultimate wisdom yet."

With that he turned and strode off up the tunnel. Father Simon said another prayer and then went back to the human place.

The guards came again later that evening. Four of them, with lasers ready. Without a word they moved into the common room where the humans were eating and arrayed themselves along the wall.

"Fathersimon come with us," their leader roared out.

Father Simon placed his spoon on the table and rose.

"*No!*" Sharon screamed and jumped up. The guards leveled their rifles and stepped forward. The humans on either side of her grabbed her and pulled her down again.

"It's all right Miss Dolan, they won't hurt me." The priest stepped around the table and the aliens closed in around him.

Father Simon was led through the tunnels far beyond his normal haunts. The guards neither spoke to him nor answered his questions. They simply hustled him along, forcing him to match their long springy strides until the human was huffing and panting to keep up.

Finally the guards hustled him up a ramp and through an air lock guarded by two more of their kind with lasers. They shoved him further into the room and stood back along the wall, holding their guns ready.

The room was one of the largest Father Simon had seen since he came to this place and it was certainly the most luxurious. The floor was covered with soft matting and there were the sling-like contraptions the aliens used for seats everywhere. What's more, there were growing things! The plants were almost black in the reddish light and they stretched their spindly, frond-like leaves up close to the lights set over them, but they were real plants. Their leaves and soil gave an odor to the air that was alien and atavistic all at once.

There was a Colonist in the center of the room. He was dressed in neither the smock of a prisoner or the harness of a guard. Instead he wore the long tunic Father Simon had seen on the Colonists he dealt with over the *Maxwell*'s screens—how long ago.

"I am the elder of this place," the alien said without preamble. "Here I command in the name of my lineage."

"You are the warden then? I am Father Simon."

"I know who you are. You are the Cult Leader among the humans," the warden said through his translator.

"I am a priest, yes. Most of the humans are not of my religion."

"You spread your cult among the Colonist prisoners without permission."

"I teach those who ask it. I do not seek converts."

"A quibble. You have no permission."

The priest was silent.

The warden fluffed his fur/feathers. "This thing that happened today was a bad thing. It cannot be allowed to happen again."

"I agree," Father Simon said. "It was a very bad thing."

"You caused this thing to happen. You made this one act wrongly."

"One-Eye did what he believed he had to. He was not of my religion and I urged him to prudence. I am truly sorry for this."

"After today I cannot allow this," the warden told him. "You have perturbed the orbits here and that cannot be permitted. You are to cease meeting with these others. You are not to go to them in their roosts."

It comes to this, Father Simon thought. "No. I cannot do this. I will not talk about religion, but I must continue to visit the sick."

The warden turned his head and stared at the priest; a hard, fixed stare as if he meant to leap at him.

"You defy me?"

"I must do as my conscience directs," the priest said. "I will not teach my religion, for I am forbidden to do so by my superiors. But there are those who need my help. I cannot abandon them."

The warden continued to stare, his arms stretched forward and his talons wide.

"Very well," he said at last. "If you are disobedient, so be it. From today forward you will have guards about you always. Two at all times." He gestured and two of the guards who had brought him here stepped away from the wall.

"Now go. Leave me. And do not try my patience further."

Outside in the corridor the two chosen closed in beside him. Father Simon gestured at the Colonists. The guard on his right moved threateningly.

"Why did you do that?" he demanded.

"I blessed you," Father Simon told the alien.

The guard waited a long time for the translation, then cocked his head to one side as if studying the priest.

"Shall we go?" Father Simon asked.

"You need not ask permission," the other said. "You have authority to go anywhere the common prisoners go."

"It is politeness to wait until one's companions are ready, is it not?"

"We are not your companions," the alien bellowed. "We are your guards!"

"We go about together, do we not?" asked the priest and set off down the tunnel. The guards followed after, obviously fuming.

Most of the time he got the same pair of guards. One was large, unyielding and gave the impression that he was looking for an excuse to rip the priest apart. The other was smaller, more slender and less threatening. Privately he nicknamed them the Grim One and the Young One—although he had no way of knowing which guard was actually older.

The presence of the guards largely cut Father Simon off from his fellow human prisoners. They were uncomfortable around the aliens and tended to avoid his company because of them.

Oddly, the guards seemed to increase his stature with the Colonists. Although they kept clear of them just as they did for other guards, they didn't shrink away from the priest any more. Somehow the guards gave him a legitimacy he had lacked before.

Except for the guards and the isolation from the other humans, life went on largely as before. Every day Father Simon went to see the sick, the hopeless and the dying, to sit with them and talk to them and perhaps bring them water from the communal tap if they were too weak to get it themselves. If guards always at his back made him less welcome, they also brought him more respect from the prisoners.

Most of those he visited died within a day or two. But sometimes a prisoner would turn away from the wall after the priest's visits. Father Simon was always careful to point out that he personally had nothing to do with what happened, but his stature increased even more. Even his guards began to treat him more respectfully and to hang back when he talked to the prisoners.

The little alcove where he had talked with Jawbone and One-Eye became crowded with Colonists who wanted to meet with him. Some simply wanted his blessing, some wanted to discuss philosophy and some had questions. Father Simon sat on the ledge with the Young One and the Grim One on either side. True to his word, he did not discuss religion.

It made for long days. Where the other humans spent most of their time asleep, Father Simon was out with the aliens fourteen to sixteen hours a day.

"If you can't teach Christianity why do you keep talking to the aliens?" Sharon asked him one evening as he sat alone at the table eating the cold porridge the other humans had saved for him.

"Remember One-Eye? I don't want that to happen again. Besides, I can perform acts of corporal mercy, even if they are small."

Sharon eyed him. "You're a remarkable man, Father. Most of us can't stand the sight of the Owlies and you're wearing yourself out trying to help them."

"I think I got involved with them differently," Father Simon told her. "I was the first one to speak to them and I spent more time talking to them—before—than any of the rest of you."

"So you love them in spite of what they do?"

He stopped eating and frowned. "No, I can't say that I love them, though I know I should. But there is something in them that is worthwhile."

Sharon snorted, almost as loud as a Colonist.

"I have trouble with that," she said, ignoring the Grim One and Young One standing by the wall. "They won't even look after their own here. They leave that to you."

"That's not really fair, you know. The prisoners here are terribly demoralized. They've been deprived of everything, even their names, and this place is worse for them than it is for us."

"Father, you're full of it! They're at least in their own system among their own kind." She stopped, her fists balled and her arms pressed tight to her sides. "Sometimes you're nearly as bad as Aubrey!" she blurted and ran from the room in tears.

Father Simon watched her go. Then he sighed and sadly returned to eating his cold porridge.

"These things you do are not approved of by the other humans?" the Grim One asked the next morning as they started out on their rounds.

"Generally not. They feel I am too close to you."

"Then why do you do them?"

Father Simon pursed his lips. "I'm trying to remember something Saint Paul said about this," he sighed. "It's times like this I really miss my Bible. Anyway, the gist of it is that you do what is right no matter what your friends may think."

"This book you mention. It is the wisdom book of your cult?" the Grim One asked.

"You could put it that way, yes."

The guard snorted and looked even more willing to tear into Father Simon.

Four days later the Grim One sidled up to him while the Young One was several steps away down the corridor.

"Here," the guard said roughly and thrust a cube into Father Simon's hand. "It is a copy of the special book of your lineage. But keep it close."

"Thank you," the priest said fervently. "May God bless you."

Without another word the Grim One turned and stalked after his companion.

"The guards make you more important," Jawbone told him one day as they made their rounds visiting. "Among us it is the habit for elders to go escorted. Those ones cannot distinguish between an escort in consequence of your dignity and guards to keep you close." He hissed in laughter.

"I don't understand why he didn't just lock me up."

"He dares not. You and all your kind are too valuable to damage. The Other One says that confining you too tightly or injuring you might kill you or make you turn your face to the wall." He twitched a shrug. "So he does this instead."

"The Other One?"

"The one of your kind who is kept separate from you."

"Aubrey! He's here too, then?"

Jawbone shrugged.

"Do you know if our ship is still in the system?" the priest asked as they walked on.

The alien hissed. "How would I know such a thing? Fathersimon, in this place it is best to forget that there is a place outside.

"We are dead and buried here," Jawbone told him. "For those elsewhere we do not exist."

"God knows we exist," Father Simon told him. "He never forgets us."

"Then God is truly alone," Jawbone said. "For there are no others who would bring us out of this place."

"Hope, Jawbone. Where there is life there is always hope."

Captain Peter Jenkins faced the President of the Colonial Council on the screen.

"Can you locate the humans on Hasta exactly?" he asked.

"There is only one base on the planet," the Council President said. "They must be there."

"How much overpressure can that base stand?" Jenkins asked.

The Council President paused and stared fixedly for a second. "Approximately twelve pounds," the voice came out of the speaker. "I can find out more precisely if you need to know."

"So more than twelve pounds per square inch of overpressure would utterly wreck the base?"

Again the glassy stare. "Say about fourteen to be certain."

"Thank you," Jenkins said and broke contact.

So they plan to destroy the base, the Council President thought as the human's image flicked out of existence. *Crude, but then they are a crude lineage. Yes, that would solve the difficulty. And nicely weaken 246.* With that settled he turned away to other business.

PART VIII: SEMEAI

Billy Toyoda came caroming onto the bridge. "I got it, Captain!"

Jenkins looked up annoyed. "Well, Mr. Toyoda? What have you got? *And put your damn feet on the floor!*"

Billy drew himself up and touched the floor with both feet. "Yessir. I've got the answer sir." Then he lapsed back into his more usual enthusiasm. "Look, the Owlies want the drive, right? So how do they know if we give them the real thing or something that just looks good?"

"A forgery?"

"Sure. With some help, I can rig up something that will look so good they won't know they've been screwed until we're well outta here."

"It might work at that," Jenkins said thoughtfully. He reached over and hit a stud. "Ask Dr. Takiuji to join me in my office, will you?"

Suki listened impassively as Billy spun out his plan of deception.

"What do you think?" the captain asked when Billy finally ran down.

Suki smiled apologetically. "Very clever. But there are perhaps difficulties."

By now Jenkins knew the Japanese well enough to know what that meant.

"Could you enlighten us, Dr. Takiuji? Please speak frankly."

Suki nodded and Billy Toyoda fidgeted. "Two things. First, we do not know how much physics the Colonists actually do

254

know. It is very hard to know how much we can lie to them. If we tell too big a lie . . ." he made a fluttering gesture with his right hand, like a bird flying away.

"They are very good. Very clever. It will be hard to lie to them believably."

"Hey, by the time I get through, it'll take them weeks to figure out which end is up."

"Perhaps this will be not so easy with physics," Suki said politely.

"You mentioned a second reason. What is that?"

"A more subtle difficulty. By what we do not tell them, we give them clues as to where to look."

"Huh!" Toyoda snorted.

"Consider. We do not wish them to know the truth of the drive so we must lead them away from that knowledge. But in doing so we leave gaps, openings. When the false information is examined, what is missing points our enemy toward the truth. A lie that leaves no clues at all is a difficult thing."

"Yeah, but if we make it confusing enough they'll never figure it out."

"That may be so," Suki said politely. "However I foresee difficulties."

Jenkins scowled down at his desk. Toyoda's idea had seemed so logical. It had looked so much like the key he needed to unlock the situation. He looked up at the two Oriental faces in front of him, the older one calm and smiling slightly and the younger one scowling.

Two Oriental faces . . .

"Mr. Toyoda, you may be on to something."

Billy beamed. "Then we'll do it?"

"We'll do something like it. If you're willing."

"What do you mean?"

"I've got a notion. But there's a risk. A lot of personal risk for you. Would you be willing to volunteer?"

Billy shrugged. "Sure."

"You could get killed."

"No biggie," the computerman said breezily. "I just get run through the simulation again."

Jenkins hesitated. *The kid doesn't have the faintest God-damn idea what it means to die,* he thought. *He's as innocent of death as a puppy. Or one of his computers.*

Still, he needed Billy for this one.

"I've got an idea," Jenkins told DeRosa. "I think I know a way to get our people back!"

"Deal with the Colonists?" Iron Alice asked.

"After a fashion. What are the chances of getting our shuttles repaired?"

"None, none, none and none," the pilot told him. "Jewett's little surprise packages wrecked them good. Number One is scrap and the other three aren't much better. All of them lost the same critical parts so we can't even cobble a good one together out of the wrecks."

"Damn! I've got to have shuttles to make this work."

"Well, ours aren't going any place. Say! What about the Colonists?"

"No good. They don't have craft designed to land on a planet. Well, 246 does, but I doubt Derfuhrer is going to give us any shuttles."

"Maybe not," Iron Alice said thoughtfully. "But who do you suppose controls the Colonies' gas mining ships?"

"Those things that fly down into the Jovians' atmosphere and scoop in gas? They're not designed to land anywhere."

"No, but they've got an aerodynamic shape, they can take lots of stress and they've got plenty of power."

"Yeah," Jenkins said. "It just might work at that."

The team gathered hastily in the small conference room, buzzing about the sudden summons. They quieted expectantly as soon as the captain came through the door.

"Mr. Kirchoff," Jenkins began without preamble, "can we use the drive to get from here to Hasta?"

"Nossir. The drive doesn't work well this close to a star."

"Forgive me, I was under the impression that the drive functioned adequately in a gravity well. That the problem was in the positioning."

The engineering officer shrugged. "It comes down to the same thing."

"Perhaps not in this case."

"Captain," Carlotti interjected, "you cannot use a KOH drive this deep in a star's gravity field. The distortions of space increase the quantum uncertainty and it becomes impossible to determine your position accurately enough."

"But it will work, physically?" Jenkins persisted.

Carlotti looked as if he had bitten into something unpleasant. "Physically, yes, but the positioning problem is insuperable."

"Need I remind you that we have had the gravity array deployed and functioning for some months?"

"No, Captain, you don't need to remind me of it. So far that's been the only astronomical science we've done on this entire trip. And yes, you're right, that helps because it gives us a pretty good gravity map of this system. But that's not enough."

"What that comes down to is that position and velocity will be even more uncertain than they usually are. If you're willing to accept that, you can use the drive."

"Yes, but you're going to have a *lot* of uncertainty. It's not safe, especially not when you get close to a planet."

"All right. Assuming you *had* to jump. How would you minimize the uncertainties?"

"Well," Carlotti said slowly, "we could do it by a series of small jumps. That would cut the observational error. But there's nothing we can do about the quantum uncertainty. There is an excellent chance we could emerge from the last jump within the atmosphere."

"Can we choose which side of the planet we approach?"

He shrugged. "Of course. We would approach the side of the planet that was turned toward us. But I don't see why it matters on which way we're facing when we go to glory."

Captain Jenkins smiled grimly. "It matters a lot if the explosion smashes the base and sprays the survivors with hard radiation. Not as clean as a rescue, but satisfactory enough."

No one said anything.

After the meeting broke up, Jenkins called the Council President.

"Can your gas mining ships land on the surface of that planet?" Jenkins asked as soon as the alien came on the screen.

Again the fixed stare the Earthmen had come to know so well.

"Yes," the President said finally. "If you added landing gear. It would probably damage them, but they should stay atmosphere tight and be able to take off again."

257

"Fine. I need six of them. As quickly as you can get them to me."

"To what end?"

"The defeat of 246," Captain Jenkins told him.

"The humans have made some arrangement with the Council," the Master of Bounds told Derfuhrer. "As part of that agreement they receive six gas-mining ships."

Fear clutched at the leader's heart. Then he forced himself to relax. *No*, he thought, *they would not trade their secret for so little.*

"What are the terms?"

"The humans are trading general information. The nature is not specified but it does not involve the star drive."

"Find out what the terms are of that trade." The Master of Cities indicated assent.

"What do the humans intend to do with those ships?"

"Use them to replace the shuttles they lost in the attack."

"To what end?" Derfuhrer asked sharply.

The Master of Cities "shrugged." "Not even the Council knows. Who can say what is in the mind of this lineage?"

"Who indeed," Derfuhrer said. "Who indeed?"

Normally the room was used as an auxiliary mess for the crew. Now it was filled with men and women drawn from the crew and the technical staff.

Carmella looked around and realized she knew about two-thirds of the people here. They were pilots or associated with the pilot force. But some of the faces were strange.

What in the world is this all about? she wondered.

At precisely 0900 by the clock on the bulkhead, Iron Alice DeRosa strode to the front of the room.

"Okay, listen up. We've got a little job to do and you pilots are going to be part of it."

So that was it, Carmella thought. All the people in the room must be qualified pilots. All the crew was cross-trained and the ones she didn't know must be the ones whose secondary specialty was piloting.

"You all know the shuttles and most of the scooters got trashed in the raid. Well, we're getting some replacements." She reached out and flicked a switch. An image coalesced in the tank on the table and the audience gasped.

The thing managed to be sleek, powerful looking and ugly all at the same time. And it was obviously not a human design.

"Jesus," Carmella said softly. "They want us to fly *that*?"

"This," Iron Alice told them, "is one of the Colonists' gas-mining ships. They're designed to dive into upper atmosphere of the Jovians and scoop up gas. We're modifying four of them for this mission. The controls may be a little funny, but the mission is simple and these things have plenty of power."

The image in the tank rotated slowly, showing the stark, streamlined shape of the brute. DeRosa pointed to the stern.

"The engines burn hydrox. Engineering is fitting these things with extensible landing jacks. Only two of you are supposed to land, but you never know."

"How much practice time will we get?" one of the other pilots asked.

"None," Iron Alice told him. "We can't afford the risk. We have a simulator tricked up to respond like the alien shuttles— or how the alien shuttles should respond. You'll do your practicing in those."

"Jesus," Carmella muttered again.

"All right," Iron Alice said. "The rest is in your briefing books. Any questions?"

"Yeah," said the tall blond pilot. "How do we know we can trust the Owlies? How can we be sure those shuttles aren't gimmicked or something?"

Iron Alice DeRosa smiled at him. "Because the captain made them an offer they couldn't refuse. And we've got to be alive if they're going to collect."

Carmella barely made it to the bathroom in time. Once in the stall she heaved and heaved until there was nothing left in her stomach. *Jesus*, she thought. *Oh Jesus*.

Weak and sick, she staggered out.

There was another pilot at the sink, combing her short brownish hair.

"You all right?" she asked.

Carmella looked at herself in the mirror. Her face was pale and blotchy and she was still bent over from the after effects of the cramps.

"Yeah," she muttered. "Fine. Just something I ate."

"I hope no one else ate any of it," the other woman said. "You look like shit."

Carmella shook her head. "Just allergies. I pushed it too far." She leaned over to rinse the bitter taste of vomit out of her mouth.

"Well, don't do it again, okay?"

Carmella nodded.

It took time, of course. Getting the gas-mining ships back to the *Maxwell* from the outer system required a voyage of several months. The laws of orbital dynamics will not be mocked, even travelling in a high-energy trajectory with strap-on fuel tanks.

Even before the ships arrived, the humans began work. The ruins of the shuttles were eased out of their bays. The bays themselves were enlarged by consolidating storerooms aft of them. They were deepened by eliminating the corridors beneath them. The bay doors were extended and enlarged. What had been a neat and ship-shape collection of spaces became an ugly void of openwork and girders.

Once the ships arrived they had to be modified. Crews of humans swarmed over them, adapting them to their new roles. Structures had to be strengthened, landing jacks added, the cabins needed to be completely redone. Engineering and other services spent weeks studying the plans and developing modifications while they waited for the ships to arrive. Everyone from vacuum jacks to astronomers worked as construction crew. But even so, it took a long, long time.

Meanwhile, there was other work to be done.

"I wish to make a trade," Captain Jenkins told Derfuhrer. "I wish to get my people back."

Derfuhrer didn't even bother to deny that he had them. "I will entertain an offer."

"The knowledge of our star drive?"

"Just so."

"This was forbidden," Jenkins said, thinking out loud. "But I have my duty to my lineage. I cannot shirk that for the concerns of other clans."

Derfuhrer said nothing, waiting.

"There are those who fear that with the drive you will come ravening our home planet."

"But you do not?"

"It will take you time to learn to build the drive, even with the help we could give you. When you get it you are more likely to seek out other stars to colonize rather than bother us. It does not make sense that you should come to our home system, except perhaps to trade."

"And you would permit that?"

Jenkins shrugged. "It is not mine to permit or prohibit. I am concerned with my ship and my crew."

"What do you propose?"

"That we trade. Knowledge of the drive for my crew."

"I already possess what knowledge your ship has of the drive."

"You possess what knowledge was in active memory when you attacked. That information was stored separately and not in the computers."

Derfuhrer paused. Yes, his people said that the humans did not keep everything in memory at one time. An odd, crude system. But then they were an odd, crude lineage. It was possible, just possible, that this captain was telling the truth.

"I will give you all knowledge of the drive we possess."

"Full knowledge?"

The captain hesitated. "We do not have that."

"It is not enough," he said at last. "I must have more."

"I have no more to give," Jenkins protested.

"There is Takiuji-san."

"You expect me to worsen my position by giving up another crew member?"

"I would trade him for the others."

"His lineage would not like it," Jenkins objected.

Derfuhrer made the Colonists' equivalent of a shrug. "It is easier to satisfy one lineage than many. Especially if a suitable weregild is available."

It was Jenkins' turn to pause while he called up the meaning of "weregild."

"I must think on this," he said. "May your lineage prosper."

"And yours," replied Derfuhrer and broke the connection.

"Said the spider to the fly," Jenkins muttered under his breath as he stared at the blank screen.

*   *   *

Peter Jenkins looked up and down the table at his assembled advisers. "Lady, gentlemen, I have made arrangements with Derfuhrer for release of our hostages," he said bluntly.

"On what terms?" Carlotti asked.

"The Colonists have agreed to exchange all the humans for one man, Dr. Takiuji."

"That's madness!" one of the others burst out.

"It would be madness if the trade actually took place. However it will not. The trade will be a cover for an attack on the Hasta base."

"Storm the base?" Carlotti said stiffly. "Captain, may I remind you that we are not soldiers."

Jenkins drew back his lips in a tight, hard smile. "Wrong. We are soldiers. Because we have to be."

"Still, their guards are trained for military operations. We are not."

"You ever pull guard duty?" Iron Alice asked sharply.

"Why, no," Carlotti said, surprised.

"Well, let me tell you something. It is the fastest way in the world to make even good troops sloppy. Want to bet the bozos on that planet weren't that good to start with?"

"We have another advantage, Doctor. Gravity."

"Gravity is the same for all of us."

"Now, but not historically. Have you noticed the way the Colonists maneuver their ships?"

"Eh?"

"Their maneuvering, did you notice anything about it?"

"Well, they seem to do it very deliberately."

"Slow, Doctor. The word you are looking for is slow. For thousands of years they have lived at very low gravity. Their home planet probably had a gravity less than half of Earth's. They're weaker than we are and their reflexes are much slower."

"Their machines aren't," Carlotti said grimly.

"We have ways of dealing with their machines," Jenkins told him. Then he outlined his plans.

"There's one little thing you left out of that briefing," Iron Alice said after the others had left.

"Oh?"

"How are you going to get your trade goods back?"

"He'll have a chance."

262

"This is insanity and you know it. If it goes wrong they could still end up with Dr. Takiuji and win the game."

"I guarantee you that won't happen."

"How can you be so bloody sure?"

"Dr. Takiuji and I have made arrangements to prevent it."

Iron Alice DeRosa stopped cold. "You mean suicide. He'll kill himself like Ludenemeyer did."

"Death in a good cause is part of the Japanese culture," Jenkins said carefully.

DeRosa didn't say anything.

"We are making arrangements to pick him up."

"If everything goes just right and we have more luck than we deserve. Otherwise he dies down there. Or worse, they squeeze him like a grape."

"There is a calculated risk. Now if there is nothing else?"

Iron Alice DeRosa opened her mouth, closed it and saluted very deliberately. "Nothing else, sir. Do I have the captain's permission to go?"

"Granted," said Jenkins and watched her turn and head for the bridge. Suddenly it felt very cold and lonely up here.

Now or never, Carmella O'Hara told herself as she approached the door to the executive officer's office. *Now or never.* For the first time in weeks she was wearing her uniform. It was clean, neat and as pressed as she could make it.

She took a deep breath and knocked.

"Come in," the familiar voice said from inside. Carmella let out her breath and went in.

Iron Alice DeRosa was sitting behind the desk, waiting for her. "You requested an interview, pilot?"

Thank God, Carmella thought, *she's not going to bring family into this.*

"Ma'am, I request to be relieved from pilot duty for the coming mission," Carmella said formally.

For a minute, a long minute, Iron Alice DeRosa just sat there, looking at her niece and saying nothing. It was as bad as Carmella had imagined it would be. She wanted to die where she stood, or at the very least sink through the floor and vanish forever.

"You're making the request to the wrong person," she told her at last. "You should go to your immediate superior."

"Yes ma'am," Carmella said woodenly.

"However I will pass this request on to your superior without recommendation so that he can make the decision."

"Yes ma'am."

"Then if there's nothing else?"

"No ma'am." Carmella prepared to leave.

"Then would you tell me what's wrong, Cammy?" Iron Alice said softly. "Just between us?"

"I—I'm just not competent to fly the mission," Carmella blurted out, confused by the sudden turn of events. She stopped and looked down at the deck. "I'm sorry to let you down," she mumbled.

"You're not letting me down," DeRosa told her. "You're making the best choice possible if you don't think you're up for the mission. Better to say so now than have things go sour later. But would you mind telling me why?"

"You wouldn't understand it," she said keeping her eyes on the floor. "It's something you'd never understand."

"Try me."

"Because I'm scared," Carmella said defiantly, blinking back tears. "I'm not like you and I'm scared out of my Goddamn mind."

"And you think I'm not?" Iron Alice grinned like a wolf. "Lady, I've been scared ever since I went out for this job. And right now I'm fucking terrified."

Carmella stared. "But you said you'd lead the flight your-self," she protested.

"That's something different," her aunt said. "You don't send people out to do something dangerous if you aren't willing to do it yourself. Besides," she added simply, "it's always easier to go out and die yourself than to send people out to do it for you. But I can't go. I know too much and I don't have the reflexes any more. So I get to sit here on the ship and be afraid."

"Mom always said you were never scared of anything," Carmella said wonderingly.

Iron Alice smiled. "Your mother is nice, but she's not too perceptive."

Carmella nodded. "Aunt Alice, why did I get a pilot's berth?"

"Why do you think you got that job?" she asked carefully.

"Because I'm your niece."

"Wrong!" Iron Alice DeRosa roared. "You got it because you're the best damned pilot I could find. You've got the training, you've got the experience, you've got the reflexes and most of all you've got the piloting sense.

"I didn't get you this berth. You got it for yourself by being one of the best small ship pilots there is."

"But I thought . . ."

"That I pulled strings? Don't put too much trust in latrine gossip."

The older woman took Carmella by the shoulders.

"Cammy, listen to me. Don't ever do anything for me. Don't do it for the family pride. Do it for yourself, for who you are and who you want to be. And if it isn't for you, then don't do it."

"I don't know what I want right now."

DeRosa sighed. "We've got time. Give me your decision by 0800. If you want to go, then go. If not, I'll square it with your commander. *But decide for yourself, girl!*"

Carmella nearly collided with Captain Jenkins in the corridor. She threw him a quick salute and then hurried past him.

"That was your niece, wasn't it?" Jenkins asked as he came into DeRosa's office. "I understand she's quite a pilot."

"Yeah," Iron Alice DeRosa said proudly. "She's a hell of a pilot."

"Spun down and ready, Captain."

Jenkins looked around the bridge and out at the spangled sky in front of them. The air was chill against his skin and the armrests of his couch icy to his touch. They had been running the air conditioners full out for the last twenty-four hours and the temperature on the bridge was approaching fifty degrees Fahrenheit.

"Very well. Pilot, execute."

DeRosa leaned forward and flipped a switch. "Executing . . . now." And the universe blinked.

The star field had shifted subtly and wheeled about them as the *Maxwell* dashed through space on a new vector. The navigator began to call out their direction and speed, but Iron Alice DeRosa was already playing the sidestick, wheeling the ship about so the torch faced the direction they headed.

The torch flared and Jenkins was rammed back in his seat as the *Maxwell* lost velocity. The numbers reeled off on his console as speed fell away from them under the raging force of the reaction.

"Lining up," DeRosa called out. She played the thrusters like a piano, feeding a bit less here and a little more there. The stars slowed and stopped their movement. The computers rechecked their position, drank in new data from the gravity array and applied corrections to the data.

"On course. Executing. Now."

Again the stars blinked and then wheeled madly. Again the starship slewed about and once more the fusion torch roared to kill unwanted velocity. Jenkins noticed he was sweating inside his suit and hoped it was nerves.

"On course. Executing. Now."

The universe spun crazily and the room had become noticeably warmer. *A bad one*, Jenkins thought. *We can't take many like that.* The spinning stars slowed and then began to precess as the computers and the pilot got the ship under control and lined it up for the burn to kill their accumulated velocity.

Then the fusion torch kicked in and Jenkins was rocked back in his seat. The straps bit hard into his already tender shoulders, but he barely noticed.

"Correcting, correcting. Stand by. Executing. Now."

They couldn't escape detection, of course. Too many eyes had been watching them and even if they hadn't been, the electronic storm they stirred up in their wake crashed upon the detectors all over the system at the speed of light.

But even light takes time to traverse space and even an M5 solar system is a vast place. It took minutes and hours for the tortured particles and waves bearing the news of the *Maxwell*'s passing to reach those detectors. And in this case, even minutes was too long.

"Correcting," Iron Alice sang hoarsely. Sweat ran down her face and the force of the fusion torch bucked her into the straps. "Correcting. Correcting." Then a pause. A long pause. "Stand by. Now."

Five times the *Maxwell* jumped. After the fourth she was hung in real space for nearly ten minutes as her pilot and computers corrected her heading and velocity to the absolute best of their abilities.

The air in the control room was stifling in spite of the dull roar of the air conditioners. Jenkins pressed his jaws together to fight down the nausea. From somewhere on the bridge he heard the sound of retching and knew not everyone had been as successful as he was.

He concentrated on his display because he could not close his eyes. The stars out the port gave him vertigo.

"Correcting," Iron Alice croaked. "Correcting, correcting, correcting." She held the sidestick between her right thumb and forefinger and moved it with nervous jerky motions. Through the hull Jenkins could hear the bow thrusters cutting on and off, like a car spluttering out of gas. The pilot stilled her hand and studied her own display for a moment.

"This is as good as it gets, Captain." Her voice was so hoarse and strained it was almost unrecognizable.

"Very good, pilot," Jenkins was hoarse too. He thumbed his mike onto the ship's main comm circuit. "All hands stand by. Jumping . . . Now."

And the stars blinked again.

Hasta was looming out the port window. Too large, far too large and closing too quickly on a crazy corkscrew path. Iron Alice hit the sidestick hard and the *Maxwell* bucked sideways under maximum impulse from the thrusters. Then the torch cut in with a great whooshing roar that carried through the entire ship. The planet spun away behind them and Jenkins held his breath. But the *Maxwell*'s engines were more than a match for the gravitational forces and their steady roar lessened then stuttered, then stopped and started again and then stopped for the last time.

Even before the crew unstrapped the next phase had begun. As soon as the *Maxwell* broke out for the final time, thirty small rockets took off in all directions from her hull. As DeRosa fought to get the ship back under control they exploded at distances of a couple of kilometers to several hundred kilometers from the ship. And suddenly the *Maxwell* wasn't alone in the sky.

Iron Alice relaxed her grip on the stick as the ship slowed its mad rush to nowhere.

"We're stable," she croaked.

"Crews execute," Jenkins called over the comm channel. "Shuttles standby." He thumbed the circuit off. "Get me a position as fast as you can."

The 1200-meter length of the ship was boiling with activity. Spacesuited workers scrambled from improvised acceleration couches and out the locks, lugging equipment with them. Access compartments crudely carved in the ship's hull were thrown open and apparatus was rigged. Vacuum jacks and astronomers alike labored frantically to get the pieces into place. Others formed human chains to pass the contents of the lockers forward.

The *Maxwell* was not armed and was never intended to be armed. But simple rockets are easy to mount and easier to launch. And every vacuum jack and rock crawler in the Earth system knows how to make them. Within minutes of Jenkins' order the ship was surrounded by an expanding cloud of projectiles, most of them heading for Hasta hanging blue-gray above them.

The bridge crew ignored the activity, concentrating instead on getting a precise position in relation to Hasta.

"Better than I thought," DeRosa said. She was still hoarse, but her voice was coming back. "We can launch the shuttles whenever you're ready."

"Get them out of the bays," Jenkins said. "Then get me an ETA and update it constantly."

"Want them to start in?"

"No. Let's let Hasta stew in its own juices for a bit."

From their makeshift bays in the flanks of the *Maxwell*, four ungainly craft rose and turned their noses toward the planet. They were ragged and a little hesitant as they used their maneuvering jets to clear the great ship, as if their pilots were not used to them. They stood along side their mother ship like remoras escorting an enormous shark.

The blue-black sky over Hasta blossomed. Flares of all colors blazed, turning night into day and day into summer's noon. Higher up the spectrum other radiation sources sprang out in streaks and splotches. Lines of light streaked through the sky as tons of chaff burst in low orbit, burning on reentry with magnesium radiance. Down in the atmosphere other chaff containers burst, distributing silvery clouds everywhere.

"Pity we didn't rig a few nukes," DeRosa said thoughtfully. "A string of EMPs would mess them up nicely."

Kessner, their communications officer, snorted. "Against a space civilization? Forget it. Their stuff is so rad hard they wouldn't even notice."

"Well, they'll notice this all right. It must be hell out for the Fourth of July down on the surface now."

"Well, let's see if we can mix some substance in with the sparkle," Jenkins said. "Launch the rocks," he ordered.

Out on the hull, other work groups swung their launchers to the azimuth and elevation the computers gave them. These were larger, sturdier constructions. Unlike the lighter missiles, which were being fired as fast as they could be passed up, these projectiles were brought out of the hatches by jury-rigged cranes. They had no weight, of course, but they had plenty of mass and the men who maneuvered them into their launch frames moved slowly and carefully.

One after the other, the "rocks" left their launchers. Lost in the electromagnetic riot kicked up by the bombardment, the transmitter signals from the rocks gave the *Maxwell* a precise fix on each of them. Down below, Billy Toyoda's computers translated that into an orbit track for each rock and an elongated oval footprint that moved across the surface of the planet beneath each of them.

"What are you doing?" the Warden demanded without preamble.

"You didn't expect us to risk our ship unprotected did you?" Jenkins replied coldly. "We are jamming and we will continue jamming."

"That was not in the agreement!" The Warden shouted. The voice emerged in a normal tone but on the screen Jenkins could see his chest heave.

"That is the way it is. Now tell your crews to stand away from their defense stations."

"*What?*" the Warden was dancing in fury.

"Warden, in just a few minutes the first rocks are going to come plowing into those batteries. If you want to lose the crews, that's your business."

The Warden hissed once and forced himself to be calm. "No. This is far in excess of my instructions. Unless I am directly told to do this, I will open fire."

"Warden, your instructions were to exchange prisoners. We do it this way and no other. I do not think Derfuhrer would like it if we left without making the trade. And at the first sign, the first *quiver* of hostile action or noncompliance we will be out of here and in interstellar space."

The Warden's jaw muscles twitched, but his eyes stayed wide. This was nothing less than a full-scale attack on his station. An act of war unthinkable. *But the prize. But the prize!* And he had very little doubt that this squat ugly creature was right about his fate if it should fall through.

"I must contact 246 for instructions," he said finally.

"Warden, use your head! There is no time. Already this system is boiling like a hornets' nest. We have to make the exchange and get out of here before all hell breaks loose." In a back part of his mind Jenkins wondered what the metaphors would translate into. "Your colony is on the other side of the Sun. It would take hours to get this straightened out.

"You don't have hours, Warden. You have, at most, minutes, or I recall my shuttles and we're out of here."

Again the jaw muscles jerked convulsively. "Very well," he spat. "Have your damn defenses. I will instruct my crews accordingly."

"Very good, Warden. Expect our shuttle within the hour." Jenkins cut the connection and opened another circuit.

"Okay people, here we go. Showtime, and make it good!"

The four ships accelerated quickly as they dropped away toward the surface of the planet.

"Shuttles away," Iron Alice called out.

"Okay," Jenkins said. Then he cut in the general circuit. "They're on their way. Let's give them all the cover we can." *And please God, let this work!* he added to himself.

The makeshift shuttle bucked and rocked as Carmella pointed its nose deeper into the atmosphere. The cockpit was crude, the software was worse and half the controls couldn't be reached with the seat harness buckled down, but oh, what power!

Her hands played lightly on the controls and her lips drew back in a tight hard grin as she concentrated on the instruments and keeping this beast on course.

The forces slammed her from side to side against the loose harness as she brought her shuttle in at the steepest possible angle. Outside the nose of the ship was glowing dull red from the friction. Inside the combination of hull heat and poor air conditioning made the cabin an oven, but she didn't notice.

An outside observer, if there had been one in the cabin,

might have noticed that suddenly Carmella O'Hara looked very much like her aunt.

"I'm not sure I like this, you know," Andrew Aubrey said as he stood beside the Warden in the main air lock.

The Warden stifled his first response. He *knew* he didn't like it. "Why not?" he asked.

"It's the reasoning. Captain Jenkins was adamantly opposed to releasing the secret of the drive. Now he's willing to trade the one man on the ship who understands the drive."

The Warden said nothing, preoccupied with his own thoughts.

"He's right, of course. You're not a threat to Earth. But I'm very surprised that he came to see that. And now this." He gestured toward the sky where the flares and chaff still burst and bloomed. "It's just not in character."

"Treachery then?"

"I would be very surprised if Dr. Takiuji got off that shuttle. But what does he gain if he does not?" He shook his head. "Most puzzling."

"We will know soon," the Warden said. Through the earth came the faint rumble of a shuttle setting down.

The lock was big enough to admit a land train. The group of humans and Colonists were dwarfed in it. Slowly the great doors swung open, revealing the bleak gray panorama outside. In spite of her suit, Sharon shivered involuntarily.

The guards pressed even closer about them, forcing the humans into an even tighter group. Aubrey remained at the side of the Warden.

"It's a trap!" Aubrey hissed suddenly. "That's not one of our shuttles!"

The Warden looked down at him disgustedly. "Your shuttles were damaged. That is a modified gas-mining ship."

Aubrey started to say something, then settled under the Warden's glare.

The radio crackled. "Move the prisoners out into the open," a human voice said.

One by one the humans were moved out through the massive lock door and stood there in a tight little knot.

A lone figure emerged from the lock and started down the ladder.

One of the squad leaders moved as if to go forward, but the Warden gestured him back.

"It is my vocation," he said to the squad leader. *And if we botch this my life isn't worth a shed feather*, he thought grimly as he stepped forward.

Cautiously, the Warden advanced over the slate-gray gravel to meet the human.

Halfway between the ship and the lock the human stopped and waited. His helmet's sun visor was up and his features were clearly visible.

The Warden checked the picture he had brought with him and nodded. Over the last several days he had studied it carefully until he could identify the person positively. Fortunately this human had a distinctive combination of features. The eyes were different and the hair was pale with age, growing in a fringe around the back of the head.

The warden turned and signaled the squad forward. They double-timed across the field, fell in around their new prisoner and the whole group trooped back toward the great gaping airlock.

"Release the prisoners," the Warden commanded over the radio. The guards fell back from the knot of humans, bringing their weapons up to rest position from the ready.

The humans stood stock still for a few seconds after their guards moved away from them. Then one of the guards shoved a human in the small of the back with the butt of his rifle and the human stumbled forward. Reflexively, the prisoners milled forward, slowly at first and then faster and faster.

One of the humans broke into a clumsy run and then suddenly they were all bounding across the plain toward the ship towering against the dark purple sky, heedless of the danger of falling or tearing a suit.

Free, Sharon Dolan exalted as her breath rasped in her ears. *We're free!*

There were other humans waiting at the base of the ship, humans in human-designed spacesuits, who urged them up the ladder and into the lock.

They crowded into the lock until there was not room to breathe. Then the outer door closed leaving others clinging to the ladder outside. Sharon first felt the pump's vibration as it forced air into the lock and then she heard it as the air grew thick enough to carry sound.

As soon as the pump shut off, she reached up and cracked

her visor. The air she sucked into her lungs stank, but it was a human stink, rich with the odor of human beings and tainted with the tang of human chemicals. Her cheeks felt damp and she realized she was crying.

They were all squeezed even closer together as the lock swung inward. Then they tumbled out into the ship and saw another human, the first new face they had seen in months.

"Get the hell on board," Carmella bawled. "All hell's gonna break loose in just a couple of minutes."

Count it out. The numbers reeled off on the head-up display inside his helmet, marking off the time in tenths of seconds. *Slow and easy. Slow it down.* He moved across the rough plain toward the gaping maw of the station lock as slowly as his captors would let him. And always with an eye on the numbers.

Behind him he heard the roar of the first shuttle lifting off and the weight on his chest eased. *Mission accomplished. Now for the hard part.* Still he kept the slow pace, hoping that he would not have to enter the great lock.

A small party of Colonists stood just outside the lock and in their center a single human. He did not have to be told who that human was.

As the party came up to the lock, the human stepped forward to meet them.

"Dr. Takiuji . . ." Andrew Aubrey began, and then stopped short.

Billy Toyoda, his head shaved, temples and brows whitened, smiled back at him through the helmet faceplate. "Hiya Doc."

Aubrey's jaw dropped. "This isn't Dr. Takiuji! You've got the wrong man!" he yelled into his suit microphone.

The Warden gaped and then his beak clacked like a gunshot. "*Stop them!*" he bellowed.

Billy watched his readout and held his breath. *Three two one now!*

Suddenly the sky was alight with lances of flame.

In spite of their name, the projectiles were not rocks. They were cylindrical billets of nickel-iron, turned smooth and with blunt noses.

Not that nomenclature mattered. They weighed about a ton each and they came down fast. The rockets did not slow them down to let them enter the atmosphere, they only changed the apogee of their orbits so they coincided with the surface of the planet at the appropriate spot. Whatever was at that spot got the equivalent of several tons of high explosive.

First to go were the two weapons installations overlooking the field. They vanished in streaks of radiance and boiling clouds of dust. Microseconds behind them another dozen chunks of nickel-iron struck the field in a tight pattern.

Some of them were backups, designed to take out the gun installations in case the first wave failed. A few were originally aimed at the prison itself, to destroy everything if the rescue effort failed. Most of them were targeted for the plain from the first. The missiles kicked up tons of alien soil and threw it high into the thin air, creating a dense cloud as gray as the plain.

Billy knew what was coming. His captors did not. At the first explosion, he broke free and dashed through the air lock and out into the gloom.

"*Stop him!*" bellowed the Warden, but Billy Toyoda was already lost from sight in the roiling gray cloud. A dozen Colonist guards stumbled into the dust cloud after him, blind in the roiling dust.

Billy was equally blind, but he knew exactly where he was going and he had used his slow trip to the lock to memorize bearings and distances. He put his head down and charged full-tilt through the dust cloud.

Beams shone purple through the dust around him, but Billy ran on, unheeding. The tenths of seconds ticked off in his faceplate display as he dodged and groped through the murk across the broken gray plain.

He made the base of the second shuttle with fifteen seconds to spare.

He swarmed up the ladder and flopped into the air lock. "Let's get the hell out of here!" he yelled to the unseen pilot and hit the switch to close the lock door.

Billy was still in the lock when the second shuttle roared skyward through the dust cloud.

On the surface of Hasta, the Warden watched him go, pursued by the futile beams from his guards' rifles.

He was ruined, he knew. His life forfeit and his lineage forever degraded. With the odd, calm clarity that follows truly major disasters, he watched his future flee into the purple sky on two searing pinpoints of flame.

The Cult Leader had escaped with the others. He found a strange sort of peace in that thought.

Out of the corner of his eye, he saw one of the guards cross himself as he watched the departing ships.

Captain Peter Jenkins stared at the screen so hard his eyes hurt.

There. One point of light. One shuttle was off and climbing strongly for orbit. The hostages were free.

But Jenkins didn't relax. He kept his eyes on the screen, watching and hoping desperately.

There! The second point of light. The second shuttle was up and away. But with or without its passenger?

Jenkins clenched and unclenched his hands on the arms of his couch. Watching for some sign. He knew the pilot would transmit a status report as soon as the ship was clear of the cloud of manmade interference surrounding the planet, but the seconds dragged interminably while he waited.

"Mission accomplished. 100 percent."

"I presume it is safe to come out now." Floating in the door was Sukihara Takiuji, looking uncharacteristic in one of Billy Toyoda's coveralls.

DeRosa's jaw dropped.

"Then who the hell did you send down there?" she demanded.

"Billy Toyoda. I figured in makeup he could pass for Suki long enough."

The whole bridge broke up in cheers.

"You tricky son of a bitch!" Iron Alice whooped. "Why didn't you tell me?"

"I was afraid the Colonists might still have ears on this ship. That was the one detail that couldn't leak under any circumstances. Only Suki, Billy and I knew that part of the plan."

"You son of a bitch," DeRosa repeated, shaking her head. "What now?"

"As soon as we've got the shuttles aboard, we get out of here. There's some unfinished business and we've got a debt to pay."

PART IX: DAMEZUMARI

"Ruined," Derfuhrer bellowed. *"Ruined!"* His subordinate cowered at his master's wrath.

News of the rescue of the humans had flashed across the system and in its wake, Derfuhrer's coalition was falling apart. Colony after colony was seeking to ally with the Council.

The shift showed that 246's position was built upon sand. Without the promise of the faster-than-light drive, 246 had nothing to offer its allies. Meanwhile, the alliance between the humans and the Council was growing in significance.

Even worse than the political implications was the humiliation. The complete story wasn't widely known, of course. But all the Colonies knew enough to know that Derfuhrer had attempted a deal with the humans and gotten his feathers singed.

Worst of all, and unthinkably, Hasta was gone. The commander of the garrison had traitorously surrendered the remaining installations to the Colonial Council.

The combination was more than Derfuhrer could bear. For days he had remained in seclusion in the Citadel, stalking endlessly up and down, sleeping little.

The Master of Forests knew all this, but he was still astonished at the change in Derfuhrer when he was ushered into his presence. He looked lean and haggard and not at all well.

Derfuhrer was looking out over the colony, seeming to stare through the mists to the workers town where they had all started their climb toward the Inner Grove.

"Well?" Derfuhrer turned from the vista to stare challengingly at his subordinate.

"787 has defected," the Master of Forests said simply. "They will not abide by their agreement with us and they have begun open negotiations with the Council."

The Master of Forests braced himself, but there was no beak-snapping explosion of rage. Not even a frozen pause for thought. Derfuhrer took the news quietly, almost calmly. As if he did not care any more.

"So," he said at last and that was all. Then he turned back to the view from the terrace.

The Master of Forests hesitated. He had been given this mission because the Master of Bounds was in disgrace. After days of bearing bad news to his master, he was unwelcome in Derfuhrer's presence. The Master of Skies was no more. He had been taken immediately after the alien raid on Hasta and a replacement had not been appointed.

"The sooner we begin proceedings quickly to new alliance with the Council the more advantageous the terms," the Master of Forests suggested tentatively.

"No!" Derfuhrer commanded. He turned from the window to face the Master of Forests. "No, better to cut our own throats. We have an option left. They make open war against us? Well, then, we will make war against them."

In spite of the difference in status, the underling's beak clacked in surprise.

"If we strike now before they can absorb the news, we can destroy the usurpers." He spread his talons for ripping and his jaws locked in a fighting rictus. "They think to polish our bones, do they? Well, we will see whose carcass lie for the picking!"

"That is a most unusual course," the Master of Forests said as emotionlessly as he could, "and a most dangerous one."

"We have nothing to lose," Derfuhrer pointed out. "That gives us the advantage. Once we strike a few of the colonies, the rest will fall back into line. Thus will justice and True Order be restored and we will regain our rightful place."

"The other colonies will surely retaliate."

Derfuhrer made a sweeping gesture. "They will be divided as they always are by their own dissension. None of them dare move on their own. And while they squabble, we shall act! With unity and firmness of purpose we will prevail over

277

all of them. We will split them off faction by faction and take them under our shade."

Derfuhrer began to stride up and down the room, moving nervously, restlessly.

"Fail? No we have not failed. Instead our so-called 'failure' has set the stage for our greatest triumph. We do not need creatures from beyond our system to prevail. With the unity and the single will of our lineage expressed directly in one person we shall emerge victorious!"

As he left the hall The Master of Forests cleaned his teeth reflexively. This was terrible, unprecedented. *But it might work,* he admitted. Derfuhrer had risen so high by working in ways which were unprecedented. Often and again sheer audacity had allowed him to triumph over unbelievable odds. Now, again in a crisis he chose the outrageous. Perhaps, just perhaps, it would again prove successful.

Besides, he admitted as he bounded along the corridor, *what other chance do we have?*

Things have changed, Sharon Dolan thought as her eyes swept over the crowded lounge. The room had been opened up to three times its normal size, but it was still jammed. Nearly everyone on the ship was here to honor the rescued captives.

Over in one corner the pilot of the rescue ship was surrounded by a crowd of admirers who seemed to be hanging on her words. At the far end of the room she could see Billy Toyoda in animated conversation.

It was hard to put your finger on the differences. The crowd seemed leaner, somehow harder, than the people she had travelled with out from Earth. Everyone was having a good time, but there was a seriousness about them that she didn't remember seeing before.

Well, she thought, *I've changed too.*

She saw Captain Jenkins coming through the crowd. Heads turned and people drew back to make room for him so he moved in his own bubble of space. *Now that is really different*, she thought.

Since she had been back she had heard almost nothing about the Ship's Council, but she had heard a lot about the captain.

278

No one seemed to mind, she noticed. There was no trace of hostility toward the captain or the crew and none of the tension between crew and non-crew that had been so marked when she left. Everyone seemed to be mixing and having a good time as if there had never been any differences.

Almost everyone, anyway. Father Simon was sitting in the corner, looking almost as worn and stressed as he had been in captivity. The others had bounced back, at least superficially, but the priest still looked as if something were dreadfully wrong.

Sharon started toward him, but at that moment the captain came up to her.

"Welcome back, Dr. Dolan." Was it her imagination, or was the greeting just a shade warmer than it had been for the other captives?

"Thank you, Captain," Sharon replied equally warmly. "Believe me, it's a pleasure to be back."

Captain Peter Jenkins smiled. In his own way, his smile was just as infectious as Autro DeLorenzo's had been, Sharon thought. She smiled back with what she hoped was the right degree of warmth.

"It is very good to be back with friends," she said.

"We believe that God, in His infinite love, is concerned with every being," the image on the wall said. "First and foremost, He is a personal God who sent His son to die for all intelligent beings."

The Master of Cities for the Council President flicked a switch and Father Simon vanished in mid-word.

What an odd belief, the Master of Cities thought moodily as he stared unseeing at the blank wall. That Heaven controlled the lives of all beings just as it controlled the motions of the planets and colonies, he could accept. That was an old, old belief among his species. But this . . .

The Master of Cities prided himself on being a seeker of truth. He had sampled many philosophies and been initiated into many cults in his lifetime. Here was something strange and new. A combination with pieces taken from both cult and philosophy, blending and integrating them into an odd, alien notion.

And yet, was it such an odd belief after all? Were not intelligent beings an integral part of the universe? And other thinkers had speculated that the symmetries and regularities of the universe could be best explained by some intelligent guiding principle. And if all that were so, was it so far-fetched that this intelligence should take interest in individual beings?

The Master of Cities rose from the seating sling and began to pace. Yes, the Warden had been right. This was no ordinary cult leader and certainly no ordinary cult. This had resonances he had never found in a cult or philosophy before.

He sat down again and turned the projector back on.

Far, far out, beyond the last of the gas giants, the signals were received by certain seemingly unremarkable chunks of rock. They were scattered through an enormous area of space where the combination of high inclination orbits, their separation and their composition made them unlikely candidates for exploration or mining.

At the signal, certain mechanisms buried within them went into operation. Slowly the rocks stopped their tumbling as they swung through the heavens. Gradually, and without any outward sign of motive power, they swiveled around until their long axes were pointing inward toward the sun and the ring of fragile colonies that orbited it. Now certain other mechanisms were brought to readiness.

In the space of a few hours what had once been a typical collection of small asteroids became missiles, each aimed to strike at a different colony. The mighty engines that would accelerate them on their mad dashes into the solar system remained quiescent, awaiting only the final order to start them on a high-acceleration course that would take them to their targets in just a few short days.

Further in, other small objects began to shift their orientation and orbits. The changes were subtle and by themselves meaningless. Taken together they were both meaningful and threatening.

Within the system, other preparations went on. Here a 246 ship suddenly spurted ahead and disappeared from the tracking screens. At another place, spare lasers were taken out of storage, ostensibly to replace units that had failed. Everywhere agents were alerted.

It all went forward in the greatest possible secrecy, but no screen is perfect, especially against beings who have played the game of shadow war for millennia. Most of 246's moves were undetected, but enough of them were seen that other colonies began their own preparations.

Slowly at first and then with increasing speed, the entire system was converted into an armed camp with everyone on a hair trigger.

"Chaos impends," the Council President announced as soon as he appeared on the screen.

Jenkins had never seen the Owlie so agitated, even when he had threatened to take the *Maxwell* away in the dark days after the raid.

"What chaos?" Jenkins asked.

"The orbits move into unpredictable configurations. Outcomes become chaotic. You must prepare to act for your own safety."

Whatever was going on, the translation software wasn't doing a very good job with the concepts. This could be a very long session—and an important one, from the way the Council President was acting.

"What is happening?" he asked.

"246 moves to violate the Covenant. They will soon openly apply force against the other colonies."

"War? You mean 246 is going to attack the other colonies?"

There was a long pause while the computer struggled with the unfamiliar notion.

"That is of a certainty, yes."

Jenkins checked to make sure DeRosa, Carlotti and Kirchoff were in the circuit. He was going to need advice on this one and he might want to kick in the drive immediately.

"When?"

The Council President hesitated. "Three days. No more."

"Just a minute." Jenkins cut the alien out of the circuit and brought the others up on his screen.

"How dangerous would a war be to us?" he asked.

"Assuming we're not a target, it could still be extremely dangerous," Carlotti told him. "We don't know what they would use for weapons, but we do know they have powerful laser batteries on all of those colonies."

"They also have very efficient mass drivers," Kirchoff said. "One way to take out one of these colonies would be to hit it with a bunch of high-velocity rocks in close formation. Of course the ones that don't hit the colony would keep going and there's a real good chance we'd be in someone's line of fire."

"Okay. How fast can we get out of here?"

Kirchoff extended a hand off screen as if toward a button and looked quizzically at the captain.

"Not just yet. But don't get far from that button, Mr. Kirchoff." He looked at the others. "Okay. Anything else?" There was nothing, so he cut the Owlie back onto the screen.

"I'm sorry about that. I had to confer with my advisers. Now, is there anything we can do to help? Short of risking the safety of my ship or my crew, I am willing to do what I can."

The Owlie relaxed slightly. "We must renegotiate our agreement," he said.

"I hope you know what you're doing," Iron Alice said.

"Nope," Jenkins said curtly, "but I hope to hell the Council President does." He looked up at the indicators across the top of his screen. When they showed all the relays were in place, he reached out and adjusted the microphone. He licked his lips, took a deep breath and began to speak.

"People of Limbo, this is the captain of the human ship *Maxwell . . .*"

The signal was picked up and relayed again and again. From the solar power stations near the star to the mining installations near the gas giants and out to the hidden bases orbiting in the outer darkness, Captain Peter Jenkins' words were carried.

· "We came to your system in search of knowledge. In spite of certain unfortunate events, knowledge is still our goal. To that end, we have struck a bargain with your Colonial Council."

"We will make you a trade for our star drive, to all the colonies equally in return for your knowledge of space engineering, star catalogs and certain other information from your libraries. In this way we shall both receive what we want."

Jenkins licked lips gone dry and wished he could take a drink from the water bulb on his console. But the act of drinking might confuse the translation routines concerned with the gestural part of the aliens' language. He ignored his dry mouth and concentrated on speaking.

"Our terms are simply that we shall make the trade in our home solar system.

"We are prepared to take the nucleus of a new colony back to our system. There they will be allowed to establish a free colony while they teach us what we would know. At the same time they will be learning about the drive. Not only how to build it, but the physics and mathematics behind it as well. We agree to teach them everything we know about the drive.

"The colony will receive honored status as an equal within our people's confederation. But the Colonists will not be allowed to leave our system. Instead we will assist them in building an interstellar laser to send the information back to you.

"The message will be sent uncoded for every colony in this system to hear and profit from. Once the information reaches you, our mutual debt is at an end. You will be free to use the drive in any way you see fit.

"We will not return to Limbo until the trade is complete. Instead you will send a colonizing ship out along a path we will give you. Some time after the ship has left your system, one of our starships will rendezvous with it and carry its crew and cargo faster than light to our home system."

The news was received everywhere in the system as close to simultaneously as radio communications would allow. On every colony alien ears listened intently to the strange creature and his announcement. Even on Colony 246.

"In this way both of us will gain what we want. Both of us will profit with minimum risk. We will leave soon to prepare the way to fulfill our end of the agreement. May we both profit from it." With that Jenkins leaned forward and cut the connection. Then he slumped down with a "whoosh."

Instantly DeRosa popped up on his screen. "Do they know it's going to take that laser message over seventy-five years to get here?" Iron Alice asked.

"They know," he sighed. "Or at least the leaders do. It doesn't seem to make a lot of difference to them. They take the long view and besides," he shrugged, "consider the alternative."

Derfuhrer was standing on the balcony, looking out over the colony when they came for him. He did not turn when they entered, although he must have known why they were here when his guards did not announce them.

The Master of Bounds advanced across the room until he stood on the edge of the terrace.

"We have come as representatives of our lineage . . ." he began, but before he could go further, Derfuhrer whirled and leaped at him, talons extended and beak agape. Taken off guard, the Master of Bounds could do no more than flinch away before the great claws opened his belly and took his life.

The Master of Forests did not hesitate. Derfuhrer had barely landed from his spring when the beam from the hand laser darted out and caught him square in the chest. Derfuhrer opened his beak to scream a final challenge, but his lungs were already gone and nothing came out. He tottered for an instant and then fell forward over his still-writhing victim.

The Master of Forests stayed where he was, laser still in hand, as the others crossed to the door to examine the body.

"Well and properly done," the Master of Seas said as he looked up from the corpse. "The head is untouched."

The Master of Forests lowered the laser and stared down at the corpse of his ally, leader and sometime friend. He knew he should feel something, but he could feel nothing at all.

PART X: YOSE

Gray.

Gray and vast and gloomy. The low-ceilinged chamber was hewed out of Hasta's rock. It stretched off to grayness in all directions, lit blood red by the glow of the aliens' lamps.

One-Eye was there, blood on his feathers and the great gaping wound still fresh in his chest. There were others there too, ranked behind him in shadowy legions.

Behind the dead philosopher the crowd shifted and stirred. "We wait," One-Eye said. "We wait in Limbo."

Father Simon woke up bolt upright in bed with the sweat pouring off his body.

It only gets worse, he thought as he waited for his pulse to settle toward normal. He sat alone in the darkness and concentrated on breathing regularly. The display beside his bunk told him it was 2:30 in the morning. He knew from recent experience he would be lucky to get back to sleep tonight.

He threw back the covers, got up and knelt in the darkness at the side of his bed.

Oh Lord, he prayed, *show me what You want me to do.*

"They say something big is up."

"Any idea what?" DeRosa asked.

Jenkins shook his head. "All I know is the Council President is very excited about something that happened eight or nine days ago. He said we have to have a representative on Meetpoint in fifteen hours."

Iron Alice nodded. In the last three days a number of

285

Colonist ships had docked at Meetpoint. All of them had come in on constant velocity drive. Clearly something big was stirring and it had to involve the humans.

"The Council President wants me to come in person."

"And you're going?"

"I think it's safe enough. But I want this ship ready to go into drive at the least little sign of trouble."

"Are you taking a scooter over?"

"No, a shuttle and one pilot." He smiled self-consciously. "As befits my dignity. Now take over. I'm going aft for a while."

DeRosa nodded and Jenkins left the bridge.

Sharon Dolan met him in the corridor.

"I understand you're going to Meetpoint to meet with the Owlies tomorrow," she said without preamble.

"That is the plan, yes."

Sharon bit her lip. "I wish you wouldn't."

"Why not?"

"I don't trust them."

"I don't trust them either. But they have a lot more to lose if something happens to me than we do."

"They could be planning something tricky. Or just plain crazy."

"If they are, the most they can gain is one starship captain. Commander DeRosa has orders to yank us out of here at the least little sign of any trouble."

"I still don't like it," Sharon said firmly.

"You think they might figure out a way to grab the ship after all?"

"That." Then she added more softly. "But mostly I'm worried about you." She placed her hand gently on his arm.

For a moment Jenkins couldn't control his face. Then he smiled and placed his hand over hers, pressing it softly to his bicep. "Dr. Dolan, this is neither the time nor the place to discuss that. But when we get back to Earth I would be more than happy to take the matter up with you, if you are still so inclined."

Sharon smiled back. "You do that, Captain. Meanwhile, be careful."

* * *

286

Be careful, Jenkins repeated to himself as he shifted in the co-pilot's chair. Oh yes, he was going to be as careful as he could be—under the circumstances. Beside him, the pilot kept her eyes on her instruments as the golden shape of Meetpoint grew ahead of them. He watched it swell and fidgeted inwardly. He had worn his dress blues for the occasion and the uniform pulled and bound in unfamiliar places.

"I make three Colonial ships there, sir," the pilot reported from the right-hand seat. "The two that came in last night are directly docked to the station and the one that's been there a while is laying off a couple of klicks."

"Any signs of activity?"

"Nossir. The drives of the two new arrivals are hot, but they're cooling. The other one shows minimal radiation and there are no signs of scooters or smaller vehicles. The docking signal is on at the third port."

"Then take us in."

"Is he there yet?" Sharon Dolan asked as she came into the conference room.

"Just docking on the station," someone told her. "So far, so good."

All over the ship, men and women were clustered around screens watching the mission to Meetpoint. The group in the conference room was the official evaluation team, the people who would advise the Acting Captain on the significance of what went on.

"I wonder what the hell they are up to," Carlotti muttered as the group in the conference room watched Mootpoint swell on their screen.

Jenkins swam down the golden corridor alone. The air had a strange tang, very different from the taste of the air on the *Maxwell*. The air currents in the corridor gently pushed him onward, deeper into the alien space station. He knew that nearly a thousand pairs of eyes were on him through Meetpoint's video system, but that only increased his aloneness. He had developed a psychosomatic itch between his shoulder blades that wouldn't go away.

There had been no honor guard waiting for him at the lock. No greeting committee at all. *Probably just as well*, Jenkins

287

thought. *Considering what happened the last time we met Colonists face to face*.

He passed through the rotating joint and into the station proper. The first faint stirrings of weight tugged him gently toward the floor. Only one corridor was lit. The rest were completely dark without even emergency lights. There was no hint of motion, no sound, no stirring anywhere. Except for the gentle motion of circulating air, the station could be dead and deserted.

On the *Maxwell* the watchers followed his progress in silence.

"Evaluation?" DeRosa asked over the screen.

"Hard to say," Sharon answered. "I think the lack of activity is supposed to be non-threatening." She looked expectantly at Father Simon.

"At the very least it isn't a bad sign," the priest said.

Jenkins forged ahead down the lighted corridor, trying not to bounce in the one third gravity of the station. Ahead of him a door swung silently open and he caught the hint of motion in the light beyond.

The door was enormous, perhaps three times Jenkins' height. The room beyond it was scaled to match.

"I don't remember anything like that," Carlotti whispered. "They must have rebuilt the entire inside of the station." Sharon motioned him to silence.

The captain came through the door and there, ranked around the walls, were the Colonists.

There were perhaps 200 of them in that enormous room. They were dressed in elaborate robes of a sort Jenkins had never seen before. The robes were stiff with embroidery and fringed and slashed in fantastic patterns. To the aliens' eyes they were probably gorgeously colored, but to the humans they appeared as drab, oddly contrasting browns, greens and grays with an occasional splash of lemon yellow.

No heads turned when Jenkins entered the room. No one moved, no one made a sound. It was as if he were alone in a gallery of statues. The captain paid them no heed and strode on. His footsteps echoed oddly off the gleaming brown floor.

At the center of the room within a black circle inlaid in the floor stood a single alien.

"I think that's the Council President," Carlotti said in an undervoice.

"It is," Billy Toyoda confirmed.

Jenkins advanced to the edge of the black circle and stopped. Still none of the Colonists moved or said anything.

Jenkins waited. The Colonists waited. Finally Jenkins took a step forward and crossed the circle boundary.

All around the room the aliens seemed to relax imperceptibly.

"What the *hell* is going on?" Carlotti demanded in a whisper.

"I don't know," Sharon whispered back. "Now be quiet."

Another alien moved away from the wall and advanced toward the pair in the circle. In his hands he held a box perhaps fifty centimeters on a side.

"Who is it?" Toyoda whispered.

"It's an official of some sort, I think from 264." Carlotti frowned. "I can't be sure though. Their colors are all muddy to us."

Toyoda punched a couple of buttons. "Those are 264 colors," he confirmed, glancing at the screen inset. "He's a very high-ranking official."

"Who?" Carlotti hissed back.

Billy shrugged. "No information. We've never dealt with him before."

The box was gilded and elaborately carved, they saw now. It was borne carefully by the Colonist in 264 colors.

Impassively, the Council President waited. There was still no movement from him.

Slowly the Colonist advanced to the Council President, always keeping both feet on the floor and moving with a slow gliding step that must be murderously difficult in the low gravity. He made an elaborate gesture of respect and withdrew behind the line inlaid on the floor.

This must be ancient, Jenkins thought. *A ritual that goes back to their planet-bound days, perhaps.*

Without any intervention, the sides of the box teetered, quivered and then fell away on the floor.

"*Jaysus,*" breathed Sharon. Father Simon crossed himself. Jenkins simply gaped.

There on the floor of the council chamber lay a severed Colonist head. The feathers showed not a spot of blood and the great yellow eyes stared fixedly ahead. Not even the humans needed to be told whose head it was.

"The order of Heaven has been restored," intoned the emissary from 264. "The balance is preserved."

"The balance is preserved," agreed the Council President.

There was a long frozen pause. Finally Jenkins realized what was expected of him.

"The balance has been preserved," he repeated.

"In the end game, first, always look around the board to see what the most valuable remaining plays are," Dr. Sukihara Takiuji admonished Father Simon. The Japanese swept his hand over the board covered with lines and black and white stones. "This is very important. But always try to keep sente. Sometimes you should sacrifice a profitable play for sente."

Father Simon nodded, trying hard to keep his mind on what Suki was saying. The onlookers gathered around the table in the Pine Lounge also nodded as Suki pointed out the places where an order of moves had made a difference in the outcome. It was more interesting than most of what was going on aboard ship as the *Maxwell* made ready to go home.

There were still a few preparations to be made. The mad dash to Hasta had overloaded some of the ship's equipment and Kirchoff and Clancy were trying to get them repaired. There were some other things to do as well.

This time the *Maxwell* would use its fusion torch to climb out of the system's gravity well before using its drive. It was slower, but much safer than the kind of manic jumps the ship had been making since it entered the Limbo System.

The crew was busy, as usual. But the scientists and technicians had little to occupy their time, and time and tension weighed heavily on them.

Father Simon and Sukihara Takiuji had resumed their marathon go games in the Pine Lounge. As usual Suki was conducting post mortems on the sessions.

"Hey Father, the bridge wants you on the phone," one of the other lounge habitues called from the far side of the room.

Father Simon excused himself and made his way to the phone. As soon as he sat down, Captain Jenkins himself appeared on the screen.

"We have a message from the Colonists," the captain told him, with an odd expression on his face.

Father Simon's stomach contracted. "I'll give any advice I can."

Jenkins shook his head. "No Father, they want to talk to you."

The face on the screen was strange. Or maybe only slightly familiar. The priest still had trouble telling aliens apart unless he knew them well. He realized his hands were shaking and his breathing was ragged. This was the first time since the rescue he had talked to an Owlie face to face.

"I am the Master of Bounds for the President of the Council," the other said as soon as he moved in front of the camera. "You are Father Simon?"

The priest nodded and glanced to the side. The captain and Pete Carlotti were standing off in the dim red light of the bridge to answer questions or give guidance if needed.

"I am commanded by the President of the Council to say this. There are those among us who wish to know more of the matters you began to teach on Hasta. For that reason, the Council has given its permission that you may stay to show more of these things to those who desire to be initiated in this wisdom."

Father Simon's jaw dropped. "I'm sorry," he said shakily. "I'm sorry, but that's, well, it's impossible."

"The President of the Council commands me to ask this of you most urgently."

"I cannot."

The alien paused and his face contorted in a way the priest had never seen any Colonist's face work before. Then he made the sign of the cross on his breast. "Father Simon, come back. We need you."

Once more, Sharon Dolan hung in zero gravity to sing to the stars.

Only this time she couldn't decide on a song. She felt like singing and she wanted the release that putting her feelings into song gave her.

But what do I feel? she wondered. Relief, of course, and sadness for the ones who had died. But beyond that there was a sense of loss in the leaving. She hated this place for all the suffering she had endured here, hated it as she had never hated anything in her life. And yet she knew that the bloody sun outside that bubble and a tiny frigid world that circled it were more deeply a part of her than her beloved Ireland ever was.

As she tried to frame her thoughts into song, she realized she wasn't the only one in the bubble.

"Father Simon. I didn't see you there."

"I'm sorry," the priest said apologetically. "I didn't mean to startle you. It's just that I came here to be alone. And pray."

"I didn't mean to disturb you."

"Oh no, please. I'm glad you're here."

The priest moved into the light and Sharon saw he was still haggard and worn. It was as if he were still living his ordeal, even here on the human ship.

"I was trying to sort out the way I feel about Limbo," Sharon told him. "It's odd how a place you detest can become so much a part of you."

"Forsan ed haec olim meminisse juvabit," the priest said.

"I beg your pardon?"

"Roughly 'Mayhap even the memory of these things will cause men to rejoice in times to come.' Vigil."

"I see," Sharon said slowly. "Yes."

Once more they hung in silence, watching the stars.

"I'm glad you're here," Father Simon said at last. "I've been meaning to talk to you anyway, Miss Dolan. I have a problem and I'd like your advice." He stopped and gathered himself.

"The Colonists sent a message to me, you know."

"I had heard."

"They want me to stay and teach them about Christianity."

"What? You mean that the other prisoners still want to learn Christianity?"

The priest grimaced. "It's worse than that. You know that nearly everything we said on Hasta was recorded by the translating machines? Well, after the rescue and the fall of Derfuhrer those records seem to have been spread all through the Colonies." He stopped and shook his head. "Apparently my message is as effective recorded as it was in person."

Sharon's jaw dropped. "You mean watching those tapes converted the Colonists?"

"I think conversion is much too strong a term," Father

Simon said. "Say rather that a number of the Colonists were very interested in what they heard and want to learn more. Some of them are even trying to practice Catholicism based on what they saw there. Besides, of course, some of the other prisoners have been returned to their home colonies."

"Jaysus," Sharon said at last. "I mean, I'm sorry Father, but, well . . . Jaysus."

"I explained that I was completely unqualified," the priest said miserably. "That I don't have a missionary license and that I'm not the person to teach them what they want to know. But that doesn't matter. I'm here and they want to learn."

"Couldn't the Church send regular missionaries?"

Father Simon sighed. "It will take us almost a year to get home, it would take at least a year to get another expedition organized and then another two years or so to return. That's at least five years. At best."

He bit his lip. "But if Captain Jenkins' plan is accepted, it will be a century or more before we make full contact with this system again. After what happened to us, no one is likely to risk a starship near the Colonists, especially not to bring in missionaries."

He looked out at the stars and fidgeted. "I've got to decide soon. We'll be leaving in a few days."

"Even if you wanted to, do you think the captain would let you stay?"

"I don't know. I don't think he would be very happy about it. He might well forbid it." Father Simon fell silent, staring out into the depths of space.

"So Miss Dolan," he said at last. "What do you think I should do?"

Oh Lord, thought Sharon. *Me, who was raised a good Protestant and the granddaughter of the Master of an Orange Lodge, counseling a Papist priest!* She paused and collected her thoughts.

"Frankly I don't see that you owe them anything," she said after a moment. "You didn't ask to be kidnapped and you didn't deliberately try to convert them. I wouldn't trust the Owlies for an instant and I think they'd more likely kill you than listen to you. If they want you back, bad luck to them!"

The priest considered. "Yes, I suppose you are right," he

said at last. "What happened wasn't my fault. Thank you, Miss Dolan."

With that he turned away and swam through the door. That was the only logical answer, Sharon thought, but he didn't seem at all happy with it. She turned back to the stars and tried to frame a song.

"Come in."

Sukihara Takiuji was kneeling on the mat. His hakima and kimono were brown with contrasting patterns of white. A pot of hot water sat on a hotplate beside him and a tea set sat to the other side. The go board was in front of him, the stones scattered on its surface seemingly at random.

"I'd like your opinion on something," Father Simon said.

The physicist gestured him to sit and the priest sat down crosslegged on the mat. Then Suki poured tea while Father Simon told him the story.

". . . And so, Dr. Takiuji, I don't know what I should do." He drained the cup of tea the physicist had offered him.

Suki was quiet for a long time. Father Simon waited expectantly.

"No," Suki said.

"I beg your pardon?"

"I do not think you need advice," Suki said. "I think you already know what you will do."

"I assure you I do not."

"You know," Suki repeated. He gestured at the board. "Father, how many times have we played?"

"I don't know," Father Simon replied, nonplused. "Hundreds of times, I should imagine."

"And how many times did I beat you?"

The priest smiled slightly, nervously. "Almost every time."

Suki grunted and nodded. "In go you must know your opponent to triumph, maybe better than he knows himself. Father, do you know 'makuto'?"

"I don't believe so."

"It is a Japanese word. Very hard to translate into English. It means 'sincerity.' But perhaps more it means 'steadfastness' or knowing one's mind and always acting accordingly. You have great makuto, I think. You will act rightly."

"Thank you, but I'm not sure I know how."

Suki offered more of the fragrant jasmine tea and the priest

294

declined. Then he poured more into his own cup and regarded Father Simon over the rim.

"You are," he paused, considering, "I think the word is 'stuck.'"

"I certainly feel trapped."

"Excuse me, not that kind of stuck. You are . . ." again the pause while he looked for a word. "Let me give an example.

"Father Simon, in the sword art you do not cut with the sword alone. Your spirit cuts. You put your whole spirit into each cut. But once you have cut, you do not hold on. Each cut is the best you can possibly make and when it is over, it is done. You go on to the next thing. Your spirit must be free, not sticky.

"Now, today, your spirit is stuck between. When you let go, free your spirit, you will know."

"But do you think I should stay or not?"

Sukihara Takiuji shrugged. "I did not say I knew. I said you do."

Lettuce tonight! Sharon Dolan used the tongs to scoop up the pale green leaves bejeweled with drops of water from washing and piled them on her salad plate. *And spinach and fresh tomatoes.* She heaped the darker green leaves and the flesh-pink slices of tomato on top.

"I used to dream about salads," she said to Father Simon, who was following her through the line. "Then we get back and find the gardens were shut down for so long we can only get them every third day," she wrinkled her nose. "There's just no justice!"

"Quite right," Father Simon said abstractedly. He had taken nothing but salad, she noticed, and not much of that.

He looks awful, Sharon thought, *like he's aged twenty years.* She noticed his hands were shaking, as if with palsy. She wished there was something she could say or do to comfort him as he had comforted her so many times with the Colonists. But she knew there was nothing she or anyone else could do to help him.

The planetographer and the priest joined three other ex-captives at a table in the far corner of the cafeteria where the former prisoners had taken to eating together. It wasn't so much a conscious act of separation, it was just that they felt more comfortable in each other's company. Sharon noticed that everyone else at the table had taken big helpings of greens too.

There wasn't much talk. The five of them just squeezed together elbow to elbow and got down to the business of eating.

Sharon took three bites of her salad, savoring the crunch and sharpness of the greens contrasted to the juicy acid sweetness of the tomatoes. It was wonderful, but it really did need dressing, she decided.

"Father, could you pass me the oil and vinegar?"

Wordlessly, the priest reached to his right and picked up the holder containing the plastic bottles.

His shaking hand betrayed him. The holder slipped from his grasp and the bottles tumbled out onto the table. The stopper flew off the oil bottle and oil splashed out onto the priest's right hand.

Father Simon righted the bottles and picked up a napkin to wipe up the spill. Then he looked down at his oil-splattered hand and his face went white.

"Please excuse me," he muttered. Then he threw down the napkin, rose from the table and practically ran from the cafeteria, bouncing uncontrollably under the low gravity.

The others at the table looked at each other. Then Sharon got up and followed the priest out.

"Father, what is it?" she said when she caught up with him in the corridor. "What's wrong?"

The priest looked down at his right hand, still glistening with spilled salad oil. "Vouchsafe, oh Lord, to consecrate and sanctify these hands by this unction and our blessing. That whatsoever they bless shall be blessed and whatsoever they shall consecrate shall be consecrated and sanctified in the name of our Lord Jesus Christ."

"What?" Sharon took his arm. "Father, are you all right?"

Father Simon let out a long, deep sigh, as if he had laid down a heavy burden.

"Yes, Doctor Dolan, I am fine. It's just that I had forgotten who I am." He looked up at her. "I got lost, you see, and it's taken me some time to find my way back."

"Father, will you please talk sense!"

"It is sense, Dr. Dolan. The oil . . . you see, part of the ritual of ordination is anointing the priest's hands as a token of his new office. His call *ad onus presbyterii*, to the burden of the priesthood."

"And?"

"And I had forgotten that. Or rather I never let myself think it through. What I had promised and what it meant.

"It's been nearly twenty-five years since I was ordained. I never had a parish, of course, and the only thing I ever taught was astronomy. Somewhere in all that, I just strayed away."

He straightened up and pulled out a pocket handkerchief to wipe his hand. "But once I remembered that I am a priest and what the duties of a priest are, it was simple."

"You mean go back to the Colonists. I thought you said you didn't have a license to do missionary work."

Father Simon nodded. "And acting as a missionary without a license from my superiors is a violation of canon law, which is a sin against obedience. But the Church enacts ordinances to enable her to carry out her divinely mandated role. If I refused to perform the duties I accepted when I was ordained, it would be an even greater sin."

Sharon was silent as Father Simon finished wiping his hand and put his handkerchief back in his pocket.

"Look, Father, let's talk about this in the morning, shall we? Meanwhile promise me you won't do anything until we talk again?"

Father Simon smiled his old warm smile. "There isn't much I can do tonight, is there?"

He looks better, Jenkins thought as Father Simon came on to the bridge the next morning. *He looks calm and refreshed again.*

"Captain, may we speak privately?"

"Sure, Father. Come into my office."

Once in, Father Simon carefully closed the door and then turned to face Jenkins. He didn't bother with the straps on the arms of the chair.

"I understand we are leaving very soon," the priest said by way of opening.

"Forty-two hours and counting," Jenkins said with a grin. "We need to tidy up some last details. Then we blast."

"You've done a remarkable job, Captain, bringing us through so much."

Jenkins thought of Ludenemeyer, puffed and blacked from decompression; of DeLorenzo with his guts torn out by a samurai sword; of Lulu Pine, psychotic and defiant at her courtmartial. "Not so remarkable. We have twelve fewer people going back than we came with. Eleven dead in the morgue and one who's probably dead and staying behind."

"By any account that is still remarkable, but that was what I wanted to talk to you about," Father Simon told him. "You will leave two humans behind. I am staying too."

"What! Why?"

"I have work to do here," the priest said. "Ministering to souls thirsting for the word of God."

Once again, Jenkins damned the expedition organizers who had sent the *Maxwell* out without a psychiatrist.

"Do you mind if I ask why?" Jenkins asked neutrally.

"Because the aliens need me. Because they have asked me to stay. Because it is my duty to stay."

"When did you decide all this?"

"It has taken some time. I came to the final decision last night."

"Are you sure you want to do this?"

Father Simon shook his head. "No, Captain, I don't *want* to do it," he said vehemently. "If I had completely free choice in the matter I don't think I would do it at all. But as a priest and as a man I am not free to follow my own whims regardless of the needs of others."

He sighed. "I'm perhaps the most unlikely evangelist you will ever find. But that doesn't really matter. I am here and I am the one who was chosen. Captain, back on Hasta I started something. It wasn't intentional. I fought against it as hard as I could, but nonetheless it happened. Now I have a responsibility." He looked straight into Jenkins' eyes.

"I am through trying to avoid my responsibilities, Captain."

"But even so . . ." Jenkins began. But Father Simon cut him off.

"There are practical consequences as well. Captain, these people have only the most rudimentary knowledge of Christianity. Without guidance there is no telling what they will turn to."

"And you're afraid they'll become heretics."

"I am less concerned with heresy than the effect on their entire civilization," the priest said stiffly. "This is a very

298

tightly knit culture and what I have released is a very powerful force. What do you suppose would happen if they interpreted what little they know of Christianity as a cult of suicide, or ritual cannibalism, or just as a quietistic retreat to the contemplation of God?"

"You're assuming that your teaching will take."

"It has taken. There are converts on Hasta, 246 and I think several other colonies by now. These people were ready for the word of God."

"Oh my God," Jenkins said softly.

"Precisely."

Jenkins shook his head. "I don't know. Preaching a human religion to aliens."

"Would it surprise you to know that most of Jesus' followers felt that way when Saint Paul started preaching His message to non-Jews?" Father Simon asked him. "It's a very old story, Captain."

Jenkins was silent, watching the priest carefully. He wasn't back to his old self at all, he realized. There was something very different about him now. He had a serene quality that somehow hinted at dynamism beneath. For some reason, the captain thought of Sukihara Takiuji at his sword exercises.

"You know what your life expectancy is likely to be once we leave, don't you?" he said at last.

"I'm afraid that is rather out of my hands," Father Simon said.

"Father," Jenkins said desperately, "how the *hell* am I going to explain this to my superiors?"

"I'm afraid I hadn't considered that," the priest said. "But I will give you a message to my superiors and they can explain it to your superiors."

". . . so he's staying," Jenkins told Iron Alice DeRosa several hours later when she came on watch.

"You're not going to stop him?"

The captain shook his head. "I don't think . . ." his screen chimed and he hit the stud.

The window expanded on his screen and there was Andrew Aubrey.

The flesh seemed to have melted from him. The smooth

polished surface was gone and what was underneath was a rawer, harsher version.

"Good day, Captain," Aubrey said.

Jenkins glanced over to make sure Iron Alice was in the circuit.

"Dr. Aubrey," he said neutrally. "Where are you?"

"Colony 246. I felt I should tell you that I am staying here to learn what I can from the Colonists."

"Nonsense!" Jenkins snapped. "You're coming back with the rest of us."

"No, Captain, I am staying," Aubrey said firmly. "There is nothing for me back on Earth and so much that these people have to teach. The new leaders of 246 have offered to let me stay and I have accepted."

"Like Hell! You're part of this expedition and you're coming back with us."

"So you can have your show trial when we get back?" Aubrey smiled his old superior smile and shook his head. "Captain, isn't there something somewhere about never giving orders you can't enforce? I am staying and there is really nothing you can do about it."

He was probably right, Jenkins realized. Unless the Colonial Council was willing to use force, there was no way to bring Aubrey back. He doubted the Colonial Council would press the issue.

"Captain, I have a job to do here," Aubrey went on. "The Colonists have so much they can teach us about constructing a truly just society, one without war."

"I would have thought by now even you would see just how wrong you were," Jenkins said bitterly. "If you want more proof I have eleven bodies down in the morgue from the last time you welcomed your 'unwarlike' friends aboard."

"Derfuhrer was an abberation," Aubrey said. "I didn't realize that and I made a terrible mistake." His face clouded. "Believe me, I am truly sorry for that and I will have to live with the consequences of that for the rest of my life.

"But one mad being doesn't change the fact that the Colonials are still our cultural superiors."

"You'll pardon me if I am not impressed," Jenkins said dryly.

"Do you think we would have done better if the tables

300

had been turned?" Aubrey retorted. "How long do you think the *Maxwell* would have survived if this had been a human society? What horrors would we have been willing to commit to gain the secret of the drive? And yet, except for a single abberant individual, none of the Colonists attempted to use violence against us."

Jenkins thought of the bombs in the shuttle bays, the worms in the computers and Lulu Pine, driven to paranoia and murder by alien voices.

"I like to think we would have done better," he said.

"We all like to think well of our species," Aubrey agreed.

"These people behaved like a gang of pirates and you call that 'culturally superior'?"

"We tempted them beyond bearing," Aubrey said with a trace of desperation. "And when they responded they were extremely efficient at it. They came within a hair's breadth of taking your ship, Captain. And as it was, they got what they wanted." Again that superior smile.

"They got it on our terms," Jenkins reminded him, "and they would have gotten that anyway. There was never any question that Earth wouldn't make a deal with them for the secret of the star drive. The only question was the terms."

"Ah yes, the terms." He shook his head. "Your offer was brilliant, you know," he said somewhat ruefully. "I would have preferred something that would have brought us together sooner, but this will be sufficient."

"Sufficient for what?"

"Sufficient to integrate Earth into the Colonial culture," Aubrey said. "You didn't think far ahead, did you? But what do you suppose will happen when Earth, with all its petty, competing sovereignties is exposed to the Colonial culture? Why, the same thing that always happens when a backward culture meets a superior one. In a century or two the *Maxwell* expedition will be acclaimed as the beginning of a new era in human civilization."

Jenkins wanted to smash his face.

"Don't be too sure of that," he said tightly. "We're having an effect on the Colonists as well. Apparently Father Simon has made a number of converts. He's staying behind to preach Christianity and the Colonists seem very receptive."

The captain cut the contact before Aubrey could get the look off his face. Then he punched up his second in command.

"That slimy, sanctimonious sonofabitch," DeRosa said as soon as her window opened on his screen. "I think he really believes all that shit."

"He's got to justify his actions to himself somehow." Jenkins looked unhappy. "He may have something, though. Even one shipload of Colonists and their technology is going to raise hell on Earth."

Iron Alice snorted. "Aubrey's crazy. You did what you had to do to save your command and head off a war. Nobody could ask for more than that. Besides, you're not the one who makes the final decision. It's up to Earth to decide to send out a ship to pick up the Colonists."

"Yes, but they will probably accept my recommendation," Jenkins said. "Sharon Dolan was right. The Colonists have so much to offer us that it would be insane for us to turn it down."

"So you're going to let a traitor play with your head."

"One way or another it comes down to my decision." He sighed. "Father Simon told me once I should start acting like the Master Under God of this ship. But nobody made me Master Under God of Earth's future."

White and shaking, Jenkins punched up Father Simon's cabin. The priest answered with a pile of underwear in one hand, neatly folded and ready to go into a space bag.

"Father, you're going to have some company," Jenkins said without preamble. "Aubrey is alive. He's staying behind on 246."

"That is news," the priest said and laid the underwear down out of range of the camera. "Did he say why he intends to stay?"

"Because he wants to learn from the 'superior' culture of the Colonists."

"Oh my," Father Simon chuckled. "Oh my."

"What's so funny?"

"I was just enjoying the irony. He stays behind to learn from the Colonists' superior culture and I stay behind to teach them ours."

"You'll excuse me if I don't share the joke," the captain said with a slight edge in his voice. "You know what he told me? He said that I'm going to start the 'integration' of Earth into the Colonial culture!"

The priest considered. "I think he overstates the case, but there is something in that. Earth culture will change because of this. But then Earth culture would have changed anyway.

"There is an old conundrum about never stepping twice in the same river. Dr. Takiuji could undoubtedly put it more elegantly, but it is still true. We were bound to meet the Colonists and to be changed by them. At the very least, what you did was to prevent Major DeLorenzo's nightmare of exploitation."

"And I'll be responsible for bringing Colonists into the Earth system. Great."

"Under more controlled conditions than would have happened otherwise," the priest told him. "We will have a century or so to adapt. Consider that if you had not acted as you had, Earth might have been tempted to bury its collective head and ignore the Colonists until they came to us. Besides, whether my mission succeeds or fails, the Colonists will be changing under our influence."

"You really believe we're going to change them?"

"Oh, there's very little question of that," Father Simon said. "Contrary to popular belief, old and stagnant cultures do change when confronted with outside influences. We're already changing them and in the next few decades we will change them even more."

"You think it's a two-way street?"

"That's usually what happens when two cultures come in contact, I believe. They mix."

"You know, with you and Aubrey here and the Colonists coming to Earth I wonder where it will end."

"Probably better than we fear and perhaps worse than we hope. We aren't given to know the future, Captain, and I think that's a blessing."

PART XI: AJI

"You're sure you'll be all right?" Captain Peter Jenkin asked for the hundredth time.

He sucked in the oddly tainted air of Meetpoint for the la: time. Above him, the *Maxwell* swung in comforting proxim ity. As soon as this last chore was done he would reboard th ship and set out for Earth. Even as he and Father Simon sai their goodbyes, Iron Alice was making the final calculatior and Kirchoff and Clancy were bringing up the fusion torch.

"Quite all right," Father Simon reassured him. "The Cour cil President has agreed that I will be allowed to continue m ministry. I will have to stay on his colony, of course, but . . . he shrugged. "I will be able to preach and teach electron cally and he assures me arrangements will be made so I ca administer baptism and communion to visitors."

"There is still time to change your mind."

Father Simon smiled and shook his head. "I think not."

"I still don't like this. You're trusting the word of th Council awfully far and you're going to be vulnerable onc the *Maxwell* is gone."

"Vulnerability isn't new to someone with this calling. And for trust, well, it is not the Council I am placing my trust in.

"You're a brave man, Father."

The priest looked embarrassed and for a second a flash the old Father Simon showed through. "No. Just someon with a job.

"What about Dr. Aubrey?" Father Simon asked quickly cover the moment. "You've talked to him again, I understand.

"He says he is content where he is with the Colonists. I probably should take him back for trial, you know.

"I should take *you* back as well," Jenkins said. "But no, leaving both of you behind was a captain's decision. In his case, it's the best thing. He doesn't want to come and Derfuhrer's successor doesn't want to give him up. Besides, as Aubrey is fond of pointing out, he is a civilian. Once he is off the ship he is no longer my responsibility."

"How is he?" Father Simon asked.

Jenkins thought of the pale, drawn face on the screen with the lines etched deep around his mouth and the glint in the eyes. "Surprisingly well, all things considered. He's determined to learn all the Colonists have to teach him about their methods of conflict resolution." Jenkins shrugged. "Who knows? He might even learn something useful."

"I hope so," Father Simon said. "Poor man."

Jenkins turned toward the sunward view port. The ruddy star of Limbo System glowed red through the filters. Hanging off in the distance he could make out the Colonial ship that would carry Father Simon to his new home.

"I wonder what the Pope is going to make of his new converts."

Father Simon smiled. "His Holiness is most adaptable."

"I hope Earth is equally adaptable," Captain Jenkins said. "They're going to need to be when they find out what I've gotten them into."

"I think you'll be surprised, Captain."

"That seems to be the theme of this trip," Jenkins said wryly. Then he sighed.

"Well, goodbye Father. And good luck."

"Thank you, Captain. I hope you have a safe voyage." They shook hands and then Captain Peter Jenkins turned toward the door and ultimately home. As he reached the port, he put a hand on the jamb and turned back to the priest.

"Oh, Father, one other thing."

"Yes?"

He grinned. "Are you sure *your* name shouldn't be Peter?"

Father Simon smiled back. "Time will tell," he said.

Here is an excerpt from the new novel by Timothy Zahn, coming in October 1988 from Baen Books:

TIMOTHY ZAHN

DEADMAN SWITCH

I was playing singleton chess in a corner of the crew lounge when we reached the Cloud.

Without warning, oddly enough, though the effect sphere's edge was supposed to be both stationary and well established. But reach it without warning we did. From the rear of the *Bellwether* came the faint *thunggk* of massive circuit breakers firing as the Mjollnir drive spontaneously kicked out, followed an instant later by a round of curses from the others in the lounge as the ultra-high-frequency electric current in the deck lost its Mjollnir-space identity of a pseudograv generator and crewers and drinks went scattering every which way.

And then, abruptly, there was silence. A dark silence, as suddenly everyone seemed to remember what was abut to happen.

A rook was drifting in front of my eyes, spiraling slowly about its long axis. Carefully, I reached out and plucked it from the air, feeling a sudden chill in my heart. We were at the edge of the Cloud, ten light-years out from Solitaire . . . and in a few minutes, up on the bridge, someone was going to die.

For in honor of their gods they have done everything detestable that God hates; yes, in honor of their gods, they even burn their own sons and daughters as sacrifices—

A tone from the intercom broke into my thoughts. "Sorry about that," Captain Jose Bartholomy said. Behind his carefully cultivated Starlit accent his voice was trying to be as unruffled as usual . . . but I don't think anyone aboard the *Bellwether* was really fooled. "Space-normal, for anyone who hasn't figured it out already. Approximately fifteen minutes to Mjollnir again; stand ready." He paused, and I heard him take a deep breath. "Mr. Benedar, please report to the bridge."

I didn't have to look to know that all eyes in the lounge had turned to me. Carefully, I eased out of my seat, hanging onto the arm until I'd adjusted adequately to the weightlessness and then giving myself a push toward the door. My movement seemed to break the others out of their paralysis—two of the crewers headed to the lockers for handvacs, while the rest suddenly seemed to remember there were glasses and floating snacks that needed to be collected and got to it. In the brisk and uncomfortable flurry of activity, I reached the door and left.

Randon was waiting for me just outside the bridge. "Benedar," he nodded, both voice and face tighter than he probably wanted them to be.

"Why?" I asked quietly, knowing he would understand what I meant.

He did, but chose to ignore the question. "Come in here," he said instead, waving at the door release and grabbing the jamb handle as the panel slid open.

"I'd rather not," I said.

"Come in here," he repeated. His voice made it clear he meant it.

Swallowing hard, I gave myself a slight push and entered the bridge.

Captain Bartholomy and First Officer Gielincki were there, of course: Gielincki because it was technically her shift as bridge officer, Bartholomy because he wasn't the type of man to foist a duty like this off on his subordinates. Standing beside them on the gripcarpet were Aikman and DeMont, the former with a small recorder hanging loosely from his hand, the latter with a medical kit gripped tightly in his. Flanking the helm chair to their right were two of Randon's shields, Daiv and Duge Ifversn, just beginning to move back . . . and in the chair itself sat a man.

The *Bellwether*'s sacrifice.

I couldn't see anything of him but one hand, strapped to the left chair arm, and the back of his head, similarly bound to the headrest. I didn't want to see anything more, either—not of him, not of anything else that was about to happen up here. But Randon was looking back at me. . . .

The days of my life are few enough: turn your eyes away, leave me a little joy, before I go to the place of no return, to the land of darkness and shadow dark as death . . .

Taking a deep breath, I set my feet into the gripcarpet and moved forward.

Daiv Ifversn had been heading toward Aikman as we entered; now, instead, he turned toward us. "The prisoner is secured, sir, as per orders," he told Randon, his face and voice making it clear he didn't care for this duty at all. "Further orders?"

Randon shook his head. "You two may leave."

"Yes, sir." Daiv caught his brother's eye, and the two of them headed for the door.

And all was ready. Taking a step toward the man in the chair, Aikman set his recorder down on one of the panel's grips, positioning it where it could take in the entire room. "Robern Roxbury Trembley," he said, his voice as coldly official as the atmosphere surrounding us, "you have been charged, tried, and convicted of the crimes of murder and high treason, said crimes having been committed on the world of Miland under the jurisdiction of the laws of the Four Worlds of the Patri."

From my position next to Randon and Captain Bartholomy, I could now see the man in profile. His chest was fluttering rapidly with short, shallow breaths, his face drawn and pale with the scent of death heavy on it . . . but through it all came the distinct sense that he was indeed guilty of the crimes for which he was about to die.

It came as little comfort.

"You have therefore," Aikman continued impassively, "been sentenced to death, by a duly authorized judiciary of your peers, under the laws of the Four Worlds of the Patri and their colonies. Said execution is to be carried out by lethal injection aboard this ship, the *Bellwether*, registered from the Patri world of Portslava, under the direction of Dr. Kurt DeMont, authorized by the governor of Solitaire.

"Robern Roxbury Trembley, do you have any last words?"

Trembley started to shake his head, discovered the headband prevented that. "No," he whispered, voice cracking slightly with the strain.

Aikman half turned, nodded at DeMont. Lips pressed tightly together, the doctor stepped forward, moving around the back of the helm chair to Trembley's right arm. Opening his medical kit, he withdrew a small hypo, already prepared. Trembley closed his eyes, face taut with fear and the approach of death . . . and DeMont touched the hypo nozzle to his arm.

Trembley jerked, inhaling sharply. "Connye," he whispered, lower jaw trembling as he exhaled a long, ragged breath.

His eyes never opened again . . . and a minute later he was dead.

DeMont gazed at the readouts in his kit for another minute before he confirmed it officially. "Execution carried out as ordered," he said, his voice both tired and grim. "Time: fifteen hundred twenty-seven hours, ship's chrono, Anno Patri date 14 Octyab 422." He raised his eyes to Bartholomy. "He's ready, Captain."

Bartholomy nodded, visibly steeled himself, and moved forward. Unstrapping Trembley's arms, he reached gingerly past the body to a black keyboard that had been plugged into the main helm panel. It came alive with indicator lights and prompts at his touch, and he set it down onto the main panel's front grip, positioning it over the main helm controls and directly in front of the chair. "Do I need to do anything else?" he asked Aikman, his voice almost a whisper.

"No," Aikman shook his head. He threw a glance at me, and I could sense the malicious satisfaction there at my presence. The big pious Watcher, forced to watch a man being executed. "No, from here on in it's just sit back and enjoy the ride."

Bartholomy snorted, a flash of dislike flickering out toward Aikman as he moved away from the body.

And as if on cue, the body stirred.

I knew what to expect; but even so, the sight of it was shattering. Trembley was *dead*—everything about him, every cue my Watcher training could detect told me he was dead ... and to see his arms lift slowly away from the chair sent a horrible chill straight to the center of my being. And yet, at the same time, I couldn't force my eyes to turn away. There was an almost hypnotic fascination to the scene that held my intellect even while it repelled my emotions.

Trembley's arms were moving forward now, reaching out toward the black Deadman Switch panel. For a moment they hesitated, as if unsure of themselves. Then the hands stirred, the fingers curved over, and the arms lowered to the Mjollnir switch. One hand groped for position ... paused ... touched it—

And abruptly, gravity returned. We were on Mjollnir drive again, on our way through the Cloud.

With a dead man at the controls.

"Why?" I asked Randon again.

"Because you're the first Watcher to travel to Solitaire," he said. The words were directed to me; but his eyes remained on Trembley. The morbid fascination I'd felt still had Randon in its grip. "Hard to believe, isn't it?" he continued, his voice distant. "Seventy years after the discovery of the Deadman Switch and there still hasn't been a Watcher who's taken the trip in."

I shivered, my skin crawling. The Deadman Switch had hardly been "discovered"—the first ship to get to Solitaire had done so on pure idiot luck ... if *luck* was the proper word. A university's scientific expedition had been nosing around the edge of the Cloud for days, trying to figure out why a Mjollnir drive couldn't operate within that region of space, when the drive had suddenly and impossibly kicked in, sending them off on the ten-hour trip inward to the Solitaire system. Busy with their readings and instruments, no one on board realized until they reached the system that the man operating the helm was dead—had, in fact, died of a stroke just before they'd entered the Cloud.

By the time they came to the correct conclusion, they'd been trapped in the system for nearly two months. Friendships, under such conditions, often grow rapidly. I wondered what it had been like, drawing lots to see who would die so that the rest could get home . . .

I shivered, violently. "The Watchers consider the Deadman Switch to be a form of human sacrifice," I told him.

Randon threw me a patient glance . . . but beneath the slightly amused sophistication there, I could tell he wasn't entirely comfortable with the ethics of it either. "I didn't bring you here to argue public morals with me," he said tartly. "I brought you here because—" he pursed his lips briefly— "because I thought you might be able to settle the question of whether or not the Cloud is really alive."

It was as if all the buried fears of my childhood had suddenly risen again from their half-forgotten shadows. To deliberately try and detect the presence of an entity that had coldly taken control of a dead human body . . .